Annie leant fo
her friend's arm ink
that you had ev model
family. I so wante

Roz began to lau this unbearably
funny and then unbe psetting. Tears flowed
down her cheeks, tears sorrow and regret . . .

Susanna Jackson was born in Battersea. She has had several careers, starting as a teacher and moving into educational writing before becoming a freelance copywriter. She was the company writer for The Body Shop, working closely with Anita Roddick on anything and everything, including campaigns and customer information. She is now writing fiction full-time. She lives in London with her husband, son and daughter.

Living Other Lives

Susanna Jackson

An Orion Paperback
First published in Great Britain by Orion in 1996
This paperback edition published in 1998 by
Orion Books Ltd,
Orion House, 5 Upper St Martin's Lane,
London WC2H 9EA

A CIP catalogue record for this book
is available from the British Library.

ISBN: 0 75281 635 7

Typeset by Deltatype Ltd, Birkenhead

Printed and Bound in Great Britain by
Clays Ltd, St Ives plc.

For David

BEGINNING

I

Roz Harper stood at the kitchen window and gazed out over the back garden, a warm coffee mug in her hands. She'd made it herself at pottery class and it was comforting to hold.

Nothing moved outside. Complete stillness. A heavy snowfall overnight had transformed everything in the garden into soft, curved white shapes. The children had been so excited, wanting to get out in it immediately, to lie in it, throw it around. She remembered those childhood feelings of surprise and delight on looking out of the window on a winter morning, and seeing snow. She barely felt that now. Where had those feelings gone? Were they still there, merely dulled, buried under layers of adult experience? Or had they completely vanished?

The thought saddened Roz. She realised that she no longer felt things so keenly or so spontaneously. She resisted the idea that this was inevitable, that the highs and lows of youth would naturally be replaced by something else – a steadiness, a comfortable predictability. She had always considered herself to be a passionate person, open and alive to experiences.

Yet now it seemed as though she too were covered in snow – disguised, her edges blurred.

The day had begun chaotically and she'd had to make an enormous effort to be calm and patient and smiling. She'd pulled Matthew in from the snow (still in his pyjamas), tried to get an over-excited Katy to eat some breakfast and dress in suitable layers, searched for hats and gloves and boots and extra pairs of socks, sympathised with Geoff as he cursed the weather for the effect it would have on his journey to work, shouted again and again up the stairs to Sam to get up, coped with Polly's bad temper at not being able to find her copy of Keats – it was a flurry of noise and bustle and demands.

At last she was alone, savouring the quiet and her solitude. Roz usually liked January, a new year, offering new possibilities, time for reflection. Christmas was over, all the hype and hysteria – much as she loved it – packed away with the decorations. And she'd just had her fortieth birthday.

She and Geoff had celebrated by eating out at a favourite Italian restaurant. They had spent most of the evening talking about the children, although there were other things that Roz wanted to discuss. They agreed, as always, how fortunate they were and how well things had worked out. What did we ever talk about before the children? she wondered. In bed they had turned to each other and made love, following their usual familiar moves, and it was friendly and pleasant and satisfying in a way – rather like the meal they'd had earlier. Roz tried to remember what sex had been like with Geoff when they'd first met, but again her memories were hazy, as if a curtain had been drawn and she couldn't quite see through it. But she could remember that sex had mattered a lot. It seemed much less important now.

Now she was forty. Forty. She practised saying it and found her lack of reaction surprising – it held no terror. Other people made so much fuss about it, falling into depression as the day approached, questioning what life was about, searching for answers . . . But Roz didn't really feel any different.

She still felt young – well, youngish – and she still looked fine, didn't she? She had noticed recently that an extra fold of skin seemed to be developing over her eyelid. Its appearance had initially shocked her: she'd thought there might be something wrong, and surely it must be temporary? But there it remained, and she saw it every time she looked in the mirror.

No more contemplation, Roz decided. She must *do* something. Something worthwhile, something for *herself*. She must utilise her time creatively. She could sketch the snow shapes outside to use as ideas for pottery . . . Or she could read the newspaper properly, overseas news included, even the financial pages, and become more informed. Then there was that new book on birthing methods to read before her next batch of classes. So many things she could do.

Although maybe Geoff was right, perhaps she did have more than enough to do already. Before Christmas she had received an offer of work from a woman she knew, who was on the local council's pre-school committee. Hilary had rung her to ask if she'd help compile a parents' guide to facilities in the area for young children. She'd thought Roz would be perfect for it, she had just the right experience. I've got an English degree too, Roz had thought wryly, but she was interested and said so. After all, it was something different, and mentally stimulating. Unlike a lot of what I do, she thought.

Geoff had reacted strangely when she told him about the offer. He had been hostile to the whole idea, saying that surely she didn't have the time? What about the children, the house, everything? He went on about how she was already spending more and more time on her childbirth classes, not to mention all the spin-offs – answering the phone at all hours to advise those desperate post-natal women having problems with their breastfeeding or stitches or whatever . . . Roz had looked at him in disbelief. He sounded angry, resentful. She'd tried to say that she'd be doing this from home, it wouldn't affect the children, and who knows where it could lead her? It would be valuable experience for the future. He repeated what he'd said before, more forcefully. Roz dropped the subject, vowing to return to it later, then Christmas had got in the way. But she'd thought about it a great deal, and especially Geoff's response. What on earth was the matter with him?

Last night, in the restaurant, she had tried to talk it over. He had resolutely changed the subject and, meekly, she had let him. What on earth was the matter with *her*? She must try again. She had to give an answer soon, and she wanted it to be yes.

Now positive thoughts and positive action were needed, otherwise the morning would be wasted. She had until lunchtime, when her friend and neighbour Annie was bringing Katy home from playgroup.

Then she recalled what Geoff had said as he'd rushed out of the door, something about an architect coming this morning, about the loft. They were thinking of converting it – they wanted more living space as the children grew older. Roz did wonder if the loft might turn out to include space for Geoff too – so many men they knew had a 'den' or 'study', even if they didn't have to work at home. A place to hide, that's what they had, but where did women hide? Were they allowed to?

She might need space to work anyway, if she took on this project. She imagined a room of her own – a small one would do, with a desk, a notice board, a picture or two, a typewriter, or should she invest in a word processor?

OK, Roz, back to reality. What had Geoff said about this architect? Recommended by someone at the health club, some Greek guy, meant to be very good, usually did much grander things than suburban loft conversions . . . Geoff had scrawled the name on the calendar by the kitchen phone. Roz couldn't decipher it, but the time said ten-thirty.

Damn, it was nearly that now. She consoled herself with the thought that the snow on the roads would probably prevent him coming, and she'd still have some time to herself. She turned away from the breakfast débris on the table, she'd clear it later when Katy was home.

The doorbell rang, making her jump. She sighed and went to answer it. A man filled the doorway. He registered her silence and expression of alarm.

'Hello – I'm Alexander Kostakis. I made an appointment with Geoff Harper about a loft conversion. You are Mrs Harper?'

Roz managed to smile.

'Yes. Please come in. I'm sorry to seem so surprised – I thought the snow would prevent you from coming.'

He grinned and stamped on the doormat.

'I'm well prepared for it – snow chains, snow boots, the lot.'

She could see an olive green Range Rover parked outside the house.

'More than most people! It always seems to cause such chaos. Here, let me take your coat.'

He handed her a heavy sheepskin. He looked smaller without it but his presence still dominated the hall. He wasn't much taller than her, but he was – well, chunky, with broad shoulders and lots of black curly hair. She thought he looked Greek, especially with those very dark brown eyes. She found herself smiling at his boots: they were elaborate and padded, in two shades of blue, the kind she associated with après-ski. His trousers were tucked into them, making him look like a strange kind of cowboy. He glanced downwards too.

'I'll keep my boots on, if that's OK. There's no snow left on them.'

That grin again. He had very good teeth.

Images of astronauts in big foolish boots bouncing round her house zoomed through her mind.

She resumed the role of efficient, capable wife – the part Geoff liked her to play. 'Come and have a cup of coffee and I'll explain what we want done. Then I'll take you up there.'

He followed her into the kitchen, carrying his briefcase of soft brown leather, more like a bag really, very different from the kind Geoff and his colleagues sported, which were hard, black and aggressive, with complicated codes as locking devices.

'Excuse the mess,' she said predictably. He dismissed it with a smile and a wave of his hand and sat down at the table. Roz hoped that wasn't the chair where Katy had spilled her juice at breakfast – it would play havoc with his black corduroy trousers.

She made sweeping gestures at the clutter on the table, wiping the sticky patches of marmalade and crumbs and milk. She could feel him watching her.

She muttered something about the rush this morning, the children and the weather, all the while cursing herself for not clearing up earlier. All that nonsense about sketching or reading . . .

'How many children do you have?'

'Four. Two of each. The eldest is sixteen, the youngest is four.'

It was a well-rehearsed reply.

'Lucky you.'

She was taken off guard by this response. She looked at him but his expression was perfectly serious. She stuffed the cereal box into a cupboard.

'Oh. People usually sympathise when I say how many children I – we – have, and I find myself apologising and insisting that they were all planned, well, certainly wanted anyway. And we aren't Catholics – some people automatically assume that we must be . . .'

She paused, aware that she was prattling on and that it wasn't necessary or appropriate, but he was still listening, regarding her face intently.

'Perhaps four children seems a lot here. It's not so unusual in Greece.'

Roz was about to ask him if he had any children, but the look on his face stopped her: a fleeting glimpse of wistfulness, even sadness. Instead, she asked him how long he'd lived in England, and he told her that it was a long time, more or less since he was a student. She sat down opposite him with the coffee and wondered how old he was. It was hard to tell, with his kind of strong looks. Probably late thirties, perhaps even her age . . .

He put a large notebook and a covetable fat black fountain pen on the table. He talked about the work he'd done recently, including the loft design for Geoff's acquaintance. He expanded on the possibilities of loft spaces and moved his hands in the air a lot.

Roz was happy to listen, and to look. She watched his hands. They were large and broad, their backs covered with dark hair. She tried to concentrate on what he was saying. It wasn't that he was boring or that she wasn't interested, it was just that she was distracted by him, by his physical presence. She began to feel warm.

Her eyes kept locking with his. She'd glance away, and so would he, then bang, their eyes collided again. She was conscious of the empty house around them, no sounds, no other people. Then she realised he was asking her about the loft, what they had in mind. She told him. He said it sounded very straightforward and stood up, suggesting he went up to look at it. She was relieved he had not stuck to the chair.

The three flights of stairs seemed interminable, so acutely was she aware of the man close behind her. At least she was wearing her newish jeans, not the old ones which were fraying at the inner thigh seam. She tried to walk naturally, but the more she thought about it, the more her hips seemed to sway. Why was she feeling so self-conscious? An answer began to form within her, as if arriving from a great distance. She found Alexander Kostakis attractive. That was it! Very attractive. Yes, she had to admit, as she looked at him at the top of the stairs, that he was – well – sexy.

Normally Roz didn't think of men in this way, or she hadn't for a very long time. She knew other women had fantasies about actors or sportsmen or television personalities – they talked about it, jokingly. Some even had affairs – often with the husbands of their friends. But she wasn't like that, was she?

As he climbed into the loft he put his pen in his trouser pocket, and asked her to hold his notebook and tape. As she handed them up to him their eyes met again and their hands touched. She left him up there, and hurried down to the floor below where she attacked the mess in the bedroom, tossing shoes into the wardrobe, hanging up the two clean but now crumpled shirts that Geoff had decided not to wear this morning, picking up his bathrobe from the floor (for the thousandth time), shaking the duvet more than it needed.

She stopped and surveyed herself in the mirror. How do others see me? How old *do* I look? She stood tall, turning sideways, holding her stomach in. But that made her breasts jut out too much. She teased her hair up and out from her face with her fingers – she never brushed it as it was curly and she preferred it to look natural. It needed the minimum of attention.

Like me, she thought. That's what I give myself.

Alexander Kostakis came into the kitchen as she was bending over, filling the dishwasher. She stood up quickly.

'I've made some preliminary measurements and a few sketches – enough to get me going. There's plenty of space and potential. Only problem might be the water tank. I'll put some ideas down on paper, then come and discuss them with you – and your husband of course.'

His tone was efficient and she responded in the

same way, talking about when Geoff would be free, when they'd be in contact, taking his business card. But all the time she was listening to his voice rather than the words and noticing how long and thick his eyelashes were.

They were in the hall now, he was pulling on his massive coat. He dropped his pen and she quickly bent to pick it up. He stooped to retrieve it too. They bumped heads painfully and laughed, apologising, and again their eyes connected. They shook hands. His enveloped hers and were warm and dry. She watched him crunch down the path in his boots, then quickly closed the door. She could hardly stand and wave goodbye.

It was snowing again, so prettily. She watched it through the kitchen window, although there were so many things she could – or should – be doing. She turned his card over in her hands and read the words. He was an attractive man and he was friendly and nice, but so what? There were plenty of nice attractive men in the world; it was just that she wasn't used to being alone with them.

She dismissed her response to him – it was what you'd expect from someone who led a fairly sheltered life, revolving around her husband, children, home, especially someone who that very morning had been thinking about age and identity . . . A perfectly normal reaction but, for her, an aberration.

'Mummy, mummy!'

Katy was shouting through the letter box. Roz opened the door to her daughter, standing in the snow with Annie and her son Tom. They came in, stamping their feet, and the usual routines took over – admiring Katy's soggy painting, organising a hurried lunch. Annie was always hungry for news, gossip, anything, so Roz mentioned the visit from the architect, but she said nothing about her reaction to him, for how would she begin to describe it?

2

Annie lived across the road from Roz, but while the Harpers' house was detached and double-fronted, like a Victorian doll's house come to life, hers was smaller and terraced. Annie thought of it as being a lesser, meaner model, and often thought of herself that way too.

Annie and Martin had moved in a few years ago, and Annie, who had caught glimpses of Roz on her initial visits to the house, had been ready to dislike this woman from the start. She'd seen Roz working in the front garden surrounded by helpful, happy children; Roz energetically cleaning windows; Roz leaning over the gate listening attentively to an elderly passer-by. Those first sightings had been enough to fuel Annie's feelings of inadequacy. Earth mothers, Annie labelled Roz and other women like her; they made her resentful and angry with herself, everyone, the world.

The day after they'd moved in, when Martin had abandoned her by fleeing to the comfort of his office, Roz had arrived on Annie's doorstep, bringing a thermos full of homemade soup, a pot of parsley for the garden, and a warm welcome to the neighbourhood. She had taken Annie off guard and completely disarmed her.

The true state of the house, its dinginess and

worse, had been revealed by its emptiness, and Annie and Martin had very little money to spare to put it right. No wonder I'm depressed, Annie had thought, gazing at the turquoise swirls and endless bamboo patterns on the walls, interspersed with blotches of mould and grease stains. A husband who preferred to be at work, a baby who wouldn't sleep, and a three year old constantly demanding attention. She'd never found motherhood easy: the enormity of it engulfed her, yet its minutiae defeated her. She constantly asked herself, Is this all?

She managed to maintain some sort of equilibrium, filling her days, getting on with it. That was the best she could do. And she began to think, thank God for Roz, or whichever goddess provided her. Roz invited Annie over, listened sympathetically, and looked after the baby while Annie slapped white paint on the offending walls. They fell into a pattern of meeting regularly, usually in Roz's house, with Tom and Katy playing at their feet. One of those amiable female friendships grew, built upon children and proximity and practicalities. It was useful to have a friend across the road.

Martin once asked her, on hearing that she'd spent most of the day with Roz, what they found to talk about.

'Oh, children, babies, lack of sleep – the usual things,' she'd replied, a little defensively, seeing that he wasn't really interested, but was reading, catching up with advertising gossip. She didn't add that they could hardly finish a sentence, or attempt to have a serious conversation, as they were continually being interrupted by one child or another.

'I do envy Roz,' she said to the back page of *Campaign*. 'She seems so – so content.'

He looked up slowly, as if it took a great effort.

'Well, why shouldn't she be?'

'Well, come to that, why shouldn't I be?'

'Aren't you, then?' He was being provocative – he knew the answer.

'No, I'm not content. I have moments of happiness, but I'm not happy in the way Roz seems to be. I'd like to be content –'

'It's just temperament, Annie – you're different from Roz, you're more brittle, more edgy –'

'Oh I see, thanks a lot.'

'Come on, I'm not saying that's bad or good, just that you're different. And perhaps you want different things out of life.'

She was about to challenge him, to take it further, but he walked out of the kitchen, saying over his shoulder, 'Can we skip any further discussion of the meaning of life, or your life? I'm just not in the mood right now. I'm shattered, I've been at it all day, you know.'

The sound of the television ended the conversation, as it so often did, and Annie slammed around the kitchen, as she so often did.

'So what,' she muttered, 'I've been at it all day too . . . And I don't have assistants to bring me coffee and say how wonderful I am, and I don't get long lunches in nice restaurants. I may not bring in any money, but I keep the whole bloody show going here. Who makes sure there's food in the fridge and soap in the bathroom and a constant supply of underwear and ironed shirts and trousers pressed just so, and who looks after the children and makes sure they've got the right size shoes, and takes them to the library and gym club and does everything else and all the things you wouldn't know how to do and don't even recognise as important?'

Martin couldn't hear, but then, he wasn't listening. Annie sat at the kitchen table and smoked, and wondered (not for the first time) how she had come to this point. Martin, marriage, house, children – the whole bourgeois works. Was this really what she'd wanted?

Anni & Martin, Anny + Martin, annie and martin, she used to doodle in her sketch book, just to see how it looked. Then she'd scribble over it, in case he ever saw it and realised that she had designs on him. That wouldn't do. After all, they were both art students, and it was crucial to be – or appear to be – cool.

They had become aware of each other during their foundation year. Martin was a bit of a loner, spending more time than was necessary working in the studio, painting or creating 3-D constructions with black and white wooden shapes. Anni (as she spelled it then) used to watch him, from a distance. She didn't spend much time working. She hung around the refectory, seeing and being seen, smoking and talking, looking for opportunities to flirt. She thought of him as Mystery Man until she knew his name. He was usually dressed in monochrome: black leather jacket, black Levis (almost impossible to get then), black polo-neck (or a white T-shirt as a concession to warm weather), black Chelsea boots. His hair was collar length, straight and streaky blond (she'd later learned it wasn't natural), he was broad-shouldered and he swaggered, just a little. There was a certain look he had which attracted her. She'd sit and blow smoke rings, her eyes fixed on him, and sometimes his eyes would meet hers, then slide away.

Anni was the opposite of Martin. Extrovert and loud, wanting to be noticed. She made many of her own clothes, using remnants of Liberty fabrics or old curtains, or pieces of material she found in bins outside rag-trade showrooms near Oxford Street. She dashed off tiny skirts and dresses on her ancient Singer machine, paying little detail as to how they were finished, as she often only wore things once. It was important to keep changing her look, to stay ahead. She rummaged for things in army surplus stores – sailor's trousers, webbing belts, army vests, and she'd find collarless shirts and old buttons in markets. She'd dye things in a tin bath to achieve sludgy browns and deep aubergines and often, unintentionally, the clothes would shrink but she wore them anyway. As she was so thin she could wear anything, and it was the look of the time – hollow thighs, concave body. It was a competitive business, trying to distinguish yourself from the crowd.

Anni and Martin finally connected one Saturday morning in Deptford Market. They were both picking through a pile of pinstriped jackets and musty overcoats, when they looked up at each other.

'Oh, hello,' she said.

'Hello,' he said, and smiled a little.

She tried to think of something to say to keep his attention, but all that came was small talk. 'Not much here today, is there?'

'No. Too many bloody art students for any bargains.' He smiled some more.

She laughed, relieved to find that he had a sense of humour. They drifted away from the stall and walked slowly through the market, discussing college, work, lecturers, people. They used each other's names – there was no point pretending they didn't know them.

Past the stall overflowing with second-hand shoes; past the old woodworking tools and bits of radios; past the corner pitch where ex-school furniture was haphazardly displayed, the small desks and chairs looking forlorn, until they reached the café near the station. Anni couldn't clearly remember who had suggested going in for coffee. She thought it was her, but if you'd asked Martin he would claim that it was him. Steamed up windows, the smell of bacon, the usual incongruous mixture of locals and students. He had tea and a bacon sandwich, she had black coffee and a fag.

She doodled on the window, he thought she was trying to be cute. She noticed how blue his eyes were, and he thought, I wonder what she's like in bed, is she as good as they say? Perhaps I'll give her a go, though it's a shame she has no tits . . .

Anni tried to be amusing, but their conversation was stilted until she discovered Martin's enthusiasm for film. (He enunciated the word seriously, with a capital F.) Then he talked. And talked. He raved about Jean-Luc Godard, was shocked to hear that Anni had not seen any of his films. While he concentrated on chewing his bacon sandwich, Anni said sweetly, 'Perhaps I could come with you, I'm sure I'd get more out of it with you to explain things.'

He nodded. 'If you like.'

He was flattered. That was what he needed. Someone to appreciate him, understand him, want him . . .

Martin had been engaged in the process of creating himself in his own image, and he was trying to do it carefully but quickly. He knew the sort of person he wanted to be, and he had become accomplished at projecting the superficial aspects – looking right, behaving cool. But there was a lot still to do. He didn't want to be found out, to be seen as an ignorant boy from Wales, provincial and unsophisticated, for he neither valued nor took any pride in his Welshness.

He worked hard at everything. He spent a lot of time browsing through art books in Zwemmer's (which he could not afford and was not bold enough to steal), and at the Tate and the National Gallery, and going to films, usually on his own. He was used to that. Sometimes he was lonely, but that was preferable to trying to be friendly with people and failing. And as for girls . . . He'd had little experience, and wanted more, but did not find it easy getting to know women, or getting to know them enough to screw them. And he was very fussy – they had to look right, be sharp and aware, be nice to him, and preferably have big breasts. But here was Anni, obviously interested in him . . . Her reputation intrigued him, and she met most of his criteria, so why not?

What had kept them together? Annie asked herself again and again. They had discovered each other's vulnerabilities and how to assuage or exploit them . . . They had enjoyed being a couple, combining forces to surprise and delight the rest. The sex had been interesting, occasionally great, and familiarity brought its own rewards. Familiarity, she thought, perhaps it all comes down to that. But we're not particularly comfortable with each other, and as for familiarity, that was definitely becoming a disadvantage.

She and Martin were now linked by all the usual commitments, which once had never been high on their agendas. Ambition had been. What happened to my ambition? Annie thought. What had she wanted?

Annie knew that she *had* wanted Martin, wanted him to be hers. She had wooed him, stroked his ego, listened to his monologues, let him think he was brighter than her, encouraged him in bed, bought him drinks, cut his hair, washed his clothes, even learned to cook so that she could feed him . . . She had done all she could to please him.

And now she asked herself, At what cost? Was it all worth it? She wasn't sure where Anni or Anny, or whoever she was, had gone. Her anger and discontent flowed like an underground river, usually out of sight, occasionally bubbling to the surface. Martin, if he was aware of it, saw it as Annie's problem, not his, and chose to disregard it.

Meanwhile, Annie spent time dreaming in the kitchen, standing at the sink, hovering over the washing-up, smoking, watching life or what passes for it, going by in the street. She increasingly saw life as a spectator sport.

She watched Roz coming and going. Roz didn't shout at her children, or drop her car keys down the drain (Annie did, twice); she never locked herself out of the house, or dropped milk bottles, shattering glass and milk everywhere; she never argued loudly with urban missionaries who called wanting to talk about God . . . Annie did all these things, and more . . . Sometimes Roz would catch Annie's eye, and reward her attention with a smile, a wave, and a mimed 'See you later', and Annie would sigh and feel little better. She'd douse her cigarette under the tap, and wish that some of Roz's contentment – or was it the ability to cope? – would rub off on her. And if she kept trying, perhaps she would attain it by association.

Roz has heard the story more than once of how Annie and Martin met. That was fine by Roz; she could understand Annie's need to excavate the past, to try to make sense of the present. She was starting to feel that way herself. Sometimes, as Annie reconstructed early scenes with Martin, Roz's mind would drift off to the beginning of her relationship with Geoff.

It was at a party in Southwark, in a scruffy Georgian house in a left-over terrace, stranded amongst warehouses and car dealers, one-way systems and the oily darkness of the Thames. Roz thought of Chaucer and pilgrims as she and her friends made their way from London Bridge station. The house was a beacon of light with every floor and staircase stuffed with students shouting above the barely recognisable music (what was it? Marvin Gaye?), wandering about clutching bottles of Algerian wine, congregating around the plastic barrel of beer in the kitchen (mainly men), dancing wildly (mainly women), chatting each other up . . . At the top of the house some had managed to pair off and were murmuring and fumbling on mattresses covering bare boards.

Experiencing a sense of *déjà vu*, Roz wondered why she'd come – though she knew the answer. It was Saturday night, party night. Any party would do. She could have stayed in to work on her essay on T.S. Eliot but here she was, a student in London, and like everyone else she wanted some fun. No one stayed in on Saturday nights.

She collided with Geoff while dancing; she was dancing and he was squeezing by to get to the wine.

They would have fallen over but Geoff had caught her. They laughed and began to talk, shouting over the music. She liked his looks – taller than her, feathery fair hair, skinny, in tight velveteen jeans. They went into the back yard to get some air and talk some more. For an economics student, he was surprisingly interested in literature and poetry (but, as he told her later, he was really interested in her). She liked the way he listened.

So that was it, the beginning – talking, flirting, kissing (she also liked the way he kissed), in cafés, pubs, parks, the cinema. As the weeks went by, more and more they wanted to be a couple. The sex was good and easy; they were supple and energetic, and they could never get enough. Frustrated by roommates, lack of privacy, single beds, student regulations, they began to dream of having a place to be alone together.

But why Geoff? Roz now asked herself. She tried to recall the spark, the recognition, that had made him special. Did she just drift into it, could it have been anyone who was attractive and reliable and well-behaved?

For at twenty-one, in her final year of university, she'd had many boyfriends, some of whom she'd slept with, but they'd turned out to be domineering or boring or unfaithful or lacking in some other way. All around her, in her tutor group (mostly female), her hall of residence (all female), girls were showing off rings on their fingers and boasting about getting engaged, or even married. That's how it was.

Was that what she'd wanted? A man of her own, a husband, a father for her future children – and Geoff had been highly suitable, was that it?

Roz had not consciously thought that way, but consciousness had hardly come into it then. Now she looked back and saw her younger self, impulsive and impatient, making decisions: to get married, have children, give up the library job she didn't much like anyway – without comprehending just how significant and consequential those decisions were.

So when Annie talked of how and why and what was it all about, it struck a chord with Roz. Me too, she thought, but did not say so directly. She'd hardly admitted her uncertainties to herself, so how could she speak of them to others?

3

On the day of Alexander Kostakis' visit Geoff arrived home even later than usual. It was around nine, the children were in bed or in their rooms, the house had been cursorily tidied. Roz felt that she could now sit down to watch the news.

He let himself in quietly, a habit from earlier days when he hadn't wanted to wake one baby or another. Roz no longer rose to greet him as once she would have done. There was no urgency in their relationship any more, though she and Geoff were friendly, caring, in tune with each other. She saw their lives running along parallel railway tracks, sometimes converging, then diverging. At times Geoff seemed to be on the express line, while she was stuck on the slow one with all the stations.

He stuck his head round the door.

'Hello love. The snow played havoc with the trains. I'll be down in a minute.'

He went upstairs to change and reappeared in sweatshirt and jeans. Roz stirred.

'Stay there, Roz. I'm going to have a drink. Want one? Any red wine open?'

'Yes, I think there's some Beaujolais.'

She wasn't concentrating on the news pictures of snowploughs and cars stranded in snowdrifts. She joined him in the kitchen, feeling that was where she ought to be anyway. They kissed each other on the cheek.

'Are you hungry? I could make you an omelette. There's not much food in the house – I didn't venture to the shops in the snow.'

'An omelette's fine. I had a large lunch. Douglas forced me to that new French restaurant near the office.'

'How was the rest of your day?'

She beat the eggs, added herbs, ground some black pepper.

'Oh, the usual really. A last minute panic meeting on the Tunisian project. I may have to go to Tunis next week.'

Roz was used to his frequent trips abroad. Geoff was an economist, working for the London end of an American oil company. It had expanded into other fields (partly as insurance for the day when the oil ran out), investigating resources of all kinds and their viability, and it now hired out its skills and people to agencies and governments worldwide. So off Geoff would go to assess the potential market for peat or bark or water hyacinth, anywhere from Poland to Nepal.

They sat opposite each other at the long pine table, where she had sat with Alexander Kostakis that morning. She thought about him as she watched Geoff eat his omelette.

'How was everything today? Children all right?' Hearing about the children was always a priority.

'Fine. Loved the snow, of course. We built a snowman after school, even Polly joined in. Oh, by the way, she needs some help with her maths homework –'

'Yes, she told me – I saw her when I was upstairs. I'll go up in a minute.'

'Oh, and that architect came today, despite the snow.'

'Ah, good. What was he like?'

Roz paused, a mixture of emotions confusing her. She sieved through them, selecting what Geoff would like to hear. She showed him his business card.

'He was nice, seemed competent, efficient. He looked in the loft, and said he'd be in touch soon with some ideas and drawings.'

Geoff thought no more about the loft or the architect, reassured that he could rely on Roz to do whatever was necessary. He went upstairs to see Polly, eager to help her, keen for her to do well. He was always generous with his time when it came to the children. Patient too.

He's a good father, thought Roz, and a good husband too, she supposed. He was steady, faithful and kind, and she assumed that he loved her. It wasn't anyone's fault that the excitement and passion had been ironed out of their relationship by domestic routine. That was life. It happened to everyone, didn't it?

Later, in their bedroom, Roz felt she must talk to him about the new work project. Never mind that it was late and they were tired.

'Geoff, I've got to decide about that work I was offered. They need an answer very soon.'

He turned from hanging up his trousers, holding them straight against his chest. 'What do you mean? I thought we'd decided.'

'Decided? When? Decided what?'

'That you had too much to do already and that you couldn't take it on.'

His back was towards her as he painstakingly hung his suit in the wardrobe. Roz felt as if her brain would explode. How dare he!

'We decided no such thing. We were going to discuss it further – remember? And actually I think it's up to me to decide if I have too much on, and I want to do it –'

Carefully he removed his watch.

'Roz, be reasonable. I think we should decide these things together. They affect us both, and the children. I'd be very reluctant for you to do more – partly for your sake, but I think we'd all suffer.'

He spoke steadily, calmly, as if addressing a stubborn child. Bloody patronising, thought Roz. She clenched her fists in her palms, unused to feeling so much anger. Fuck him, she thought. She glared at him, trying to understand. Was it just that he disliked change? Did this idea threaten him in some way? Or did he just want to keep her in what he considered to be her place – at the heart of the home?

She tried to be reasonable.

'Geoff, listen. I can give up my pottery class, that will give me an extra evening a week. And I can cut down on the ante-natal classes. I haven't signed anybody up for the Spring course yet – and there are other trained people in the group who can take them . . .' Her voice trailed away.

'You seem determined to take this on, despite what I think.' He paused, staring at her. 'I have to get some sleep, I've got a very early start in the morning – I'm going to Brussels for the day.'

He turned his attention to his alarm clock.

'Oh, you never said –'

'I haven't had the chance. Are you coming to bed or what?'

She mumbled something about needing a drink of water, and told him to put out the light. She went downstairs to the kitchen, fuming. Why was he being so cold, so censorious? She got a whisky, something she rarely drank, and sat at the table and cried. She didn't cry often, and wasn't sure why she did now. She felt sorry for herself, yes, but it was more than that – something to do with the loss of an illusion? She had thought of her marriage as a partnership, of equals. No more.

She poured another whisky. She wished she could call Annie, but it was after eleven – too late. They'd have much to talk about, tomorrow.

Roz felt lousy the next morning. A cab called for Geoff at some awful hour – she presumed he was catching the first plane to Brussels out of Heathrow.

She took Katy to playgroup, then stood at the kitchen window, watching melting snow drip from the trees. The snowman was losing its shape – soon it would be just a shrivelled carrot, an old scarf and some twigs in a pool of slush.

The phone rang. It was Alexander Kostakis. He said that he was nearby and wanted to show her some photographs of his work, it might be useful . . . Roz agreed. He said he'd be with her in twenty minutes and rang off. Roz stood still, holding the phone.

I'll be with you . . . She said the words to herself and sighed.

She went upstairs, ostensibly to make a bed or two, but took the opportunity to check how she looked. Tired and pale, she thought, but passable. She went back downstairs, pulling in her stomach muscles, wandering from room to room. She decided she'd avoid the domesticity of the kitchen this morning, and bring him into the living room.

The doorbell rang. There stood Mrs Baxter, her cleaning lady, who came three mornings a week to help out.

'Oh, Mrs B – hello! Come in. Do you know, I'd forgotten it was your day. Silly me.'

They'd known each other for years, but despite Roz's insistence, the other, older woman still preferred to call her Mrs Harper, or just 'dear'. In return, she was happy to be called Mrs B by all the family. She did have a key, but only used it when she was sure that the Harpers were out.

'Hello, dear. I'll do some ironing this morning, shall I?'

She hung her serviceable coat in the hall.

'Ironing would be great, Mrs B. There's a pile in the utility room, I didn't get round to it yesterday.'

Mrs Baxter went off to the back of the house. Roz knew she'd stay there for an hour or more, ironing resolutely, tuned in to Radio Two.

The doorbell rang again. Alexander Kostakis was holding a large black portfolio under his arm. He smiled. He has a lovely smile, she thought, again.

'Have you got time for a coffee?'

'Yes, why not?'

His coat joined Mrs Baxter's. Today it was long brown leather. She looked at his boots, Timberlands this time. He noticed that she noticed and grinned.

'There's not much snow left, so no excuse for my moon boots today.'

She wondered if the boots might become a running joke between them. Between them? Forget it, Roz.

She showed him into the living room and went to make the coffee.

When she returned he was standing in front of the bookshelves, his hands thrust into the back pockets of his black cords, his head on one side, intently reading the titles. He turned to her.

'I really like this room. There's a lot of interest in it. And so many books!'

She thanked him and put the tray down on the large square coffee table, moving aside the shells and driftwood which Mrs B cursed as they were so fiddly to dust.

She sat on the long sofa bought in Heal's ages ago, now covered in a deep blue chenille throw. He dragged himself away from his scrutiny of the books, and sat next to her, though there were two other sofas to choose from.

He took a mug of coffee (black, she'd remembered), holding it in both hands, one hand gently stroking its curve.

'So, tell me, who is it who's interested in art and photography and archaeology?' he asked, gesturing towards the bookshelves.

'Oh, me mainly, I suppose.'

He settled back into the sofa, one leg crossed over the other, and looked at her. He seemed so relaxed and at ease. He spoke of his favourite paintings and artists, and asked Roz about hers. They discussed the relative merits of different museums and galleries in London and elsewhere. He seemed in no hurry to talk about the loft, and his portfolio remained unopened, leaning against the wall.

She watched as she listened. He was talking of Donatello's *David* in Florence (she had heard only of Michelangelo's statue), one of the first nudes of the

Renaissance. He described the exquisite form of the body and his hand swept downwards through the air, demonstrating the curve of the back.

She found talking to him, listening to him, as natural as if she'd been with a female friend. She tried to imagine sitting here with another man – one of Geoff's colleagues perhaps, or Annie's husband Martin. It would be very different. This man wasn't awkward or tense or impatient to get back into his own world. He wasn't patronising her, or flirting heavy-handedly. Her mind flew back to reading D.H. Lawrence at university; an essay on male and female, the he and she principles, the male in the woman being attracted to the female in the man, and vice versa . . . She ought to re-read it.

'Mrs Harper? Would you like to see the portfolio now?'

'Oh, yes. And do call me Roz.'

'Roz. Is it short for something?'

'Rosalind.'

'From Shakespeare? Is it *As You Like It*?'

'My mother once played the part in an amateur dramatics production!'

'Please call me Alexander – or Alex, my English friends tend to call me that.'

'Yes, I will. Who are you named after, Alexander the Great?'

'Possibly! Though of course, I'm really Alexandros. But since I've lived here so long, it's become anglicised.'

He was still holding the empty mug, his broad thumb stroking up and down the curved handle then resting in the thumb-mark at its base imprinted by Roz.

He held it up.

'This is very pleasing. Handmade pottery can be so good to hold and touch, don't you think?'

'I made it. I go to pottery evening classes –'

'Ah, did you? A woman of many talents . . . Roz.'

'Hardly! Or only minor ones –'

'Don't underestimate yourself.' His tone was serious.

She found herself telling him about all the other things she did – apart from the children and the house – the natural childbirth classes, and the informal advice sessions that resulted, and now this new project she was going to get involved in . . . She intimated that her husband disapproved, without actually criticising Geoff or being disloyal, and he listened, regarding her intently, his eyes not leaving her face. She broke off, suddenly anxious that she may be boring him.

'I'm so sorry. I don't know why I'm telling you all this. And we haven't even discussed the loft!' She tried to laugh off her embarrassment.

'There's nothing to be sorry about. Sometimes it helps to talk to someone who is outside it all.'

He stood up, looking at his watch.

'I must be going. Shall I leave the portfolio here? It has lots of photographs of my work for you to look at. Both of you. Then you can think about what you want.'

They agreed that he'd ring in about a week. He told her to call him if she had any suggestions or questions. They shook hands, a lengthy handshake, their eyes locked, before he walked off down the path, his open coat flying behind him.

Roz went back to the sofa. There was a faint lemony fragrance in the air, it must be his aftershave. She put his portfolio beside her, turning the heavy plastic pages. They revealed simple buildings with stunning interiors. There was a white stone house, which had to be in Greece, the sky behind it was so blue. Then a windmill with circular rooms. Bliss.

At the back she found some pictures of a loft conversion, lots of wood, triangular spaces and corners. It looked fine. She returned to the white house, and the windmill, dazzling in the sun. Blue shutters, thick walls, a courtyard. Cool and shady spaces beckoned, with floors of stone and marble, alcoves and recesses filled with sculpture and plants. The light in the photographs was magical.

She roused herself, and put the portfolio away. Back to reality, she thought, as she went to make Mrs Baxter a cup of tea and listen to the latest report on her husband's bad back.

4

Flying over France, on his way to Tunisia, Geoff gazed at the swoops and drifts of clouds and fidgeted in his seat. Normally he made good use of plane journeys by working and catching up on research, avoiding the food and drinking only water, but today he'd eaten the lunch and was now on his second brandy and soda. He should have been re-reading briefing documents in preparation for meetings with government officials, but he was distracted. He gazed out of the window, thinking about Roz.

They'd hardly seen each other during the past week, let alone spoken. Then yesterday she'd informed him that she'd rung her contact and would soon be starting work on the new project, once the funding had been finalised. It shouldn't take up more than ten or twelve hours a week, working from home, she said, spread over a couple of months. She'd added sarcastically, 'There, that's not so bad is it, Geoff?'

He was trying to be reasonable, but he couldn't understand why she wanted to do this extra stuff. Surely she had everything she needed? It wasn't for the money, so why?

Roz was fortunate, he thought. She had a comfortable life, filled with simple satisfactions, lived snugly in the security of home. Home. He loved the word.

His own childhood had been lonely and barren. The only child of older parents, both doctors, he vowed that one day he would have a large happy family, living in a warm welcoming house, full of love and laughter. And he'd done it, he'd got it, and that had taken some of the chill out of his childhood memories. But he had never really forgiven his parents, especially his mother. She had been devoted to her career, competing with his father, staying up at night to write a paper on this or that, rarely giving him attention or a smile or cuddle. Roz had once expressed admiration for her, commenting on how much she had achieved, especially for a woman of her generation. He had frozen, unable to say the words, 'But at what cost?'

Women confused Geoff more and more these days. Increasingly he found his views being challenged, and not just by Roz. At the office last week a junior executive had even dared to laugh at him and call him old-fashioned.

But some things didn't change. For one thing, women still found him attractive. Sometimes women he met through work, or when he was abroad, came on to him. Occasionally he followed it through, but he was cautious and highly selective. He did not go with anyone whom he thought might cause trouble later.

He'd had sex, and just sex was how he saw it, with several women over the past few years. They had all been one-night (or one-day) stands. He did not tell anyone, he did not boast to the guys at the office. He was not immersed in that male camaraderie, the winks and nudges, the eyeing-up of every female as a potential conquest. He was more subtle.

Of course, Roz did not know and he would never tell her. He saw these encounters as entirely separate from his life with her, and he was careful to do nothing that would endanger their marriage. He liked things the way they were.

Geoff wished he'd had the chance, or made one, to talk to Roz before he'd left. Things had been so strained between them. He remembered that in their very early days, Roz told him that he was unlike other men she'd known, she could talk to him, he'd listen. Geoff could picture her now, sitting up in her narrow student bed, her knees tucked up to her chest, her bare breasts squashed up and sideways. He had wanted to gaze at them, but had to keep meeting her eyes as she told him earnestly about something she'd been reading by D.H. Lawrence. When he could bear it no longer he'd tickled her, pushed her down, kissed her. They had often spent all Sunday in bed, making love four or five times in a row. He thought about the uninhibited Roz he had fallen for, so vibrant, so giving, so very sexy. She had inspired him to overcome his natural shyness.

But that was then. And now? What had happened to the sensuous and sensual Roz? He explained it away easily – age, children, fatigue, lack of time. It was inevitable that their sex life had diminished over the years – it happened to all long-time marrieds, didn't it? It was still pleasurable, but it lacked excitement, so sometimes he had to seek that elsewhere. And sometimes he just needed a screw.

Now he needed distracting from the distractions. He reached into his briefcase and took out some papers. Work. You could always rely on that.

*

As Geoff unpacked in his hotel room in Tunis, Roz was waiting for Alex Kostakis to arrive. He'd rung earlier, saying he'd like to come round to show her his ideas for the loft. She told him that Geoff had just left for a trip, but never mind, come anyway.

Geoff wants me to handle this, thought Roz, so I will.

But first she had to handle the children, satisfy their different needs and demands. She played elaborate puppet games with Katy; talked to Matthew about school and the fight he'd had in the playground, and tried to help him with his ambitious Lego model; she insisted Sam leave his video game to discuss his homework with her, otherwise it might not get done, not properly anyway, and then had to find the ingredients for a home economics lesson he'd suddenly remembered he had the next day; she sympathised with Polly who was sure she had a cold coming, made her lemon and honey, and agreed that Jane Austen wasn't as easy as everyone seemed to think. She cooked an early supper that everyone would like and eat (extremely difficult), explained where Dad was yet again; bathed Katy, read her a story and sang her her favourite nursery rhymes.

By the time she paused for breath it was nearly nine o'clock. Katy was asleep, Matthew was in bed, Sam was upstairs, theoretically finishing his homework, Polly was reading in her room. Roz did a whirlwind tour, then rushed to her bedroom to get ready. But ready for what?

She avoided the answer, concentrating instead on what to wear. Her newish black trousers, yes. What on top? She chose an aubergine silk shirt she'd had for years. She tucked it in, but her waist wasn't small enough and it made her look too bosomy. She left it casually loose, that was better, she didn't want it to look as if she'd gone to any trouble. She put some large silver hoops in her ears, slipped on soft black flat shoes from Hobbs, dabbed on some mascara and that was it.

Alex looked like the archetypal tall dark handsome stranger, standing under the porch light. Yet he wasn't quite a stranger any more, and he wasn't that tall. They greeted each other as he hung up his coat. He was carrying his brown leather bag and a large sketch pad.

'Would you like a drink before we get started? Wine, or something else?'

He followed her into the kitchen. 'Red wine would be good.'

He stood against the worktop, his arms folded, and watched her fetch glasses, a bowl of nuts, the tray.

'So where are the famous Harper children? I thought I might meet them tonight.'

'The two younger ones are in bed. The other two are doing their homework. They might be down later.'

She carried the tray into the living room. As she handed him his wine their fingers touched. Their eyes locked, yet again. A familiarity was growing between them, she knew it. Did he find her attractive? Suppose she were misreading the signs? She was so out of practice at such things.

She fetched the portfolio and, simultaneously, they sat down on the same sofa. Closer than before.

He drank some wine, stretching back with one hand behind his head. He massaged his neck under his long curls. He reminded Roz of a large magnificent cat.

He was wearing a soft navy woollen shirt, which looked Italian and expensive. It was open at the neck, and she could see curls of hair leading down to his chest. Corduroy trousers, tobacco-coloured this time, were tight across his strong thick legs. His legs were spread open, for comfort she assumed. He caught her glance and held it. What did that look mean?

She leaned over to pour him more wine, and she could feel him looking down her shirt at her breasts. Oh God.

She thought she'd better ask him about his work, and they spread the portfolio across their adjacent laps, its weight joining them at the thigh, and he talked her through the photographs.

Eventually they reached the end and he propped it against the sofa. Her thighs felt bereft. He reached for his sketch pad. His plans, only rough drawings he insisted, looked fine to her. Practical but imaginative, keeping interesting corners while making the most of the space. She tried to ask a few intelligent questions, including cost, which he side-stepped, so that she could delay the moment of his leaving.

The bottle of wine was finished. She suggested coffee, and they went into the kitchen. This is becoming a routine, she thought. She realised that she knew very little about him, and resolved to change that.

'Where in London do you live, Alex?'

He prowled around the kitchen, hands in his pockets.

'Near Regent's Park. Well, I have a view over it. You could say I live at the back of Camden Town – some of my friends say that to tease me.'

'Very handy for Greek restaurants anyway.'

She sat at the table and pushed down the plunger of the cafetière. He watched.

'Do you like Greek food?'

'Yes, though it's a while since I had any. I tend to exist on marmite sandwiches and fish fingers nowadays, particularly when my husband's away.'

He looked puzzled.

You silly woman, she thought. What does he know of children's eating habits and convenience foods and messy meal-times?

'Have you any children Alex?'

He looked down into his coffee, then up at her. A wistful look?

'I do have a child, a daughter. She lives in Athens with her mother. We're separated.'

'Oh, I see. I'm sorry.'

He smiled. 'No need to be. These things happen. Why do the English always say they're sorry, about everything?'

'Actually, I think it's women, English or not, who are always saying sorry. Especially to men.'

He raised one eyebrow. He was very good at doing that. Then he leaned back, raised his hands and laughed. 'Well, that puts me in my place!'

Sam charged into the kitchen. 'Mum, I'm starving – oh, hi.'

'Sam, this is Alex Kostakis, the architect I told you about. Alex, this is Sam, my elder son, who's nearly always hungry.'

Sam frowned at her. Why did she have to say that?

Alex stood up and shook Sam's hand. 'Hi, Sam.'

Sam mumbled and headed for the cupboard where the crisps and biscuits were kept.

'Do you want a sandwich? Or why don't you have an apple or a bowl of cereal?'

'It's all right, don't worry, these'll do. See you later.'

He disappeared out of the door as fast as he could, a blur of shaggy blond hair, big trainers, baggy T-shirt, with a packet of crisps and a Kit-Kat and a small carton of orange juice clutched to his chest.

'And how's your homework?' Roz called after him.

'Done it. Don't fuss!' He called back down the stairs.

'Honestly, you'd think I never fed him. I suppose it's because he's growing so much.' Here I go again, she thought, prattling on in this mumsy way.

Alex looked amused. 'How old is he?'

'Thirteen, nearly fourteen. A difficult age.'

'All ages have their difficulties, don't you think?' he said, standing up, preparing to leave. Roz wished he wouldn't.

'Roz – about Greek food – I've an idea. Let me take you to a Greek restaurant one evening. How about Friday?'

She was dumbfounded. He was asking her out. Did he feel sorry for her, a poor little housewife stuck at home while her husband was away? Or was it something else?

There was a rush of eagerness within her and she smiled brightly.

'Thank you – that would be lovely.'

'Would be, or will be?'

She wasn't sure what he meant.

'I'm teasing. But I do still find your English tenses a bit complicated at times.'

'Oh, I see! But your English is so good, you'd hardly know you were –'

'Greek! Yes, I know. That's what my family back in Greece say. They complain that I'm more English than Greek now, but I don't think so.'

She sensed layers of experience, even sorrow, behind his words. She said no more, thinking that she'd probably learn more the next time she saw him. Oh, the next time!

She saw him to the door. They agreed he would collect her on Friday night. She said there was no need, she could drive to meet him, but that seemed to offend him. He hesitated before leaving, and for a moment she had a weird feeling that he was going to kiss her hand.

But he just said, 'Until Friday, Roz.'

'Until Friday. Bye, Alex.'

She stood against the closed front door for a few moments, taking deep breaths.

Polly came slowly down the stairs, sneezing and feeling sorry for herself.

'Oh Polly! That was the architect just leaving. Not feeling well, darling?'

Back into the motherhood routine. A hug for Polly and soothing words that it was only a cold, and yes, she was sure it would be gone by the weekend. She packed her off to bed with a hot water bottle and some mentholated tissues.

She looked in on Katy and Matthew, sound asleep as they should be, then nagged Sam to put out his light. She tidied up the ragged ends of the day: dishwasher on, doors locked, cat in conservatory, lights off.

The luxury of the bed without Geoff. She stretched out, this way, that way, and allowed herself to think about Alex and the prospect of a whole evening out with him.

Only one more day, and then it would be Friday. She felt like a child looking forward to a very special treat. She tormented herself with questions. Suppose she caught Polly's cold? Would Alex have invited them both if Geoff were here? What if Geoff suddenly returned? Was she mad?

Was Alex doing this merely as a professional courtesy to get to know his client? No, it was more than that. She could feel it. And Geoff? Would she tell him about Friday on his return? That would depend on what happened.

5

Alex was puzzled by his own behaviour.

Part of him could not understand why he had asked Roz Harper out for dinner. Admittedly, she was attractive, intelligent, even interesting, but she was also married with four children. A flirtation was fine but surely that should be all. And he was a man who resolutely steered away from emotional difficulties. He loved women, he loved being with them, he loved to make love to them, but ever since his marriage had failed he preferred his pleasures to be straightforward and uncomplicated.

He had married too young, then had insisted that they live in England, ignoring his wife's obvious unhappiness and yearning for Greece. Foolishly, he'd thought a child would be the answer.

In a way it had been the answer for Melina: she'd returned to Athens to have the baby, and had remained there, emboldened by the support of her mother and sisters, resistant to his efforts to get her back. He did not try for long. It tired him. So he stayed in London and accepted the estrangement. Perhaps he was even relieved.

He regretted that he barely knew his daughter, but it was a mild regret. Sometimes he reflected on his brief marriage and unreal fatherhood, and privately felt that he had learned from the situation, but what?

A deeper understanding of women? How to listen as well as to charm? How to be more open and sensitive?

He thought so. Not that he necessarily let it show in his many and short-lived affairs, but it was there, this awareness and way of being, if need be.

And now, Roz Harper. Another part of him wasn't surprised at all that he had invited her out. He felt a strong pull towards her, deep and instinctive. He connected with her. It was sexual, yes, of course – he'd like to get into her bed. He felt she'd like it too, he sensed she'd be exciting and passionate with the right man, and those breasts . . . But it was more than that. He couldn't put a name to it, not yet, but it was something that made her marriage, children, whatever, irrelevant.

Roz was finding it hard to focus on anything but the extraordinary fact that she was going out with Alex Kostakis on Friday night. *Going out*. Such a teenage expression. How ridiculous!

She somehow managed to function, controlling the surges of excited anticipation that kept intruding on her thoughts. Dealing with the mundane took over – the unavoidable round of depositing and collecting children, going to Sainsbury's, cooking, refereeing disputes over the use of the phone or television . . . Add the wisdom of Solomon to the qualities needed for motherhood, she thought.

Friday morning came. Katy had alarmed Roz by being sick in the night. She watched her daughter anxiously over breakfast, but she seemed healthy enough, even eating more than usual. She turned her attention to the others – encouraging Polly to overcome her cold, squeezing her fresh orange juice, checking that she would be in tonight to babysit. (Roz said she was going out for a meal with some people from pottery class. Lie number one.) She got them all out of the house, despite Sam being half asleep, took Matthew to school and Katy to playgroup and didn't stop to chat to Annie. Back home, she confronted her wardrobe yet again, the question screaming at her, What shall I wear?

She rushed to Brent Cross in Geoff's Saab, ignoring builders in white vans who wanted to race on the North Circular. She dashed in and out of clothes shops, trying not to lose patience with the bored young assistants who raised eyebrows at the things she asked to try on, facing despair in the fourth – or was it the fifth – shop, where she battled with the ferocious swing doors of a tiny changing cubicle that opened on to the shop, only hiding her from neck to knees. Telling herself she was pathetic, she took refuge in Marks and Spencer – someone in her family always needed underwear and buying some would retrieve this trip from being a total waste of time. Even though she only ever bought plain white cotton pants, she picked up some satiny French knickers, brown with peach lace, and threw those in the basket too. Then a bra to match. What the hell, she could always bring them back . . .

At home she tried them on. Ridiculous, she thought, and abandoned them in a pile on the bed, impatient with herself and the time-consuming silliness of it all, and went to collect her daughter.

Roz was reluctant to linger at playgroup, but Katy was still occupied, even though most of the children were spilling out. She was carefully folding dolls' clothes, tidying the Wendy house. Roz sighed, regretful that her daughter was involved in such stereotypical female activity – why wasn't she putting away the woodwork tools, or not tidying at all, like the many small boys already going home, leaving their tidying to others. But then, she rationalised, this is what she sees *me* doing at home . . .

After lunch she proceeded to turn out her wardrobe, letting Katy try on her clothes and shoes and jewellery and experiment with her make-up, while she concentrated on finding something acceptable to wear tonight. Part of the problem was that she didn't know what sort of evening it was going to be. She could hardly ring Alex, and say, Well, Mr Kostakis, what did you have in mind? What do you suggest I wear?

By the time the other children returned from school, Roz had laid some clothes on the bed – white shirt with embroidered collar, long black skirt flared from the hips, burgundy velvet waistcoat decorated with beads, black leather belt. She'd risk wearing the shirt tucked in as the waistcoat would hide any bulges. Her black buttoned boots with a slight heel stood ready. It was a gypsyish sort of look, but what the hell, it suited her.

Geoff ordered another cognac from the hotel bar. He sat on a high stool, dipping his hand into the pistachio nuts, glad to have a few hours to himself. He'd been to a drinks party at the British Embassy, the usual mixture of businessmen, local politicians, the odd academic, politely sipping their drinks and eating awful vol au vents, in an atmosphere which was pure Surrey, lovingly created by the ambassador and his wife. Geoff had been to countless such functions in different countries, yet they always felt remarkably similar.

Someone slipped on to the stool next to him. It was the French doctor he had met twice at breakfast. They had already chatted as they'd poured themselves orange juice at the buffet, then again while spooning fresh fruit salad into bowls. She was from Paris, here to monitor a birth control programme. She was his height, slim, striking, with good bones and a wide mouth, in her early thirties he guessed, elegantly but simply dressed, and she spoke excellent English – better than his French.

Tonight she looked tired, with shadows under her eyes. He ordered her a drink too, and they compared their day, sympathising over the difficulties in getting things done.

They had more cognac. They were both a little bored and lonely. They discussed Europe, and how the French and English felt about each other. They found things to laugh at. They relaxed. As she pushed her glossy brown hair off her face, Geoff thought how beautifully and bluntly cut it was, swinging and falling like expensive curtains. Her jacket fell open, and through her white linen shirt he could see the outlines of her bra and her small breasts. He imagined them to be perky and brown-nippled. He wanted to see them. Touch them.

She caught the direction of his glance, then looked him in the eye. Their faces were close. She wondered what he would be like in bed – she had never had an English lover. He visualised their long lean bodies naked, rolling over each other on a bed. Their knees touched. She put her hand on his (she had long straight fingers, no rings) and said softly, 'Shall we go upstairs?'

In the lift they pressed hard against each other and kissed. No words, no names. Geoff remembered when he was young – twelve or so – he had thought French kissing could be done only by the French. The way she kissed him, perhaps he'd been right.

6

Annie stood at her kitchen sink ferociously attacking a non-stick pan covered with the remains of bolognese sauce. She'd had the gas on too high, which was why the bloody sauce had stuck, and she hadn't turned it down because she'd had to answer the phone. It was Martin ringing to say he'd be very late home (again), something to do with finishing an important presentation. She'd thought she could hear sounds of voices and music in the background, but she didn't feel like asking him exactly where he was . . . So she'd had to have a cigarette and a drink because she felt so pissed off, and had forgotten about the bolognese.

OK, she might be removing the surface of the pan as well as the remnants of food, but she didn't bloody care. The whole day had been shitty. Nothing particularly bad had happened – but that was just it, *nothing* had happened . . . Only the usual routines of shopping and children and domesticity. She had hoped to see Roz for coffee and a chat, but Roz had seemed in a strange mood today, unlike her usual self, preoccupied.

Annie looked up from the lumps of blackened food floating in the sink, and out of the window. By the light of the street lamps she could see someone leaving Roz's house. Was it Roz, and a man too? Then they were obscured by the Range Rover at the kerb. Annie watched, leaning against the sink, her sweater getting wet.

Alex opened the passenger door for Roz. She wished he hadn't. It made her feel even more awkward. She fumbled with the seat belt. She sensed that he was about to lean over to help her, and she imagined how their hands might touch, how he would untwist the strap at her shoulder, following it down over her breasts, across her stomach . . .

Click. She'd done it.

Mozart was on the stereo. She began to relax. Alex drove carefully and smoothly – she was surprised. But why? After all, she hardly knew him.

Yet she felt safe. She trusted him and she trusted her instincts – it was still possible to do that, wasn't it?

He sensed her watching him.

'Are you all right? You're very quiet.'

'Oh, yes, I'm fine. I'm enjoying the ride. I haven't been in one of these before. It's a bit like being in a boat, a luxury cabin cruiser you see moored in marinas . . . I should imagine, anyway – I've never been in one of those either!'

He laughed. I'm babbling again, she thought, like a brainless little woman, overawed by his big car. They were driving down the hill, past Highgate Cemetery, when it occurred to Roz that she didn't know where they were headed.

'So where are we going?'

'A place off Charlotte Street – I know the owner. He's Greek. I think you'll like it.'

They didn't speak for the rest of the drive. He hummed along to Mozart. She found it endearing rather than irritating, and began to feel a little drowsy. Cocooned, warm, comfortable, high up over the traffic, she began to wish this journey could continue indefinitely.

It was crowded and noisy in the restaurant, with too many people, the tables crammed closely together. Alex felt a flash of disappointment. This might not turn out as well as he'd hoped. It looked as though old Yanni had handed the restaurant over to his son, who was probably trying to make his mark, and more money, by squeezing in extra places and going down-market. Maybe he should have suggested dinner at his place. This was only an excuse, after all. He rarely ate Greek food himself. He had just wanted to get the delightful Mrs Harper out of her house and on her own. What he really wanted to do, what he still hoped to do, was to take her home and make love to her.

She looked very pretty tonight, very womanly and sexy, he thought. But right now she was also looking flushed and uncomfortable. The signs weren't good.

Roz tried to focus on the menu, but she was worrying about the possibility of seeing someone she knew. Suppose, for instance, a colleague of Geoff's appeared at the next table? Did it matter? Would she have to explain? What was there to explain?

The swirl of her thoughts was interrupted by Alex – leaning towards her, lightly touching her hand, making suggestions about what to eat. She wanted to say, oh anything will do. For a moment she thought of saying she must go home, this has been a mistake, but then she noticed his eagerness to please, saw just how appealing he was, and felt more drawn to him than ever.

She barely noticed the food. It came, she ate some, it went. They drank white wine. They leaned closer over the table to hear each other as the noise around them increased, creating a space of their own.

'Tell me about yourself Roz, I want to know all about you.'

She started telling him about her childhood, her sister who was a successful academic, her parents, then she moved on to the children, her life now.

'But Roz, this is all about your family. What about *you*? Tell me all about you. I want to see into your soul.'

What a Greek thing to say, she thought. But his words touched her.

He hoped it hadn't sounded too much of a cliché. But it was true – he wanted to discover her, the essential Roz. One way would be making love, but that would have to wait a while . . .

Roz regarded him seriously before answering. She saw a hint of anxiety in his expression. Was he as nervous as she was? What could he be nervous of?

She fixed on his eyes and started to talk to him, really talk. The words flowed out of her, feelings, emotions, thoughts she didn't know she had – or had forgotten. Years' worth of words, unplugged, released. His sounds of encouragement carried her along. She told him of her eighteen-year-old self, wanting to be arty, to write poetry, to paint, to travel, to *be* someone, but always diverted by superficialities, or by boys or men, by pleasing others. Or thwarted by lack of encouragement or opportunities or her own lack of real ambition –

The waiter leaned over to exchange an empty bottle of wine for a full one. Curse him, thought Alex.

He took her hand. He held it between his two hands. She felt his warmth, she felt joined to him.

'There,' he said. His voice was low, intimate. 'That will stop you shredding any more menus.'

She looked down – the menu in front of her was ripped in small straight tears around the edge. Had she done that?

'Tell me more.' His tone was coaxing. Now he was holding both hands, and he held her with his voice and his look. She could not resist him.

The sounds of the restaurant drifted around her like a breeze, nothing could break his spell. She told him about the kind of life she had dreamed about when she was younger – a bohemian life, a reckless daring life, lived with risk and passion . . .

He began to stroke her hands with his thumbs.

A recognition burst inside her – how she wanted him! The yearning, churning ache of desire that she had not felt for so, so long, that nagging craving need for sex, was back.

She was speaking of regrets about her life, but her voice floated off somewhere above her head. Their knees touched under the table. His leg pushed against hers, she returned the pressure.

'I have regrets too,' he said. 'I regret not meeting you long ago.'

And he brought her hand up to his mouth and kissed her open palm. Inside she flipped and swooped.

They gazed at each other intently. He leaned very close.

'Roz, will you come home with me? Now?'

She nodded, squeezed his hand, managed to whisper, 'Yes.'

The noise of the restaurant intensified and intruded. The sound of smashing plates, laughter, squealing. The spell around them was suspended, temporarily.

Alex stood up, pulled her to her feet. 'Come, I'll get the bill on the way out.'

The cold air in the street sobered her a little – was it the wine or the hunger for Alex that made her feel so unsteady?

He helped her with her coat. She felt a shiver of anticipation, that adolescent feeling – will he put his arm around me, will we walk as one?

He did, they did.

They fitted well together as they walked to the car. His arm encircled her tightly, as if he were frightened she might change her mind and run away.

Neither said anything, although they kept looking at each other under the street lights, smiling, not quite believing what was happening.

Roz found it easy to ignore a voice that whispered in her head about her children and husband, about loyalty and guilt. All she could think of was the moment – and the children were fine, and Geoff was far away.

All she wanted to hear was the thundering need inside her. For Alex.

He drove off towards Regent's Park, too fast, but she was glad. One hand left the wheel and stroked her hair, lifted it, caressed her neck.

Did she dare touch his knee, move her hand towards his thigh? She did.

A charge buzzed and surged between them, and the closed space inside the car was filled with impatient sexual energy.

'Nearly there, Roz,' was all he said.

7

They pulled up outside a large white house with a grand columned porch and a huge front door. He murmured something about being lucky to find a parking space. They hurried up the steps, holding on to each other. She felt giddy, a little fearful, knowing that they were moving towards the inevitable . . . He fumbled with keys, still holding her with one hand, reluctant to relinquish contact.

Her mind took in the chequered marble floor of the hall. They climbed the wide staircase, arms around each other inside their coats, their steps slowing as his fingers brushed the side of her breast. Oh, he thought, how promising. And we still haven't kissed, she thought, kiss me, oh please.

He spoke ordinary words, 'My apartment is at the top.'

She said nothing, thinking of the kiss – will we be standing, sitting, lying down . . .

They came to his front door, a dark green door, another key and they were inside, the flick of a switch, light and space, a wall of windows full of the London night.

Stylish, arty, interesting. Later, another time, I'll explore this flat, she thought, but first . . .

He removed her coat, threw it with his on to a

brown leather sofa. They stood facing each other, holding hands.

Now. Their eyes met in consent. There could only ever be one first kiss between them. Wait. The pleasure of anticipation. His hands were on her shoulders, pulling her closer closer, her arms around his back . . . The kiss. Slow . . . tender, lips together, apart, mouths open, wet tongues competing for space, twisting, turning deeply.

The joys of their bodies pressed together, the heat pulsating through their clothes . . .

He suddenly pulled back, held her at arm's length, searching her face, his expression full of desire – and anguish. They were breathing hard.

He was giving her the chance to stop, to retreat, to refer to husband, children, guilt, but her mind was empty of all that.

'Roz, Roz, I want you, you know that, but –'

She held his face in her hands,

'It's OK, it's OK,' was all she could murmur.

They kissed again, harder, mouths open wider and wider, their faces wet, almost banging against each other, on and on, as if they could discover everything about each other through kissing.

This time, Roz eased herself away. It was ridiculous, but she had to pee.

'Alex, I'm sorry, I have to – can I use your bathroom?'

He laughed, wildly, his hand on his heart. 'Thank God, I thought you were deserting me!'

'How could I?' She looked pointedly at his erection, clearly visible through his chinos. He laughed again, and hugged her. 'Go, quickly, over there, second door.'

A small lobby, coat hooks, mirror, another door.

Hurry, hurry. Black, white, chrome, masculine. Where was the flush? Continental style, pull it up, check in the mirror. What a mess, red face, blotchy.

Run cold water, black soap, wash hands, splash face, cool down. Oh I want him, want him, fuck – oh Christ, she thought – will he think I've come in here to insert a cap, check I've got condoms? Should I tell him I'm fully wired for sex, Copper Seven in place? What's the protocol these days? What about AIDS? No – hold on, be calm. Go to him.

He was sitting on the sofa. He got up, came towards her, and led her into the bedroom.

They stood by the bed, kissing again, his hands running up and down her body, pulling her into him, up against his erection, her hands on his strong back . . . Separating for an instant, panting, he stroked her face.

'Oh Roz, really I'd like to take time, to undress you, go slowly, but I want you so much – shall we be quick, this first time?'

His voice was like a breath in her ear.

She breathed back, 'Yes, yes, oh yes.'

Clothes off, tossing them anywhere. What do I care now about my underwear, she thought. Waistcoat, shirt, bra off. Breasts bare, she started to whip off her boots, fumble with the laces, how stupid to wear them. She speedily pulled down her skirt, tights, pants all in one go. She saw that he'd been faster – he had less to take off. He was covered in dark hair, and oh the size of his erection . . .

He saw her large breasts, swinging, as she took her clothes off, and he came to her and held them, he had to. Softness, abundance, creamy milky skin. He sensed a lack of inhibition in her response that thrilled him.

She saw his solid muscular body and his delicious circumcised cock, so thick as well as long . . . Cock. Such a good word for it – proud, jutting, strutting, *male*.

The simplicity of two naked bodies, free, skin against skin, flesh against flesh. Alex and Roz.

He flung back the duvet so that nothing would impede them. Kissing even more wildly and wetly than before, almost clumsy in their passion, he pushed her on to her back, kneeling over her, hard cock against soft stomach, his hands roaming over her breasts, exploring, squeezing and playing, his palms moving up and down across her nipples. She groaned, her rhythm rocking against him, waves of relief and recognition and longing. He pinioned her arms above her head, kissing her throat, moving down to her breasts, licking, sucking one then the other, but no time now, she was starting to come. His fingers found her, so wet, so open already, moving, bucking, her voice crying fuck me fuck me, moving into her so easily as if he'd always known her, filling her, thrusting higher, both moving faster, him rising up on his hands, the thrill of his body arching over her, her legs wrapped round him – YES more more more!

His eyes closed, a cry, his whole body shuddering, and she came with a scream of his name.

He sank on to her, his heavy head on her breasts. She held his head tightly, stroked his damp hair, felt wetness oozing from her, was overcome with emotion. So good, so bloody good, so long since she'd felt this way, so right.

He lifted his head, murmured in Greek, kissed each breast, rolled gently off her.

They lay side by side like two bookends, nakedness

echoed, propped on one elbow facing each other, smiling.

I do not feel embarrassed, she thought, lying here with my forty-year-old body, my breasts just anyhow, my round stomach. I want to look at him, I want him to look at me. *Me*. I feel like me again.

He caressed her face, her shoulder. She stroked the hair on his chest, so thick and dark, but softer than she'd expected.

'There was something about you – I knew you were a passionate woman as soon as I met you. I wanted you even on that first visit to your house. And you wanted me too, didn't you?'

'Yes, although I didn't really admit it to myself. I've never done this before –'

He laughed, throwing back his head. 'You surprise me!'

She tweaked some hair on his thigh. 'You know what I mean, never with anyone else apart from – well, since my marriage that is –'

'Ssh, no more talk. Come here, let me hold you.'

Soon he became hard again, and she grasped his cock, stroked its length, then his fingers were inside her, and he said he loved her body, and she threw herself on to him . . .

It was slower this time, so much to explore, pleasuring each other, with fingers and tongues, fondling and sucking and slipping and both yearning for more, more of each other and saying so.

They made love side by side, wanting to look at each other, to watch the other's face, see expressions change. He moved carefully and steadily into her, she eased him in, her legs under and over him, ankles crossed behind him, her hands on his wonderful firm bottom, his squeezing her soft one. Together they moved, eyes fixed on eyes until, heads thrown back, they came to an exquisite end, her mind a jumble of Greek gods and caves and half-men/half-horses charging down a hillside . . .

They lay very close on their backs, his arm around her gently fondling a breast (oh, he thought, I could spend days and days just doing things to her breasts), her hand on his hard stomach, smoothing down the hair, a finger tracing around his navel, the whole world in his navel . . .

'This is just the beginning,' he said.

She murmured, 'Yes, oh yes,' and felt she could drift into sleep.

He touched her hair, kissed her eyes.

'How long can you stay?'

She sat up quickly, jolted into action. 'What's the time?'

'Nearly twelve.'

'Oh God, I must go. Cinderella time! I can get a taxi –'

He turned her towards him, almost roughly. 'Oh, no you won't. Of course I will take you home.'

He seemed offended, so she apologised. He kissed her, cupped her breasts, reluctantly let them go.

'We better get dressed, Roz, or we'll start all over again.'

She dressed as quickly as she could – everything was in a tangle. As she struggled with a boot – the lace was broken – she saw him pull on his boxers, up and over . . . Tuck it in, down. Magnificent, tantalising.

But she felt a flash of uncertainty – what would happen next? Where did they go from here?

He was tender, reassuring, helping her with her

coat, lifting her hair over the collar. 'When can we see each other again, Roz?'

She noticed how he used her name a lot. It touched her.

'Do you want to?' Little me voice again, damn.

He tweaked her nose. 'Of course I do, you delicious woman. What did I just say? Do you want to see me?'

'Of course I do.'

'Well then, don't let's play games.' He kissed her forcefully on the mouth, an affirmative kiss, an until-next-time kiss. 'Now, let's go, we'll discuss the how and when in the car.'

She let herself relax against his shoulder as he drove her slowly home. She felt, simply, happy. The feeling stayed with her as she entered the house, having agreed with Alex that he'd call round on Monday morning. To talk.

All was quiet. Safe. Intact. Nothing to reproach herself for, no reason for guilt.

A note from Polly said that everything was fine, she'd gone to bed.

Roz was glad no-one was still up, she wanted to be alone. She locked up, checked Katy and Matthew, did a bit of desultory tucking in and picking up of teddies, and turned off Sam's bedside light – he'd fallen asleep reading. Polly's door was closed.

She went through the normal motions, but she didn't feel normal. I feel like someone else, she thought. No I don't, I feel like me.

She took her lenses out, dropped her clothes on the floor, didn't bother to wash or brush her teeth or even remove her make-up, wanting their smell to stay on her.

She stretched out in the bed, luxuriating in the

remembered feel of him, a faint aroma on her skin, more aftershave, a tang of nutmeg. Her nipples were sore, her vagina still wet. Oh God. She replayed the evening in her mind, step by step, scene by scene, move by move, and fell asleep, her hand resting comfortingly between her legs.

8

Monday arrived at last.

Roz started the morning on a wave of impatience, dealing with all the requests for money, lunch boxes, boots, excuse notes for games, everything, as quickly as she could. Why couldn't they do things for themselves for once? She thought she'd always encouraged her children to be independent. She sped Katy to playgroup in the car – 'Mummy, I'm the first one here!' – then flew home again.

She'd somehow got through the weekend. Saturday hadn't been too bad. She had woken very early, still in a state of euphoria. No guilt, which surprised her, no agonising. Just a feeling that it had been right, and a wonderful trembling excitement about seeing him again. She'd bounced out of bed, full of energy, feeling lighter, younger. She'd surveyed herself in the mirror – she looked well, but otherwise no different. Her mouth was sore from so much kissing, but it didn't show.

She'd been virtuous, throwing herself into tidying and housework, being busy and physical, letting Katy help (why did this child love housework?), while Matthew watched television and Sam and Polly slept. She'd cooked a proper lunch which the children hardly ate. As they'd squabbled and messed around at the table, she'd looked at them fondly and felt the urge to gather them all up and hug them, to take them out and spoil them. She supposed it was her way of trying to share her happiness.

In the end she'd taken Katy and Matthew swimming (Polly was going to Camden Lock with her friend Laura, Sam was out skate-boarding). The younger ones were delighted – she normally made all sorts of excuses not to take them to the public pool – the crowds, the germs, the verrucas.

And it had been awful there, as usual, but she did not mind. Full of adolescent boys showing off, fooling around, a substitute for sex, she supposed. Sex. That had made her think of Alex.

Back home, as she'd been rinsing swimsuits and towels stinking of chlorine, the phone rang. She leaped to answer it, sure it would be Alex, although he had not said he'd call.

It was Geoff, not sounding as far away as he should. Oh God, she thought, what if he's at the airport? But he was still in Tunisia. They'd had a brief, friendly conversation, Roz feeding him snippets of news about the children, saying nothing about herself except that she was fine. He told her of the red tape and frustrations, and how he may have to stay longer than planned (oh good, she thought). He spoke briefly to the children and rang off.

Far away in North Africa, he smiled to himself, satisfied that all was well. Then he allowed himself the indulgence of anticipating another night with Céline (he now knew her name), who had proved to be as bold and athletic and unpredictable in bed as he could possibly have hoped for.

On Saturday night Roz had watched *Blind Date* with the children, ordered a Chinese take-away (one of their favourite treats), and was scraping all the greasy trays and left-overs into the bin when the phone rang. This time it *was* him. She'd rushed upstairs to take the call in her bedroom. His voice took her breath away. She wanted to touch him, hold him.

'Alex. How sweet of you to ring. I was hoping you would.'

'I wanted to ring you all day, but I thought I'd better wait until those children of yours were in bed. Are they?'

'Oh, some of them.' She didn't want to talk about her children.

'Well, how are *you*?'

'Great! I felt wonderful today – because . . . because of last night.' Simple words. But how could she truly tell him how she felt? Should she?

'And it was so good being with you, I can't begin to tell you.'

She trembled, and gripped the phone tightly.

'Roz –'

'Alex.'

'I want to see you so badly.'

'I know, I feel the same. Are you coming here on Monday?'

'Try and stop me!'

'As if I would. About ten then?'

'Yes. I'll be there. I can't wait.'

They said good night, then lingered in silence, like all lovers, reluctant to sever the link and break the spell. They said it again, then replaced their receivers slowly, simultaneously.

The call left Roz feeling flushed, agitated. She'd thought she'd heard voices behind his. Was he with someone? Who? There was so much about him that she didn't know.

*

Alex imagined Roz in her house, with her children. He was alone listening to Radio Four. Now, after speaking to her, he had a fucking hard-on. He stalked around his flat, cursing her but wanting her. She had such an effect on him – so immediate, so intense, so needy . . . Damn it, damn her, that she was married and so attached. He wanted to rush over there right now, and spend all night in her, in her bed.

He attempted to rearrange himself inside his jeans, then poured a large whisky, looking through his stack of videos for a distraction. Something melancholy, bittersweet.

He settled for *A Bout de Souffle* (he had a penchant for European films of the Sixties), and tried to put Roz out of his mind – until Monday.

Sunday had been awful. It felt like when she was fifteen, hating the slow quiet day, wishing it away. In the evening, once the children were in bed, or upstairs, she'd treated herself to a long soak in a fragrant bath. She'd washed her hair and waxed her legs, and slapped moisturiser over every inch of her skin.

Am I doing this for him? she asked herself. She wouldn't have sex with Alex tomorrow, not here in this house – that wouldn't be right, would it? That night she dreamed of him. They were standing in the loft having sex, when the roof began to blow away, tiles flying through the air.

He arrived early. She rushed to the door, and there he was, holding up his briefcase. 'About the loft, Mrs Harper?' he said in a silly voice.

'Of course,' she giggled. 'Do come in.'

He hugged her fiercely, almost lifting her feet off the floor, surrounding her with himself and his sheepskin coat. 'I'm so happy to see you,' he said again and again into her ear, her hair.

They kissed. It started as a friendly, good morning, how are you sort of kiss, but became something different.

They came up for air after a few minutes. Alex held her shoulders.

'Oh, Mrs Harper, what are we to do?'

She moved in close to him, held him tight, decided to take his words lightly.

'All sorts of things, but not here, not yet, not unless we're desperate.'

'But I am desperate.'

'I know, I can feel you.' Her fingertip traced the outline of his erection through his jeans.

'You're teasing me, Roz.' He took her hand away and kissed it. 'But I can wait. Let's talk.'

They sat at the kitchen table, reaching out to hold hands. They were silent for a few moments, fingers entwining, gazing at each other.

'Alex, I don't know how to deal with this situation. I want to be with you yet –'

'Yet you feel you shouldn't be?'

'Well, not exactly, it doesn't seem that simple. There's a part of me which says I should feel guilty, but mostly, right now, I'm being pulled towards you. Does that make sense? I want to see you, to – to make love with you, to get to know you better, and I don't really feel guilty at all.'

'Well, why should you? You're not hurting anyone –'

'Not yet!' Her voice grew louder. 'And I mustn't hurt anyone – especially the children.'

She didn't mention her husband, thought Alex, perhaps she feels less for him than she should. Or was she being tactful?

The kettle boiled. She let go of his hands, and stood up. 'How about a coffee?'

'No. It's you I want.'

He was at her side, enfolding her in his arms. She nuzzled his neck (oh, he smelled so good) and mumbled, 'I want you too. I've thought of nothing else all weekend.'

He massaged her neck, tenderly. 'I think I know how you're feeling. I understand about your children. But let's take it a step at a time, shall we? We'll find a way to see each other, we must . . .'

His words faded as he kissed her face with soft little kisses all over. She could feel herself relaxing, giving herself up to him, opening like a flower.

He held her, looking around. 'Where can we go?' She pulled him into the hall, towards the stairs. They grabbed at each other's clothes, he pushed up her sweater and pulled her bra up and over her breasts in one swift action, so that they bounced free. There was a great wodge of clothing under her neck, she was hot and sweaty, but she loved the urgency of it, his head brushing between her breasts . . .

She whimpered, and reached for his belt, whipped his zip down, put her hand into his boxers to free him. He unzipped her jeans, pulled them down and her pants, and whispered, 'Here, now.' He eased her back against the stairs and she stretched out, one hand holding a banister, the other flat against the wall. She did not hesitate. It's all right, she thought, it's not the marital bed – this is acceptable, it's neutral territory.

He knelt on a stair below, between her legs, and

entered her quickly. She arched her back against the stairs. It was fast and rough and rudimentary, so voracious were they, coming in a rush together, sighing with release.

He nuzzled her breasts, kissed her and helped her up. They put their clothes right, grinning at each other, at the ridiculousness but importance of it all.

She made some instant coffee, with difficulty, as he continued to touch her, kiss her neck, fondle her breasts. They sat down next to each other at the table, chairs pulled close, and he stroked her hair back from her warm forehead as you do with a sick child. 'So, my Rosalind, how can we manage to have some time together?'

He looked at her with tenderness, waiting patiently for a reply.

He was going to have to do a lot of that, he knew. He was not by nature a patient man, but for her he would try. He knew it was going to be frustrating – not just sexually, though not being able to make love to her whenever he wished was bad enough – because so much was now up to her. All he could do was make himself available, and try not to make too many demands.

It was Roz who was going to have to live a lie.

She had been thinking about what she had to do. She was resolute: Alex was now her lover and she had to see him, be with him. He was not just a quick fuck, a distraction for a bored housewife (how some people – Geoff? – would probably see it). He was much, much more than that.

It was largely a matter of organisation and she was good at that.

She normally went to her pottery classes every

Tuesday evening – she'd come to him instead. Then there were all the meetings she attended – the playgroup committee, the PTA at two schools and one sixth form college; the childbirth group; environmental pressure groups . . . She didn't forget Geoff's frequent visits abroad (now she had reason to be pleased about them) and she thought they could snatch some time together during the day, when the children were at school, if Alex could manage it . . .

As Alex listened, playing with a curl of her hair, watching her lively face, he began to comprehend the complexities of her life and it unnerved him. He was used to living a life where he had to think only of himself, his own needs. How different for her: a life lived so much for others, confined by circumstances. He wanted to free her.

'Of course, if your loft conversion goes ahead, I may have to be here a lot, making sure the client is satisfied . . .'

They laughed and their gazes locked, and Roz wondered if they had time . . .

He knew what she was thinking but said he had to go, lunch with a client. And I have to collect my daughter, she said.

'So when can we meet?' he asked. 'Tomorrow's Tuesday, can you come to me then?'

She was about to say yes, she'd miss pottery, then remembered there was an open evening at Sam's school and she had to see his teachers – and as Geoff was away . . .

'I'm sorry, Alex.'

He hugged her. 'It's all right, Roz, it's going to be all right. Look, you ring me when you've worked out when we can meet. Ring me anytime, OK?'

He gave her another business card, this time with his home number on the back.

'I will, I will. As soon as I can.'

They held each other tightly, their bodies pressed together, as if trying to leave an imprint, then reluctantly drew away.

She walked to collect Katy, although it was raining heavily. It suited her mood, she felt drained. She had embarked upon an affair. She had to make arrangements to conduct it. It sounded so commonplace, so tawdry. It wasn't really like that, was it?

Katy presented her with a limp piece of card, weighed down with glue and feathers and wood shavings. 'Look, Mummy, for you. Collage.' How are we going to get this home and dry, thought Roz.

'They start them young these days, don't they? Collage indeed,' Annie remarked. She was trying to get Tom's feet into yellow wellingtons. 'Too small, told you, too small!' he protested.

They left together under Annie's giant umbrella, Katy's collage crushed in a pocket of Roz's Barbour, the children jumping in every puddle. Back to normality, thought Roz. This is what it will be like. Switching tracks.

Annie and Tom came in for lunch. The children ran into the playroom and Annie settled herself into the big Windsor chair at the end of the kitchen table.

'Coffee, Annie? Then how about some lentil soup – will Tom eat it?'

'I think so. Though what he will or won't eat seems to change from week to week.'

She watched Roz bustle about the kitchen, taking a tub of soup from the fridge to heat up, making coffee.

'Honestly, Roz, you are amazing, making your own soups, everything so cosy and under control. I don't know how you do it, no one does.'

'Ah, the trick is that it *appears* to be under control – believe me. Open my cupboards and everything spills out, my cakes don't always rise, I can't remember when I last defrosted the freezer –'

'Nonsense. Everyone sees you as the perfect wife and mother.'

Roz groaned. She did not want to be seen that way, especially now – it was hardly appropriate.

'Annie, you and I know there's no such thing.'

Annie pulled out a packet of cigarettes, and asked if she could smoke – she always did, so Roz wondered why she bothered to ask. She went through the ritual of finding an ashtray and opening a window.

Annie inhaled deeply and began to talk about herself. About Martin, his lack of consideration, her need to do something else apart from being a general dogsbody . . . She was trying. She'd recently bought some watercolours and some decent paper, but so far they'd remained unused. Perhaps she didn't take herself seriously?

Roz listened sympathetically, nodding in the right places, stirring soup, cutting bread, all the while saying to herself, like a child, I've got a secret, I've got a secret. How surprised her friend would be, she thought, Annie with her unconventional clothes and outspoken behaviour, if she knew . . .

Annie's voice, entering a different tone zone, interrupted her. 'Roz, I've been meaning to ask you –

who was that gorgeous man, the one with the Range Rover, that I've been seeing around?'

'Oh, that's our architect.' She hoped she wasn't blushing. 'Well, he might be – he's drawing up plans for the loft, you know we're thinking of converting it.'

'He looked delicious. Though of course I didn't see much of him. He looked like that guy in those old Gitanes ads, remember? Sort of gypsyish, sexy but romantic.'

She could tell all this from her kitchen window?

'Oh does he?' Roz concentrated on seasoning the soup. 'He's actually Greek, although he's lived here for years.'

'Perhaps that's what I need, a hunky man, a lover to bring excitement into my humdrum existence.' Annie dragged hungrily on her cigarette, as if she were trying to extract meaning as well as nicotine.

'Do you really mean that?'

'No, probably not. Where would I find such a creature? Anyway, I don't suppose I could handle all the lies and excuses, the aggravation.'

Roz kept her back to Annie. She couldn't trust the expression on her face.

9

Would anyone choose to be a parent if they knew what it would be like?

Roz was sitting with Sam in the hot crowded school hall, waiting to see his maths teacher, surrounded by a haphazard queue of parents, their appointment times no longer relevant as people overran their ten-minute slots. They'd already been upstairs to see his French teacher, rushed across to the humanities building to see his class tutor, then over to the science block . . . And there were still several more to see.

She and Geoff had chosen this large local comprehensive because they both believed in state education and it was, well, comprehensive and local, and had a good enough reputation. The everyday reality comprised overstretched teachers doing their best with diminishing resources and increasing paperwork, trying to teach but more often barely coping with a completely mixed bunch of adolescents.

It wouldn't be so bad, Roz thought, if I'd been hearing good things about this son of mine. She glanced sideways at Sam, hunched over, looking fed up. As he should be – she'd been hearing consistent accounts of his bad behaviour in class, messing about, answering back, not concentrating. He'd always been lively, but until now it had seemed containable.

'So Sam, what's this all about?'

'Dunno. They're exaggerating, anyway.'

'Are they? Why would your teachers do that?'

'I dunno. Some of 'em don't like me.'

He was using his school voice, she knew, in case any of his mates were around. She sighed, and said they'd discuss it further at home. He shrugged and said OK. Wish you were here, Geoff, she thought.

Back home at last, her head aching, Roz was pleased to see Polly in the kitchen loading the dishwasher. We've had a relatively trouble-free time with her at least, Roz thought. Hardworking at school, good at exams, friendly and sociable, not too many problems with boys, none with drugs, touch wood.

'Polly love – how's things?'

'Fine, both asleep. Usual bedtime fuss with Matthew, he wanted to watch all sorts of rubbish on TV. He seems to have this idea that because he's nine he should be able to watch programmes at nine o'clock!'

Roz laughed. 'I'll speak to him tomorrow.'

'Want some tea?' her daughter asked.

Sam escaped, bounding upstairs two at a time. I'll talk to him later, thought Roz wearily.

'Actually, I think I'll have a drink. I need one.'

'Was it that bad?'

'You know what open evenings are like, it all takes so long, it's nobody's fault. Then Sam didn't exactly get good reports –'

She stopped, thinking she shouldn't say too much. Sometimes she forgot Polly wasn't another adult.

Roz sat down, slipped off her shoes and sipped

some wine. Perhaps she'd phone Alex tonight . . . To hear his voice, make him real.

'Oh, Mum, Dad phoned about an hour ago. I told him where you were –'

'How is he? What did he say?'

'He's coming home tomorrow, that's great isn't it? Though he said he might have to go back in a few weeks. Oh, and he sent his love.'

'Oh, good.'

Roz wondered if Polly noticed her lack of enthusiasm, but she knew that even the most loving and giving of children were basically self-centred, and only really noticed their parents' behaviour when it impinged on them.

Polly went upstairs, to finish an essay she said. And to ring her friends, thought her mother.

Oh sod it! She cursed the fact that Geoff was returning tomorrow. She'd been hoping that she could visit Alex one evening this week – but what excuse could she give now? She couldn't use pottery night or a parents' evening, not now. Use your imagination, Roz. She was always being told she had too much imagination when she was younger, so use it now.

It would be strange to have Geoff home. It seemed so long since he went away, but it was only six or seven days. How would she feel when she saw him? Would guilt descend upon her? Would she be convincing as her normal wifely self, whatever that was?

She savoured the last night of having the bed to herself. Hot chocolate and digestive biscuits while she skimmed through *Good Housekeeping*, she couldn't concentrate enough for a book. Never mind the crumbs, she'd just move over to Geoff's side. She took off her nightshirt, to sleep naked. If Geoff were here he'd take that as a signal for sex.

She thought about Alex and what he did to her, how he made her feel. She ran her fingers lightly over her breasts. Oh Alex. As she put out the light it occurred to her that Geoff would probably want to make love tomorrow night. It would be reasonable – they had been separated for a week, and what could be more natural than a seemingly devoted husband and wife making love after an enforced absence?

She drifted into turbulent sleep, filled with exhausting dreams. In one she had mislaid Katy in a massive car park full of Range Rovers. Then she couldn't remember how many children she had when questioned by a policewoman.

Geoff arrived home by taxi early in the afternoon. He enjoyed coming home from these trips in the middle of the day – he had the chance to enter what he saw as the charmed, female, weekday world of the home. It usually meant he took the rest of the day off.

As he quietly opened the front door he felt the familiar rush of warmth. He stood in the hall for a few moments, breathing it all in. So unlike the house of his childhood, which had always seemed cold, in every sense. When he'd returned from boarding school, having struggled on the trains alone, there was never any pleasure in arriving.

Now he could smell something baking, he could hear the radio and the voices of Roz and Katy coming from the kitchen, then laughter.

He savoured the moment. I'm getting sentimental, he thought. Perhaps it's my age, or the effect of landing safely yet again. He had two recurring dreams of aeroplane crashes: one where he was in a plane going down, noise, flames, chaos, yet he remained calm, reading *Newsweek*, and always awoke before the fatal ending; in the other the whole world was swirling, heading for disaster, crashing around the plane, while he drank brandy and ate peanuts in a wide first class seat.

He shouted hello, and Katy came running from the kitchen, wearing her Miffy apron.

'Daddy! My Daddy!' She flung herself at him, hugging his legs. He lifted her up, kissed her soft round cheeks, what a sweet delight she was, and there was Roz behind her.

'Roz, darling. Good to see you.' She smiled, kissed him on the cheek, he kissed her quickly on the lips.

'Geoff, you're back. How are you?'

He enjoyed seeing her after an absence, it was almost like meeting her all over again. She was so pretty, so wholesome and healthy-looking, so – so *normal*. More and more he seemed to meet other kinds of women. Hyped-up women, pushy, in skirted versions of men's city suits, smart and edgy, lipsticked and glossy. Give me Roz any time, he thought.

She asked him about the trip, made him a cup of tea, and he sat with Katy on his knee and chatted, telling Roz some of it – filtered information. It wasn't that he was being patronising or secretive, just that much of it was just plain boring. Of course, he did not tell her about Céline.

Katy interjected frequently with her own news and demands, and Roz was relieved, as she was feeling somewhat detached from the homecoming of the husband and father and hoped it wasn't showing. Her smile was beginning to ache.

Geoff looked happy enough.

At least children oil the wheels, she thought. They interrupt, they create havoc, they provide topics for conversation, they make you too tired for sex. In her new situation, whatever that was, she felt regretful about the children, long-term, because their existence would probably be the major obstacle to her relationship with Alex. But short-term she was grateful to them – they could provide a smokescreen for her to hide behind, to avoid closeness and intimacy with Geoff.

A real family tea-time, thought Geoff later that day, looking at his assembled children around the kitchen table. Roz had made masses of interesting sandwiches, in different kinds of bread, and brought out the cake she'd made with Katy. Geoff fed the children educational snippets about his trip: he kept most of their attention for most of the time. He didn't notice that Sam had his Walkman on, his long hair hiding the earphones, and Matthew had his hamster under his sweater – every now and then a bump moved about until Matt put his hand over it. He gave them their presents – key rings for Sam and Matthew, beads for Polly, a soft camel for Katy.

Roz drank tea and observed. What a handsome, happy family they are, we are, she thought, gazing at each child in turn, then Geoff. I should be proud and glad and grateful. And I am – I was. She was tempted to fetch the camera, to record the scene before her, but did not want to move. She sat quietly, in the middle of the family yet outside it, watching a living tableau, like an elaborate Christmas window at

Selfridges. She realised that she was seeing the Harper family as others must see it – although they, naturally, would include her, Roz Harper, perfect wife and mother.

Geoff caught her eye across the table and sent her a fond smile, seeing the tears in her eyes, assuming they were tears of happiness.

Roz was dreading the moment when the children were in bed. She felt almost embarrassed at the thought of being on her own with Geoff. But they all took ages to settle down and Polly lingered, always eager to talk to her father. It was nearly eleven by the time they were alone, and it was obvious he was tired.

'Sit down for once,' he said. She was meticulously tidying, sticking close to the kitchen sink.

He gave her a bottle of Chanel No 5 – he invariably bought her some duty-free perfume – and she thanked him and kissed him on the cheek. They sat companionably on the sofa together, some Bach in the background, Geoff's arm loosely around her shoulders (I can cope with that, she thought) and talked about the children, indulging in parental pride and satisfaction. She told him about Sam and Geoff said he'd talk to him, but it was no big deal surely? Perfectly normal behaviour for a boy his age. She left it at that.

Geoff had a shower before bed, saying he felt grubby from his journey. True enough, but he also wanted some time alone, a bit of space. He wanted to think about Céline, and also to try to wash her out of his system.

He stood under the hot streams of water, recalling

their nights together. Four nights, and what nights. She had been an education, introducing him to all sorts of games and pleasures. He had done things with her that he'd never done with Roz – or with anyone else.

They spent all four nights in her room, although each time he returned to his in the early hours of the morning. Four nights full of erotic wonder and excitement. She was like a piece of elastic, supple, inventive.

She'd produced a selection of condoms from her briefcase – different colours, sizes, finishes. Samples from her birth control visits, he wondered, or does she always carry them? She chose a ribbed blue one and deftly rolled it on him. 'Pretty boy,' she said. 'Now are you ready for me?'

Different positions, different places – standing in corners, the shower, once in the lift in the middle of the night. Was it because she was a doctor that she liked to live close to the edge, to take risks?

Dancing naked, eating room-service naked, always naked. No-hands games in which they touched each other all over, but with their hands behind their backs, using lips, tongues, toes, everything.

One night they played doctors and patients. She was naked but for her stethoscope. Intimate examinations. Geoff bandaged up, then unbandaged. She had roared with laughter.

Another night was naughty night, as she called it. She teased him about his Englishness, his schooling. She said she had to spank him. All sorts of things happened that night that he would rather not think about.

This morning when he left (she was there for a few more days), she had been sweet and tender and amused. She gave him her card and said he should call her if ever he was in Paris. He reciprocated with his. Don't worry, she said, I won't tell your wife – though he had not spoken of Roz – and smiled and kissed him.

Would they see each other again? He dared not think about it. He had never had an encounter like this before – but then, he had a feeling that she was a one-off.

Even now, thinking about her, he had an erection. He turned the water to cool, gasping, and tried to turn his thoughts to Roz. Her body so soft and full, such a contrast to Céline's. Céline's body. He mustn't think about it.

He hoped Roz wouldn't expect him to make love to her tonight.

Roz lay in bed, wondering why Geoff was so long in the shower. She might pretend to be asleep when he came in, to avoid any awkwardness, but she'd have to deal with it sometime.

I can deal with anything, she told herself. I can be strong, I can play the part, I can pretend. I will do whatever I have to do, so that I can have Alex.

10

It had begun: the organisation, the arrangements, the deception. Roz felt confident that she could cope, running her two lives in tandem. The reins were in her hands, and all she had to do was make sure that they didn't get tangled.

She managed to see Alex once or twice a week, but it was never enough. First to go were her pottery classes – theoretically they continued, but in practice were actually heady creative evenings in Alex's flat, usually in bed, or on the floor or sofa.

It had felt strange the first time, leaving the house as usual in old clothes, taking a torn shirt of Geoff's she wore when pounding clay. She left it in the car, telling herself she must be back home at the normal time of ten thirty, experiencing a slight regret, but only that, at forsaking the promising bowl she was making.

She'd rushed up the stairs and was breathless when he opened the door. They had not seen each other for over a week, had only spoken in brief unsatisfactory phone conversations. He'd looked delighted to see her, and took her hand. They spoke each other's name. Was he nervous? She was. This was different from the time before. Then, although they had both had a strong idea of what would happen, they were still in a state of innocence as they'd crossed the threshold. Now she was on official business. She was here to see her lover.

He'd taken her duffel coat and hung it up. She'd gone into the living room, feeling shy and shabby, like a downstairs maid invited up to see the master. While he'd fetched some wine from the kitchen she'd looked around: white walls, large splashy abstract paintings, black and white photographs (no people, only landscapes and close shots of stones and trees and buildings, old and new). Bleached wood bookshelves held an eclectic collection, mainly in English: art books, photography, hardback novels, philosophy, poetry . . . She'd recognised many of the books – it didn't surprise her that their tastes coincided.

They'd sat on a sofa, facing each other. Alex raised his glass, 'To us.' Roz did the same. He reached forward and caressed her cheek with the back of his hand, tenderly.

'How are you?'

'I'm fine. And how are you?' That was all she could say. Why were they talking like this, so politely and superficially, when beneath the surface everything was churning and yearning . . .

'I'm fine too, now that you're here. I –'

He'd looked vulnerable. She'd held out her arms and he'd turned his face into her old woolly jumper, making a small sound. She'd stroked his thick curls, kissed his forehead, murmured his name. After a while he'd raised his head and they began to kiss wildly, pulling at their clothes. They'd made their way to the bedroom, still kissing, and had scrambled into bed, pressing together, sighing with need and appreciation. This time, they'd made love slowly, embarking on a voyage of discovery around each other's bodies. Two hours of sweetness. There were first times. The first time she did this to him, and he did that to her, and they did this or that together. She had knelt over him, traversing his chest, his stomach, with her mouth, licking and nipping . . . Down, down, she went, burying her face in the dense hair, taking his cock into her mouth, her tongue delicate and skilful. Later, he applied himself to her breasts. 'Did you feed your children?' he'd asked, huskily, as his hands moved over her. She'd nodded, and he'd groaned, 'Feed me, feed me,' and he'd latched on to her nipple, pulling and sucking strongly.

They had rocked together, joined and bound. It was unlimited, total.

Here I am, Roz had thought, with a man I barely know (yet I do, I do) making wonderful uninhibited love, and it's crazy, crazy, but I feel I have come home.

They seized what time they could.

Roz snatched extra evenings by telling Geoff she really ought to go to this meeting on the future of state education, or that talk about the protection of green spaces, or this lecture on energy-saving schemes for the home. On those evenings she made sure that, when she came home, she wore an appropriately concerned expression, as befitted someone who had just heard about the dangers of pesticides in the food chain, or the growing hole in the ozone layer. Geoff was usually too exhausted to require much more from her than a quick murmured sentence or two, and she was always careful to back up her stories with some research, scanning everything relevant in newspapers and magazines and Friends of the Earth literature.

Then there were the days. Roz had to reserve time

for work – the Parents' Guide project had started, and she was researching facilities in the borough, which meant time spent on the phone and in libraries, and occasionally visits and meetings. But she organised and juggled, as all women do, and while the children were at school and Katy at playgroup, she and Alex grabbed a few hours here, a whole morning there. They enjoyed being private in public, foolish and romantic, talking, talking, talking about anything and everything, learning all the things about each other that they had not learned in bed.

They would meet in a car park on Hampstead Heath, arriving separately, then walking with their arms around each other, speaking of their pasts, of the first time they heard Bob Dylan (how to describe the revelation?), or saw a Matisse painting, or a Bill Brandt photograph . . . They found they already shared so much. They discovered, inevitably, that they were soul mates.

On rainy days they'd visit the British Museum and wander hand in hand from one end to the other, hardly registering the contents of the glass cases, not caring if they were seen as philistines, only caring for each other. They'd end up in the galleries of Greek antiquities, beautifully displayed they both agreed, and full of light. And Alex would become a little melancholy, as he felt it was his right to do, ruing the fact that the treasures were in London, not in Greece where they belonged. Roz would debate the issue with him, trying to defend the English gentlemen travellers of the past, but her heart was not really in it. Her heart was with Alex.

In the museum café, over coffee (again! Roz joked that their relationship was measured out in coffee spoons, and Alex got the T.S. Eliot reference) he told her about his childhood in post-war Greece. About his beloved elder brother who had died as a child, his health weakened, it was said, by the malnutrition and hardships endured by the family during the war. His mother had never recovered, living a half-life as a semi-invalid, critical of her remaining son and daughter who never lived up to the memory of her first-born. His businessman father travelled a lot (not just for work – it was suspected that he had a long-term mistress tucked away somewhere) but was affectionate and spoilt his children when he was at home. Roz thought there were hints of a potential Greek tragedy and sympathised, but Alex assured her there had been a warm extended family, with jolly aunts to pinch his cheeks and a troupe of cousins to roam with. And there was obviously wealth: he mentioned an apartment in Athens, a house in the hills outside the city, a boat and a home on an island in the Cyclades.

He told her how he had always loved to draw, how as a child he'd spent hours in Athens with his sketchpad, recording the details of buildings, enjoying the textures of marble and stone. That had been the beginning, he supposed, of wanting to be an architect, although his father had wanted him to go into the family business. Roz had asked him what that was, and he said it was import and export mainly, plus property and investments. He was a little vague. His sister was now in charge, he said, since his father had retired, more or less. He looked wistful, but whether it was because of his dead brother, or heartbroken mother, or disappointed father, she didn't find out. They'd had to go, holding on to each other all the way back to his car on a meter nearby.

They went back there often. It became one of *their*

places. They liked to be out together, showing the world that they were lovers. Roz refused to contemplate the possibility of someone seeing them – nothing must spoil their precious time together, or get in the way.

Another time, on a fine spring day, a day they would always remember, they strolled through Highgate Cemetery towards the tomb of Karl Marx. Roz was talking about her childhood, and finding it difficult to describe that particular time and place: the Fifties and early Sixties, in suburban London, when everything seemed safe and nothing much happened. How could she convey the sheer Englishness and the conventionality of her middle-class home, with her father a local bank manager and her mother a housewife, how could she explain the *smallness* of it all?

They moved on to discuss politics, and, of course, they found they shared the same leftish views. They had instinctively known that. Roz thought about Geoff, who was more right wing than she was, but said nothing. She remembered her sister Maggie's words from long ago, 'How on earth can you marry a man who's practically a Tory?'

Roz admitted to Alex that she hadn't been politically involved for years, but they agreed that you could be political through the way you lived your life and kept to your principles. Alex said that he had once been very active, when he was at university at home in Greece.

'I was a real firebrand, I thought I was a revolutionary. But of course there was much to be revolutionary about then.'

'You mean the Colonels?'

'Yes. The Junta. It was a bad time and a dangerous

one too. People forget how bad it was. Some of my friends didn't come out of it intact.'

His expression didn't reveal much but the tone of his voice had changed. She remained silent, holding tightly on to his arm, close to him.

'I got out – not exactly intentionally. I was over here, studying, then stayed on for some holiday. There was lots going on in Europe over that summer, political stuff. I was reluctant to go home, I wanted to go to Paris, Berlin. Then my father got word to me that the secret police were asking about me. He advised me to stay in London. So I did. He helped arrange things so that I could continue my studies here. He sent money over, made it easy for me –'

'You sound as if you regret it, that it shouldn't have been easy for you,' Roz said softly.

'Perhaps. It wasn't easy for those still in Greece – unless you were a fascist of course.' He shrugged. 'It was a long time ago. But ever since I've more or less lived the life of an exile. I could have gone back when things improved but I found myself staying in London. I don't really belong in Greece any more and I don't belong here.'

They were passing the monument to Marx, which was surrounded by a sombre party of Chinese visitors in dark grey suits, and for a moment they too gazed at the huge magnificent head then walked on. In the shadow of a Victorian family mausoleum containing generations of grocers, Roz pulled Alex to her.

'Well now, Alex, you belong to me.'

He laughed and held her tightly, covering her face with kisses, and said, 'I love you, Roz. I love you!' And he looked into her eyes and waited.

'Oh Alex, I love you too. I do.'

There, it was said. It wasn't analysed or discussed,

it was just true. And simple. They both felt it, breathed it, knew it. The words had been hovering around them for some time, almost whispered, almost heard. Now they were spoken and acknowledged.

They held each other's faces, and smiled wide sweet smiles of happiness. They hurried out of the cemetery and into Waterlow Park, away from death. Roz laughed, 'Shall we celebrate with, guess what, a cup of coffee? There's a nice café in here.'

'Yes, why not? Anything with you, anywhere, I love you!'

They hugged and walked as one, saying over and over, 'I love you', in funny voices, different accents, and he taught her how to say it in Greek.

Roz ignored the fact that the park was not far from Muswell Hill, close to home. She sometimes brought her children here, as did many women she knew. But she and Alex were enclosed in a magic bubble of their own creation.

A mother and small child were feeding the ducks as the lovers passed by on the other side of the pond. She paused, bread in hand, noticing that the woman wrapped up with that attractive man looked incredibly like Roz Harper. She reflected on the thought that somewhere in the world there was probably a double of her too . . .

Roz and Alex sat in the café, radiating warmth and satisfaction, which was nothing to do with being indoors, or with the hot croissants and coffee on the table. She thought, this is a special day – the day when we said we loved each other; he thought how happy he was, because he did belong to her, and she to him, even if it was only part-time. For now.

*

While Roz and Alex built their secret half-life together, and fantasised about the other half, her children lived their lives: Matthew coped with noisy playgrounds, and fights and bullies; Sam squared up to teachers and tried smoking a spliff for the first time, behind the sports hall; Polly worried about getting good grades and agonised over Laura's brother Nick and whether he really liked her; Katy wanted Charlotte to be her friend, and was scared of the spider in the playgroup toilet . . . And her husband?

Geoff worked. He had too much work to do. Sometimes, for a little light relief, he would phone home, just to chat to Roz, but lately she seemed to be out a lot. He would hang on listening to the ringing, envisaging the big empty house, his home, and hoping nothing was wrong. His main thought was that they must get an answering machine. He'd organise it.

When he would idly ask Roz where she was when he called, her replies were always mundane: collecting dry cleaning, or having coffee with Annie, shopping and more shopping, or helping at playgroup, or sorting out jumble for the PTA. And lately, of course, she was involved in this new project of hers (neither of them yet called it a job).

She was nearly as busy as he was, he thought.

11

Roz was not looking forward to this at all. She had never been over-enthusiastic about Geoff's company parties, but had endured them gracefully. Since Alex she had found it harder to function as the dutiful wife. That was how she saw her life now – divided into Before Alex and After Alex, and her passion for him dominated her life like a newly found religion.

Geoff was driving too fast. He didn't want to be late. There was going to be somebody important there tonight, someone from the States who was reviewing the London operation to decide who was to be promoted to the company's head office in Houston. Geoff knew that he was being considered, but he hadn't yet told Roz.

He patted her knee. She was wearing silky trousers, and looked very presentable – no, more than that, she looked great. He told her so. His compliments are routine, thought Roz, like so much in our lives. But she knew she was looking good – being in love with Alex suited her.

Soul music, Saturday night music, was on the radio. It reminded Geoff of the first time he'd met Roz, at that party in Southwark so long ago.

'Remember this?' he asked.

'It makes me feel like dancing. Remember dancing?'

'Just about! I'll do my best tonight.'

'I might even dance with someone else.'

'Well, why not? That's what parties are for. Circulate and all that.'

'Sure. I hope you and all the other men bear that in mind and don't indulge in talking shop as usual –'

'Oh, come on, Roz, it's not that bad, is it?'

He swung the car around a corner. Despite his efficiency in other areas, Geoff was a sloppy driver.

'Yes. Sometimes it's boring with all the men in a huddle, and the wives thrown together searching for something to talk about.'

'You've never complained before – damn, bloody fool!' Geoff swerved to avoid an old Ford pulling out from a pub car park. 'Would you like it any better if the huddle as you call it, included a woman? Is it the huddle you object to or the maleness?'

'Look, I'm not really complaining.' Roz ducked his challenge, not wanting a full-scale argument about male/female roles. 'All I'm saying is that I get a little tired of merely being an adjunct. Married into the company, but not quite of it. It's a feeling of being left out. You probably don't often have that experience.'

Geoff momentarily took his hands off the steering wheel in exasperation. He was surprised at her bad temper. And he didn't bloody well need this right now, not tonight. They had to present a united front, be Mr and Mrs Perfect, as usual.

'What *is* the matter with you?'

She remained silent, feeling cheap. She didn't really feel all that strongly about these things, but was venting her irritation at Geoff for being himself, for being there, and her frustration at not being with her lover. Where is Alex tonight, she wondered, what is he doing, who is he with?

She shivered, and gathered up some remaining scraps of dutiful wifeliness.

'I'm sorry, I'll stop moaning. I don't know what's the matter with me. I'll make an effort to enjoy myself.'

'You usually do, that's why I can't understand you being like this. Oh, let's forget it. And I'll make an effort not to spend too much time talking about work, though it's difficult. Will that do?'

She gazed out at the darkness of Hampstead Heath, thinking of her assignations with Alex. Geoff was driving along the narrow strip of road between The Spaniards and Jack Straw's Castle, renowned for its history of highwaymen. She imagined Alex in a velvet coat and high boots, riding out of the trees on a black horse, hi-jacking her life.

They drove down towards the village in silence. Geoff remembered when he and Roz used to come to Hampstead before they were married. Walking, going to the bank holiday fair, kissing pressed up against trees, talking for ages in The Coffee Cup . . . It seemed so long ago, as if it had all happened in someone else's life. Yet here they were, the two of them, still together. However something wasn't quite right. He was reluctant to admit it, but lately there seemed to be something wrong with Roz. No, something different. She was sometimes brittle and dreamy, as if preoccupied. She showed no signs of wanting to discuss any problems or of even hinting at them . . . A secret? What could it be? Perhaps she was just worrying about growing older – women did, didn't they? Or was it her health? Perhaps she was feeling broody. Surely she couldn't want another child? He must try to talk to her. Make the time, alone together . . .

'Geoff, wasn't that the Downings' road?'

She was right. He swore and braked.

The house was in a wedge of streets at the foot of the Heath – still Hampstead, just. Hugh Downing worked with Geoff, and they were rivals as well as colleagues – who could be the most efficient, the most innovative, the best?

Hugh and his wife Jenny, a solicitor, had just the one child, rarely seen. Their house was tall and narrow, and lights shone from every storey but the top one. That's probably where the token child is tucked away, thought Roz. What *is* his name? Jenny greeted them, managing to be both gushing and distant and they followed her downstairs.

'Now, drinks and eats are down here; there's music in the room upstairs, above that our studies for quiet chats, whatever, then next floor is the spare bedroom for coats –'

Roz stopped listening, thinking, bizarrely, that Jenny sounded like a lift attendant. *Going up*.

Their hostess rushed off, her long flimsy batik dress following behind – Roz had seen it before, or a version of it in other colours. She glanced at Geoff. He squeezed her hand and smiled. She thought, dispassionately, how nice he looked, and how nice he was. Nice. The kind of word you might use to describe an acquaintance.

Hugh hailed them from the drinks table, looking plump and sleek, like a seal.

'Hello there, Harpers! Good to see you – what'll you have to drink? There's the usual – red or white, or there's punch. It's got quite a kick, made it myself.'

'I'll try some of your punch, Hugh.'

'Brave girl. And doesn't she look smashing tonight, eh, Geoff?'

Roz sipped her drink and looked around. The display of food was immaculate. Unlikely to be Jenny's work, thought Roz. Jenny was not known for her cooking, she was known for her career. And what am I known for? she asked herself. My children, my many children, I suppose. So far.

A soft voice at her shoulder said hello. It was Mary, the wife of Douglas, a senior member of Geoff's team, senior by age. She was a small woman with an anxious look, and clothes the colours of a sparrow's plumage.

Mary was relieved to talk to Roz whom she'd always liked. She felt safe chatting to her about nothing in particular. These occasions were a trial but Douglas insisted she made the effort, as he had to do. All she wanted to do was to fade into a corner until it was time to go, she felt so old and drab. But here was Roz looking so wonderful. She stood in the glow emanating from Roz and it warmed her like sunlight.

They talked of the people around them, mainly familiar faces (the company prided itself on keeping its staff).

'Who's that, Mary? That tall man by the fireplace with Geoff.'

'Oh, I think he's someone from American HQ, someone important.'

'American HQ!' Roz laughed. 'Such a military

term, we're like army wives, aren't we? And serviceable too, in our own way.'

Mary laughed nervously, as if mutiny had been suggested.

'I need another drink, want one Mary?'

'No thank you, Roz. I'm drinking Perrier, and a glass lasts a long time.'

Roz headed for the drinks table and Mary watched her go with regret, feeling bereft. As Roz helped herself to wine, she wondered if anything was the matter with Mary. We all have secrets, we all have problems, she thought. How would Mary react if she told her about her affair with Alex? Perhaps Mary would tell her a secret in return.

'Darling –' Geoff made her jump. 'I'd like you to meet a colleague from the States, who I worked with last year. This is Paul Petersen. Paul, this is Roz, my wife.'

Geoff looked eager to please this man, the one she'd discussed with Mary. He shook her hand firmly.

'Mrs Harper, I'm truly delighted to meet you.'

Roz smiled as charmingly as she could. 'I'm pleased to meet you, Mr Petersen, and do call me Roz.'

'Then you must call me Paul.' He relinquished her hand.

He looked like one of those superannuated astronauts, trim and tanned, an advertisement for one way of American life – the athletic, healthy, eternally youthful mode. His hair was clipped close to his head like little feathers and his eyes were light and intense. She sensed that the relaxed exterior could conceal a hard man.

'Well, I must circulate. Roz, I'll leave you to look after Paul.'

Geoff disappeared into the inevitable huddle of men and Roz reflected on why women always have to play hostess, even when they're not in their own homes. Not that Paul Petersen appeared to need looking after.

'How nice of your husband to leave me with you.'

Roz raised an eyebrow or attempted to – she was never sure if she actually achieved it. She avoided flirting and asked safe questions about where he came from (Texas), his work, his stay in London.

'Now, enough about me. What about you, what do you do with yourself? Do you have children?'

Same old questions, thought Roz, and replied somewhat wearily, 'Oh, I definitely have children. Four.'

'Of course, Geoff did tell me that. How could I forget? It's probably because you don't look like a mother of four children.'

Patronising sod, she thought, finishing her wine.

'Oh, really, how are mothers of four meant to look? Should I have two heads or something? And how do fathers of four look?'

He laughed, leaning back with his hands up as if dodging a blow. 'Hey, no fighting please! I get plenty of that back home!'

Typical of a man, she thought, avoiding the question by turning attention to himself.

'You do?'

'Sure, my wife is a real feminist. I have to watch what I say and do! Oh, rightly, of course, but sometimes it's hard for a man of my generation.'

He smiled winningly, obviously used to winning. It irritated Roz but she tried not to let it show. She made an effort and they had a superficial conversation about men and women, their differences and difficulties, batting superficialities to and fro, back and forth. I bet he's good at tennis as well, she thought.

She caught Geoff's eye across the room. He nodded slightly – she wasn't sure what it meant – was he encouraging her to carry on talking to Paul Petersen? Meanwhile she was thinking of a polite exuse to move away. Fortunately Hugh came bustling up and dragged the American off, wanting to bend his ear about some brilliant idea he'd had. Roz headed for another drink.

Petersen reserved judgement on Roz Harper. He had heard that she was the ideal wife and mother, fully supportive of her husband, enabling him to fulfil his potential in the workplace. Maybe she was, he thought, but he detected something else – an independent spirit? That was tolerable, but there was something more – a spark of recklessness? It could be that she was merely displaying what so many women – including his own wife, God help him – manifested these days: frustration, resentment, reluctance to be number two to their menfolk. If so, how would she react if Harper were posted to Houston? How would she fit in with the other company wives and the ladies who lunch? Geoff was a sound man, he thought, an excellent man in the company, but what about the wife?

In the car, going home at last, Roz looked at Geoff's profile and tried to define what she felt for him. Affection, kinship, a comfortable familiarity. No doubt many marriages survived on less. But it wasn't enough for her, not any more.

There was a growing distance between them. Was

he aware of it? She wasn't sure. She did know that lately she had been constructing an invisible glass wall, so that behind it Geoff became less real to her.

As the car slowly climbed up the hill to Highgate he asked her what she'd thought of Paul Petersen. 'He seemed to like you,' he added.

'Did he? He was all right, quite amusing in a way. But I'm not sure I got his measure.'

'How do you mean?'

'Well, what was he about? I mean, he spent a lot of time with me and I had a feeling that there might be more to it than just socialising. A hidden agenda perhaps?'

Geoff considered how to reply. He'd better tell her the truth, or part of it.

'Actually, there's a high level vacancy at Houston HQ and they're looking to fill it with someone from the London end –'

'And that someone might be you?'

'It's possible. I assume that's why Paul is over here. He heads up human resources so he's looking at those of us considered suitable –'

'And looking at wives as well?'

'Well – yes, I suppose so, in a way.'

That was it, thought Roz. I was being checked out tonight to see if I'm true company wife material . . . Damn it. Why did this have to happen now? I can't leave London, I won't leave Alex.

She stared out of the window at the darkness of Highgate Wood along the windy road to Muswell Hill. She felt chilled by Geoff's revelation but told herself to be calm. After all, she reasoned, she'd have plenty of objections to the idea even without the existence of Alex: uprooting the children, their education, her work . . .

'And if you're the chosen one? What then? Do you have a choice or any say in the matter?'

'Roz, don't worry, these are early days. If and when I'm a serious contender, then obviously we'll find out more and discuss it properly. OK?'

He squeezed her hand reassuringly. She agreed to say no more about it, not yet.

Roz couldn't wait to sleep. She went into the kitchen for a glass of water. Geoff came up behind her, and put his hands on her hips, turning her round, leaning against her, pressing her back on to the curved wooden edge of the worktop. She was surprised by the force of his action and by the sudden intimacy of his face so close to hers.

For a second she felt he was a stranger and experienced a jolt of unexpected emotion – was it fear, or just alarm that he might make demands of her? Oh, no, she thought, I can't have spontaneous sex in the kitchen, not with Geoff.

He looked into her face as if trying to fathom her mood. She asked him, lamely, if he wanted a drink – anything to defuse this moment.

'Darling, all I want is you.' He hugged her. 'You know, I was so proud of you tonight. Everyone kept telling me how well you're looking which was a polite way of saying you're bloody gorgeous.'

He loosened his grip, kissed her on the nose and held her at arm's length. 'Let's go to bed, shall we?'

'God, yes. I'm shattered.'

Geoff was about to say that sleep wasn't what he had in mind but Roz's weary, almost resigned expression stopped him. She went upstairs while he locked up and then looked in on the children. It gave him a great sense of satisfaction and well-being, knowing that his children slept peacefully while he went to bed with his wife.

He watched her removing her make-up in slow circular strokes. She looked as if her mind was elsewhere.

'By the way, do you ever feel you'd like to come with me when I go on these trips abroad?'

He was full of surprises tonight. She'd always understood that it was best for her not to accompany him, for all sorts of reasons (he'd be working, she'd be bored, and what about the children?). A while ago she might have been pleased to be asked, but now, of course, there was Alex. Geoff's absences provided more opportunities for seeing him.

She slowly wiped Vaseline across her eyelid, wishing he hadn't raised this.

'Why ask me now?'

'Perhaps it was some of the things you said tonight, plus I do miss you. And the more I go, the less interesting it is. I used to get a kick out of it all. Now it's becoming as routine as commuting on the Northern line.'

'And would it improve things if I were with you?'

'I'm sure it would.'

'Oh, great, so you want me along as your in-flight companion. Who would look after the children? And what about me? There are things I have to do. My work, for instance!'

As she snapped at him she realised she was overreacting. He looked hurt.

'Calm down Roz. Why are you so touchy? It was only a suggestion. I thought you might like a change of scenery. I don't want you to feel left behind. For God's sake.'

He climbed into bed, looking martyred. She followed him, meekly.

'I'm sorry. I'm being ungrateful. Can we talk about it tomorrow?'

'All right, we'll do that. I've a trip coming up soon. Now –'

He snuggled towards her, a hand on her breast. He sensed a lack of response and whispered, 'Are you too tired?' but his hands continued to travel over her body. She said nothing but turned and kissed him, trying to do it with good grace. She couldn't keep avoiding this, it had to be done, otherwise he might begin to have suspicions. The kiss was brief. Geoff didn't kiss her as much as he used to. Unlike Alex. Oh shit.

She opened her legs, encouraging Geoff to enter her, so that it would be over quickly. She lay back and tried to detach herself, letting him get on with it, her teeth clenched, her eyes squeezed shut, one hand clamped tightly to the side of the bed. It was awful. At last he rolled off her, murmuring his thanks. Perhaps he hadn't noticed that she'd performed with little energy and enthusiasm. She turned away with relief and fell asleep.

Geoff lay awake and thought about Roz as he listened to her breathing. What was the matter with her? As well as everything else, she'd seemed so tense when he made love to her. She used to be such a mover. Was it something to do with him? What could it be?

His mind roamed over the evening. He'd observed Roz across the room and had felt proud that she was his wife. Paul Petersen had liked her – he had told Geoff so. That was a good start.

He hadn't been completely open with her tonight:

it was highly probable that he would be asked to go to Houston and oh, how he wanted it! If you aimed to reach the top of the company pyramid, you had to prove yourself in the States. All he then had to do was transfer everything he had here – Roz, the children, some of the trappings – over there. He didn't consider that Roz would seriously object. She would support him, she always had. Petersen had been vetting her tonight and if he suspected that she drank too much or was flirty or indiscreet, or too radical politically, then she would be unacceptable. That would throw doubts on Geoff. But he was sure that Petersen had discovered none of these things. He could rely on Roz.

It took a while before he could sleep. His thoughts had turned to Céline. He enjoyed thinking about her and the things they had done together. He wondered if he'd ever experience her again. Her card was tucked inside one of the many pockets of his briefcase – he knew he shouldn't even contemplate contacting her, but it pleased him that it was there. Thank God Roz hadn't been with him on *that* trip. He regretted asking her to come with him in the future – he'd only offered it as a morsel of consolation, trying to be nice. Luckily she hadn't seemed too keen. He needed his opportunities for adventure.

12

Annie had hardly seen Roz lately but she was dying to ask her about the Greek guy, the architect. He was at the house so often. If it had been anyone else she might have suspected that something was going on. After all, extra-marital affairs were commonplace, although it was usually men that had them. Women like me at home don't really get the opportunity, she thought. Where would I meet a man? She understood the old jokes about housewives and milkmen.

Today she'd caught a glimpse of Alex (was that his name?) saying goodbye to Roz at her door. Their expressions and body language had encouraged her to watch. She sensed a closeness and familiarity which unsettled her. But surely it was impossible? This was Roz, remember – steady dependable Roz.

She mentioned it to Martin over supper. He laughed.

'You're imagining things. Roz? Hardly!'

He carried on eating, his eyes straying to the newspaper on the table. He'd made her feel foolish, so she was determined to continue.

'Well, she's attractive isn't she?'

'I've never thought about it. I suppose some people would think so. Not my type though.'

Annie stayed silent, thinking. Let him stuff his face

and read the paper. A chill went through her whenever he said something like that. It suggested that he had a type, that he still thought that way. She imagined him in the street and on the tube, appraising women with a quick look up and down, ticking them off: yes my type, no not my type.

She gripped her glass tightly and refrained from asking him exactly what was his type. He would only patronise her and say, Why you of course darling. What a ridiculous situation, she thought. Here he was, the love of her life (probably): all she'd ever wanted was him. So why wasn't she happy? Was it just women who plunged in, passionate, adoring, reckless, then ended up like her – drained, depressed, dissatisfied? She wondered.

She sometimes fantasised that she was single and childless, with a successful career and her own flat in Soho, leading a stylish and independent life. Yet she knew that she'd still want a man and want to be with him and please him. She would still couple her happiness to his. And she'd end up like this. The path of love is circular – or is it a downward spiral?

She must somehow rebuild herself. It was no use mourning the old Annie – she was different now. Children change you, she thought.

Part of her problem was money. She wanted distraction and stimulation – but lack of money was the overriding factor. She never really felt that the money Martin earned was *theirs*. If she had some money of her own it would mean independence, and she could spend it how she wanted. Clothes, holidays, the house. Especially the house – it was getting increasingly tatty. So many things needed repairing, renewing, and would just about last through the messy stage of the children's early years – and what then? Like me, she thought, I'm getting tatty too. I need some attention.

Her conversation with herself continued as she collected washing from all over the house. It wasn't as if life was suddenly going to spring into action at some magical point in the future when she pressed the restart button. This was life. Now. Yes, it did seem unfair: she felt in limbo, the real her frozen, while another self scurried around being wife and mother. And it didn't seem right that she should be getting older while her life stood still.

What the hell. Annie began to tire of her own self-pity.

Think positively, be active, she thought. Roz would help. Maybe they could go to an exhibition or art museum together during the day, or return to that exercise class they used to go to . . . She'd invite Roz over, and ask her.

Roz had her own problems. Managing all this wasn't so easy. She had overlooked the school holidays when planning her strategy to see Alex. The children had been at home for a whole week and she'd only seen him once, by pretending that her pottery class was running as usual. At times she ached for him – and not just physically. She wanted to talk to him, hear his voice, gaze upon his face, laugh with him, be wistful with him. She felt more and more that Alex was her other half and she needed him to make her whole. When she missed him she was also missing herself.

The weather was dismal. It rained non-stop. In the past, before Alex, she would have been energetic, arranging outings, organising games with the children. Not now. She moped, and felt listless, and all she could think about was sneaking into the bedroom to indulge in another clandestine, erotically charged phone call.

The children noticed her mood, and by instinct left her alone as much as they could, turning to each other. Polly asked her what was the matter and she feigned minor illness, saying maybe she had a bug or something. In the few quiet moments she snatched for herself, she brooded. It was unlike her to feel depressed but she began to. So far it had all gone quite smoothly: she'd kept the home front going, preserved her jolly and normal façade, most of the while thinking of Alex, yearning to be with him. She felt so tired. It was such an effort, this deception, running two lives. How long could she sustain it?

Yet she had no regrets, not about Alex, though sometimes she did about the rest. She punished herself with questions. Had she loved Geoff? Why did she marry him and then get pregnant so soon?

Roz glared at herself in the bathroom mirror, not liking either what she saw or the answers to her questions. She knew that she'd opted for marriage and motherhood partly out of laziness, taking the easy way out.

The role of wife and mother had been appealing because it *was* a role, a fully fledged, tried and tested, recognisable role, that saved her having to find an independent path for herself. After leaving university she'd had several temporary jobs, the longest of which was in a public library. She'd quite enjoyed it, at least she was with books all day, but her focus was elsewhere – building a life with Geoff. She'd had no great ambition to be anything (had any of her female friends?), even though she was clever and had some small talents. The few sparks she'd ever felt in any direction had been creative ones, but her parents had done all they could to steer her away from those, warning her, like ancient mariners, of the dangers that await you on the rocks of artistic endeavour.

So she'd married Geoff and everyone had been pleased. And she'd loved the excitement of finding a flat, and buying all those grown-up things like cutlery, and the excursions to Habitat (a novelty then), and learning to cook, and having people round for supper, and going to bed with Geoff every night in their very own bed . . . Oh, the whole thing. It had been enough, more than enough.

Then she'd become pregnant. One night she didn't use her diaphragm – it was such a hassle, and she convinced herself that it was still the safe time after her period . . . And that was it. (Polly, as it turned out.) Geoff had been instantly delighted when she told him. This was what he wanted, so they didn't discuss any options or alternatives, whether now was the right time, what Roz wanted to do with her life, all those issues. The pregnancy continued, and Roz began to relish this new role, happily giving up the job in the library and herself to motherhood.

She splashed her face with cold water, trying to clear her mind. So here I am, she thought as she pushed back her hair.

'Mum, Mum!' Polly was shouting. 'Where are you? Sam and Matthew are practically murdering each other over the remote control, and the hamster's on the loose, and Katy's spilt her juice, and I'm trying to do this bloody essay!'

'All right, I'm coming.'

Roz to the rescue. She dashed down the stairs, ignoring Polly's cross face as she retreated into her room, slamming the door. She knew that she must pull herself together, accept that if she couldn't see Alex, she couldn't see him, and she must pay some attention to this lot. This lot. What a way to think about them, she thought. Her children. She couldn't change her mind and say, oops sorry, shouldn't have had them, she wanted a different life now. Could she?

She waded into the struggling mass that was her sons and physically separated them, then gave them the task of finding the hamster. Changing Katy's wet and sticky clothes sodden with a full carton of orange juice she thought, if Alex could see me now.

Geoff chose that evening to discuss the move to America. He'd been thinking about it all day and it had to be done. He got back early, about seven, feeling tired and tense. Being home did not soothe him, as it usually did. Roz was irritable, the children were all over the place, things seemed disorderly. He knew she shouldn't have taken on this new job – it was too much for her. This was not how he wanted it to be. He had a sense of the household unravelling at the edges.

Roz was in the kitchen, making supper. Macaroni cheese, not everyone's favourite and somewhat dull, but she couldn't think of anything else. Geoff made himself a gin and tonic. He didn't offer her one.

'Roz, I heard this week that there's definitely a vacancy in Houston and I'm in the running. I think I'm the favourite actually, though I know Hugh is very keen –'

She stirred the cheese sauce, gripping the wooden spoon tightly. Her voice was strained.

'Oh, I see. So it's happening? Have you actually applied for it or told them you want it?'

'It doesn't quite work like that –'

'*Do* you want it?' She turned round to face him.

'It would mean promotion. If they offered it to me I could hardly turn it down, not if I want to stay with the company. And I do.'

'You haven't answered my question – do you want it, do you want to go to America?'

'Well, it's not as simple as that. It's not just about what I personally want, I know that, it's about what's best –'

God, he was annoying her. 'Best for whom?' She left the sauce to get herself some white wine from the fridge.

'Darling, that's obvious, best for all of us, as a family.'

'Oh, good, so I will have some say in it, will I?'

She gulped her wine and snatched the saucepan off the hob as it started to burn.

'Of course you will! That's what I want to talk about. Petersen has invited us out to dinner – he'd like to meet you again, and you can ask him any questions you like.'

'Wonderful. Thank you Mr Petersen, yes Mr Petersen, no Mr Petersen. Anything you say Mr Petersen –'

'Roz please –'

'Please what? I'm meant to please *him*, aren't I? I suppose he's not sure about me, wants to ask me some searching questions about how I vote or what sort of knickers I wear –'

'That's enough! What the hell is the matter with you? Why are you being like this?'

'Like what, exactly?'

'So bloody negative, as if you've already decided you don't want to go.'

She thought, I don't and I won't. I have another life now. But she tried to react like the old Roz, the one before Alex – what would she have said? Try to be reasonable, she told herself.

'I haven't decided anything. I know nothing about it, do I? I just don't want things decided for me.'

'OK, OK. Shall we talk about it more after supper? Let's try to agree on a date to meet Petersen. It matters to me.'

'All right, whatever you say.'

'Oh, and I may have to go over there soon for further discussions, then I can have a good look at Houston –'

Her spirits lifted at the thought of his absence for that would mean more Alex, but she wanted to shout at him, tell him she was not just a company wife, she wasn't going to be packed off to America . . . And more.

Geoff wanted to shake her, force her to be enthusiastic and to support him. After all, the whole family depended on him and his work. Without it, everything would collapse.

13

Alex was in his office looking over some plans but his mind was on Roz. He wanted to call her. Hearing her voice would be better than nothing but he knew her children were off school and it would be difficult for her to talk. What he really wanted was to see her. He put his feet up on his desk and indulged in thinking about her. Her soft skin, her welcoming body. He wanted more of her. Not that she didn't give herself utterly to him – she did – but their time together was so brief and hurried. He needed more of her. He wanted to have her in his bed all night so that they could fuck and sleep and fuck again and again, then wake up together and shower together ... Together. He wanted them to be together.

He was growing hard just thinking of her and all the things they could do together, given time, but then his secretary knocked on the door with a cup of coffee. He leaned forward quickly – he wouldn't want Lynn getting the wrong idea. She looked at him with her usual amused expression.

'Alex, remember to phone Jon back about the mews project. And Penny rang this morning too.'

He thanked her and watched her behind as she left the room. It seemed to have a life of its own and she would wear these tight skirts which revealed the line of her brief knickers and the outline of her barely contained bottom as well. Alex never tired of looking at it. It wasn't really sexual, just a source of fascination. Lynn was a happily married woman, as she often told him, with a builder husband and three kids living in a kind of bliss in Kentish Town. She was employed part-time and was the first to admit that she wasn't exactly overworked. Neither was Alex. He turned down more projects than he took on. At first Lynn had found that hard to understand, coming from a background where if you had the opportunity to make money, you took it. Now she accepted that he probably had his reasons. He obviously didn't want to expand either, but worked alone doing nearly everything himself, occasionally contracting out mundane tasks to freelancers.

Lynn knew something of his private life. In the few years she'd worked for him there had been a succession of girlfriends. She took their phone calls, sent them flowers on his instructions, booked theatre tickets and restaurant tables for two. They never lasted long, he seemed to tire of them quickly. The most recent was Penny, but lately he was reluctant to take her calls and Lynn assumed she was on the way out.

Alex walked around his office, trying to decide what to do about Penny. There was plenty of space for him to stride. It was part of a conversion of a Victorian furniture factory, tucked away off a now-residential street in Primrose Hill, not far from his flat. The building was a showcase for Alex's skills as he was responsible for the conversion, and he owned it too. He'd retained the central courtyard, where the factory workers would have been allowed out for a quick chat and a smoke, escaping the smell of glue and varnish. He'd installed a pebble garden with trees in pots and park benches for the use of the tenants – creative people mostly – and their clients. French windows led inside to a communal exhibition space for product launches or shows of work. Everyone agreed that Paradise Place (amazingly, its original name) was a civilised place to work.

He looked out at the courtyard. It was a gloomy day and no-one was about. This was where he'd met Penny, who was in PR and represented the hatmaker who had a workshop and office in the building. He'd seen them walking outside and had noticed her long legs. A little later he'd contrived to bump into them in the gallery corridor and a conversation had led to her phone number then dinner then bed. He'd liked her a lot. She was bright, cheerful, very funny and easy-going – an ideal partner for an affair, he'd decided. Tall with short sleek dark hair and a generous mouth, always fashionably dressed and immaculately made-up, she was one of those young women he often saw in huddles at parties and private views. Invariably short-skirted and dressed in black lycra they looked sombre but drank and shrieked and laughed a lot. He'd been delighted to have such a creature for himself.

He'd enjoyed her in bed – she was athletic and adventurous, her body taut and well-exercised. He had continued to fuck her for a while after he'd met Roz but had found he had less and less enthusiasm. His heart just wasn't in it. Little things about her began to irritate him – her toenails; the way she'd decorated her flat, all kitsch and campy; the short hair on the back of her neck; the way she called him her minotaur. Now he was running out of excuses for not seeing her. Luckily she'd landed a new account and had been too busy working and travelling to ask to see him – but he had to tell her it was over.

He rang her office in Covent Garden, knowing it was cowardly, but he didn't have the emotional energy to tell her in person. Perhaps she'd take it calmly, for they had never discussed how they felt about each other and it had been a practical, almost businesslike affair.

'Alex! How nice to hear you.'

'How was New York? Successful trip?'

'Yes, it was. But frantic. And I've got an enormous pile of stuff here to sort out. Shows how indispensable I am! How are you? Busy? When can I see you?'

He paused. There were sounds of her computer and someone yelling that there was another call for her. He spoke slowly.

'Penny, that's why I'm ringing. I can't see you any more –'

'What? What are you saying?'

'I can't see you any more, I can't –'

'What do you mean?' Her voice rose.

'Look I'm sorry, but I can't continue with this relationship, this affair –'

'Oh, was that what we were having?'

'Whatever. I can't – look, I've met someone else. It's very special.'

'Oh lucky you. I'm so fucking glad.'

'Please – sarcasm doesn't help.'

'Doesn't help *you*, you mean. Might make me feel better though – I'm the one that's being rejected here.'

'I'm not rejecting you Penny. Please don't take this personally – you're gorgeous, you're bright, you're –'

'Spare me that character reference. If I'm so fucking

marvellous, why are you dumping me? And who for? Who is she? Some blonde bimbo?'

She was crying now, raging between sobs. He wished she'd regain control and behave with some dignity, but it got worse. She began to apologise and talk about how good it was between them and what might have been. He could bear it no more. He put the phone down, consigning Penny to the past. It was Roz that mattered – she was his present and his future. But how to get her centre stage, how to make her his and his alone? As he thought of her he smiled – if only Penny knew that it was no bimbo, but a married woman of forty, a mother of four, who had taken hold of his heart – and other parts too.

Roz sat in Annie's kitchen, for a change. The invitation to come over was well-timed. It was pouring with rain and she couldn't face Sainsbury's. The two women ignored the squeals and shrieks of the energetic game rampaging through the house and settled into coffee and conversation. Annie was complaining about Amy's teacher, whom she suspected of sexism – 'And she definitely discourages Amy from doing woodwork –'

Roz regarded her fondly. Today Annie was dressed in layers of black and grey, topped by a polka dotted scarf restraining her spikes of orange hair and ending in purple baseball boots. She lit a Gauloise. This usually signalled her time-to-talk-about-Martin but she looked at Roz through the smoke and asked, 'So how's life? You look tired, Roz.'

'I am. Geoff and I were up late last night, talking – there's a possibility the company will want to move him to America –'

'No! Really? Here, have a drink.' Annie produced a bottle of wine – it was nearly lunchtime after all.

'Thanks, Annie, I couldn't sleep last night, thinking about it –'

'Well, it's a big thing in your life! It always gets me. Why should the wife have to uproot herself just because of her husband's job?'

'Well, yes. But there's an even bigger thing in my life, which could change it even more.' Roz was surprised to hear herself saying this, but what the hell, it was out now, and she wanted to tell, she wanted to shout Alex's name from the rooftops. She paused, registering Annie's puzzled expression, then announced, 'I've fallen in love.'

Silence. Then a great thud, as Annie put the wine bottle down too hard on the table.

'Roz, what are you saying? I don't understand. Fallen in love? Not Geoff?'

She stared into Roz's face, searching for enlightenment, feeling stupid. Roz laughed.

'Oh, Geoff doesn't really come into this, except that, if anything, I've fallen *out* of love with him, or grown out of it, whatever –'

'Well then, what?' Annie was impatient.

'I hadn't meant to tell anyone but perhaps I need to . . . I've fallen in love with Alex – you know – the architect, the one who's meant to be designing the loft extension –'

'Oh him – the gorgeous one! I've seen him coming and going a lot! But does he know how you feel?'

It did not occur to Annie that Roz – conventional, reliable Roz – was involved in anything more than an infatuation, like a teenage crush.

'Oh, yes! He feels the same – he certainly seems to, and he says so!'

Roz laughed again, a sound full of satisfaction, even pride. Annie got the picture.

'Ah. You mean you and Alex are actually having an affair?'

She refilled their glasses, lit another cigarette, clumsily, just on one side and inhaled deeply. Could she believe what she was hearing?

'Yes – an affair, I suppose that's what I'm having. What we're having.'

'God, Roz. I'm sorry I'm being so dense, it's such a shock – you, of all people! Oh, you know what I mean, you've always seemed so settled, so content.'

'I was. Or I thought I was, until Alex came along. And that was that.'

'Geoff doesn't know, of course?' Annie's voice dropped to a conspiratorial whisper.

'No! In fact you're the only person I've told. We've been pretty discreet so far.'

Annie was flattered that she was the only outsider to be let into the secret. She wanted to know more – all the details, the how and the when and the where, and Roz took delight in telling her . . .

'Wow!' Annie sprawled back in her chair. 'I still can't quite believe it. Though for the past month or two you have been looking so well – people have been remarking on it, especially considering –'

'Considering I've got four children, I know.' Roz anticipated the sentence. She'd heard it so often.

'Although the gossip at the school gate the other day was that perhaps you're pregnant again –'

'Christ, no!' Roz raised her voice. The strength of her reaction surprised them both.

'Oh Roz.' Annie sighed wistfully, with a touch of

admiration in her voice. She felt a strong lurch somewhere inside her – was it envy? Or excitement?

She asked one more question.

'What are you going to do?'

It was Roz's turn to look puzzled. 'Do? About what?'

'The whole thing: Alex, Geoff, the children.'

'I don't know. I haven't really thought about it, only in fantasies and dreams. I suppose I'll carry on juggling it all as best I can. It'll go on as it is, until something needs to be done.'

Annie thought this air of insouciance was almost as shocking as the original confession. Roz didn't seem to care what would happen. Part of Annie admired this bravado, part of her was not so sure.

Annie wanted to share Roz's revelation with someone – and it would have to be Martin. She could hardly wait for him to come home. She got Tom and Amy to bed then started slicing strips of chicken and vegetables for a stir-fry.

She watched him gulp down his wine and attack his food.

'Martin, you'll never guess what Roz told me today.'

'Try me. Pregnant again? Or is Geoff doing the noble thing and having a vasectomy?'

She ignored him and pressed on.

'She's actually having an affair! Can you believe it? With that hunky Greek architect I told you about. I did wonder about him, remember?'

Martin stopped eating for a moment. 'So good old Roz is not so good after all, eh?'

'Quite! I was so surprised – shocked – Roz of all people!'

'Yeah, she doesn't seem the type. But who is? Who knows?'

He turned his attention back to his plate. Annie was about to tell him more when he asked, 'And why are you so excited about this news? Do you envy her?'

'No! And I'm not excited about it. It was just so unexpected. And I can't believe she confided in me . . .' She pushed her unfinished food away and reached for her cigarettes, ready to discuss it in more detail.

Martin stopped her. 'I do have more important things to think about, you know. And I'm bloody tired of hearing about Roz this, Roz that. Oh, she's so efficient, she manages her life so well – and now look, she can even run a sordid little affair too! Christ almighty! I suppose you admire that as well –'

'How do you know it's sordid?'

'Oh, for fuck's sake! If she were a man, a man of her age with four children, having an affair, what would you say then? You'd soon be calling it sordid *and* you'd be up on your feminist high horse, saying typical irresponsible man, treating women like shit, what about his wife and children, all that, wouldn't you?'

Annie hesitated. She recognised some truth in his words and backed off.

'I suppose so. Don't let's row about this. It just seemed interesting that's all. It's probably because my life is so starved of interest –'

Martin got up suddenly from the table, leaving his untidy plate just as it was, and shouted, 'Not again! Spare me that poor little me stuff. You wanted to have children and give up work, remember? You'd better make your mind up. Decide what you *do* want.

You can't live your life through other people. I've had enough.'

He stamped off to watch television and stayed there all evening, determinedly glaring at the screen. As an advertising man he was able to justify watching rubbish to keep his finger on the pulse of popular culture. And he had to keep an eye on the ads, the competition.

Annie sat alone in the kitchen surrounded by the remains of supper. She tried to ignore it and to concentrate on thinking up ways to improve her life. She often read in magazines of women with young children, not unlike herself, who had brilliant ideas and started businesses of their own and became rich and successful and lived happily ever after.

I used to be a creative person, she thought. But creativity did not come easily these days. By bedtime all she had was a full ashtray, a thumping headache and a sense of waste.

14

Annie was in a rage. The kitchen reverberated with her anger: cupboard doors banged and bounced on their hinges, cutlery clattered into the sink, chairs fell over. She was fighting a battle, part of a continuing domestic struggle with Martin. He wasn't aware that demarcation lines had been drawn, nor that this time they related to empty milk bottles. Annie had decided to let them line up on the worktop, on the floor, wherever, to see if Martin would notice.

It was the fourth day of this particular skirmish and there were now nine bottles cluttering the kitchen. They were in her way and the sight of them irritated her beyond belief, but she would not move them. How many more will it take before he noticed, she seethed, before he's driven to pick them up and put them out for the milkman?

A mild voice in her head told her to be reasonable: why not just put the bloody things out and make life a little easier for herself? A stronger voice interjected: why should I? Who says that I'm responsible for *all* the minutiae of domestic life? Just because I don't go out to work, does that mean I have to do every single thing at home?

She began to be dimly conscious that the battle was within herself. And she could feel an undertow dragging her towards inevitable capitulation. After all, she hadn't won the Battle of the Open Drawers last month. That had been sparked off by Martin's habit of never closing a drawer after taking something out, or rather, by Annie's tolerance of this habit wearing thin. Every day, after he left for work, the large Victorian chest in the bedroom resembled a kind of sculpture, with drawers pulled out to differing lengths and the odd sock or sweater spilling over the edge. Annie felt like labelling it *'Unfinished Business'* and offering it to the Tate. One day she felt less than generously towards it and its creator and resolved to stop pushing the drawers in. That voice had prompted her again: why should I follow in his wake like a little shadow, tidying, putting things right? Just because his mother had.

That particular battle had finished on day three, without Martin even knowing it had started, as Annie was carrying a tall pile of imperfectly ironed clothes and walked straight into the bottom drawer, which protruded the most. She cursed and slammed it in, collapsing on the bed with the ironing to rub the rising bump on her shin.

In her calmer, more rational moments Annie realised that there was another way to deal with this – to tackle him directly, adult to adult. She had tried, and Martin had explained that as *he* worked outside the home (the last three words to mollify her) and *she* did not, obviously she had more time and opportunity to tidy and clean the house, and all the rest, than *he* did. Simple division of labour. Easy. Annie knew that it was more complicated than that but didn't say so. She argued with herself instead.

It was no wonder that Annie got a lot of headaches, often of migraine proportions. She floundered in the complexities of the problem – how to be a good wife and mother while constantly hearing the demand in her head: what about me?

She added the tenth bottle to the line, silent unwitting soldiers in the battle. She turned her back on them and sat down at the table, flicking unidentifiable crumbs on to the floor, and lit a cigarette.

Something had to be done. Work was the answer. She'd thought about going back to work before but child care was a problem, and go back to what? You couldn't go back to being a bright young thing in a photographer's studio if you were no longer a bright young thing.

Her art-school education in textiles wasn't much help. She could retrain, do an Open University Course, or opt for teacher training, like many women she knew. But did she want to be a teacher? And retraining would take time. She needed something to alleviate her sense of desperation and she needed it now.

Serious moneymaking appealed. She could start a business, be an entrepreneur – everyone seemed to be doing it. If she were successful and earned loads of money she'd attain some independence and achieve equality with Martin. Then she wouldn't have to worry about empty bloody milk bottles. She'd have other things to think about, more important things, and she could employ someone to deal with the minor domestic details, an au pair, mother's help or whoever . . .

Annie jumped up, fired by a vision of a new beginning and a new self. She placed three milk bottles outside the front door and stuffed the rest in a rubbish bag – she'd recycle them, whatever, later –

then sat down to consider how to launch herself into the world of business. She found one of the expensive notebooks that she was always buying but rarely used and started to list her skills and talents. She could design fabrics and make clothes, she could cook. There was her photographic experience and jewellery making and gardening . . . All of these things could be turned into a business of some sort. She daydreamed of what might be.

She was late for meeting Tom. As she hurried towards playgroup, her head buzzing with small business loans and retail opportunities, she was amazed to see Roz and Alex steam off in the Range Rover with Katy in the back. Roz was getting very bold, she thought, reckless even. Is she daring someone to tell Geoff? Annie wondered why it hadn't occurred to her to tell him. Was it out of loyalty to Roz or allegiance to a more general idea of female solidarity? She did not feel she owed Geoff anything and he'd be unlikely to believe her anyway. So she wouldn't tell him. But someone might.

Annie experienced shifting emotions as she watched the car turn the corner. Bloody cheek Roz has, she thought, flaunting her lover. How did she explain him to Katy? Suppose Katy mentioned something to Geoff? They were probably off to have lunch somewhere where the waiters were nice to lovers – and children. She felt a twist of envy and realised that there was a small part of her that would like to see Roz's immaculate tower of bricks come tumbling down.

She struggled out of playgroup with Tom's still wet painting flapping against her knees, half-listening to his lengthy explanation, 'That black bit's a spider and that blue bit's a fly but it's got magic powers so it can escape and . . .' She couldn't avoid the cluster of mothers chatting on the pavement. One, Wendy, called her, 'Hey, Annie!' Her voice dropped to a loud whisper, 'Who was that dishy man with Roz Harper?' The others turned their attentive faces towards Annie as she entered the group like a fellow conspirator, their assorted children temporarily ignored as they climbed the wall and spilled across the pavement.

Annie played for time, deciding just how discreet to be, enjoying the power of the moment.

'Well, I'm not sure that I should tell you,' she grinned.

'Oh go on, Annie. Tell us. Spill the beans – who is he?' they chorused.

'OK, OK – he's called Alexander, and he's – he's a friend.'

Their various voices shrieked together, 'A friend. . . !' 'Very special friend if you ask me.' 'I wouldn't mind getting friendly with him . . .'

Annie tried to stop what she had encouraged.

'Actually, he's an architect . . . Something to do with a loft conversion for the Harpers . . .'

Laughter spread around the group.

'Really? He can inspect my infrastructure anytime!' Wendy sniggered.

Annie decided to leave before it all got out of hand. She muttered that she had to go and walked off quickly, surprising Tom, who for a few seconds was left behind. She could hear the women joking about foundations and remodelling frontages, squeezing in as many sex 'n' architecture references as they could before reluctantly trailing home to create healthy lunches that their three and four year olds might like and even eat.

Annie tugged Tom down the street, noticing that she now had imprints of his painting over her jeans. She felt a little tacky – had she deliberately fed them titbits of innuendo to cause a stir, to start a smoulder of rumour? She told herself not to feel too guilty, for surely Roz had done that herself by appearing with her lover in public. But how eager we are to gossip, thought Annie, enlivening our existence with a bit of salacious excitement if not at first hand, then second or third hand would do. Yet we're all supposed to be conventional, respectable wives and mothers . . . Just like Roz!

Annie laughed out loud, and Tom pulled at her hand. 'Mummy, what's funny? Tell me the joke.'

'Oh, it's not really a joke, Tom. Just life. People. Everything.'

Annie left Tom engrossed in front of *Sesame Street* and sat in the kitchen and read through her list. Her earlier optimism was draining away fast. The utter ordinariness of it struck her – how many women could compile a list like this? A multitude. It amused her in a desperate sort of way. It reads like something out of Jane Austen, she thought. Such feminine skills – a little bit of needlework, some flower arranging, some delicate drawing. What was worse, she realised, was that other people had already exploited the potential of these meagre ideas. What was there left to offer?

Annie lit one cigarette from another and gazed around the kitchen, seeing messy worktops, washing-up waiting in the sink, the pedal bin overflowing. She heard Tom laughing at *Sesame Street* and was about to join him – she needed cheering-up – when the phone rang.

'Annie? Hi, it's Sally Houghton, Oliver's Mum.'

Odd how we do this, Annie thought, even women like Sally Houghton, defining ourselves as someone's Mum, not confident that we'll be recognised in our own right. Annie pictured her: tall, rangy, big tortoiseshell specs, well-groomed, something in publishing, probably ringing from her own office right now. But why?

'Annie, I'm not sure how to put this. Oliver will be four in a couple of weeks, and I want him to have a great party, and I was just thinking about how marvellously you did Tom's – that amazing cake and everything. And I was wondering if you could make a cake for Oliver's party, perhaps even plan the whole thing. I hope you don't mind me asking, hope you're not offended or anything. But it's just that I'm so busy right now, and our new au pair's not really up to it, and your party for Tom was so inspired and professional, and the cake was *so* artistic –'

She paused for breath. Annie was puzzled – Sally wasn't a friend, just an acquaintance through their children's playgroup where the boys were friends, so she couldn't be asking for help for free, could she? Then what?

'You mean you'd like me to design and make a cake and even plan the whole party?'

'Yes, exactly. That would be marvellous! For a fee naturally. But do you do this sort of thing?'

'I do all sorts of things!' Annie needed a minute to think. 'I think I could manage this. When were you thinking of having it?'

'The fifteenth. Two weeks on Saturday. Of course, I don't know what else you have on at the moment –'

Annie smiled, tempted to say that she was off to New York for a meeting next week, then of course there was a deadline that was absolutely crucial, but who was she kidding?

'Hold on Sally, I'll look in my diary.'

She leaned against the wall and took her time, glancing at the calendar decorated with cute kittens that the children had bought her for Christmas. Nothing on that day. Not much in between. A fee? Oh God, how much? What should she charge? For the whole job, or by the hour? She had a dim recollection of what Martin once said about freelance work: if you're not sure how long it will take, charge by the hour.

'That looks fine. I can fit it in, although it does depend on how complicated you want it to be, how much you want me to do.'

'Yes, sure. Tell me Annie, how much do you charge?'

Annie gulped, telling herself to go for it.

'Oh, twelve pounds an hour – plus materials and expenses of course.'

'Fine. Now, Oliver's very keen on space and robots – you know, the usual stuff.'

'OK. I'll come up with some ideas for the cake and some themed ideas for the party, plus an estimate of my time.'

'Good, good. How about Saturday morning – can you bring your ideas round then? Say about eleven? You know where we are. . .'

Annie held the phone to her chest long after Sally had rung off. She felt tearfully and pathetically grateful. It was as if a fairy godmother had waved her magic wand. So what if Sally (an unlikely fairy godmother) was high-powered and well-paid and had to pay other women to do what she had no time for. So what if Sally was just a touch condescending, that was merely part of the relationship between she who pays and she who is paid – nothing personal.

This was work, *paid* work! Annie marvelled. It was real – she was going to create something, produce something, and get paid for it. It was something she could easily do, and at home too. She grabbed her list and smiled – she'd written down children's cakes and party catering as an idea! See, you're not so useless after all, she told herself.

Tom wandered in from watching television, drawn by the sound of his mother singing. Annie hugged him. 'Come on Tommy boy, let's be creative!' He repeated her words, enjoying her mood, and she settled him at the kitchen table with a large lump of playdough on a wooden board. He was quickly absorbed in making mountains and caves for his plastic dinosaurs and monsters. She sat at the other end of the table with her notebook and pencil. Thoughts began to race through her mind, not of the cake or party, but of success: a company . . . a shop . . . a fleet of vans delivering party food to homes across the capital.

She debated whether to tell Martin about her new venture, or wait until it had developed further. She had to try not to bore him – one of the worst things you could do to Martin. She rushed around the kitchen, concocting a sauce for pasta from whatever she could find. She heard Martin's key in the door, his loose change clanging on to the hall table, the thump of his metal briefcase on the floor. 'Hello darling.' Would he notice she sounded especially chirpy?

He came into the kitchen. 'Hello love.' It was the wan, I've been-at-work-all-day voice. 'Any mail?' 'No, only the gas bill.'

She threw some capers into the pan and went to kiss him. He sat slumped at the table, looking tired and drawn, slackening his tie. 'I need a drink.' Annie poured them both a glass of wine, and sat and listened to the ritual recital.

'Bloody awful day. Looks as if we might lose the Body 'n' Bounce account –'

'Remind me, is that a shampoo or an exercise video?'

'Annie, don't you ever listen? I told you, it's a new all-in-one shampoo and conditioner.'

'Bloody awful name.'

'Yeah, well, we're working on that. Anyway, every presentation we make isn't fucking good enough, there's a madam of a Marketing Director who thinks she knows it all . . .' Annie retreated to the saucepan, standing and stirring, only half-listening. A door closed in her mind, shutting off the news of *her* day, thinking that he'd only spoil it, he wouldn't have any enthusiasm, he might even laugh at her.

She blurted out her news the following morning over breakfast (not that breakfast was a coherent or organised happening, more just a certain time of day). She told Martin, too fast, that she was going to do some freelance work as a party planner and cake designer – she'd been approached. He was flicking through his Filofax while ploughing through a bowl of bran. Martin was a great believer in it – he thought it would help him get thinner.

Annie, distracted by Tom and Amy squabbling over a free plastic animal in their cereal packet (Tom wanted it, and Amy wanted it because Tom did), managed to throw in a few buzz words which she thought might attract his attention – market, need, exploit, opportunities, entrepreneurial, money . . . He half-turned towards her and mumbled, 'Mm. Great. Fine – keep you busy, earn a bit of cash. But isn't it a bit samey for you – I thought you wanted a change?'

'Well, we housewives have to make the most of what we've got. What else can we do?'

But he wasn't really listening and missed her sarcasm, rushing out the door, 'Must be off.'

The anxieties of the man. He worked late, brought work home, then rushed to get to work early to prove how bright-eyed and bushy-tailed he was. Annie sighed and attempted to hurry the children along, promising she'd buy an identical packet of cereal so that they could both have a plastic animal.

While she plaited Amy's hair – 'Two of those thin plaits hanging down each side, you know, just at the front, please Mum,' and supervised Tom brushing his teeth – 'Up and down, not sideways' – she thought, I'll show Martin. I'll make something of this, I'll earn some money, I'll be successful – from these small beginnings, from one bloody birthday cake who knows what can grow?

DISCOVERY

15

Roz had an ache deep inside her chest. It felt as though her heart was tearing in two. She knew that was fanciful but the pain was real enough. It visited her frequently, like a spiteful reminder. Sometimes she could hardly breathe as it tightened its hold. She'd read enough health care manuals and newspaper articles to realise it was probably a symptom of stress. Self-induced. She'd created this whole situation yet now she felt so passive. Since Annie had asked her what she was going to do, she had allowed the question to surface in her consciousness. It was already there, of course, but hidden. She knew that it must be confronted, but how?

She sensed that things were moving towards some sort of crisis. Geoff wanted to exploit the opportunity of the job in America, he wanted to advance his career, his life. He expected her to fall in behind him, pliant and positive and supportive, and was becoming impatient as she showed little sign of doing so. The children unknowingly occupied the middle ground.

Alex was becoming impatient too. She went to him when she could but it was never enough. He wanted to do mundane things with her, like go to the supermarket, or decide what to cook for supper, or buy bath towels, or plan a garden, or read the Sunday papers together . . . Roz did not quite understand that

Alex had put the rest of his life into suspension – if he could not see Roz, he would rather do nothing. Weekends, when Roz was ensconced with her family, were a nightmare. He refused invitations, would not see friends. He knew it wasn't healthy, but what else could he do?

Lying unspoken between them was the question of sex – with others. He hadn't yet asked Roz what happened in her marital bed, so far he'd felt it was better that he didn't know. She assumed that there was no one but her. She dared not consider anything else.

Roz watched Katy eat her lunch, half-listening to her chatter about playgroup. She was thinking about her own behaviour. Lately she'd been acting oddly, alluding to her affair with Alex, almost telling people. She'd done this with several mothers at the school gate, no one she knew particularly well, just ordinary, pleasant women who happened to say, 'You're looking well, Roz', or asked, 'How are you, Roz?' as if they really meant it. And she'd leaped in with a twist of a smile, as if making a joke: 'That's what love does for you!' or 'Well, they say an affair can do you the world of good!'

She registered the confusion and embarrassment on their faces, the concerned glances to see if there were any children nearby to hear. Invariably they'd make an excuse and hurry away. She was startled by her words too, but still she did it.

There were other things. She'd let Alex take her to meet Katy a few times after they'd spent the morning together and had run out of time. He'd been very sweet to Katy – as she'd known he would be – explaining what an architect did and what a loft conversion was, doing funny drawings to amuse her. One afternoon they'd arranged that Alex would bump into Roz and Katy in Hampstead and they'd have lunch in the village. The next time it was in Alexandra Park by the pond . . .

She was allowing their affair to come closer to home. Was this her roundabout way of making something happen?

What she actually wanted to happen was unclear – she could not articulate it, even to herself.

It was a relief to be working. It surprised her how absorbing it was. This was the one time when she didn't think about Alex and what the hell she was doing or where it would lead. The Parents' Guide was taking shape. She worked on it at home whenever she could, spreading her files out on the kitchen table, using the old typewriter she'd rediscovered from her college days. The words flowed easily, but there was a lot of organising and editing to do. The booklet had to be accessible to all sorts of people – Roz had been made very aware of that.

She had regular meetings with Hilary, who'd originally approached her to do the work and who now monitored its progress. After a few weeks she would have to attend a meeting of the under fives committee as the Parents' Guide was on the agenda.

'It should be fine,' Hilary said, 'as long as you reassure the members that the Parents' Guide is for *everyone* and that you don't have a middle-class bias.'

'God, I hope not! But don't worry – I am aware of the issues.'

Roz picked up an agenda and saw her name by item five. She surveyed the long oval table. There were so many different organisations and interests represented: education, the health authority, childminders' association, minority women's groups ... Although at times they disagreed on details or points of policy, they all saw the welfare of women and children as a priority. Roz found it refreshing. And she enjoyed the buzz of discussion – it made her mind quicken.

They discussed the deprivation faced by children in bed and breakfast accommodation; the safety of old equipment in park playgrounds; the vetting of nursery workers' backgrounds in the light of an unfortunate incident ... Her turn came. Hilary introduced her and the Parents' Guide. Roz was nervous. Although it was this committee that had approved the funding for the project, they had not approved her personally. She took a deep breath, then outlined the planned contents and distributed sheets of information.

There were challenges. Was she taking into account all social groupings and income brackets? What about a section on Free Fun – outings for those with little money? Was she familiar with the particular needs of single parents? Should it just be aimed at parents – what about other primary carers and childminders? Was she being careful about her use of language, and did she have a copy of the council guidelines on non-sexist language?

Roz listened, fielded the questions and gave reassurances. She asked representatives of organisations to provide her with their full details for inclusion, she requested that further funds could be made available so that the guide could be translated into languages other than English, for the benefit of all. There were nods and favourable sounds from around the table. Hilary smiled at her and the meeting moved on.

As they talked of finding money to repair the Play Bus, Roz experienced a new awareness. Here she was, not as wife or mother or lover, but as Roz Harper, herself. No one had doubted her. She felt proud and fulfilled. She knew she was late coming to this. Other women had long been convinced of the value of work outside the home, but she had made a start. It felt good.

'Mummy, mummy – the phone!'

Katy, her mouth full of fish pie, moved towards it but Roz got there first. It was Alex.

'I need to see you, Roz, I really do. Before Tuesday.'

There was an urgency in his voice that she couldn't ignore.

'Oh Alex . . . Look, I'll try to think of something. Are you in tonight?'

'Yes, of course, if you think you can –'

'I'll try to be there.'

'Good. Then I'll see you later. Bye, my love.'

She wondered why he needed to see her so badly. He had rarely made such demands before, but perhaps that was changing. Katy had pushed away her plate and was watching her.

'Who was it, Mummy? Was it Daddy? I want to speak.'

'No darling, it wasn't Daddy. Just a friend. Now how about some yogurt?'

She smiled brightly to cover up her distaste at lying to her daughter. It's fortunate that she's so young and self-absorbed, thought Roz. She's my unwitting accomplice, too innocent to realise what Mummy is up to when we meet that nice man Alex, as if by accident . . . If Katy ever did mention these events to Geoff, Roz could cover up – there was always the loft, which she had his instructions to go ahead with anyway.

Now she had to think of an excuse to go out tonight. It would have to be an extra pottery session. She'd tell Geoff she needed to check on her firing – those pots which didn't exist, the ones she'd been saying she'd been working on for weeks. Yes, it was nicely consistent. She'd say she had to go as the kiln was being unloaded today . . . Then she'd come home disappointed as the pots were cracked and broken, something to do with air bubbles. That way Geoff wouldn't wonder why he didn't get to see them. It sounded reasonable – I've become good at this, she thought.

Geoff was home by seven-thirty and after a brief explanation Roz fled the house, getting to Alex's flat as fast as she could, as usual. But it was not to be an ordinary evening. As Alex opened the door he drew her into his arms and hugged her fiercely.

'Oh, Rozzi, I'm so glad you're here. Come and have a drink.'

In the kitchen a bottle of Krug protruded from an elegant silver ice bucket. She was no longer surprised at Alex possessing such things.

'Champagne! What are we celebrating?'

She watched him easing out the cork with his large thumbs, and hoped they were going to take their champagne to bed with them.

'Everything – you, me, us – oh!'

They laughed as the cork hit the ceiling. 'Like me,' he said. 'Eager.'

'Hardly like you, my love, you last a lot longer than that!'

They kissed a big wet sloppy kiss that included half their faces. As they paused for breath, gazing at each other over their glasses, Alex said, 'Let's drink to my divorce – and our future!'

He touched her glass with his.

'Your divorce? I thought you were already –'

'There was always some legal obstacle before, but apparently there is some new legislation in Greece and the fuss over property has been resolved to her satisfaction. Anyway, I heard from my lawyer in Athens today – it's now officially over.'

He seemed almost brittle in his happiness. Roz felt a touch of sadness. He hasn't shared this or burdened me with any of it, just as I don't tell him about my problems, like this business of moving to America. He must have had difficulties over this divorce, and practical hassles with it happening in Greece, yet he only tells me now. Are we – is it – so fragile? she wondered.

'Roz my love – cheer up! Why such a long face? Drink to my freedom, whatever that is!'

He stretched out his arms and began a Greek dance around the kitchen.

'Whatever freedom is!' Roz laughed.

He danced towards her, and encircled her in his arms.

'And listen – I've got to go to Athens in a few weeks, some legal matters need attention. I want you to come with me, just for a weekend, a long weekend. Say you will.'

He buried his face in her neck, his lips warm against her skin.

'I don't know if I can Alex – I mean, how –'

'Invent an excuse – I'm sure you can. Your mother or something. Think of it: you and me, together for days and nights –'

She thought of it. This was temptation.

'It would be wonderful. I'll try –'

They kissed – would they ever tire of kissing? – and he led her into the living room where they sank together on to the rug. He put the champagne in its bucket and there it stayed for the rest of the evening, largely untouched.

Their need for each other obliterated everything else. They rejoiced in each other, still discovering things the other liked to do, have done. Alex bit her left shoulder again and again. Usually she stopped him, in case Geoff would see the marks, but tonight she encouraged him. She twisted and turned under his mouth, and came to orgasm, just from this man, her lover, biting her shoulder. Briefly, she marvelled at it, but then she pulled off his last few pieces of clothing. How she adored his body, how she loved to trace the slight curve of his cock and to tease the very tip of him so exquisitely with her tongue . . .

Later they lay in his bed. She was tired and flushed, and snuggled up to him, simply happy. Why was sex, when it was so good, so much better than everything else? Alex's arm was around her and they could have drifted comfortably into sleep. That was how they both wanted it to be. But there was a clock ticking in Roz's head. She stirred and looked at her watch.

'Christ! I must go – it's after ten already.'

Alex sat up abruptly and his voice was loud and jarring.

'Sometimes I can't bear this – I hate it! These snatched hours, here and there, when you can manage it. I want more of you, more.'

He held her shoulders tightly. Her left one was sore and it made her wince. She had never seen him like this. She stroked his face, placatingly.

'Darling, I'm sorry. I don't like it either. But what can I do? We knew how it would be.'

'I know, I know.' He relaxed his grip. 'And at first it was all right but after months of meeting like this I'm finding it difficult. And look at me!'

He had another erection. Roz groaned – she wanted to stay, to stroke him, hold him, pull him into her. The urge was so strong, yet she had to resist it and resist him.

'Alex, you're magnificent, but I must go. If I'm late Geoff might suspect –'

He leaped from the bed and held her to him, with difficulty, his penis squashed between them.

'And if he did? If he knew? Maybe we should tell him, perhaps it would be better.' He nibbled her ear, and twirled his tongue inside it.

She threw back her head and gave in. This is what matters, she told herself, this is the best feeling in my life, and I must have it.

He pressed her against the wall, his hands on hers spread wide. He bent his knees slightly, she opened her legs. He steadied her and thrust upwards into her – his touch was sure, he knew her body so well. Their faces were close and neither closed their eyes. As he moved faster he murmured to the rhythm, 'Tell him, tell him, tell him –'

As they came together a few minutes later Roz was gasping, 'Yes, I will, yes, yes, yes.'

They collapsed on the bed. Alex stroked her hair. 'I

hope you mean it. I love you and I want you all to myself. We should be together!'

She looked at him, unable to deny what he was saying, but already thinking that she must hurry home. She got up and began to struggle into her clothes.

He stood naked in front of her. 'Well Roz, do you want me – or him? Sooner or later you must choose.'

He was offering himself to her and at that moment she could not reject him. She refrained from saying that things were not that simple, she dared not raise the issue of her children, she did not ask what sort of life they would have together. She merely said, 'I want you Alex, I do want you.'

He embraced her gently and she thought she saw tears in his eyes. He released her, and as she tried to reach for her bra, he put his hands over her breasts, lifting and kissing each in turn. 'And you can have me, just say the word.'

He held her once more then let her finish dressing. He carefully reminded her about the weekend in Greece and she said she'd ring him with the answer. She knew it must be yes – she felt she owed it to him. And it was easier to say yes to a weekend together than to confront the issue of telling Geoff.

As she drove home too fast, feeling wet and sore inside her pants, she envied Alex at home, probably in the bath or shower by now, finishing the champagne. Understandably, it all seemed clearer and simpler to him – the complications were all on her side. She would have to do something, sometime. But what? Perhaps she could have a life with Alex, another life, a different one. She needn't reject the children – they could live with her and Alex, couldn't they? But what about Geoff?

What a mess, she thought. She was nearly home, and had to slow down as crowds were leaving Muswell Hill Odeon, trailing across the road. She suddenly yearned for a modest and innocent pleasure like going to the cinema. But now she had to devise a plan to get her away for the weekend with Alex. More duplicity.

She drew up outside the house. She switched her mind from the imagined bliss of being with Alex for several whole days and nights to project herself into the role of innocent wife returning after an evening of frustration in the pottery studio. Duplicity piled on duplicity, she thought.

16

A weekend bag stood in a corner of the bedroom near Roz's side of the bed. In it she'd already placed underwear, a cotton wrap, a swimsuit – all new; small sizes of shampoo and conditioner and moisturiser; a guidebook hidden underneath. She was preparing for her stay in Athens.

Geoff could see the bag of course. It was no secret that she was going away for the weekend, it was just that he thought she was going to Devon for three days of intensive pottery.

Convincing him had been easy: Roz had enthused about this residential course she'd heard about at evening classes; it was at an arts centre near Dartmoor, and it focused on advanced techniques, especially firing and glazing – her weak points she said. Several others were going and Judith, their teacher, had recommended it and it was only for a long weekend, from Friday to Monday, so he could manage, couldn't he?

He'd agreed after consulting his diary and considering his work load – could he take both Friday and Monday off? – and being reassured that Roz would leave lots of food in the fridge and freezer. She said she'd give him more details nearer the time and he asked her to make sure to leave a contact number, just in case. That will be a challenge, she thought.

As the time approached she felt she would burst with

excitement and anticipation. The children were off school for the Easter holidays, so it was difficult for her to see Alex. Talking to him on the phone had to suffice, snatching opportunities whenever she could.

She worried that something would happen to prevent her going, a sign, a stroke of fate, so she threw herself into housework and cooking meals for the freezer, preparing everything for Geoff to take over smoothly. But she was also engaged in that childhood exercise: if I'm good I'll be rewarded. Her treat awaited her.

Annie had spent the morning creating a strawberry mousse in a bottom-shaped mould she'd found in an obscure gift shop in Holborn. She'd just proudly turned it out all in one piece when Roz rang to see if she felt like having coffee or a chat or whatever, so she invited her over to see it.

Roz arrived with Katy and Matthew, having left Polly revising for exams and Sam still asleep. They came into the kitchen and there, resplendent in the centre of the table, sitting on a large white plate, was a shimmering pink mousse bum. The curvy, upturned cheeks wobbled as they approached.

'Oh God, Annie – how could you?' Roz screeched with laughter. 'I was going to say how sexist it is but I suppose it could be a male bum.'

'Well, possibly! Tom – no!' Annie managed to grab Tom's hand as he was about to give the mousse a good poke. The children had collapsed into giggles, muttering about bums for lunch, so Annie suggested they all went into the garden. 'And Amy, don't let Tom go too high on the climbing frame, will you?'

'So who is this creation for?'

'I'm doing a buffet supper tomorrow for some estate

agents – a merger of two firms in Islington. They all seem pretty hooray-Henryish, so this should go down well, don't you think?'

'Oh yes, it's beautifully crass! You're doing adult parties as well as children's now?'

'So it seems! This is the first, actually. A father at one of the kids' parties asked me, so I thought why not? Coffee?'

'Yes please. Business is booming then?'

'Touch wood! Things are going well – I've had one party a week since I started, which is about all I can handle. I've had to turn a couple down, so I must think about getting some help. Especially if I'm going to do adult parties as well.'

Roz watched Annie making coffee in a machine she hadn't seen before and realised that there was a new dimension to her, a different edge to her voice. The old self-deprecating, jokey tone was still there, but underpinned by something else.

'It sounds as if you're becoming a real business woman – expanding already!'

'Why not? That's the way these days. But listen – if you can think of anyone . . . Otherwise I'll advertise, start off with a part-timer. Imagine being a boss! Who would have thought it, little old me?'

She asked Roz to stay for lunch and Roz was pleased to say yes – she needed distraction these days, however minor. Annie busied herself at the cooker. 'It's just some homemade soup.'

Roz looked around her. The kitchen appeared cleaner and tidier than usual. And Annie seemed more organised and in control. Things have changed, she thought, here I am, having lunch at Annie's, instead of the other way round. Of course, being a provider of food was her business now.

'Tell me, how is Martin reacting to your work, your business?'

'I'm not sure. He's not sure.' Annie turned and grinned. 'I think he felt threatened at first – you know he has such a fragile ego! He's having to get used to the idea. He wants it to be a success of course –'

'Of course!'

'Well, you know Martin. He approves of entrepreneurial ventures and all that. And I don't mind the money and success part either!'

Roz laughed with her. She'd always liked Annie's openness and honesty.

'And Martin won't object to what I'm doing as long as it doesn't interfere with him, his life. Which is why I think I'll have to get some help at home as well – an au pair I thought.'

'Good idea, if you don't mind someone living in –'

They were interrupted by shouts from the garden. Roz went to investigate while Annie stirred the soup. Amy and Matthew were arguing over who was in charge of the game, which mainly seemed to consist of bossing the two younger ones about. Roz attempted to intervene but Amy argued with her too. It was hard to discipline someone else's child, she thought, and didn't try, but sat on the garden bench to make her presence felt.

Annie called them into lunch, telling the children to wash their hands. They crowded into the cloakroom off the hall. More squabbles. Roz helped Annie ease the wobbling giant mousse out of the way into the fridge, which it dominated with its pinkness.

'It's not yukky soup again, is it Mummy?'

'Yes Amy. But really good yukky soup. Now lay the table please.'

'Ugh! Wish we were having lunch at your house Matt.'

Amy organised the others to set the table. This girl should go far, thought Roz.

'They're getting rather tired of me trying out recipes on them – they'd rather go back to fish fingers everyday,' Annie laughed, serving the soup. 'Voilà! Cream of artichokes. I've forgotten what it is in French. Tell me if you think it's suitable for the estate agents' do, Roz.'

'Not choking soup. We can't have choking soup!' Tom shouted. Katie joined in and they both pretended to choke, thumping each other on the back. Amy and Matthew decided to distance themselves from this babyish behaviour and carried on eating.

'This is really very good. It's highly suitable – if you can make it in bulk.'

'Thanks,' Annie smiled. 'You know, it's funny but I actually enjoy cooking again, now it's for a purpose. And it's very convenient to combine the two – cooking for Martin and the kids and trying out stuff at the same time. Although they complain that they hardly ever have beefburgers any more –'

'Beefburgers! Can I have some?' Tom interrupted.

'See what I mean?'

After lunch Roz helped Annie clear away. She'd expected Annie to sit amongst the mess and have a cigarette but that too seemed to have changed. 'Aren't you smoking Annie?'

'I'm trying to give up. I've cut it right down, just one or two in the evening at the moment. I'm worried about dropping ash in the customers' food and scaring them off! But anyway, enough about me. How are you, what's happening?'

Her interest in Roz's life, in the affair, had diminished now that her own life was more interesting, but she still felt she should ask.

'Oh, OK. The usual juggling. Things are more difficult in the school holidays –'

'Tell me about it! Trying to get anything done –'

'I didn't mean . . . Never mind. Did I tell you I'm going away tomorrow, for the weekend?'

Annie caught Roz's eye. Could she be going away with Alex? Would she dare? Roz looked away.

'It's a pottery course in Devon. Learning about raku, that sort of stuff. Getting stuck into some clay will be good for me.'

Roz felt Annie's interest wane and she sensed her impatience as she bustled briskly about the kitchen. Annie had become someone who had a lot to do.

She offered to have Tom and Amy for the afternoon. The children were pleased, Annie was delighted.

Roz settled Tom and Katy in the playroom – one advantage of having so many children was that there was a vast range of toys to play with. Matthew took Amy to see his hamster and to give it a run. Roz went upstairs to complete her packing. She lay on the bed next to the pile of clean clothes for consideration and thought, tomorrow night I will be with Alex. All night. And the next, and the next.

She retrieved her passport from the file containing insurance details and birth certificates, all the documentation of family life. (Geoff kept his passport in his briefcase, always at the ready to spring into action for the company.) There was their marriage certificate. She stuffed it back in. She hoped Geoff wouldn't need to look in here over the weekend but even if he did, it was unlikely that he'd notice her passport was missing.

She was more or less ready. She'd worked out the arrangements for tomorrow morning with Alex and discussed a different but overlapping version with Geoff. It had been complicated. She told Geoff she was getting a lift to Devon with another woman in her class, a non-existent Naomi who she said lived in Camden Town. She'd get the tube or a taxi to Naomi's house. There had been a sticky moment when Geoff had offered to drive her there but she'd insisted it wasn't necessary – after all, what about the children?

Alex, who had wanted to collect her somehow or meet her at a half-way point, had eventually agreed that he'd wait for her at his flat. Then they'd be off to Heathrow, together.

Now all Roz had to do was give Geoff a contact number. She had done some research at the library. While Katy was choosing picture books and Matthew looked for any adventure stories he hadn't yet read, Roz looked through a guidebook to Devon and found a recommended country hotel near Dartmoor. She noted the phone number but changed two digits. She'd give that to Geoff, plus a fictitious name for the arts centre – Landscape Arts and Crafts Centre, that would do. But she'd insist that she'd try to ring him – she'd say it would be better as she'd probably be spending most of her time up to her elbows in clay.

She hoped that she'd covered every possibility: she had no energy to think it all through again. All she wanted to do was to think about Alex. And tomorrow.

17

Roz and Alex sailed past the crowd at the baggage carousel, carrying their weekend bags and holding hands. Roz bubbled inside – and not just because they'd consumed a lot of champagne on the plane. She felt she'd shed a skin – everything problematic had been left behind; the other part of her life was on hold.

At the taxi rank, standing in the hazy heat, she slid her hand around his neck, where the skin was hot and the curls damp. He stroked her cheek. Two policemen wearing sunglasses and guns watched them and nudged each other, speculating on their relationship, deciding they had to be lovers.

A taxi drew up. They eased apart and Alex spoke to the driver. I must learn some Greek, thought Roz. Alex can teach me. They sat closely together in the back and Alex explained that they were going to a hotel down the coast, away from Athens.

'Oh, aren't we staying in Athens itself?' Not that she really cared. Anywhere would be perfect with him.

'Trust me – this is better. Athens is becoming so polluted and it's very crowded. This way we can have the best of both worlds.'

She relaxed against him, aware that she *did* trust him – in every way. She trusted him to love her, not to hurt or deceive her . . . All those wild things that you could imagine – she didn't. Her instincts reassured her. She *knew* this man, even if she still didn't know everything about him.

They drove along a nondescript highway, dense with haphazard traffic and lined with industrial buildings and giant billboards advertising Marlboro and Coke and Budweiser, the usual names. Access routes from airports, skirting around their mother cities, looked like this all over the world, she thought.

The smell of the driver's cigarette, the world outside coming in through the open windows, the Greek pop music on the radio sounding surprisingly Eastern, swirled about her. She was drowsy but tried to stay awake, wanting to experience every second with Alex acutely, but the journey, the excitement and the champagne were having an effect. His arm was round her shoulder, and he played with her hair, massaged her neck, stroked her ear. She rested one hand on his knee, pressed close to hers. She fought the urge to run her fingers up his leg. Soon, soon, she told herself.

The taxi increased speed, they were leaving some of the urban sprawl behind. There was still a lot of traffic but it moved faster, like a pack of snappy dogs let off their leads. Alex said it wouldn't be long now. She was aware of a landscape emerging – beyond the strip of the road she could see bare brown hills with dots of green. It began to resemble the Greece she'd imagined. She rested her head on Alex's shoulder and closed her eyes.

She half-heard the thud of the car door and Alex murmuring that they'd arrived. Sunlight burst around her. She blinked, her contact lenses dry in her eyes.

The haze had lifted and she looked up to a perfect blue sky and a shadow of a building. The hotel. Bland, pale and modern was her first impression; low profile, low key. Inside it was more striking: a shaded porch filled with tubs of flowers, a reception area with marble floors, a fountain, plants in every corner, an atmosphere of cool and calm. The man at the desk greeted Alex like an old friend, politely acknowledged Roz, then they were in a lift, out into a white corridor lined with large photographs of Greece. She walked in a daze. Everywhere was hushed.

'It's so quiet Alex,' she whispered. 'Are – are we the only guests?'

'It's still siesta time.'

A young man wearing a crisp white shirt and a model smile opened a door and left their bags. Alex closed the door, carefully and quietly. Roz stood and drank it all in. She kicked off her shoes and slowly spun round, 'Oh, this is wonderful. Wonderful!' She'd been expecting a pleasant room, but not this: an enormous suite with sofas and vases of lilies, everything in blue and white, airy and stylish, and bowls of fruit and a fridge full of champagne, and who knew what else behind the doors . . .

'You know you're fulfilling fantasies and dreams I never even knew I had!'

Alex smiled at her enthusiasm. He didn't know that she'd only seen places like this in films. When she'd travelled as a student it had been camping or cheap shared rooms, then later the family stayed in cottages or farmhouses – not luxury hotel suites, not with all those children. He took off his shoes and socks and lay on the bed, watching her. She explored.

She opened the door to the bathroom and exclaimed at the blues and greens and seashell motifs

– it was like being underwater. The bath was huge, there were two basins and a separate shower. I can play Aphrodite in here, she thought.

'Now come and try the bed, my love.' He was becoming impatient.

'In a minute – I want to go on the balcony.'

She opened the French windows and went out. Terracotta tiles, white wooden furniture, blue cotton sunshade, more plants. Below she could see a terrace, a swimming pool, gardens, a path through trees to a small beach – and the sea, clear shades of turquoise deepening into blue.

'Oh Alex, it's so beautiful.' He had joined her outside. 'Everything is perfect. Thank you for bringing me here.'

'Not quite perfect, my sweet, wait until you hear the jets as they approach the airport.'

'I don't mind, who cares? It was a plane that brought us here, after all.'

He held her, stroked her hair away from her face. She put her head on his chest, feeling the heat of him. It moved through her, sweeping away any thoughts of home, children, deceiving Geoff. She concentrated on the now. Loving Alex made everything seem simple.

They moved to the bed and lay facing each other. It was a very large bed. God-size rather than king-size, Alex said. Suddenly something occurred to Roz: 'Alex – have you stayed here before? You seem to have no interest or curiosity about this place –'

Sharp niggling thoughts entered her mind: who had he stayed here with? Did he bring all his women here? On this very bed? She reminded herself that she trusted him.

'All right, Detective Harper, I confess.' He saw her expression change. 'Rozzi, don't look so alarmed. All

I meant was that, yes, I've stayed here before. Many times. You see, my family owns the hotel and I designed it –'

'Why didn't you tell me?'

'Well, it might have sounded a bit crass. Or you might have thought me – what's that expression, so English – a cheapskate? What on earth does that mean anyway?'

'I don't know! But I wouldn't have thought you crass, or a cheapskate. Never.'

The idea was ridiculous – after all, he had paid her air fare and was taking care of the whole trip. She bent over him to kiss him.

'No more secrets.'

'It wasn't really a secret – it just didn't seem important.'

'But I want to know everything about you, everything. It's all important.'

She kissed his eyes, his nose, his long eyelashes, his bristly chin.

'You do. You will.'

They kissed long and deeply, sticking to each other despite the air conditioning.

'Roz – let's shower together, then come back to bed.'

'Yes, yes. I'll wash London and everything out of my system.'

She peeled off her T-shirt and jeans, bra and pants. He watched her as he slowly unbuttoned his shirt. She stood naked before him, making some attempt to hold her stomach in, keep her shoulders back, pull her breasts up, but she'd become used to him seeing her naked. And how many times had he kissed her stretch marks, squeezed the softness of her tummy, and revelled in her fullness? He often told her that he loved her the way she was: he loved *her*.

He took her hand and pressed it against his chest so that she could feel his heart. They stood silently together, looking at each other, enjoying the moment. For once there was no rush, no concern over time.

They walked into the bathroom holding hands, stepped into the shower, under the water. Images streamed through her mind. Adam and Eve. Deluge. Behind the waterfall. A Pre-Raphaelite sumptuousness. Water sprites. Innocence and indulgence. Wetness everywhere.

Later, between the white linen sheets, they floated towards sleep. Roz's prickly eyes reminded her of her contact lenses. She slipped out of bed and went into the bathroom to remove them with a sigh of relief. All these small practical details – we're not familiar with each other in that way, she thought. Does he shave wet or dry? How does he sleep at night – on his side, his back? What does he usually wear in bed? There were still so many things to discover about him and for him to discover about her. Some of them they would only find out if they lived together. If, she thought, or when?

The luxury of having hours alone together was overwhelming. They needed to devour the experience. The rest of the afternoon was spent in bed, dozing, confiding silly secrets, rolling over and over to see who would be on top this time, giggling, chasing, all the things that lovers do. They surfaced for interludes in the shower and room service picnics on the sofa.

It was beginning to get dark outside when Alex said he must make some phone calls – he had to talk to his lawyer, arrange to see him, and he wanted Roz to meet his sister, what did she think? At that moment Roz felt happy to do anything. She would have been content to spend the whole weekend in their suite, their temporary home, but she did not say so. She'd told him to do what he thought best, arrange anything he liked. She felt placid and peaceful.

While Alex talked on the phone she stood on the balcony, watching the sky change colour, streaks of purples on grey and pink. The air was soft, still warm, and there was a herby fragrance rising from the gardens below. Rosemary? Thyme? She took deep breaths of it. The sea was flat and luminous and hardly made a sound.

She heard Alex's voice change tone. Was he going to speak to his ex-wife while he was here, she wondered. And his daughter? Did he ever see her? Roz realised she did not even know her name. He never spoke about her and Roz sensed that it was best that she did not ask. She went inside to get dressed, hoping the clothes she had with her would be appropriate. Alex wanted to take her into Athens for the evening.

A black Golf convertible with the top down was parked in the hotel driveway.

'Aren't we going by taxi?'

'No Madame, I am driving you myself.' A mock accent, a teasing bow. He explained that the family kept the car here for his, and anyone else's, use. Roz began to wonder about The Family.

The drive into Athens was romantic, despite the traffic and fumes and noise: her hand on his knee, her hair billowing around her, his arm sometimes across her shoulder or caressing her neck – he was very deft at driving with one hand. A feeling of intimacy, despite being open to the world. Roz imagined how this would look if she was standing at the roadside and saw this couple in an open-topped car flash by. It was as if she were watching someone else's life.

In Athens Alex cursed until he found a parking space at last, squeezing the car into a corner of a large square, surrounded by banks, offices, apartments, the pavements filled with people – tourists strolling, Greeks hurrying home from work.

It could be any European city, Roz thought.

'They say that Athens is the noisiest city in the world,' he said.

'I can believe it!'

He guided her across a road clogged with hooting cars and aggressive drivers, gripping her arm as if afraid he'd lose her. She loved this constant physical contact. It occurred to her that she and Geoff rarely did this: there were always children's hands to hold, or buggies or shopping. And before the children – had they then? She didn't think so: physical contact in public had never come naturally to him, she had had to initiate it. But why was she thinking of Geoff now? She flicked the thoughts away.

'Where are we going?'

'We'll wander towards the Plaka. People have lived there for over three thousand years –'

'Yes – I read in my guide book that it's the oldest part of the city.'

'Ah, you don't need me then?' He feigned disappointment and began to withdraw his arm, but she laughed and snatched it back, cuddling close to him.

'I need you for all sorts of things, as you well know.'

They turned into a side street, then another, then another, each narrower than the last. Alex led her into a maze of alleyways, some so narrow they could not walk side by side. They stepped in and out of shadows, light coming from the small houses they passed, through open doors and windows, revealing glimpses of ordinary lives. They climbed past fine houses with shutters and wrought iron balconies (nineteenth-century, Alex said). There were sudden surprises: a courtyard filled with pots of geraniums and other flowers she did not recognise, scenting the air; turning a corner there was a tiny church (Byzantine, Alex said), and then a sunken garden, with a thin cat regarding them seriously. She held his hand tightly, imagining the horror of being separated, unable to find him.

There were fewer tourists now, only the occasional person who would wait while they squeezed by, and they would nod at each other in acknowledgement of a shared taste and experience. After another flight of steep steps they came to a small square, and there it was: the Acropolis crowning the top of the hill, floodlit, with some extra help from the moon. They leaned on an old stone wall and gazed at its magnificence. All the words that Roz wanted to say sounded trite: breathtaking, incredible, amazing . . . We use them to describe such everyday things and experiences, like a pair of shoes or a TV programme, so there's no vocabulary left for those things that are truly so, she thought.

'Oh! What can I say? It's, it's –'

'I know, takes your breath away, your words away, doesn't it? I love seeing it like this, at night.'

Roz had seen photographs of the Acropolis, but nothing had prepared her for this. She was moved by the past; by glories, defeats, tragedies; by all those other lives . . . She sighed, full of yearning for things she could not recognise or name; touched by melancholy; swamped by complexities only half-understood.

'I'll take you up there in daylight, this weekend if we can. Oh Roz, there are so many things I want to show you, to share with you.'

She took his face in her hands. The moment was transfused with feelings of awe, some of it connected to her love for him. They kissed, tenderly and slowly. It was an affirmative kiss which said, we belong together.

They walked slowly back down. Snatches of Greek music filtered through the air, and the streets were wall to wall with people, jostling, laughing, shouting. Alex bought a bag of pistachio nuts from a stall and they ate them wandering along in a random way. Roz paused outside a shop to look at the rows of worry beads and jewellery hanging on stands. For a second she wondered what she should buy for the children, then remembered with a jolt that she was supposed to be in Devon. Alex dashed into the shop, reappearing a few minutes later, telling her to close her eyes and put out her hand. There was a key ring with a plastic Parthenon attached. 'Oh Alex, it's great! Thank you. I'll always treasure it.' And she meant it. The key ring, the night, the place.

They sat at a table outside a bar, Roz sipping iced coffee, Alex an ouzo, watching people go by. Two young men approached, walking in that exaggeratedly male way with the emphasis on the pelvis. They stopped, looking surprised, greeting Alex loudly. He rose, obviously pleased to see them, and there was a lot of back-slapping and hugging and laughing. The three of them shadowed the table. Roz was unsure whether to stand or not, so sat still, feeling herself shrinking into insignificance. Alex eventually turned to her.

'This is my friend, Roz Harper, from London.'

Two pairs of dark eyes looked her over.

'And this fine pair are my cousins, two of my many cousins: Christos, Andreas.'

Christos, the taller one, shook her hand.

'Hello, Roz Harper. I am sorry but I do not have very good English.' His smile was wide and practised. Andreas, further away from her, bowed slightly in her direction, 'Good evening. We are pleased to meet you.'

Their curiosity was obvious. She guessed they were wondering what Alexandros was doing here with this woman, who was she, did she share his bed?

Alex asked them have a drink and she hoped they would refuse. But they managed to find two extra chairs and squashed around the table somehow. Everyone's knees were touching, it was unavoidable. Christos and Andreas asked her how she liked Athens, had she ever been here before, polite stilted questions. She tried to smile and answer in a friendly way but she resented their presence; she felt like a child whose birthday treat has been ruined. She retreated into silence and her drink.

The three men slipped into Greek and their conversation became louder, gesticulating and punching each other on the shoulder. She had no idea what they were talking about: family? The government? Her? She withdrew further, her fingers playing with the key ring, her mind straying back to home, wondering how the children were, and even how Geoff was coping . . .

Alex's hand was on hers. 'Roz, shall we go now? I know you're tired.' She nodded, saying a quick goodbye. They shouted after Alex as he propelled Roz along the street and he shouted back, raising his hand. Neither he nor Roz said a word to each other until they reached the car.

'Christos and Andreas asked us to eat with them but I said you were tired and we should go back to the hotel.'

'Yes, I think that's best.'

He pulled the top up on the car, put some Vivaldi on the stereo, and drove fast. Roz closed her eyes. She had a headache. Back in their room, Alex stood in front of her and held her arms.

'OK, now what is it? Are you upset, or what?'

She refused to admit how she felt – how she had felt – and said, 'I'm just very tired, that's all, it's been a long day.'

He would not let her go. 'Yes but it's more than that, isn't it? I think you're sulking, in your quiet English way.'

'I'm not! What the hell makes you think that?'

'I know you, remember?'

'All right then. Why did you have to talk to your Greek friends and ignore me?' She knew she sounded childish and pathetic.

'Oh, Rozzi, come on. They're my cousins, they're family. I couldn't ignore them, nor would I want to. I haven't seen them for a while, and it was only a short chat. We've got plenty of time, now relax.'

'But we haven't, Alex! Our time, this time, is precious, it's limited.' She moved away from him, kicking off her shoes, removing her ear-rings. He sighed deeply, then sat on the end of the bed.

'Don't you think I know that? But tonight – it's such a small thing and this is my home town, remember? It's likely that I'll bump into family or friends. This is part of me, you must recognise that.'

She nodded and bowed her head, feeling chastised. She felt ashamed for being so unreasonable and possessive, but part of her still burned, wanting him all to herself. She sat down next to him and he gripped her by the shoulders, his face close to hers.

'I have to share you all the time. You don't know what it's like when you leave me after an hour or so of being together. You go home to your cosy house, with your children all around you, and a husband you can take or leave, but he's there! I can't even bear to think about what you do about sleeping with him –'

'Oh Alex –'

'I have to deal with being without you. I have to fill my life. I stay in, I brood. I don't want other women, even though they're available. I only want *you*, but I have you in strictly limited amounts – and you have your other life, without me.'

He paused for breath, looking upset. She took him in her arms, his head on her shoulder, and rocked him gently.

'I'm so sorry, so sorry. I'll come to you, I'll be with you, I will, I promise.'

They went to bed exhausted, with a distance still between them and held each other briefly, without making love. Alex fell alseep but Roz lay increasingly awake – and this was their first night together. She resisted the urge to weep, not wanting to wake him, not wanting to yield to the feelings of self-pity which were threatening to engulf her. She told herself that things could not be perfect between her and Alex all of the time – they were bound to feel the pressures of their situation.

She lay listening to his breathing, to occasional voices on the terrace below and the droning of a late night jet overhead. At last she relaxed, touched his warm arm for reassurance and fell alseep.

18

Geoff glared at the television without really registering what he was watching. It was Saturday night and he was dog-tired. Roz had rung earlier, sounding cheerful and chirpy; she was enjoying her course, she said. Lucky her, he thought.

He wished she was here. Two days of children and domesticity already felt like more than enough. There was tomorrow to get through, and Monday, but at least they were back at school then and he hoped to get to the office for a few hours.

What a day. It wasn't until after nine that he'd been able to sit down, alone, and have a drink. He'd already had several glasses of wine through the evening, on the run while doing something else, and had left a trail of half-full glasses all over the house.

He'd been fairly relaxed yesterday, telling himself that it was good to be with his children. He was someone who enjoyed spending time with his kids, wasn't he? But today his patience had begun to wear thin. He'd wanted things to be organised and under control, but he met with passive resistance. Polly said she had revision to do and was probably going to do it with Laura, or they might go to Emma's house, but she didn't know until they'd all spoken on the phone . . . Matthew was meant to be going to his Saturday morning junior football club but said he didn't feel like it, he felt a bit sick, and retreated to watch television, and Katy joined him. Sam did not get up until lunchtime. Geoff was making the others scrambled eggs when he ambled into the kitchen, ignoring everyone else, pulling out packets of cereal, monopolising the toaster, finishing a carton of orange juice.

Geoff tried not to lose his temper, telling himself the usual things – he's adolescent, it's not easy . . . He looked at Sam shovelling cornflakes into his mouth and had to remind himself that this was his son, whom he'd taught to ride a bike and to swim, who used to demand to have *The Jungle Book* read aloud . . . Where had that lovable blond-haired innocent gone?

Nowhere, thought Geoff, he's right here, just changed almost beyond recognition. He might have managed to remain calm if Sam hadn't suddenly announced that he needed new trainers.

'What's wrong with the ones you're wearing?'

'Wrong colour. Gotta have black ones.'

The others bent their heads over their plates, sensing a storm brewing. Polly prayed for the phone to ring.

'Do you mean we've got to go shopping for trainers *today*? Why didn't you get them in the school holidays? Did your mother know about this?'

'Look it's not a problem Dad. I can –'

'Can we get them locally?'

'No, they won't have the ones I want. Oxford Street –'

Geoff exploded. Oxford Street? On a Saturday? Why didn't Sam think about someone else for once? Why couldn't he plan ahead?

Sam began to argue. Polly disappeared to use the

phone, Katy and Matthew dived back into the playroom, leaving their eggs, by now cold and rubbery.

Eventually a compromise was reached. Sam was allowed to go to Oxford Street with his friend Josh, as long as they were back by seven. As Geoff handed over a wad of notes for the trainers he wondered what Roz would have done, how she would have handled it if she'd been here. But she wasn't.

He had to go shopping in the afternoon. Although Roz had assured him that she'd left plenty of food, there were still some things they needed. They were low on toothpaste and toilet paper. Why hadn't Roz noticed that? She seemed to have less and less time for shopping and housework these days. Geoff recognised that running the house, as he called it, required time and effort, but he felt it should be Roz's time and effort, not his. He held things together from the outside, she should do the same from the inside.

He wandered around Sainsbury's with Katy and Matthew, buying all sorts of things he didn't even know existed. It took a long time, partly because he couldn't find things. They must have moved everything since he was last here. When was that? He couldn't remember. He piled lots of treats into the trolley – chocolate bars, cakes, puddings, ready-made Chinese meals, plus simple things he thought he knew how to cook: chops, sausages, chicken, pasta. There was an element of pride involved: he wasn't going to use all the stuff Roz had left in the freezer and he wanted to avoid going to McDonalds.

The shopping came to just under a hundred pounds. God, did it always? They had to queue to get out of the car park, then Muswell Hill was completely blocked – some problem with a bus on the roundabout. As they sat in the traffic, Katy said she needed to pee, Matthew said, 'Don't do it on me', and Geoff began to worry about the four tubs of expensive American ice-cream he'd bought – would they start to thaw?

Back home, with the six bags and two boxes of shopping strewn over the kitchen and Katy and Matthew telling him they were starving, searching for items for the freezer to put away first, Geoff couldn't help thinking, was it always like this with children? Constant interruptions, being pulled this way and that, having to make major and minor decisions and do so many things at once? Was this what it was like to be Roz?

19

Roz woke before Alex, experiencing that second of wonderment, where am I? There were no William Morris print curtains, no Chagall prints on the wall, no sounds of children. That familiar scene was far away. The brightness streaming into the room told her she was in Greece.

She propped herself up on her elbow to look at him. His eyelashes brushed the top of his cheeks, one eyebrow arched more than the other. She wanted to get to know every pore of his skin, every small scar and minor blemish, but she did not touch him, she let him sleep. She wrapped her peignoir around her and quietly stepped outside on to the balcony. The sun was already up, the wall was warm to her touch and the sea shimmered. It was so still but she kept watching for the merest movement, the hint of a wave.

Alex appeared, wearing boxers and yawning. How would it be between them this morning? she wondered. He stood behind her, his body pressed against hers, his head over her shoulder. They gazed at the sea. The calm expanse of water had a hypnotic effect. Neither spoke, the events of last night were not mentioned. Harmony was restored. Alex held her tight. As the noise of an approaching plane shattered the tranquillity they laughed and went inside, back to bed, eager to make up for the lost opportunity of their first night together.

The weekend passed in a blur of happiness. Time galloped past, then inexplicably slowed right down, so that small details of each moment were illuminated and could be savoured. Months later a smell, a taste, a certain light, would take Roz back in an instant.

Alex made suggestions and arrangements and she let him. Her sister Maggie had always said that she was too reliant on men, but Roz felt that this didn't count. This was Alex, this was their weekend together.

His lawyer had come to the hotel on Saturday morning and Alex went downstairs to see him while Roz soaked in a steamy fragrant bath. When he returned he rubbed his hands with glee, saying that now business was over and everything was signed and sealed he could enjoy himself. He unwound Roz from the bath-towel and began.

He insisted on taking her into Athens to shop. He wanted to buy her things: clothes, jewellery, anything she wanted. She acquiesced, what else could she do? She couldn't say that they seemed to be conforming to the stereotypical behaviour of lover and mistress. That would hurt him.

They went in a taxi to avoid parking problems. Athens was heaving with even more noise and fumes than the night before. Yet he made it magical: his enthusiasm for the city was infectious. He kept up a non-stop commentary on the history that lay behind what she could see – Socrates did this; Aristotle was here; in the war this happened . . . She marvelled at his knowledge – perhaps he cherished his heritage more keenly because he no longer lived here?

He began diving into clothes shops, leading her by the hand. This was the Knightsbridge of Athens, he said. She hid her reluctance, for his sake. The saleswomen alarmed her: no part of them untouched by improving hands. From hair to eyebrows to their sleek shaved legs they represented a testimony to effort. She let Alex deal with them while she pretended to flick through rails of clothes. They were happy to chat to Alex – who wouldn't be? – and after a few minutes she appeared at his elbow and murmured his name, saying there was nothing she wanted. This was repeated three or four times. She wanted to ask him if he wished to change her, if he wanted her to look different, or even, was he ashamed to be seen with her? But she said nothing, not wanting to introduce any hint of conflict into the day, telling herself not to be so insecure.

'Roz – they weren't really your sort of places, were they?'

She smiled. He understood her.

'Not really!'

'How about a department store? Would you prefer that?'

'Yes – if you still insist on wanting to buy me things.'

'Yes, I do insist. When do I ever have the chance to do this?'

The store was reassuringly large and crowded. At least this should be more anonymous, she could browse and help herself, she thought. Alex knew his way around. He steered her towards stands of French designers, names she hadn't heard of, and persuaded her to try some things. The clothes surprised her. She knew the axiom that you pay more for less, that simplicity is expensive, but she'd never really experienced it in practice. The cut, the fabric, the details like the tiny wooden buttons . . . She came out of the changing room to show Alex, wearing loose linen trousers and a white cotton shirt, a linen waistcoat, and over it all a long jacket cut like a man's but somehow different. She felt great, she had to admit.

She let him buy her the lot, guessing it was very expensive. He insisted on adding a black duplicate of the white shirt and she didn't argue. This was real spoiling – being treated to two of something.

As they headed for the shoes, passing the lingerie, for a moment she thought he might want to buy her some fancy frilly underwear, the kind of stuff she hated. But he said nothing – perhaps he knew her better than she knew him.

She'd always loved buying shoes and as a child would often sleep with a new pair beside her bed to relish the look and smell of the leather. Now she concentrated on flat pumps and ended up with some of the softest, chocolate-brown leather, with cut-outs at the sides to lift them out of the ordinary. They at least were made in Greece.

Alex scooped up the glossy bags and took her down shady side streets lined with fur shops, their windows flaunting animals' coats styled into grotesque styles and colours. Jewellers displayed masses of gold: chains, rings, brooches, shining like booty, newly created treasure. Roz began to feel a little anxious. This wasn't her sort of thing either, but Alex pressed on until they arrived at a shop more subdued than the rest.

An elderly man came out from behind the counter, greeting Alex as if he'd been here before, with a brief nod to her and a gesture which suggested that she should look around. What she saw surprised her. This was more like a gallery than a shop. There was silver as well as gold; great chunks of it crafted into beautiful pieces: ear-rings, bracelets, armlets, chains, rings. She turned to Alex. 'This is all so beautiful.' He looked pleased. 'I thought you'd like it. There are some lovely silver pieces – isn't that what you like best?' He did know her well.

This reminded her of all the teen magazines she'd read; films she'd seen; the romances she'd devoured at an early age; even the literature she'd studied, in which women were wooed, swept off their feet, courted, spoiled . . . Life had never been like that, the reality had been different – until now. And although her intellect rebelled and questioned, another part of her melted and gave in to the indulgence and enjoyment of it all.

Eventually she left the shop with three new bracelets on her wrist: simple silver bands which fastened ingeniously like handcuffs. They clunked satisfyingly as she walked. Shopping makes you hungry, Alex said. Spending money does, thought Roz. They went to a small chic restaurant nearby for lunch, so discreet you could hardly see what it was behind the tinted glass doors in a white wall.

They toyed with swordfish and green salad but their real hunger was for each other. Their eyes and touch acknowledged it and they hurried out to get a taxi.

The hotel was still and quiet, the air seemed heavy with expectancy. Alex whispered that they had hours to do what they wanted, hours to spend on each other. And he began to move downwards, down her body with his mouth, his tongue. They stretched and curled end to end, closing the circle, entering a bubble of their own making. Liquid, languid sensations. Without those two fierce cores of concentration – him on her, her on him – she felt as if she could float away. When they paused, coming up for air, their need collided, they twisted and turned together and he entered her, to seal and finalise what had gone before.

When they woke late in the afternoon they lay for a while gazing at each other, their fingertips touching. Alex suggested a swim. 'Yes, why not? It would be good for us – all we've done all day is sex and shopping.' She said it teasingly. They both knew it meant more than that.

Roz wanted to feel the sea around her so they ignored the pool and walked down to the beach. It was a private one for the hotel and there were few people on it and even fewer in the water. She swam out through the clear water until she could no longer touch the sand then floated on her back, staring up at the sky. Alex was impressed by her swimming. They played in the water, chasing, ducking, splashing – innocent pleasures. Less innocently, they embraced underwater and played lovers' games, Alex momentarily releasing her breasts from her swimsuit. My mermaid, he called her.

They stretched side by side on the sand, talking idly of holidays they'd had as children. They were filling in gaps, pouring cement into the foundations of their relationship. As they strolled back to the hotel he spoke of his sister, who was joining them later for dinner. He talked of her proudly: she was two years younger than him, so bright and capable, and was now running the family businesses. Businesses? thought Roz. How many are there?

While Alex shaved in the bathroom Roz phoned home. Thank God for direct dialling, she thought. She spoke briefly to Geoff, making up details about the pottery course, telling him about the surrounding countryside, sending her love to the children. He remarked on how close she sounded. She thanked the god of telecommunications again. Afterwards she congratulated herself on her performance, but her hands were shaking.

Roz wore her new clothes and shoes and new bracelets and concentrated on being a new person – Alex's lover. Not a wife, not a mother. I'm with Alex, she thought, that's it. She wondered how much Alex had told Tina about her – would she disapprove?

Tina arrived alone, looking chic and cool but she allowed Alex to envelop her in a hug. Brother and sister were obviously delighted to see each other. He introduced the two women. A slight flick of Tina's eyes, up and down, assessed her in an instant. Roz kept her eyes on Tina's face, but had already had a good look at her as she came in. She was petite, dressed in a green linen trouser suit with cream fabric shoes with square toes, and lots of matt gold jewellery. Her hair was cut in a sleek bob, framing dark eyes, wide mouth, strong eyebrows. She had the sort of looks Roz had always admired: the Eurolook of seemingly effortless style and elegance. She could be Spanish or Italian or French. We British never seem to achieve it, however hard we try, thought Roz.

They went outside to the terrace. The sky was a

glorious display of dramatic colours, evening becoming night. They paused to appreciate it.

Alex and Tina spoke in English: hers was nearly as good as his. She gave him news of her husband – in Zurich on business – and her son Miki. Roz wanted to ask all the things one mother usually asks another, but she held back, as she could hardly reciprocate by talking about her own children – it wouldn't be appropriate.

They were diverted by waiters, menus, food. Roz was hardly aware of what she ate, except that there were many courses and the cuisine seemed more French than Greek. They talked about Athens, Tina and Alex disagreeing affectionately about the places you had to see, or not, the restaurants you should eat in, the things you must buy. Tina laughed, and briefly touched Roz's hand with her carefully manicured one, the nails coloured a deep red.

'Roz, next time you come to Athens you must come out with me, instead of this pretender. He's practically a foreigner now, what does he know?'

They indulged in several desserts at Tina's insistence, dipping their spoons into one another's bowls. Well, this is OK, thought Roz, feeling a hurdle had been passed but not sure which or why.

And Tina, what did she think? She saw a warm, attractive woman who appeared nervous and a little distracted. But she saw someone she could like and more importantly, she saw someone who was making her brother happy. For too long he had seemed lonely and isolated, drifting without purpose. Alex had briefed her on the phone so she knew about Roz's circumstances; she also knew that she could not mention it – not tonight anyway. It was obvious that they adored each other, so who was she to question whether it was right or wrong?

Over the brandy she raised her glass and risked a toast, 'To you two – to Roz and Alex.'

Alex smiled sweetly at her, Roz looked surprised. They raised their glasses then repeated the toast in Greek, as if for luck.

When Tina left, she and Roz kissed each other on the cheek. It was an acknowledgement of acceptance and a signal that they could be friends. Alex watched his sister as she left the restaurant, the waiters paying her lots of attention – she was ultimately their boss, after all.

'She's probably resisting the urge to go into the kitchens and discuss tonight's food . . . She pays such attention to detail, my dear sister, and she works too hard.'

He turned his gaze back to Roz and raised his glass in another toast, 'To tonight.' Their hands met across the table.

Their second night together was how the first night should have been. Long, unhurried love-making. It amazed them how it was different every time. Holding each other, talking in low voices, speaking words of love and encouragement, making promises. Falling asleep still holding each other, together in the middle of the vast bed, unlike long-married couples, who compete for space and tug bed covers possessively.

They had the pleasure of waking together in the early morning, finding each other there. Making love again, side by side this time, not caring about unbrushed teeth or unwashed faces and bodies. Oh, to start every day like this . . .

*

Alex, perhaps spurred on by Tina's comments, was determined to take Roz places. After showering together – 'I must have had this in mind when I stipulated non-slip tiles' he said – they headed for Athens once more. It was still early. He'd hurried her through breakfast, wanting to get up to the Acropolis before the coach loads and the crowds. They almost succeeded.

As they climbed the hill in the developing heat Alex never let go of her hand, talking and talking about the buildings, the different periods represented, the mathematics involved in creating these masterpieces – rules and ratios, things Roz found it hard to grasp. He attempted to explain the difference between Doric and Ionic and Corinthian columns – and she listened, trying to see what he was describing.

She searched for a moment to reflect on it all, taking deep breaths as she saw the caryatids, the maidens supporting a portico of the Erectheion temple. Alex's words – about the difficulties faced by the architect (were there architects in 400 BC?), the challenges of the site – faded as Roz gazed at the statues. She knew they were copies – the originals had been moved to the museum as air pollution had been eating away the marble – and wondered at their significance. Maidens. What a word. Had she ever been a maiden? And why maidens? Why not Spartan youths with muscles and spears? She resolved to do some reading, the world of mythology beckoned.

They walked back down into the city and lingered in a café. Roz was about to suggest a return to their hotel room but Alex said they must go to the flea market so they were off again, to Monastiraki Square.

It felt as if the whole of Athens, and then some,

was out on the streets. The market was sprawling and chaotic and it was almost too noisy to talk. Alex and Roz wandered through the stalls, eating slices of fresh coconut. There were ceramics, 'old' copper kettles, ceremonial daggers, worry beads, goat bells; images of Greece served up for tourists.

Roz wished she could buy some presents for the children – she realised that she'd mentally begun to pick out suitable things. It was automatic.

They decided they'd earned lunch. Roz silently willed Alex to suggest they could eat back at the hotel – she wanted to take her shoes off, her clothes off, lie on that wonderful bed, but he found a taverna nearby and they perched on rickety chairs and drank Greek beer and ate souvlaki and salad.

Next stop, he said, was the National Archaeological Museum.

'We'll just see the highlights,' Alex assured her. 'There are so many wonderful things – over seven thousand years' worth. Some people spend a lifetime studying here.'

She could believe it. It *was* an impressive museum. Alex led her through it by the hand, weaving in and out of the crowds, stopping at pieces he thought she should see. Her feet began to rebel and her head began to ache, but she had to show an interest.

'You seem to know your way around Alex.'

'I should do. My father used to bring me here regularly.'

She imagined him as a child holding his father's hand as she now held his. The museum passed in a blur. Later, she recalled gold death masks; bronze statues, pots, coins, frescoes, and vases, so many vases . . . She began to feel a philistine, not appreciating what was around her. All this history, all this culture – and what did she know of it? She said as much to Alex and he stroked her cheek, said there was plenty of time to learn, he would teach her.

Back in their suite, she flung herself on the bed, kicking off her shoes at last, trying to ignore the headache. Alex loosened her clothes.

'Darling, I've exhausted you. We did too much, I'm sorry. What can I do to make you feel better?'

'Oh Alex, you're so good to me.' And she burst into tears. He enfolded her in his arms and asked what was the matter. All she could do was shake her head. How could she express the great jumble of emotions she was experiencing?

She was tied to her children and her husband; she was bound to Alex, yet she felt adrift, like a small boat with no engine, no oars, tossed on a turbulent sea. All these feelings welled up inside her; she'd tried to keep them at bay, but now she failed . . . And, it was already Sunday afternoon, nearly the evening, and tomorrow she had to go home and face reality. The sweetness of the time here with Alex was becoming bittersweet; everything was tinged with melancholy. She sobbed. He comforted her.

He could sense some of the things she was feeling. What could he say? He was not impartial, after all. Instead he gave her love. He held her gently, rocked her like a baby, dried her eyes, made her blow her nose, ran her a deep warm bath.

She submerged herself in the water. She wanted to submerge herself in Alex, to merge with him. She lifted her head up, her hair dripping. My sea nymph, my Aphrodite, he said. He sponged her shoulders, her breasts, then made himself stop. She was smiling now. God, he loved her. What could he do to make it easier for her?

'How about some champagne, are you up to it?'

'Yes please, I think I am. Will you join me?' She seized his hand and kissed the palm, then held it to her breast. He left her for a moment to fetch the bottle and the glasses then he knelt by the bath and they drank champagne.

'To us, my love, and the way forward.'

She repeated his words and they proceeded to get a little drunk.

'How are you feeling now?'

'A lot better, thanks to you. Now, aren't you going to join me?'

'In the bath? I thought you meant join you for a drink –'

'Alex don't tease! Get your clothes off, I want you in here.'

'OK, prepare for a tidal wave!'

She watched him strip off his clothes, enjoying the moment when his penis was set free. In he stepped. Water slopped over the edge and they giggled. They lay back with their hands along the side of the bath, and explored each other with their toes, their eyes locked, each daring the other to do more. His toe entered her and she quickened and moved against it. He watched her excitedly, then her feet curved around his cock, stroking, moving up and down until he arched his back and shouted as he came into the bath water. They smiled at each other.

'Fresh bath water now, don't you think Roz?'

'Yes and more champagne!'

She clung to him all night in bed and he was touched by the depths of her emotions. She wanted him to do all sorts of things to her, as if she could weld him to her with passion. Again, again, Roz would say if Alex showed any sign of stopping – she was abandoned, tireless, arousing him with any means. There were no barriers between them, no inhibitions. What they did together served to obliterate the horrors that had seeped into her mind: the horror of losing him or of losing her children, the horror of having to choose between them.

Round and round it went in her mind and round and round they went until nearly dawn, when he slipped out of her and into sleep. She followed him. They lay sprawled on their backs, his hand resting on her breast, her hand cradling his penis, as if for comfort. They held on to each other and held on to the night, not wanting it to end – for when would be their next night together?

20

Geoff congratulated himself that Sunday was going well; it was how a Sunday ought to be. He was more than on top of things. The sun shone, he read the papers in the garden while Katy and Matthew played on the climbing frame; the chicken he'd cooked for lunch turned out fine and all the children ate it. He'd even managed to get Sam out of bed at a reasonable time (though Sam considered it unreasonable).

After lunch he mowed the lawn and removed daisies and dandelions from the grass. He was permitted to do that, he felt, but was careful not to touch the rest of the garden – that was Roz's domain. Once, when he'd decided to tackle it, cutting here and pruning there, tidying it up, she'd become emotional. She seemed to prefer it to look wild around the edges.

He inspected the lawn with Matthew who delighted in pointing out a row of ants' nests which had taken hold. Aggressive action was needed, he said – they'd go to the garden centre to buy some lawn food and ant powder. Matthew got the giggles, imagining the lawn tucking into sausages and chips, and Katy wanted to know if ant powder was like talcum powder. Sam suggested setting fire to the ants' nests, it was more fun.

Polly was in the bathroom doing something secret

and complicated to her hair and Sam had science homework to do, so Geoff took Katy and Matthew off to the garden centre at Alexandra Palace. It was packed and they had to wait ages for a parking space. 'We should have walked, Dad,' Matthew offered as Geoff tried to manoeuvre into a tight corner.

He let Matthew go into the adventure playground while he and Katy squeezed through rows of bedding plants and rose bushes and terracotta pots. He found himself looking women up and down as they passed in the aisles and had to brush against him. Whole families discussed the merits of garden benches, couples argued over marigolds – vulgar or not? Elderly women squinted at the small print on seed packets. The place was an event, an excursion, thought Geoff and picked Katy up to hurry in search of what he'd come to buy.

'Geoff?'

He turned. A fortyish woman, attractive in an arty sort of way, hair spilling out of a pile on her head, was speaking to him. Did he know her?

'It *is* Geoff Harper, isn't it?'

'Yes – but I'm sorry, I don't –'

'Don't worry, I didn't expect you to remember me, we only met once. It's Roz who I know – I'm Judith Reed, I teach pottery at the institute.'

'Ah! Hello. So you haven't gone to Devon too?'

'Devon?'

Katy squirmed impatiently in his arms. She'd spotted some hedgehog-shaped boot-scrapers she wanted to investigate.

'The pottery course. Where Roz has gone this weekend . . .'

His voice tailed away as he saw the look of

bewilderment on her face. He carefully put Katy down.

'Oh really? Not one of mine! Look – why I stopped you, it *is* to do with pottery. I've been meaning to phone Roz, but perhaps you can ask her for me – does she want to carry on with it? It's just that she hasn't been for so long and there's a waiting list of people who want to join the class.'

She looked up at him brightly and he agreed to mention it, his voice sounding as if it came from outside his head. She seemed satisfied and dashed off to join a man with a beard who'd been calling her from the racks of trellis panels.

Geoff stood very still. Everything had slowed down. His brain wouldn't work. He knew there were questions he should ask her but he couldn't find the words and anyway she'd gone. What was this all about?

He grabbed Katy, who protested, 'But Daddy I want that hodgehog!'

He corrected her automatically, '*Hedge*hog. And you can't have it.'

He shouted for Matthew, who came reluctantly, complaining that he would miss his turn on the slide. He whisked them into the car, ignoring inquisitive glances from people who saw a man starting to lose control. All he could think about was that he must get home, he must think this through.

Later he would look back on this Sunday as That Sunday, the day when everything changed. It would remain painfully etched into his mind. He saw the day cut in half by a chance meeting in a garden centre. Before was light, after was darkness.

*

The children were confused. Why was Dad so grumpy? He'd seemed in such a good mood before. Sam asked for help with his homework (partly to show that he was actually doing it) but Geoff snapped it would have to wait. He shouted at Polly through the bathroom door asking how much longer she'd be in there. She muttered that she'd be out soon. (The hair colour had to stay on for twenty more minutes but she didn't tell him that.) He told Matthew to read Katy a story and left them trying to find a book that Matthew could read and that she would like.

Geoff went into the bedroom and closed the door. He tried to get things straight in his mind. That Judith woman seemed to know nothing about this pottery weekend, yet he was sure Roz had said she'd recommended it. Perhaps he was mistaken – he hadn't been listening that carefully. And Roz had phoned him yesterday, had chattered about the course and the people and the place. It must be a simple misunderstanding. But what about the other things she'd said – that Roz hadn't been going to pottery classes? Weird. Roz *had* been going! She'd left the house on Tuesday evenings, she'd come back talking about her pots, her bloody pots, week after week. It didn't make sense.

He sat on the bed and rubbed his hands over his face and through his hair, again and again. He felt as if there were something just outside his reach, something shadowy and formless that he couldn't grasp.

There was one way to sort this out – he'd ring Roz, she'd left him the number. He went down to the kitchen – there it was, on the notice board.

A male voice barked Hello.

Geoff asked what the number was – he hated it when people didn't tell you.

'What number did you want?' The voice was belligerent.

Geoff consulted the piece of paper and told him, then asked if that was the Landscape Arts and Crafts Centre.

'What? This is that number but we're no artsy craftsy centre. Ha! This is a farm!' And whoever he was banged the phone down.

'Dad, like a cup of tea?'

Polly had come into the kitchen, her wet hair swathed in a towel. He said he would and went to tackle the squabbling he could hear in the playroom, almost pleased to have a distraction. What should he do next?

He rang directory enquiries. The woman said she had no place of that name listed in that area. He asked her to double check, to widen the area. She was helpful but still came up with nothing.

He was stumped. The one person who could clear this up was Roz – and he couldn't reach her. There *was* something to clear up, that he was sure of. Had she just needed a weekend away on her own? If so, why hadn't she asked?

He tried to think laterally. Who else might know where she was? Possibly Annie, but he couldn't face going over to ask her if she knew where his wife was. Too humiliating.

He made the children sandwiches and cut the cake he'd bought in Sainsbury's, attempting to create a true Sunday teatime. Afterwards he must check that they had everything ready for the return to school tomorrow – there were bound to be things that were missing or clothes needing washing or ironing. And he must approach Sam, offer to look at that homework, and show an interest in Polly's revision. He also had stuff of his own – a budget to work out, a project proposal he should read.

There was so much to do. He didn't need the extra hassle of worrying about Roz. But where the hell was she?

21

Roz quietly let herself into the house and briefly checked her appearance in the hall mirror. I'll do, she thought, there's nothing to suggest how I've really spent the weekend. Her skin was flushed, but that could be due to the Devon air.

She had meant to return earlier but had gone to Alex's flat from Heathrow for an hour which became two. She hung her new clothes in one of his cupboards, placed her shoes next to his. That's a start, he'd said. The bracelets she would hide at home.

They had to force themselves to say goodbye. Being in Athens together had been like releasing a cork from a bottle – and now it was impossible to replace it.

Geoff waited. He'd been waiting all day, practising what he'd say to her. He needed an explanation. What time had she said she'd be back? He thought it was late afternoon. If she didn't appear, should he call the police?

Roz breezed into the television room where he was watching the news calling, 'Hello, Geoff, I'm back.' She didn't register his lack of response, but went into the kitchen, talking loudly. She'd rehearsed the lies in the taxi.

'It took ages getting home – some awful accident on the motorway, dreadful traffic. I need a drink. How are the children? Where are they?'

He turned the television off abruptly, came into the kitchen and closed the door carefully behind him. Roz looked at his face: something was wrong. Oh God, had someone died?

'Geoff, what's wrong? The children –?'

'The children are fine. Katy and Matthew are in bed, though they wanted to see you. They may still be awake. Sam's upstairs, Polly's on the phone.'

His voice was flat. He seemed angry.

'I'll go up and see them, tell them I'm home.'

She rushed upstairs.

He waited. When she reappeared he was walking around the kitchen drinking whisky.

'Where have you been, Roz?'

'Seeing the children, the little ones *were* asleep –'

'Oh please! I mean, where have you been this weekend?'

Surely he couldn't suspect anything?

'You know where I've been –'

'I'm not sure that I do.'

He related the chain of events, starting with bumping into Judith Reed. As he narrated the details – quite unlike him, he usually got straight to the point – she felt immobilised, the expression on her face froze, she was unable to move her lips to respond. But her mind raced. Could she still cover up and brazen this out?

She couldn't think fast enough. No ideas came. The chill spread through her, as if she'd been jettisoned on to a cold alien planet and was insufficiently programmed to deal with the situation. She watched Geoff's fists clenching, his knuckles turning white, his mouth moving faster and faster. She listened to the thudding tick of the wall clock – it seemed louder than usual, as if trying to send her a message.

His face reddened and now he was shouting.

'Well? Where *were* you? And where did you go when you said you were at pottery classes? What the bloody hell is going on?'

She had to face that he knew she'd been lying. This was it. How much should she tell him? Everything? She experienced a sense of high drama and could not stop a small self-conscious smirk from sneaking across her face.

'Is something funny? Come on, share the joke –'

'No, there's no joke, I'm sorry –'

'So get on with it! Cut the crap! Something's going on – you've been lying to me and I can't imagine why, so tell me, damn you!'

He had grabbed her arm and she could feel his desperate need to know. She sighed and spoke in a very small voice.

'Sit down Geoff. I'll tell you.'

He let go of her and sat down clumsily, bumping into the table. She sat down slowly opposite him, trying to postpone the moment when she would have to begin.

Words flashed through her mind like the pictures on a fruit machine. How should she phrase this?

'I wasn't in Devon. I was away. I haven't been going to pottery classes on Tuesdays, I've been seeing someone . . .'

There, it was out: limp, pathetic. She trembled, knowing that whatever else she said would have to be filleted. Geoff would never be able to handle the true tale of her and Alex in its raw entirety.

She wasn't prepared for the strength of his reaction, though she should have been. His hands slammed down hard on the table.

'What? What do you mean? Seeing someone? Someone else? Another man? Are you trying to tell me you're having an affair?'

Jackpot, thought Roz.

'Answer me! Is that it, is there another man?'

He struggled with the words, pronouncing them with distaste. Roz was reluctant to think of Alex as 'another man' but now was hardly the time to argue about terminology. So she quietly said, 'Yes. I'm seeing another man, having an affair. I was away with him this weekend. In Athens.'

Geoff pushed his chair back violently and began to pace the room, hitting his thigh with his fist.

'I can't believe this, I can't believe it . . . Athens? You've been in Athens this weekend? When I thought you were in Devon! While I looked after the kids you were in Athens with your – your lover?'

He came towards her, shouting in her face.

'Who is he?'

She jumped and began to prevaricate. She could lie, of course, but perhaps now, at last, she should tell Geoff the truth, or most of it anyway. He shouted even louder, 'Tell me! You owe me that! Who is this shit you've been sleeping with?'

She let that pass and replied simply, 'All right then. It's Alex Kostakis, the architect who –'

'I know who he is, for God's sake. Oh Christ.'

He stopped pacing and slumped in a chair, leaning

forward head in hands, saying over and over again that he couldn't believe it, he didn't understand.

Roz traced the familiar and comforting grain of the table with her finger. She and Geoff had bought it in Camden Passage long ago, their first big purchase as a couple for their home.

Guilt and shame seeped through her but that was not all. Relief too: he knows, he knows, she thought; it's too late to turn back.

Geoff raised his face to her. He looked thoroughly wretched.

'Why, Roz? Why? Aren't you happy? I thought you were. Us, the children, everything – isn't it, wasn't it, enough?'

'It's not that. It was enough. Or seemed to be. I wasn't unhappy. Oh I don't know. I wasn't consciously looking for anything else, anyone else. It just happened. He – Alex – happened. We fell in love.'

She realised as she said it that she should have omitted that last bit. Geoff exploded with rage and stood up again, looming over her.

'Fell in love? Fell in love? What's the matter with you? You sound like a teenager or a character in a sloppy romance! You're forty, for God's sake, you have four children, remember? And you dare sit there and tell me you fell in love! What about me? Don't you love me?'

'Yes, yes. I do love you.'

She had to say that, even though she no longer knew if it was true or not.

'Oh sure, like you'd love a faithful old retainer, a family pet. The tame bloody spaniel who does everything he's expected to, everything you want. Then I get kicked in the teeth with "we fell in love". Christ!'

He groaned and leaned against the fridge. She felt real sympathy for him. His world had cracked wide open, revealing another world that he'd rather not see.

She sat very still with her hands in her lap and her head bowed, like a penitent, not wanting to move or speak in case she made it all worse. She tried to hug the thought of Alex to her, to reassure her that all this was worthwhile.

Geoff had tears in his eyes. She was shocked. She had never seen him cry apart from tears of happiness at the children's births. He opened his hands towards her and spoke in a voice obscured by emotion, 'Doesn't all this – what we've created – mean anything to you? Our children, our home? It's so precious to me but doesn't it matter to you?'

'Of course it does. But what I have with Alex matters too.'

Again she had provoked him when she should have kept quiet. His anger burst out and spilled into the room, eddying around her.

'What exactly *do* you have with your darling Alex?' He spat the name. 'Tell me! Is it sex? Is it good? Are Greeks any different?'

'Yes, it is good, if you must know! It's bloody fantastic! But it's not just sex – I told you, we love each other.'

'So tell me, what does he do that I don't? Not that I ever get much chance. What's the trick? Tell me what he does!'

She backed away from him, sickened. 'Oh, Geoff, don't.'

He mimicked her, 'Oh, Geoff don't . . .' He laughed bitterly. 'You've got a nerve, you know. I discover that you've been deceiving me, having an affair, and now you dare to defend it, and tell me how wonderful it is – it's unbelievable!'

Polly was in the bathroom, rubbing at the splashes of hair dye on the wall. She'd cleaned up yesterday but had missed these. It was amazing – Dad hadn't even noticed the mess or her hair, he'd seemed so preoccupied. She'd been expecting a fuss.

She loved the new colour, a deep plummy red. It made her look different – not different from everybody else because loads of people she knew dyed their hair, but different from her usual self – the Polly everyone expected her to be – sensible, hard-working, straightforward. She looked at herself in the mirror. Perhaps she should have more holes in her ears – it was so boring to have ordinary pierced ears, one hole on each side, even her mum did.

Sam tried to come in. She opened the door.

'You're not doing something to your hair again, are you? It looks gross already.'

'Thank you Sam. What do you want?'

'I need to pee.'

'Go downstairs. I'm busy in here.'

'I can't. Mum and Dad are having a row and I want to stay out of the way.'

She listened. He was right – there were angry voices and slamming noises coming from the kitchen. They leaned over the banisters and whispered.

'Can you hear what it's about, Poll?'

'No. Not really. Perhaps Dad's just letting off steam because he had to cope with everything while Mum was away.'

'Yeah. As long as they're not splitting up.'

'Sam, why do you say that? Of course they're not.

They hardly ever argue, so don't assume that one row means they're splitting up –'

'OK. OK, don't give me a lecture. But nearly everyone's parents are divorced –'

'Don't worry about it. Now shouldn't you be going to bed?'

'Why are you always so bossy?'

He dived into the bathroom. Polly closed the door and turned her sound system up. She didn't want to hear her parents arguing and she didn't really want to know what it was about. Perhaps they were both suffering mid-life crises, they were about the right age.

Geoff swung from tears to anger. It confused Roz but she supposed it was naive of her to expect him to behave any differently. She'd never seriously considered how he would react if he found out, she had never tried to put herself in his place.

She got up and asked him if he wanted a drink.

'No, I don't but I suppose that means you do. You can bloody well wait – you've lots to tell me first. I want to learn all about this affair of yours. So sit down.'

He was gripping her arm tightly. She did as she was told. His anger alarmed her and there was now a coldness about him which made her feel weak. He questioned her for an hour or more across the table. The familiar surroundings of the kitchen began to blur. She felt like someone in an interrogation room helping the police with their enquiries. He wanted all the details: when it did start? Where? How often? Typical Geoff, she thought wearily, he has to research it thoroughly, discover all the facts, try to take control. She relented under his pressure and gave him the answers he wanted, choosing her words carefully, trying not to provoke him further.

There was one big question that they did not explore: the issue of 'What happens next?' remained untouched, for by one in the morning Geoff had suddenly had enough. He rubbed his eyes and announced that he had to sleep, *he* had to go to work in the morning. He stumbled out of the room.

She sat for a while in the silence of the house. She thought of the kaleidoscope she'd had as a child which she'd loved. Changing, shifting patterns, never quite the same. Their lives were like that.

She stiffly climbed the stairs, debating whether she should join Geoff. The spare room was messy and the bed wasn't made up and she couldn't face sleeping on the sofa. Besides, the children might discover her sleeping separately from their father and she wasn't ready for that. So the marital bed it had to be.

Geoff was already asleep but was grinding his teeth – he often did when under stress. She lay as far away from him as possible.

22

Roz and Geoff overslept. They were woken by the noise of the children and Polly shouting, 'Mum – are you getting up? It's late!' Roz dragged herself out of bed, Geoff charged into the shower, swearing. He reappeared briefly and drank some fruit juice standing up while Roz organised the children, then he hurried out calling goodbye to everyone. Katy deserted her cornflakes, running into the hall to kiss him. He and Roz had not spoken a word to each other.

She blinked back tears over her mug of coffee. She suddenly felt so sorry for herself, for Geoff, for everyone. But she couldn't let it show, things must appear normal for the children's sake. She pulled herself together, got the children off to school and left Katy at playgroup.

Annie came bouncing up, looking bright and perky.

'Hi! Feel like coming in for coffee? There's something I want to show – Roz, what is it? You look awful – are you all right?'

'Just tired. Didn't get much sleep last night.' She carried on walking, eager to get back home to be alone, even ring Alex.

'Yes, I noticed your lights were on very late.'

Annie sounded both concerned and curious. Roz

thought she might as well tell her, otherwise Annie would insist on having coffee and asking questions.

'Geoff found out last night, about me and Alex.'

'Oh no! How? Or did you want him to know – did you tell him?'

Roz paused as they walked past an elderly neighbour waiting for her dog to finish squatting at the kerb side.

'I had to tell him, he'd discovered that I hadn't been going to pottery classes, but somewhere else instead. And he found out I wasn't in Devon at the weekend, I was away with Alex –'

'Where were you?'

'Athens. Anyway I couldn't bluff it out so I told him. I confessed.'

'Bloody hell. How awful. What are you going to do?'

'God knows. Right now I think I'll go back to bed.'

As Roz walked wearily up her path she remembered that Annie had wanted to show her something. Another time, she thought. She heard the phone ringing and rushed into the house, thinking it might be Alex. It was Geoff. No greeting or pretence, just a question.

'You aren't going out tonight, are you?'

'No. Geoff –'

'Not planning to rush off to your lover?'

'No.'

'Right. So we'll talk tonight.'

It sounded like a threat.

She ignored the mess in the kitchen and went back to bed. She set the alarm for two hours' time so that she could meet Katy, then stretched out, her head thudding, and fell asleep.

*

Annie was amazed at Roz's nerve. Imagine pretending to go to Devon then flying off to Athens with her lover. The difference between the lie and the truth was almost absurd.

She experienced her usual ambivalence towards her friend, thinking it served her right while also feeling sorry for her. There was nothing worse than being found out. But perhaps that was what Roz had wanted.

Enough about Roz's life, she thought, get on with your own. She climbed to the top of the house to what she only half-jokingly called her office. This was what she had wanted to show Roz.

It was the smaller of the two spare rooms up in the attic, the one Martin had always said he wanted as a darkroom, but never did anything about. Over the Easter holidays Amy and Tom had helped her clear it out. Boxes of old clothes and baby things and magazines went to the recycling centre or the Oxfam shop. They slapped white paint on the walls and she'd bought some second-hand office furniture: an old wooden desk, covered in cigarette burns and carved initials; a slightly battered filing cabinet and a swivel chair. It would do, for now, she thought.

Annie sat at *her* desk and spun round a few times in *her* chair, allowing herself a few moments of self-congratulation on how far she'd come in such a short time. It was just as well that Roz wasn't here – there was so much to do. She consulted the planner on the wall and her action list. This morning she must finish planning a party on a pirate theme – would the cake work as a skull and crossbones? This afternoon she had to make one in the shape of a dragon. Then there were phone calls to make, the party shop in

Primrose Hill to visit. She made a note that she must track down wholesalers of candles and streamers and goodie bags.

Annie was in demand. The business was taking off, spreading by word of mouth. Her very first client, Sally Houghton, to whom she was eternally but silently grateful, had been delighted with everything and had actually given Annie credit when other parents had complimented her on the cake. She'd even given out Annie's phone number. The whole thing had snowballed from there.

The more she did, the more she thrived. She buzzed with energy and enthusiasm and felt she could tackle anything. Naturally there were occasional mishaps, like the party in Totteridge for a four year old. Annie had arrived at a hacienda-style mansion with the cake and all the other food and found that she was expected to stay and organise and entertain as well. She wanted to cut and run, but found it hard to be firm and insist it wasn't part of her services, and she didn't want to antagonise a client. (Anyway, she'd charge for the extra hours.) So she did her best, played Hunt the Thimble, Oranges and Lemons – all the games she could think of. At the end, as she packed away her plates and bowls, exhausted, the overdressed mama had murmured how nice it was to hear all those traditional songs and games again – how quaint. Annie resolved that in future she would make the extent of her responsibilities very clear.

It was all part of the learning curve, as everyone seemed to say. It taught her that there was a market for entertainers, so she began to research possibilities: she visited the clown school in Highbury and the juggling classes at the community centre and noted people who seemed suitable. Either she could recommend them or offer them as part of a complete service. Meanwhile she had other things to organise: help in the business and help in the house. At least she now had her room – what the hell – her office! Tonight she was going to surprise Martin with it.

After supper she took him by the hand, almost pulling him off the sofa.

'Martin come with me. I want to show you something.'

He grumbled but followed her, intrigued a little despite himself, thinking it might be something sexy she had in store for him. They climbed to the top of the house. She paused outside the room, partly for effect, but also to allow Martin to get his breath back, then flung open the door.

'Voilà! My office! What do you think?'

Martin's mouth dropped open. He walked into the room.

'What did you say? Your *office*? Since when? And why didn't you discuss it with me?'

She hadn't expected this reaction.

'Yes, my office. I wanted to surprise you –'

'Obviously. But what about me? I had plans for this room.'

'Now wait a minute. You'd only vaguely talked about it as a darkroom and you've never done anything about it, so I –'

'Never have any bloody time, do I?'

'It was just full of junk, so I thought I'd use it, only temporarily if you like. I need some space to get organised for my work as there's more and more of it coming in –'

'What do you mean, junk? Some of the stuff in here was mine. Where is it now?'

'Oh, anything important I put in the loft. Don't worry, it was only old toys, things like that, that I threw out.'

She had to lie. She prayed that he would not ask specifically where his collection of *Sunday Times* magazines was.

He grunted and sat down in her chair, turning slowly.

'And how much did all this cost?'

She told herself to keep calm, speak slowly, explain everything to him as if he were a child, otherwise she was likely to scream and shout at the selfish sod.

'Martin, please! It's only a desk and a chair and a filing cabinet, all of which I need. It didn't cost much – as you can see it's second-hand and I paid for it from my takings and in cash, which brought the price down.' Why should she have to justify herself to him like this? Over a few measly bits of old furniture. 'And I'm keeping account of everything I make and everything I spend – look.' She showed him the large accounts book.

'Yeah, I see.'

'I know it's not much compared to what you earn but it's just the beginning. This is the time of the small business, isn't it? I'm creating something – a product that people want and a job for myself and perhaps for others too in the future.'

He smiled indulgently. 'You sound like a convert to good old Thatcherism, I'd never have believed it!'

She pretended to swipe him with her accounts book.

'You know what I mean. I am serious about this – it won't just be a sideline for little old Annie at home . . .'

'Hey, come here.' He drew her on to his lap, holding her hips.

'Watch out for my executive chair!' They laughed. She was pleased that she'd managed to change his mood, even shift his attitude – but why, she thought wearily, do men have to be managed in this way?

He tweaked her nose.

'Well, if you're really determined to make a go of this –'

'I am!'

'Some extra money can only be a good thing. You'll have to think about all sorts of things – where you bank it, VAT, and you'll need an accountant at some point. Have you found out about small business loans?'

She diverted him with a kiss. She didn't want him taking over, telling her what she should be doing. This was *hers*.

'What I really need is some help. Someone who could help in the house and with the party side when need be. An au pair –'

'What, to live in?'

'That's what they usually do! She could have the room next door.'

'Bang goes my studio.'

'Oh come on – it's just another junk-room at the moment –'

'I know, only kidding. I suppose there are compensations – can we have a sexy Swedish au pair? Can I choose her?'

'You're so bloody predictable!'

They went back downstairs to have a drink. Martin slapped Annie's bum playfully as she bent down to get the brandy glasses.

'Have you come up with a name for this business yet?'

'People tend to refer to me as Annie's parties, but I'd like a proper name. Most of the obvious ones are already taken – Party Planners, Party Piece, that sort of thing. But I was thinking of The Party Line or The Party Spirit. What do you think?'

'Quite like The Party Spirit. Or be straightforward and actually call it Annie's Parties. The personal touch – reassuring and people think they know what they're getting.'

'Not too boring?'

'Sometimes the most obvious and boring things work best. I should know!'

'I'll sleep on it.'

'When you decide, we'll talk about the stuff you need – business cards, letterheads. I could knock something up for you or get someone at work to do it.'

'Great, Martin, thanks.'

And they went to bed feeling positive and friendly towards each other. They even made love, although having sex was a more accurate description, Annie thought.

They turned towards each other to satisfy their mutual needs, each assertive, even aggressive, in getting what they wanted. Annie placed Martin's hands over her breasts; he pulled her head down to his cock. She thrust herself down on top of him; he rolled her over so that he was on top. It was energetic and enjoyable, if not particularly loving.

Annie was glad that they'd made it. What was that phrase – take your pleasure where you can? But he was at least beginning to be supportive of her work. And she'd do it, she'd show him.

Martin fell alseep quickly, thinking about the new girl at work, Amanda, with the shortest skirts and longest legs, who seemed keen to learn all she could from him, who said she admired his work. There was lots he'd like to show her. He could start tomorrow, over lunch.

Roz went through the day in a daze. She had work to do and a deadline to meet: a complete draft of the Parents' Guide was required by the end of the month, but her files remained unopened. She couldn't remember when she'd last felt this tired.

She'd rung Alex several times but couldn't get hold of him. Maybe it was better not to speak to him yet anyway, perhaps she should wait until after the talk with Geoff this evening – but what would happen? What could possibly be resolved in one evening?

'What did you say, Mummy?' Katy looked up from her Duplo pieces.

'Oh, nothing, darling. I was probably thinking aloud. I've got a bit of a headache.'

'Poor Mummy. Take some headache pills.' Katy added another storey to the house she was making. Roz laughed and ruffled her hair. 'Yes I will, darling.'

She looked at her daughter, at the way her lips pouted as she concentrated, the soft curve of her cheek, her rounded arms. How much does she need me? thought Roz. How much do any of them need me?

Questions buzzed in her head.

The children – how would they react if she told them? What exactly would she tell them? Supposing she did have to choose between Geoff and Alex? Choosing Geoff would mean choosing the rest of the package: her life as it had been before Alex; the children; everything. If she chose Alex, she couldn't take the children, or could she? Alex had often said that he'd have the children too. Did he mean it? How would they feel about that? But she couldn't push Geoff out of their lives and attempt to replace him with Alex: he was their father and whatever else, he was the innocent party in all this.

She began to comprehend, reluctantly, that if she wanted a life with Alex she would have to leave the children and go to him alone. After all, she told herself, if she was killed in a car accident or if she got cancer and died, Geoff and the children would have to manage without her. It happened. Children are flexible, they adjust.

Sam and Matthew arrived home, dumping their bags on the floor, pushing and arguing. Their presence ended her opportunities for introspection. As she made sandwiches and asked questions about school and suggested doing something other than watch television, she reflected on motherhood, how it combined the menial with the managerial.

She started to tidy the kitchen but gave up, thinking it would only get messy again. She sat down and rolled her head slowly around in circles, trying to relieve the tension in her neck and the pain in her head.

Polly called out from the hall and came into the kitchen – she always had a cup of tea before ringing her friends.

'Hi. What's up, Mum? You look very pale.'

'Just a headache, darling.'

'Poor you. I'll make you a cup of tea.'

They sat companionably at the kitchen table. Her hair really is very bright, thought Roz, but she said how much she liked it, as she hadn't had much chance last night. Polly said she had to use the phone but she'd come down soon and make some supper. Roz told her she was an angel. An angel with a red halo.

Polly announced to the others that Mum wasn't feeling well and that she was making them baked beans on toast. Take it or leave it, Sam, she said. She told him to butter the toast and Matthew to lay the table while she patiently helped Katy grate some cheese without grating her thumb.

As she watched her children Roz's eyes filled with tears. She turned away and stood at the sink drinking a glass of water until the moment passed. The noise level made her shrink into her headache. Polly suggested Roz should go to bed for a while, that she'd look after everything and though Roz was tempted she declined, thinking how appalling it would be if Geoff came in and found her lying down, seemingly neglecting her children.

She was eager for Geoff to arrive home, though dreading it. She wanted to tackle things, to move on. She remembered how she used to feel when she'd committed some misdemeanour as a child, shrinking from her mother's anger expressed through clenched teeth: 'I've a bone to pick with you, Rosalind.' How she'd hated the phrase, how it had confused and alarmed her. Then her mother would postpone the moment of reckoning. 'We'll talk about this properly later.' The waiting was the worst of all.

23

Geoff came in late, around nine. After getting the younger children to bed Roz had decided to make some soup. She found chopping vegetables very soothing. Sam was engrossed in a teen horror book in his room, Polly had gone to Laura's, ostensibly to consult on some homework. Everything is as ship-shape as I can make it, thought Roz. She was ready for the onslaught.

She caught her breath as she heard Geoff in the hall, hanging his coat up, putting his briefcase down. He put his head round the kitchen door and said hello in a quiet, polite voice. Probably because he thought Polly or Sam might be here too. He said he was going upstairs to change.

Her stomach churned, her head throbbed. She mechanically stirred the minestrone. She heard his footsteps.

Geoff poured himself a glass of Evian and stood with his back against the counter, looking at her.

'I've told Sam to go to sleep. He stays up much too late. And where's Polly?'

'Gone round to Laura's. Something about her history homework. I told her to be back by ten.'

'Mm. I suppose that's in order, but I worry about her out on her own at night.'

'So do I. But it is only a few minutes away.'

'I know, I know.' He watched her stirring the soup. She was holding on to the large wooden spoon as if she'd collapse without it.

'You don't usually wear an apron – I'd forgotten you even had one. What is it – playing the dutiful wife? Isn't it a little late?'

She flinched from his sharpness.

'Geoff, I'm – '

'If you're about to apologise – don't. And don't try to explain. Nothing you can say will make me feel any better, or repair the damage you've done.'

Roz gave up on the soup and leaned against a different counter from Geoff. 'I won't try to explain – I don't think I can anyway – it all comes out so trite and clichéd.'

'Well it is, isn't it?'

'What?'

'Your affair. It *is* trite and a cliché. You know, the usual stuff you read about on the *Guardian* women's page: you're forty, wondering what happened to your youth and what life's all about, so you have a final fling to reassure yourself that you're still attractive – all that.'

'That's *not* what it's about! It's not like that!'

She realised she was still wearing the ridiculous apron so she ripped it off, breaking the strings, then threw it at a chair and missed. Geoff continued in his cool controlled tone.

'Really? So what is it about then? I could try to be sympathetic if those were the reasons – I could try to understand, even try to forgive you.'

'I've told you – it just happened. Alex came along – and we fell in love.'

'Oh no, not that again!' He laughed bitterly. 'I find that very hard to take. You're not an unattached teenager or a merry widow, for God's sake. Even if it's true, and it's not just lust or infatuation, which is much more likely – let me finish – how can you fall in love? You're not in a position to, are you? You're not available.'

'Who says? Love, passion, who says it can't happen, even to me at my age? And it has happened!'

Geoff began to shout. '*I* say it can't bloody well happen! Don't you get the point? It's not appropriate – not because of your age, but because of your situation. You, me, the children. You've got responsibilities, real ones – four of them to be precise! What you're doing is downright irresponsible, by anyone's reckoning. And please note that I'm avoiding mentioning me. I realise I don't count – you've written me off, that's obvious, now that you love *Alex*.'

She was about to respond to his final sneer when the front door banged. Polly was home. She thought she'd heard her parents arguing and her instinct was to go straight up to her room, but that might alarm them so she peeped tentatively into the kitchen. 'Hi Mum, hi Dad. I'm back.'

Her father beamed at her. 'Hello, Polly love. How was your day?'

They chatted for a few minutes. Her mother offered her some minestrone. Polly thought she looked a bit stressed out. She muttered something about homework – always an acceptable excuse – and escaped upstairs.

Roz lamely offered Geoff some soup but he said he didn't feel like eating. Nor did she. They sat at the table, keeping their voices down, all too aware of Polly moving about upstairs.

'Well?' He leaned towards her. 'What about Polly and the others, your responsibilities?'

'I don't know what to say. You're right about the children. But what about me? This has happened to *me*! Don't I have any rights? It's my life, my only bloody life!'

He sighed deeply and ran his hands back through his hair. 'But as I keep saying, you shouldn't have let it happen to you nor should you have wanted it to happen.'

'What you're saying is that I've made my bed and I've got to lie on it. One choice made a long time ago rules out all other choices for ever, is that it?'

'Unfortunate choice of words, but yes . . . You *do* have responsibilities, I'll keep saying that – if not as a wife then as a mother – '

'Don't lecture me! You're so pompous – '

That made him furious. He jumped up and shouted.

'How dare you criticise me! Whatever I say or do is nothing compared with what you are or what you've done! Don't you see, you selfish bitch, that I've been trying to be civilised about this. I've avoided using all those words I'd be justified in using, the ones that kept coming into my mind all day. What are you? You're a liar, a cheat, and you've become so – so dirty. Thinking of you and that Greek fucking . . .'

He made a noise which was an expression of pure raw feeling, almost a howl. He sat down again as if defeated, took a breath and added, 'Think of the children. That's all I'm saying – is that pompous?'

She recoiled from the strength of his emotions and the tears in his eyes. She must try to handle this more carefully and gently, although right now she wanted to run away and hide, to leave it all behind. He seemed to know what she was thinking.

'You can't avoid the consequences of your actions.

What *are* you going to do? Have you thought about it? Are you going to stop seeing him?'

'I don't know.'

'Will you stop seeing him – for the sake of the children, if not for me?'

Her pause was too long.

'Well?' He demanded some sort of answer.

'I don't know!' It was all she could find to say.

'Come on – you must have given it some thought – what happens if poor old hubby finds out? You must have discussed it in those quiet moments in bed together, after all the fantastic fucking. Planning your golden future together, all that crap.'

She wanted to cover her ears but merely protested.

'Stop it! And no we haven't – we didn't, not really. It would have been presumptuous to go so far as planning a future together, I know that.'

'Ah! Presumptuous indeed!'

'You know what I mean. I've been irresponsible, I admit it, and I've been foolish. I didn't think about the future, I didn't really want to – I was just taking each day as it came – '

'Lucky you.'

'Being sarcastic doesn't help.'

'OK, OK.'

'I – we – must consider what to do, I know. I *am* concerned about the children, truly I am, whatever you might think. But if I stop seeing him while I feel like I do – it just wouldn't work.'

'Couldn't you make it work?'

'No I don't think I could. I have to be realistic. I'd feel resentful and angry: having let myself out, as it were, I can't tuck myself nicely away again, like a freshly ironed shirt! I know I'm being selfish but I must think of me too.'

'*Me me me*. Do you really think we have a right to find personal happiness come what may? To lead a perfect life, with every need satisfied – '

'Would it be better if I denied my needs, my wants, then? Devoted myself to others and the great cause of self-sacrifice? Is that what you think women should do?'

'Oh it's the feminist path you're pretending to follow now, is it? But other women find themselves by getting a job, or doing a degree or starting a business. *You* choose to express yourself or let yourself out as you so graphically put it, by having an affair. It just doesn't make sense to me – does it to you?'

'It feels right, that's all I can say.'

Geoff poured himself some whisky but did not offer Roz any. He stared at her and eventually spoke.

'All right. We could go on and on. You seem to be saying that you can't – or won't – stop seeing him. But I have a right to know, and I'll keep on asking you, what are you going to do?'

She shook her head. He continued.

'OK. If you won't tell me, I'll tell you what I think should happen. Go if you like. Go with him, if he wants you, but leave me with my children – '

'They're my children too!'

'I didn't say they weren't. But what I'm saying, Roz, quite definitely, is that I'm not going anywhere. I'm staying here with the children where we belong. If you want to leave, do so, but you're not taking them with you. If you go, you go alone.'

24

They had more or less the same discussion again and again over the days that followed. Roz began to feel as if they were following a script.

Geoff was unceasing, forcing her to consider her position in a hard cold light when all she wanted to do was retreat into silence, performing simple everyday tasks while thinking of Alex. She was already nostalgic for the time before Geoff knew.

She was desperate to see Alex but it was more difficult now. She even felt uncomfortable ringing him. They'd spoken briefly on the phone and she'd told him that Geoff had found out, that things were difficult, that she'd see him when she could.

When they weren't discussing The Situation, Geoff and Roz hardly spoke. They got through the weekend by turning to the children. Geoff helped Sam mend his bike and taught Matthew to play chess and talked to Polly about exam techniques and took them all to Parliament Hill to fly the family kite collection. Roz cooked vast quantities of nourishing family meals and made fairy cakes with Katy and busied herself around the house, dusting off the air of neglect it had acquired lately. She felt as if she were preparing for a siege or some other momentous event. And meanwhile she was in limbo, they all were.

The effort of trying to behave normally all weekend

was exhausting. Neither had any energy left for further discussions about their futures, separate or otherwise. Even Geoff left the subject alone as they went to bed early and silently on Sunday – another night spent lying rigid with tension along the edges of the bed.

The next day Geoff burst in late from work. He seemed furious, his face was grey and taut. Roz supposed he'd had a bad day, on top of everything else, but it didn't seem appropriate to ask.

He poured himself a whisky and went into the television room, asking about the children. She followed him meekly.

'It doesn't surprise me that Polly's out,' he snapped. 'Have you noticed how she never seems to bring her friends here anymore? Perhaps it's the atmosphere – '

'I don't know if she's aware of anything – '

'Don't be a fool, Roz! You just don't want to face up to the consequences of your actions. You ought to be thinking about what you're going to do now.'

He faced her aggressively with his legs apart, hands on hips.

'But it's not entirely up to me.'

'Yes, it is! God, this is so frustrating! There's very little *I* can do. I could attempt to throw you out but I don't know where that would leave me legally, and what would it do to the children? It is up to you – you caused this, remember, you've changed our lives, you and – '

He was reluctant to say the name.

'Alex.' She said it forcefully.

'Yes – and some of it's up to him so what does he say? Does he want you to live with him?'

She hesitated. Geoff sat down on the sofa with a

sigh and waved his hand dismissively. 'It's OK, I'm past hurting. I've reached saturation point. Well?'

'Alex has said he'd like me to live with him. But we haven't discussed it recently, not since you found out.'

'You'd better see him and discuss it then. Decide. Because quite honestly I can't live like this – the strain is enormous, and it's all so messy, so unsatisfactory. So if you're leaving I want to know as soon as possible – I'll have arrangements to make for the children, all that sort of thing. And if it's going to happen, then the sooner the better, make a clean break.'

He turned and abruptly left the room, muttering that he was going to have a shower. He wants to wash me out of his system, thought Roz. She began to weep, sitting in her favourite chair, the comfortable but shabby Victorian armchair by the bookshelves. The William Morris fabric she'd covered it with was fading now. She'd often breast-fed the children here. It was large enough to accommodate an extra child and a storybook as well as her and the feeding baby.

The children.

The reality of leaving the children had begun to hit her. Before, if she'd thought about it, she retreated. It was as if she teetered on the edge of a vast canyon with the opposite cliff a mere blur in the distance. She had to draw back and stop thinking about it, otherwise she would topple over and fall down, down, down. But now she wiped away her tears, took a deep breath and tried to confront the idea of leaving them.

Geoff had forced her into this by his insistence on

decisions and sorting things out. She realised what he was doing, she knew him well enough. After his initial reaction, he was now dealing with the situation in the only way he knew how – as if it were a crisis at work. He wanted to be in control. He wanted it resolved with a neat and tidy solution so that he could file the problem away. And I'm the problem, she thought.

But she knew that something must be done, they could not continue like this. And Alex had to be part of the decision, she had to talk to him. She'd ring him, see him tomorrow – hadn't Geoff said she should?

Geoff was in the bedroom drying his hair. The phone extension made a small sound – no doubt Roz was calling her lover. He rubbed his hair vigorously, as if banishing all thoughts of Roz and of loving her from his mind. He must not be weak, he must not be sentimental, he told himself. He just needed her to make the decision to go, and he'd make sure that she did. Even if she suddenly vowed to relinquish this man and begged for forgiveness, he would not relent: he could no longer live with her. He would manage, they were his children, he would make sure that they were all right.

Geoff was up very early the next morning, even before the children. He was being hyper-efficient: organising everyone, making porridge in a large saucepan, providing piles of toast and mugs of hot chocolate, most of which the children would leave untouched. When Roz appeared in the kitchen, still in her towelling robe, he turned from stirring the porridge to announce, 'I'm taking the children to school and Katy to playgroup. Is that all right with you?'

He glared at her, daring her to disagree.

'Fine, if you say so.'

She busied herself making some tea, trying to keep out of his way. She felt tearful and she quickly squeezed her eyes shut to make the tears disappear. Think of Alex, she told herself. At least she was seeing him this morning.

'Hey, Mum, wake up!' Matthew's voice, obscured by toast and marmalade, brought a weak smile to her face. She must try to act normally, for the children's sake, even though nothing felt normal any more, she told herself. And she mustn't feel rejected, just because Geoff had decided to take charge this morning. She knew that he was developing a strategy to deal with her, with the situation. It was a display of power. He was taking over, saying, look, I can do it! Me – Geoff, Tarzan, Superman, hero. You – Roz, bad woman. Who needs an errant wife and mother?

She sat at the table amidst her noisy, bickering children and let him get on with it. Polly said she had to go. She liked to leave early to meet her friends.

Roz wondered what they talked about – she realised that she knew very little about parts of her daughter's life.

Polly interrupted her. 'Mum? I said goodbye and did you hear that I'll be late home? There's a drama workshop after school.'

'Oh sorry, darling. Yes, fine. Bye – have a good day.'

Roz thought she saw a look of concern, or was it puzzlement, on Polly's face as she closed the door. Perhaps it's because I look such a wreck, the strain and lack of sleep are showing. Or it's more likely that Polly can't understand why I'm sitting at the table instead of being my usual busy self. So much for behaving normally, thought Roz. For a moment she felt like putting her head on her arms and weeping. The full enormity of it all engulfed her. Her life, the children's, Geoff's, perhaps even Alex's, thrown out of kilter. It was as if a giant had walked through their lives, scattering the pieces, and it would be impossible to put them back together again.

Geoff muttered sharply as he began to clear the debris of breakfast from the table, 'Come on, no self-pity – this is your doing, remember?'

Then he spoke loudly to the children.

'Right, get yourselves together. Anyone not yet brushed their teeth? Come on, Katy, I'll help you.'

Katy looked up from the absorbing task of encouraging Teddy to eat up all her porridge.

'Is it time for playgroup, Daddy?'

'Nearly, darling. We'll take the boys to school first – you can come with me, then we'll go on to playgroup.'

'But Mummy usually – '

'I'm taking you this morning. Now where's Teddy going?'

Geoff took her firmly by the hand and left the room. The boys were clattering around, filling their school bags, looking for things. Roz sat quietly in the middle of all the activity, feeling like an outsider. She was so used to being the producer, the one in control. She wondered if Geoff would care if she loaded the dishwasher with the breakfast dishes, or if he would want to do it all himself later. She decided to wait until he'd left, then she'd do it.

'Roz?' Geoff was impatient. 'I said, is there anything special that the children need today – is it football or swimming or anything else?'

'Right.' She stood up, holding her robe together. 'What's today? I think Matthew needs his football kit – he should have it ready. Oh, and Katy is meant to take something yellow to playgroup – '

'Something yellow?'

'Yes, they've got a yellow table at the moment. You know, a display with things that are yellow. They're doing colours at – '

'I see, I see.' Geoff shook his head. She could see him struggling to cope with this unfamiliar trivia but he managed to turn patiently to Katy and ask, 'Now what are you going to take to playgroup that's yellow?'

'Mm. What about my yellow spade, Daddy?'

Roz groaned inwardly, knowing that the said spade was somewhere in the garden, covered in mud. But she tried to remain the silent onlooker and merely mouthed 'Football' at Matthew as he came down the stairs two at a time. He held up his kit bag triumphantly, and she felt a disproportionate rush of relief and gratitude.

Geoff continued his display of patience. 'And where is your yellow spade, darling?'

'In the garden?' Katy looked at Roz automatically for help. She was the one they turned to when they needed something found or washed or bought or sorted out, thought Roz. Geoff has no idea about all the small crises and events which make up the fabric of children's lives – and hers. He couldn't keep it all running smoothly – could he?

Sam was urging everyone to get a move on. He took Katy's yellow sou'wester from the hat stand and assumed a jolly Playschool presenter voice. 'Hey what about this Katy? It's very *yellow*!'

The scene in the hall degenerated into chaos as

Matthew tried to grab the hat from Sam and a tussle ensued. Geoff's patience finally ran out and he turned on Roz.

'This is too much! Why are things so disorganised? It would help if everything was written down – who does what on which day – anything extra that's needed – '

'It is – there on the notice board.'

'Is it? Not very clearly. Get it sorted out – '

Geoff stopped, suddenly aware that he was shouting into silence. The children stared in surprise, unused to him raising his voice, especially at their mother. Roz felt sympathy for him: he was thrashing around in deep, uncharted waters of misery and confusion and he felt out of control, something which he hated. How different it was from his world at work, she thought, where everything is planned and efficient, smooth and orderly.

She hurried the children along and Geoff let her, until at last they were ready. She bent to kiss Katy who was clutching her yellow sou'wester. The boys were already halfway down the path towards Geoff's car.

'Bye, Katy darling. Don't forget you're going home with Miranda and her mummy today, for lunch.'

'Oh no, I don't like Miranda any more, Mummy, she's not my friend.'

Roz couldn't help sighing. 'Well, she was your friend last week, when we arranged this.'

'What's all this? Why is she going there?' Geoff asked.

'Because she's been invited – she often goes to friends' houses for lunch or tea or they come here, as you well know.'

'Convenient for you, isn't it?'

'Geoff please.' They faced each other over the small figure of their daughter. She looked up at one face then another. The boys were shouting from the front garden, wanting to leave. Geoff turned to go.

Roz bent down to Katy's level. 'Darling, I've already told Jane, Miranda's mummy, that you're going for lunch. It would be rude to say no now.'

'All right. I do like playing with all her Little Ponies. She's got lots, and the stable.'

Roz hugged her daughter and said she'd pick her up sometime after lunch. At last they were all gone.

She ran a bath, leaped in and out, deciding there was no time to wash her hair. She frowned at her face in the mirror. She was looking dreadful: her skin was blotchy, her eyes red and puffy. She gave up, thinking how she looked was probably the least of her problems.

Alex held her tight, tighter, and kicked the door shut with his foot. His face was so warm and his voice was soft in her ear, 'Oh it's so good to see you, it's seemed so long.' She hugged him back, as hard as she could, reassuring herself with his reality.

They walked slowly into his kitchen, their arms around each other.

'I'll make some coffee Roz. Sit down – you look tired.'

'I am. I've hardly slept since Geoff found . . . Do I look that bad?' She bit her lip, feeling tearful and sorry for herself again.

'No! But how could you look your usual gorgeous self with all this stress? And you know I love you whatever you look like!'

'Do you?' She sounded pathetic. He kissed her in reply.

*

They sat on the sofa and he said, 'Tell me everything.' She started with that awful moment when she'd returned home, babbling to Geoff about the journey from Devon. Alex looked increasingly grave as she continued.

'Geoff says I must decide what I'm going to do. He wants me to leave, he wants me out of the way. As far as he's concerned I've blotted my copybook, been a naughty girl. So that's it!'

She laughed nervously. Had she been talking about Geoff too much?

Alex smiled. 'The English! Isn't he going to fight for you? Where's his passion?'

She smiled weakly. She knew they were merely skating on the surface. Alex took her hands in his.

'So he wants you to leave. But what about you? What do you want?' He regarded her calmly, waiting for her answer. Her stomach churned. This was it, this was for real: people's lives hung in the balance.

'This is so difficult for me . . . All I do know is that I want you – I can't give you up, I told him that.'

He looked at her with great tenderness. 'Did he ask you to stop seeing me?'

'Not exactly. But he's asking me to give up the children! He's a good father and that matters to him, he needs that. What he really feels is that I'm – I'm tainted and I'm no longer fit to look after them, to be their mother.' The last words came out in a rush, a panic. He held her protectively to his chest and rocked her.

'But you *are* their mother. You always will be, whatever happens, whether you live with them or not.' She closed her eyes and listened to him. She surrendered to him, wanting him to take over.

'I love you, Roz. I want you so badly. You know I'd

have the children but they may not want me and it's clear that Geoff will not let them go. But I want to build a life with you. Can you come to me without the children?'

She nodded against his chest. His voice murmured, 'We needn't live here – we can make a fresh start somewhere else, wherever you like. I'll do whatever it takes to make you happy, Roz.'

The tears came, her voice was distorted.

'Oh Alex, you're so good to me. I know there's no turning back. I have to leave Geoff, and if he's determined to keep the children, what can I do? I have to leave them too.' She sobbed.

He stroked her face and tried to find some reassuring words. 'I know it's painful. There will be pain whatever happens. We can't make everyone happy and if we want to be together, certain things have to be done.'

They sat silently together on the sofa for a long time. They wouldn't make love today. She was too exhausted, too distressed, and he sensed that. She was also feeling uneasy. It was not specific, not straightforward guilt about Geoff and the children, but more a pervasive unpleasant feeling that undermined her. A kind of shame.

have the children but they may not want [illegible]
[illegible] that [illegible] will [illegible] want to
[illegible] Can you come to me without
[illegible]

[illegible]

[illegible]

[illegible] and [illegible]

[illegible]

[illegible]

LEAVING

25

Roz narrowly missed a builder's van which suddenly pulled in front of her. At the next traffic lights she drew alongside and glared at the driver. He refused to look at her, but his mate leaned across and laughed and gestured with two fingers. She cried all the way home.

She climbed into the unmade bed fully clothed, promising herself that she'd just close her eyes for an hour. Katy would be having lunch with Miranda about now. She'd have to get used to that, she thought as she hid under the quilt. Imagine: after she left, she'd look at her watch and would think, it's time for Matthew's recorder lesson, or Katy's bath-time, or what time is Polly due home today, or Sam will be late for football practice . . . A panorama of experiences spun before her, displaying the world she would no longer have. The everyday details of life with children – bedtime stories; comforting them when they were ill; laughing at their ridiculous jokes; tussles over shoes and clothes, getting them to eat healthily; cuddles and affection – would be wiped away.

Could she bear it? She balanced the question with the thought of not seeing Alex again. She told herself that she would still see her children even if she left them, she was still their mother, it would just be different, and she curled up like a foetus and fell asleep.

She woke from the recurring dream in which she was searching for her car in a vast, never-ending car park, knowing that she'd left Katy strapped in her child seat inside. The sound of the phone brought her to consciousness. She grabbed it.

'Roz?'

Oh God, it was Jane, Miranda's mother. Christ, what was the time, she'd forgotten to set the alarm before she fell asleep.

'Jane, hello! I'm sorry – '

Jane interrupted her in a clipped voice, 'I was just wondering what we'd actually arranged – '

'Yes, of course – we said I'd collect Katy after lunch. I'm so sorry, I got held up. Problems with the tube, as always. I was just about to come – '

'Fine, because I have to go out this afternoon. See you soon then.'

Jane sounded frosty. I'll have to make it up to her by having Miranda for a whole day in the holidays, she thought. She rushed out of the house, tugged on her trench coat to cover her creased clothes. She wondered if Jane knew that she had a lover and might suspect she'd been with him. She may have heard it on the grapevine – real juicy gossip spread fast – Roz Harper of all people having an affair! She wished now that she'd been more discreet.

'What's up Mum?'

Polly was making herself a sandwich to take up to her room. Roz was waiting for Geoff to come home. Lately she'd begun to fantasise about a disaster on the underground or a bomb at his office or a bus crash. No more Geoff. What if . . .

'Oh nothing really, darling.'

'Have you got a headache?'

'Yes, but I'm fine.'

'But you're getting so many headaches these days. Perhaps you should see the doctor.'

Roz could see the anxiety on her daughter's face. The children were always uncomfortable when she was ill or appeared to be vulnerable, but this was more than that.

'If they continue, I will. It's nothing serious – don't worry.'

'I can't help it. You're having headaches and looking stressed out, Dad seems – seems different somehow. And you two are arguing a lot. You never used to.'

Geoff was right, thought Roz, I was naive to think the children hadn't noticed anything. What could she, should she say?

'Everyone goes through these patches, darling. It's just life. There's so much to do, to think about. Dad has a lot to cope with at work. We're bound to get a bit ratty sometimes – '

Polly looked at her as if not quite satisfied.

'How about your work – ?'

'Well, obviously that means that I have more to do! If you decide to combine work and children – '

'I'm not going to have children! Too much hassle –'

'Oh Polly.'

Roz hugged her daughter, squirming inside. Pretending that there was nothing seriously wrong would make it even worse when Polly learned what was actually happening. Another betrayal.

They drew apart.

'Mum, I want to go to Glastonbury this year, the festival – '

'I do know what Glastonbury is – I'm not that ancient!'

'Anyway, I really want to go. There's a load of us from college, we'll all go together and we can take our big tent, can't we?'

'We'll see – '

'We've got to buy the tickets soon. It's at the end of June.'

'Mm. We'll see. We'll have to discuss it with Dad. And I'm not sure what state the tent's in, it's ages since we used it – '

'But there's no reason why I can't go, is there? I'll be sensible, you know you can trust me.'

'I know, Polly, but there is a lot to talk about – how much it costs, who you'd be going with. Now don't look like that. I haven't said no. We'll talk about it later.'

Polly stomped upstairs. Roz sighed at the persistence and determination of youth. She held her head. It was spinning.

Tonight she must tell Geoff that she'd decided to leave. She ran the words through her mind, as if trying them on for size. It seemed unreal. *Had* she decided? Was it only this morning that she'd seen Alex and they'd agreed she would go to him without the children?

The familiar feeling of unease swamped her. Everything felt wrong. Should she have intimated something of the truth to Polly, to prepare her? As the eldest should she be told first? Was that fair or unfair? Geoff would be outraged if she said anything without discussing it with him. Geoff. Why did she feel that he was orchestrating the whole thing even though she had initiated it?

She thought about Geoff and their marriage. *The Marriage*: it was like a third being that had grown between them, with a life and needs of its own. He drew power from it, for he was in control. He led, she followed. He was the manager, she was the deputy, she saw that now. It displeased him if she ever stepped out of line. Look how he had been about her work. He had just about tolerated her childbirth classes – to him they were merely a bunch of women cluttering up the house, lying on cushions in the living room, talking and practising breathing. But he hadn't wanted her to take on the Parents' Guide because that was different – it was outside the home, it was official and even quite well paid. It had some status. It challenged his concept of the marriage and family which required Roz to be at its heart, at home.

She felt as if she were looking at her marriage down a telescope, bringing it into focus. When did these tiny cracks start appearing in the perfect façade? she wondered. She had either not seen them or had chosen to disregard them, but now she could see clearly. Being with Alex had a crystallising effect.

Geoff tried to adjust his position so that he wasn't pressing against the woman by the door. She'd already caught his eye and glowered but whether it was at him personally or men in general, he didn't know and didn't care. It wasn't his fault that there weren't enough trains, that the tube was crowded, that he was male and bigger than her . . . Nothing was his fault. This business with Roz and her lover – that certainly wasn't down to him.

He swayed with the movement of the train, thinking of them together. He'd demanded that Roz tell him where they'd fucked in the house – *his* house

– in which room, on which piece of furniture. She'd insisted that they hadn't used the bed – but he didn't know what to believe. So many lies. Such treachery. It still took his breath away thinking of her in Athens – Athens! – when he'd thought she was in Devon. And this man, this Alex. He was faceless. Geoff imagined him with Roz, a dark form moving around her. What did he look like? Geoff was consumed with curiosity. There was so much he didn't know.

He went over the last few months again and again in his mind, searching for clues he might have missed. He wondered about this new job Roz had – could that have been a front to see her lover? But he had seen her files of work, she had showed him what she was doing and he'd feigned interest. She'd even waved her first payment cheque triumphantly in front of his nose. The job seemed real enough.

Geoff shifted, trying to avoid someone's newspaper tickling his cheek. The enforced intimacy of these tube journeys was alienating. The only way you could cope with being so close to strangers was to cut off, detach yourself. Lucky old Roz has never had to do this, he thought sourly.

Her resistance to the possible move to America now made more sense. Obviously she couldn't bear to leave lover boy. And now she wouldn't. Geoff considered what he should do. Take the kids and go to America without her? But how would the company feel about that? Most irregular, not acceptable. Petersen had faxed him only this morning, saying he was arriving in the UK next week and was looking forward to meeting him and his lovely wife. Oh shit.

The woman next to him was trying to read through a travel brochure, squashed up against her chest. He looked over her shoulder and saw a beach in Goa. It suddenly occurred to him that there was no summer holiday booked for the Harper family. Every year, soon after Christmas, Roz would begin her research, accumulating piles of brochures and guide books. She'd present suggestions to him, then they'd narrow the choices down and discuss them with the children. None of that had happened this year – of course not! Why hadn't he realised, why hadn't he asked her about it?

His mind buzzed with questions he hadn't asked her and probably never would. Oh Roz.

He didn't feel he knew her any more.

He had no one to share this with, no one to talk to. He had no close friends – did any men? He'd always thought of Roz as his closest friend and never thought he'd need anyone else. It was a lonely experience.

The train clattered into Camden Town and the crowds thinned. He made determinedly for a seat. Opposite him was a young woman in boots and leggings, not much older than Polly. Her head was down, she was reading – he couldn't see what – and frequently flicked back her hair with a turn of her head. It mesmerised him. Read, turn, flick, read, turn, flick. Her hair reminded him of Céline's. God, how he'd like to see her and repeat their adventures. Perhaps he could find an excuse to go to Paris and dare to ring her. Would she remember him?

Roz would never know about his little escapades. Why should she? His minor infidelities were nothing to what she had done. In fact, he barely considered them to be comparable. He'd always kept that part of his life separate and would never have let it threaten the marriage. Whereas Roz had allowed the infidel to enter the gate.

*

Geoff spoke to Roz in the now familiar voice: cold, expressionless, unforgiving; the voice he reserved for her.

'Well? Been busy today? Have you seen him?'

'Yes. We talked about the situation and I've decided – I think I have to leave.'

'Oh. That's it is it – you're going to leave me, leave the children? Just like that?'

She held on tight to the wheelback chair she was standing behind.

'Yes. Isn't that what you want, Geoff? Isn't that what you told me to do?'

'How dare you?' His anger burst through. 'How dare you talk about what I want? What I want! Has that ever been considered in all this? I'll tell you what I want – correction, what I wanted was things as they were. I was quite happy. But you've changed all that and now everything centres around what *you* want – '

'Not entirely. I want Alex and ideally I want the children too, but – '

'But you're not taking them, I won't let you!'

'I know, I know that. I know it wouldn't be fair to them or you – '

'And *I'm* not going anywhere. I'm not moving out to let you get on with your love life and still have the children and the house! Why should I?' He was shouting now.

'Geoff please, I don't expect you to. I've never suggested that you leave, have I?'

'No.'

'So I've got to leave. I see that.' Her voice faltered. 'Unless – unless we could work something out, come to an agreement so that we can both stay and share the children.'

He laughed, a brief bitter sound which made her wish she hadn't said it.

'Oh how wonderfully civilised! Go on as before you mean? The happy family but with a difference – dear wifey and mummy also has her lover on the side. What fun – I could have a mistress too!'

She must have flinched, both at his sarcasm and his use of the word mistress – how she hated it.

'Oh yes, and why not? Plenty of men do, after all. And some women would want me, even if you don't.'

She sat down, bereft of words. She wasn't sure what to say or do next, but waited for Geoff to continue. After a pause, he sat down too, bringing the whisky bottle with him.

'I think about this – us – all day at work. I can't concentrate. I snap at people, I forget things, mislay reports.'

'I see, so you want things settled, is that it, so that you can get on with your work as normal? I'm upsetting your routine – '

'You can sneer, Roz, but remember my job keeps this whole show going. The lifestyle which you've become accustomed to, and up to recently enjoyed, is due to my work and effort! And when you go, when I'm a one-parent family, I'll have to find the money to employ someone to do all the things I don't have time to do, won't I? But of course, that won't be your problem, will it?'

He drank some more whisky and regarded her steadily. She found it hard to meet his gaze. At last he spoke, as if summing up. 'So, right then. You're going. When?'

'I haven't thought about the details yet. There's so much to decide. We'll have to discuss it all, won't we? How best to do it – '

'Now I'm confused. Which "we" are you talking about – you and him or you and me?'

'I meant you and me. Whatever else has happened, we're still the parents of the children – we share that.'

He snorted. 'You're only just, I'd say. Haven't you somewhat abdicated that position?'

'No! I'm still their mother, I'll always be their mother!'

She was echoing Alex's words but they were true. Geoff did not disagree. He slumped at the table, drained of energy.

'Yes, yes, you're right – we've got to work out how we're going to do this. How to tell them, what to say. We must do it so carefully to try and minimise the damage. And we'll have to arrange how you're going to see them, all that . . . Oh Christ – '

He covered his face with his hands as his voice shook. 'What a mess.'

They sat silently, contemplating with horror what had happened to their lives. She experienced a yawning void, an abyss, somewhere inside her stomach. He was completely unnerved at the way his world had crumbled, and panicked at the vision of a future without Roz.

On impulse she stood and went to him, sensing a mutual need for some basic comfort, putting her hand on his shoulder. He jerked under her touch and stood up. She thought he was rejecting her gesture but he swiftly turned to her. They held each other and cried.

26

It was a strange time. Roz tried to describe to Alex what was happening at home with Geoff. It wasn't exactly a truce, she said, more like a lull in the fighting. Alex listened, understood and waited. He kept telling himself that she was leaving, she was coming to him, but he felt as if he were adrift in no man's land.

Roz waited too. She had to wait for Geoff to come to an agreement on the details of her leaving, but first she had to wait for him to want to discuss it. She circled around him, assessing his mood. Sometimes she fantasised about packing a few things and calling out, 'I'm off!'

Geoff rode an emotional roller coaster. One day he'd be high on anger and self-righteousness, the next slumped low in self-pity. Uncharacteristically, he needed to talk about his feelings. How he hated her at times, how he wanted her to stay yet go, how he yearned for things to be back the way they were. Once he asked wretchedly if there was really no hope or future for their marriage and she'd had to say no and comfort and console him.

At other times he would behave as if nothing had happened and talk about normal everyday things. The children, his work. There was the issue of Polly going to Glastonbury (they eventually agreed, with certain conditions); concern over Sam's reports from school.

One night he came in and launched into an account of something that had happened at work. Douglas had called from a phone box practically incoherent, shouting that he felt trapped, begging to be rescued. He was just round the corner from the office – he'd gone out to get a sandwich but had begun to panic. They found him cowering on the dirty floor, hiding his face, with a crowd of people outside. They rang Mary, who came to collect him, saying she'd call their doctor, and that was that. Geoff said they probably wouldn't be seeing him back at work in the near future, if at all.

The incident seemed to have upset Geoff, he didn't stop talking about the company all evening: how ruthless it was; how stressed out everyone had become; how Douglas – in his fifties – was seen as being over the hill; how any sign of weakness or human frailty or not pulling your weight meant you were out . . . Roz listened sympathetically.

He said he was feeling disenchanted and had begun to wonder if there was life after work. Sometimes he thought he was like Matt's hamster on its exercise wheel, going fast and keeping busy, but not going anywhere. Then he'd smiled and said perhaps he and Douglas should start a fish farm together. She'd never heard him talk like this before.

Meanwhile Roz concentrated on *her* work. It was neutral and safe. She finished the first draft of the guide by the deadline and delivered it to Hilary, who seemed pleased with it and with Roz. It now had to go before a sub-committee for approval, which Hilary said should be no problem. Then it would come back to Roz for final polishing, and planning of illustrations or photographs if funds permitted.

Roz watched Hilary pour coffee at her desk. This is what I need, she thought, a haven like this where I can be me. The office was tranquil and attractive with prints on the walls and a large plant in the corner, although the block was an ugly tower so beloved by councils in the sixties. Hilary was saying that there might be more work of this sort – she had some ideas – if Roz was interested. Roz said that she certainly was. She started to tell Hilary how grateful she'd been for this opportunity to prove herself, especially as she'd had no proven work record. Hilary waved this aside. So many wives and mothers, she said, were in a state of voluntary unemployment. It was to do with men's control over women and women's dependence on men. She herself had been in that position once, and if she could now help others break out of it, she would.

Roz drank her coffee and thought about this. She realised that she'd never really discussed her work with Alex. What place would it have in her life with him?

Roz saw Alex once or twice a week, but always during the morning while Katy was at playgroup. Right now she didn't feel she could come out to see him in the evening – it didn't seem appropriate. She had to stick it out at home, listening to Geoff, waiting.

They had desperate times in Alex's bed, amazing themselves by discovering still new things to do together, to each other. They walked in Waterlow Park, imagining how it would be when she came to live with him. Alex made her laugh by revealing the things he did to distract himself when he wanted her, needed her. Driving around the M25 at night; crossing the bridges over the Thames one by one, memorising the names; immersing himself in English history books; even working! He described the times when he had an erection just from thinking about her and he'd have to press himself against the clothes she'd left at his flat . . .

At home she practised detaching herself from the children. She did all she should, she cared for them as usual, but told herself that she was behind a glass wall. She placed herself at one remove. It wasn't easy, but nor should it be, she knew.

One evening she'd finished reading a story to Matthew and had given up trying to talk to Sam and went wearily downstairs. Polly's door was closed and Roz could hear her laughing and screeching on the phone extension in her room. She rarely ventured into her daughter's territory these days. Conversations were conducted from the doorway, which provided a glimpse of piles of clothes, make-up, books, magazines strewn anyhow. Roz let it be.

She heard Geoff's key in the door and she knew by the sound of him in the hall, something to do with the way he put his case down, his voice when he called out, that tonight was the night it would begin.

Geoff thrashed around the house, barely speaking even to the children. He faced her furiously in the kitchen. She tried to ask him about his day. He said the highlight was a conversation with Paul Petersen, who'd been pushing to meet Roz again – so he'd had to tell him about the imminent breakdown of their marriage. Geoff also informed him that there was no possibility of him going to America in the near future and by the look on Petersen's face he doubted if he now had any future with the company. He said he wished he didn't have to care.

Roz made a sympathetic noise. He turned on her. Try and keep your cool, she told herself. Retreat behind the glass wall. Think of Alex.

'So Roz. I've got to sort my life out. I want to get on with it. It's time that you and I got down to business – '

Polly came in with a collection of mugs and glasses for the dishwasher. God, she hated it when her parents froze when she entered the room and they'd been doing it a lot lately. She had the distinct impression that she wasn't wanted, despite their cheerful efforts to ask about college and homework. Phoney, she thought. There must be something wrong, even though Mum denied it. Still, they'd said she could go to Glastonbury, that's what mattered right now.

She knocked on Sam's door and warned him not to go downstairs because the parents were at it. No Sam, not sex. Arguing. Oh shit, he said. And he was hungry, though luckily he had some crisps stashed away. What simple needs you have, Polly said, and took refuge in her room.

Geoff continued.

'Right, this is how I see it. We have to make plans: when you leave, how you leave; how you – or we – tell the children; what I do about help in the house; what you take with you . . . Then I suppose at some point we have to discuss divorce, the house, money, all that.'

'Geoff – '

'Don't look like that, Roz. Come on. There's no point feeling sorry for yourself – remember who caused this. And you want to leave – '

'OK, OK. So what do you – '

'We'll start tomorrow night, after the children are in bed. I have no energy for it now.'

He left the room. She held on to the table. The way he talked, it sounded like a strategic military campaign. She half expected him to open a file on the computer, marked Operation Separation. Yet how would she suggest they did it?

She rang Alex, risking interruption by Geoff. She whispered into the phone that it had begun, they were getting down to the nitty gritty. She'd be with him, really with him, soon.

She climbed the stairs, feeling as if she were dragging a large burden marked Misery behind her, while ahead was the light of happiness and freedom. She crawled into bed and hid under the duvet. The noise of water from their bathroom meant that Geoff was having one of his long showers. She wished she could be alone. If only they didn't have to share the same bed. But it wouldn't be for much longer, not now.

Alex roamed around his flat. He was deeply moved by the thought of Roz relinquishing everything for him and excited by the prospect of having her all to himself at last. A new life with her. He hoped he'd be up to it, he'd have to make sure he made her happy. This was what he needed – a commitment. He'd be committed to Roz and, who knows, there was still time to have a child. A son?

His impatience made him restless. He thought of

going out for one of his nocturnal drives but he'd been drinking. He sprawled in front of the TV in his boxers, flicking channels, feeling like a slob, his hand at his groin. Now he had a hard-on – all this thinking about Roz. She was the most uninhibited woman he'd ever known. He groaned and cursed, wanting her *now*, and had to resort to jerking off in the shower, closing his eyes and imagining her there with him. Or even watching him. Now there was an idea . . . As he dried his body he consoled himself with the thought that soon (how soon?) she'd be here, with him, and they could indulge in all sorts of things, together.

27

Matthew was in bed with a high temperature and a sore throat, requiring regular doses of attention and Calpol. Roz succumbed once more to the duties of motherhood. So much for keeping a distance, she thought.

Annie came in to talk when she brought Katy home from playgroup. As they sat in the kitchen Roz realised that they would not be doing this much more. She would be gone.

'Are you OK, Roz? You look a bit down. Nursing the male of the species can be so exhausting!'

'True! They're so demanding, aren't they? But it's not that. It's – it's crunch time, you see.' She looked around to make sure that the children were in the playroom. 'I'm leaving. I'm going to live with Alex.'

'Oh Christ. Are you? Are you really? I can't believe it.'

'I really am. I can't believe it myself but – but if I want to go on seeing Alex then I haven't any choice. I can't give up Alex – I can't. But the horrible part is that I have to leave the children. Geoff insists on it.'

She took a deep breath. Her head was down, she did not want to look Annie in the eye. The moment was tense. Annie paused before breaking the silence, putting her hand on Roz's.

'Oh Roz. This is a bloody impossible situation. I'm sorry, anything I could say would sound so trite.'

Roz returned the squeeze of Annie's hand. She was thankful that Annie didn't try to moralise or point out that this was all of her own making. She was grateful to her for simply being a friend.

Annie didn't know what to say. She could see Geoff's point of view, she could understand how he felt. Why should he lose everything? On the other hand, didn't the children need their mother? What was best for them? Annie's eyes filled with tears. She couldn't help it. The awfulness of it all was overwhelming. She pictured Roz's children in her mind, the kids she knew and liked. What would this do to them?

On the other hand, they would have their father. She had always propounded the view that parents should take equal roles in bringing up children (not that she and Martin had ever done so) but she couldn't avoid the fact that the Harper children would be minus a parent. Roz. Their mother.

Annie put her arm around her. Words poured out of Roz, how she told herself that children were resilient, they were survivors, she'd still be around, they'd just have to have a different sort of relationship with her. Plenty of children managed with just one parent – what were the statistics? And being a two-parent family was no guarantee of happiness or success, was it? There was no way of knowing how they'd react to her leaving – perhaps it wouldn't be as traumatic as she expected . . . Perhaps. Anyway, Geoff insisted that she had to go.

Roz sobbed. Annie sobbed with her, hoping none of the children would come in. What a mess, she thought. And I used to think I was screwing up my life. Which reminded her – she had things to do, a party to organise, a cake to make.

They drew apart, wiped their faces, blew their noses.

'Roz – if there's anything I can do, anything. You must tell me.'

Roz made an attempt to smile. 'Thanks, Annie. There probably will be. Though I know you're so busy now. Stay for a while, tell me all about what you're doing – is it going well?'

'It's going really well, amazingly. I'll just stay for a quick coffee then I must go home and get on with things.'

Once she would have lingered for as long as she could. But not now. She was a woman with a business, with work and clients. She told Roz briefly about developments – it was good to have an audience. Roz was glad of the diversion and, she had to admit it, was impressed. Who would have thought it possible – Annie getting it together like this?

Annie talked about having to deal with VAT and finding out about food and health regulations, and that she was getting an accountant, and she'd contacted an au pair agency –

'Ah! I just remembered I've arranged for her, Eva Berstin, she runs it, to come round this afternoon. Probably to check me out! I'd better go and tidy up a bit and think about what questions to ask her. God, is that the time?'

'Leave Tom with me if you like, Annie. I'm here all afternoon at Matt's beck and call. Which reminds me, I'd better go and see how he is. And let me know how it goes with this woman – I've got to start finding out about such things, whether we should get an au pair, or nanny or whatever.'

'But surely you won't need – '

'Geoff will. Someone to help, to be with Katy, the others, after – after I've left.'

'Oh of course. Sorry, wasn't thinking.' Annie hugged Roz and dashed back to her house, relieved to leave all that pain and anguish behind. Roz watched her go. She would never have believed that she could envy Annie, but she did, in a small way. But she had Alex, she told herself, they had each other. That was what this was all about. And it would all be worth it in the end, it must be.

That evening, the organisation of The Leaving began. It was nearly ten before Roz and Geoff sat on opposite sofas to talk. He had a determined look and a notepad on his knee. She resisted the urge to make snide comments, to ask why he didn't have his secretary with him to take notes, that kind of thing. She knew it would be cheap. But he made her feel defiant: it was a reaction to his taking control as usual, dominating and making decisions, leaving her with little opportunity to express her opinions.

Geoff read out his list of things to be considered and action to be taken. She tried to concentrate and nodded attentively. Some of the words had washed over her but she didn't ask him to repeat them.

'I'll be making my own list as well, of course,' she said.

'Yes well, we have different agendas – you've got a whole new life to plan, haven't you? While some of us – me – are being left to pick up the pieces of your old one.'

She decided to say nothing. She just had to take the bitterness and anger he threw at her and tell herself it could be worse. And she wouldn't have to listen to it for much longer.

'Now let's prioritise. First we've got to decide when you leave. Next, how you tell the children – or if you tell them – perhaps I should? Then there's the manner of your leaving. And by then we must have whatever help I'm going to need in place.'

She noted his formal language – a refuge from the rage of emotions he felt inside? She heard how he slipped from 'we' to 'I'. Soon Geoff and Roz Harper would no longer merit 'we'. But she and Alex would. Alex, Alex. How she wanted to see him, hold him. Perhaps tomorrow if Matthew was back at school. Unlikely. But could she ask him here?

'Roz? Are you listening? Can we deal with at least some of this tonight?'

She took a deep breath, stepped behind the glass wall, and focused her mind. 'Right, my leaving – when should it be . . . ?'

They decided it would have to be after Polly's exams in June. They were important, and mustn't be disrupted. Once they were finished the children would be told, and Roz would move out soon after – perhaps even immediately? Now they had a deadline.

They discussed how to tell the children. Neither of them could face the reality of those words, the look on the children's faces, their reactions. They closed the door on that horror, for the moment.

Geoff shuffled his papers. She said she'd look into all the varieties of help with the children and mentioned Annie and the au pair agency. He nodded, not looking at her. They went to bed in silence, despair hovering over them.

She lay awake, wishing she had someone to turn to, someone wise and kind who could advise her. The thought of her mother didn't enter her head – she didn't see her mother in that role. Roz had neither requested nor received any help or advice from her in her adult life, unless you counted practical tips on how to get grass stains out of clothes or when it's best to prune roses, things like that. What Roz wanted was an expert, someone in the Dr Spock mould, who would accept the situation then tell her the best way to leave, how to break it to the children . . . She yearned for a how-to manual. But no, those books she'd fled to in the early years of motherhood, those volumes that had sat by her bed and even accompanied the family on holiday (just in case), they included nothing which would help her now. How to leave your children: that had no place in the normal, optimistic world of how to be a good parent. Bereavement perhaps, abandonment, no. Perhaps she'd write it when this was over. (Would it ever be?) But would anyone want to read it? How many women left their children? Many men did. But women? Mothers?

Roz dreamed that Polly held a baby roughly, like a doll, limbs trailing. Was it Polly's baby or hers? She had no time to work it out. Polly dropped the baby and there was a sickening bang and crunch as its skull hit the ground and Roz shuddered at the damage, it vibrated within her. She woke up, trembling. Would she ever be able to put the pieces of her life back together again?

28

Roz debated whether to ring her sister Maggie in Bristol – she had years of experience of different sorts of child care. They weren't in the habit of phoning each other, their relationship was not close. Roz had always been slightly in awe of Maggie who, even as a child, had been serious and determined, with a logical mind and a clarity of intelligence. She knew what she wanted and went after it. That had applied to school prizes, exam results, travelling scholarships, a first-class degree, an academic career. Later, when she was ready, she'd acquired an equal partner (not a husband) and a child (just the one). Their mother always said that the two sisters were like chalk and cheese. Roz felt she was the cheese, Maggie the chalk. She was soft, Maggie was hard.

Roz sensed that Maggie disapproved of her: for having so many children and no career, for being dependent on a man, for being lazy and unambitious. She'd never actually said so, but Roz picked up the signals. Nevertheless, after much prevarication, she decided to ring her – wasn't that what other women and especially sisters were for, to give each other support and advice in times of need?

She rang early one evening. Kezia, Maggie's seven-year-old daughter, answered in precise tones. She was very confident, her social skills highly developed. Roz asked for her mother.

'Maggie? Hi, how are you?' Roz flinched at the sound of her own voice. Damn, she'd forgotten to call her Margaret. A few years ago Maggie had told Roz that it was demeaning to be called by diminutives, as so many women were, and that she should be called by her full name and she would call Roz Rosalind. Roz understood the point, but couldn't quite see why Maggie was making so much fuss about it.

'Oh, Roz, it's you.' (Even Maggie forgot her own edicts sometimes.) 'I'm fine. And you?'

'Oh, OK. How's work?' Roz knew she had to acknowledge the importance of Maggie's job – she lectured in social history – before getting on to other matters.

'Busy as always. More students, less resources. And my head of department is still a rampant sexist – he makes life more difficult than it should be . . .'

Roz listened for a while then got to the point. 'Maggie, I'd like to ask your advice. Is this a good time?'

'Sure – I was just catching up on some reading. Kezia is meant to be practising the flute and Howard's still at work, so go ahead.' She was intrigued – what could Roz possibly want to ask her? Their lives were so divergent. Was it to do with their mother?

'Right. It's to do with child care – well, help in the home – with the children, and I know you've tried various sorts of help, and we're going to need some – '

'Roz! Are you getting a job? That's great! Tell me more!'

Roz had to tell her briefly about the freelance work she was doing for the council on the Parents' Guide.

Maggie sounded surprised and interested and if the circumstances were different Roz would have savoured her reaction. But she pressed on.

'Actually it's not because of that – I'm managing. It's – er – Geoff's going to be needing help because – '

'Geoff? Why? I don't understand!'

Roz gritted her teeth. Why doesn't she just let me explain? Being a lecturer she's so used to talking, being listened to. This was a bad idea. Still, persevere. She'd have to tell her sometime, anyway.

'Geoff will need help because I'm leaving. Leaving him, leaving home. And the children. They're staying put, with Geoff.'

For a moment Maggie was silent. No words came, although Roz could hear a sound at the other end, a breathy sound, the sound of her sister's amazement, shock, whatever it was.

'You're leaving? But why?'

'In some ways it's very complicated but in a way it's simple. I've been having an affair, I *am* having one. I can't give him up, I love him. Geoff insists on having the children. So I'm leaving to live with Alex, my – my lover.'

'What? I can't believe this! I can't believe what you're saying.'

'I know – it does seem unbelievable. I didn't mean this to happen – '

'But how – how could you? I mean, actually *leave* your children?'

'I don't have much choice – '

'Oh come on! Of course you do – '

'Maggie, I didn't ring for you to moralise or give me a lecture. I'm getting enough of that from Geoff – '

'Poor bastard.'

'Oh, thanks. What about me?'

'Look, I'd be more sympathetic if you were leaving to find yourself after all those years of domesticity, to make a career, live on your own. But you're just going from one man to another – I suppose you'll be kept by this – this Alex, he'll look after you, support you – '

'I didn't ring you for this. I'm not like you and you resent me for that – '

'You've always had it so fucking easy, you've never stood on your own two feet, you've never worked or struggled for anything – '

Roz slammed the phone down. She was shaking and upset. Not that she needed her bloody sister's approval. She tried to calm down and to return her mind to the issue of nannies.

Maggie thrashed around her study, disturbing the papers on her desk, trying to analyse why she was so affected by this news. Did she envy her? Was it merely sibling resentment? But how could she, how could Roz do this? It just wasn't – she searched for the word and could only come up with – decent. Not a word she normally used.

Half an hour later she rang Roz back, apologising and saying that because she'd been so surprised she'd over-reacted. She knew it wasn't really any of her business. Roz apologised too though she wasn't sure what for – everything probably.

Maggie switched into brisk, professional mode and gave Roz a brief rundown on the child care situation, as she saw it. (She didn't mention that she was actually no expert, that her own arrangements were far from perfect and that the more help she hired, the less Howard did.)

Au pairs *could* be great, she said. She'd always had

Scandinavians as their English tended to be good even before they arrived and she approved of their value systems at home. But they were only teenage girls, usually eighteen or so, and perhaps they wouldn't be up to coping with the – how could she put it? – potentially fraught situation in the Harper household. English nannies were more expensive and if they were trained they liked to take over and do things their way, and you had the whole sociological thing to deal with – the fact that their background and lifestyle could be very different from yours and there could be regular boyfriends on the scene . . . She recommended trying Australian or Kiwi girls who were usually nurses or students or teachers travelling round the world, stopping in England for a while to earn some money. They tended to be cheerful and easy-going, but after a few months, six if you were lucky, they moved on to Greece or Italy or back home via India . . .

As she talked, Roz's head began to ache. She wished to be far, far away from all this.

There was an awkward pause before they said goodbye, as if they wanted to edge closer but weren't able to, or perhaps they just felt they should want to be closer. Roz thanked her sister and they promised to keep in touch. Maggie asked Roz to let her know what happened. She replied that she'd send her new address when she moved.

How weird that sounded, but she'd have to get used to saying it.

Roz realised that now she'd told Maggie, she ought to let her mother know the news. She opted for a simple, straightforward letter, which took several attempts to get right. Her mother lived in Cornwall and regarded any long-distance phone calls as an extravagance, whoever made them. She was a bit of mystery to her daughter – Roz wasn't sure what made her tick. She'd seemed typical of her generation, born between the wars. Her life had revolved around her husband (he had died about ten years ago). He had come first, his comforts and routines and interests, and her girls had come second. It was a quiet tidy household with everything in its place. Her father liked it like that. When he died Roz and Maggie had puzzled over who or what they were mourning. They weren't sure how their mother felt. As always, she'd seemed very reserved.

Then, a year after being widowed, she'd surprised everybody by selling the suburban family home, abandoning her bridge club and the flower rota at the church and moving far away, to the most western part of Cornwall. She didn't show much interest in her family, even her grandchildren. Her cottage was too small to have anyone to stay and she never came to London. There were birthday cards and presents, and the same at Christmas, but little real contact.

Roz wondered what sort of response she'd get from her letter, if any. She couldn't imagine what her mother would think and it occurred to her that they barely knew each other now – and had they ever?

Maggie was restless after she'd spoken to Roz. Her mind churned, and she kept thinking of questions she wished she'd asked. She alarmed herself by wanting to know more, to hear details, of Roz's affair. Her lover. What a thought. It unsettled her. She snapped at her daughter and at Howard, and couldn't get to sleep that night. She wanted to make love – she felt really randy but Howard was disinclined. He was pissed off: he'd had a bad day with a long faculty meeting on top of tutorials and lectures and troublesome students demanding higher grades, or so he said.

Maggie decided she would see Roz, she wanted to talk to her. She had to go up to London soon to visit the British Library so she'd suggest they meet for lunch. If Roz had moved by then she could propose that the lover came too. She fell asleep at last trying to imagine what he looked like.

29

Roz met Alex in the basement café in Liberty's. It seemed daring and romantic to sit among the ladies up from Surrey, the French tourists, and the occasional office worker. To sit and plan their future together – the next few months at least – to sit as lovers at ten thirty in the morning, every touch across or under the table charged with significance.

They talked of the deadline, the date agreed with Geoff for her leaving. It was only a few weeks away. Alex said how wonderful it was but he was sensitive to the less wonderful aspects of it. He clasped her hands tightly with his and told her how happy he was. He counted the days. Roz delighted in his enthusiasm, it was infectious. She said she was happy too but they both knew it was more complicated than that.

It was like being on a swing boat in a fairground, she thought. Whoosh, up she went, high and happy, Alex and love and a future together, then whoosh, down she swung: children, Geoff, leaving . . .

They wandered through the store. It had always been one of her favourites, even as a student when she had little money, she loved to experience the style and taste and richness. It had always been one of Alex's favourites too, which he'd discovered soon after coming to London. It was where he went to buy presents for his mother and sister, to send back home. They were in a haze of happiness, as if they had all the time in the world (they had a few hours – Annie was collecting Katy) and all the world was at their feet (and it was, the world they were creating for themselves). They meandered through displays, agreeing to ignore the formal glass and china – not their sort of thing, into the kitchen department, admiring the lemon squeezers, chopping boards, the Italian plates and Spanish glasses: the everyday elevated into something else.

They had fun with the soaps and bath oils from Japan and France and California. Alex insisted on buying a collection for Roz, for when she bathed at his place.

'I know how much you love your baths, you water baby.'

'Ah yes, but do you know how much I love you, Alex?'

She kissed him on the nose. They didn't pay any attention to the sales assistant but he observed them and thought, all right for some, and counted the hours until his lunch break, regretting the row he'd had with his boyfriend that morning.

Roz and Alex waited for the wood-panelled lift and went up to look at Persian carpets and Arts and Crafts furniture and avant garde one-offs. Down in jewellery and scarves Alex wanted to buy her this, then that, but she managed to resist him.

'You can buy me things when we're properly together. You may have to. I may have to leave with very little.'

They were standing on the pavement. He put a protective arm around her – she needed it.

'It's OK. Everything's going to be all right. I'll look after you.'

'It's true enough. I'll be leaving with more or less nothing. I'll come to you as naked as the day I was born, well not literally, but you know what I mean, no assets – '

'Roz, Roz.' He nuzzled his face in her hair, her ear. People walked around them. 'That sounds wonderful, you're exciting me. Let's go back to bed.'

They had been planning to walk all the way back to his flat through Regent's Park as it was a fine sunny day, but they abandoned that plan. As they looked for a free taxi Roz suddenly remembered her official reason for being in town: she had to collect some of the freebie magazines for Aussies and Kiwis in London. There were always some on news-stands around Oxford Circus. They hurried, grabbing more copies than she needed. Alex hailed a cab and for once the traffic seemed to be elsewhere and within fifteen minutes they were in his flat, their clothes off, in his bed, making each other feel good and whole again.

He insisted on driving her home. She went straight to Annie's to get Katy. The two women had a rushed conversation on the doorstep. That's how it was now: Annie was too busy and too conscious that time is money, for lengthy lunches or leisurely coffees with gossip and chat. She noticed Roz's armful of magazines.

'Hey – you're not planning an overland trip to Australia, are you?'

'Who knows?' Roz made sure Katy couldn't hear – she was swinging on the gate with Tom. 'I'm finding out about Australian girls, you know, as Geoff's helper. My sister Maggie thought that might be best, but I haven't ruled out alternatives. What's happening with you?'

'I've got an au pair arriving on Friday! It was more difficult than I thought. Apparently they tend to arrive en masse in September, and you're hard pushed to get one at other times. But Mrs Berstin knew about this one – Carina – she's unhappy in the family she's with. She came round last night, and seemed to like us. She says the woman where she is now checks on her cleaning and follows after her when she hoovers . . . I told her it wouldn't be like that here!'

'What's she like?'

'She's Swedish. Tall, dark hair, seems a serious girl. Her English is really good, thank God. I'm in the middle of getting her room ready – I'd better go.'

Roz reluctantly crossed the road to her own house. Home. It seemed less and less like home. She tried to settle Katy doing something on her own. She didn't want to paint, she didn't want to draw, she said she'd done that at playgroup. She wanted Roz to read to her, play with her. Roz agreed to read a story but said that afterwards she must make some phone calls. Luckily Katy chose *Rosie's Walk*, a short book with few words though they usually spent ages discussing the pictures. This time they whizzed through it then she encouraged Katy to go out to play in the sand pit.

She stood at the kitchen counter and skimmed through the magazines she'd picked up, keeping an eye on her daughter through the window. In the Wanted columns people pleaded for Nannies and Mother's Helps, offering inducements such as own TV, use of car, en suite bathroom, holidays with the family in the USA. What could the Harpers offer? Single Dad, four children, recently abandoned by mother, require extra tender loving care . . . No chance. She'd have to go through an agency – there were plenty of them. She picked one more or less at random, though she quite liked the name: Non-stop Nannies. She hesitated as she lifted the phone. Should she reveal the true circumstances? Would the idea of a single father put them off? (She and Geoff had agreed that she should make the enquiries as it might seem creepy or suspicious if he did, being a man.) She could hardly say that she wasn't going to be around, and in fact the girl was going to be a replacement of sorts. She decided to play it by ear.

A voice announcing herself as Clarissa answered, young and enthusiastic, sounding as if she should be organising hunt balls or charity events. Roz explained that the Harper family wanted a live-in help, non-smoker, driver, good with kids, able to cook, easy-going – and more . . . It was surprisingly simple. Clarissa asked some questions, like the ages of the children; where they lived, the facilities in the house – meaning number of bathrooms, that kind of thing; the hours the girl would be expected to work, how much time off she'd get and so on. She said she'd pop a form in the post straight away and when Roz returned it they'd find some suitables and send them for interview. Then she mentioned terms. Terms, thought Roz naively, what does she mean? Basically it meant money. Roz was shocked at how much this was going to cost Geoff but she said that was fine and that was that.

She repeated the experience with two more agencies then joined Katy in the garden, feeling drained by her efforts. And this was just the beginning. There would have to be short-lists and interviews and decisions. Meanwhile she had to start thinking about where to put this girl. There was a small basic room at the top of the house which they occasionally used when the children's friends came to stay. She'd have to tart it up a bit. Me and Annie both, she thought, but for such different reasons.

She wandered round the garden, with secateurs in hand, jabbing savagely at anything that got in the way.

'What are you doing, Mummy?' asked Katy. 'Can I do some?'

'This is pruning, darling, and no, these are too sharp for you.'

And I'm pruning my life, she thought. Cutting some old bits off, so that new bits can grow.

At least she had something to report to Geoff tonight; she felt like a child who has done her homework on time. Not that Geoff would be giving out any merits or gold stars – not in her direction, never again.

The phone never seemed to stop ringing. It would be either Clarissa or Charlotte or Plum, the young women from the agencies, and they'd say, 'I've got a super girl for you, Mrs Harper.' She had a hard time distinguishing one from another.

She and Geoff agreed that they'd interview no more than four. They fixed the times for the next Saturday morning, telling the children that they were thinking of having someone to help out with everything. It was plausible enough. They didn't seem that interested or surprised – many of their friends already had nannies or au pairs. Katy didn't seem to grasp the idea and Polly grumbled, 'Do we have to have someone in the house? Couldn't she live somewhere else? It means sharing everything and the bathroom.' Roz avoided Geoff's eyes and insisted firmly that it wouldn't be that bad and there would be advantages. She was relieved when she wasn't asked to list them.

Geoff had drawn up a list of questions he wanted to ask these girls and points to consider, things to look for. Roz let him. She was going to trust her instincts.

They were all Australians. The first girl turned up with a friend. That was a surprise but it appeared that they both needed a job. Roz and Geoff were a little confused – which one were they meant to be interviewing? Suppose they liked the friend better?

The next one was late. She was blonde, kittenish, a little fey, didn't always meet their eyes when talking. They weren't sure about her. Number three was nice but older (late twenties) and trained as a nurse. Roz found that reassuring but as the conversation went on, she began to seem *too* capable and professional. Geoff worried that he might find her bossy – she might start to take over the house, his life.

They had some time before the last one. They made some coffee and felt depressed, barely speaking. None so far had been right, they agreed on that. They tried to be optimistic.

Roz liked Kim the minute she opened the door. She was tall, a bit scruffy, with big black boots on – the Aussie equivalent of Doc Marten's Roz assumed. She had a wide open face, a big smile. Geoff asked his questions, they looked at her references. (She'd been a nanny back home and the family wrote of her glowingly and were sad to lose her.) She was nineteen but seemed older, and could cook (she'd also worked in a restaurant). Roz watched her as she answered Geoff. She was natural, at ease, with no affectations. She felt sure the children would like her. The only drawback was that she might only stay a few months – she still had a lot of Europe to see, she said.

Roz showed her the room and said they may get a television for it.

'No worries,' said Kim. 'I don't watch it much. There's so many other things to do.' She said the room was fine and she loved the house and asked to meet the children. Roz could hardly refuse, but left out Sam who was still asleep. They stuck their heads round doors and saw the other three although Polly was on the phone. Kim said she had a sister about the same age. Roz thought that this would work.

They said they'd let her know tomorrow. Kim said she'd ring them as it was hard to get through on the phone where she was staying and they shook hands.

'Well Geoff, what do you think?'

'I think it has to be Kim. She'd fit in well and she seems easy-going but capable. And mature for her age. I wish she could commit herself to longer though.'

'But we don't know how long any of them will stay – I mean some might say a year, but not mean it.'

'I know. So we'll have to accept that she can only stay a few months. That'll be longer than you, anyway.'

She didn't want to argue. There was enough to cope with already.

'Perhaps you can persuade her to stay longer, you never know.'

'No indeed – you never know what will happen, do you? Look at us.' His face flickered with anger. 'I can't bear the thought that the children are going to have to get used to being attached to people, like Kim, then they leave. Think about that.'

He left the room. He didn't want Roz to see him

upset – he had to keep his dignity, his self-control, if nothing else.

Roz attempted to gather the remnants of a family Saturday around her. She woke Sam, made a shopping list and canvassed each of her children to see who would come out with her. Geoff she left alone. As she walked to the shops with Katy and Matthew, promising that yes, they could go to the Galt toy shop *and* Woolworth's, she counted in her head how many more family weekends there were to go before The Leaving. And then what would her weekends be like?

30

Kim was keen to start straight away – she was living in a crowded hostel in Bayswater, which wasn't cheap. They agreed she could start the following weekend and worked out her hours and how much they – no, *he* would be paying her. Roz tried to hint that there may be changes and flexibility would be needed . . . Kim had replied 'No worries' as she often did.

Geoff sat buried behind the Sunday papers, feeling he ought to take the children out or do something with them, but he felt so tired. It preyed on his mind that they hadn't yet decided on what to say to the children or how. And now they'd chickened out of telling this girl Kim the truth. Nearer the time would do, he supposed. The time. The Leaving. When he thought of it his stomach flipped with distaste and anxiety but with a touch of excitement too, for he wanted Roz to go. He did.

He grumbled at her over the top of the *Observer*. 'Apart from the emotional cost, you realise that you leaving is going to cost me a lot, don't you? A hundred pounds a week to Kim, plus the exorbitant agency fee! Not only will we have to cope without you but we'll be poorer too. Have you thought about that?'

She could have answered him with information on

how much insurance companies considered wives and housewives to be worth – there had been a case recently, in which the true market costs of what someone like Roz did had been totalled: it amounted to far more than he would be paying Kim. The price of motherhood. She could have said something about her being unpaid all these years, so he'd got off cheaply hadn't he, and gone on to open the debate on the wages for housework issue. But she didn't. She took it as usual. She was the bad girl in this scenario and had to be rebuked, didn't she?

'If I had any money, I'd help, I really would,' was all she said.

'And that's another thing – are you going to be kept by lover boy, is that going to be your role? I wouldn't have thought you'd sink so low.' Today the anger was seeping out of him in nasty poisonous droplets.

She was saved from trying to respond by Sam bursting in, asking for some money and could he go out with Josh on his bike? The normal routine of questions ensued. Where are you going? How long for? What happened to your pocket money? How much do you need? And what for?

Roz let Geoff deal with it and wearily climbed the stairs to the room she had prepared for Kim. She lay on the bed and tried to empty her mind. It was quiet and peaceful up here, a neutral space. Perhaps this was what she needed for a while, a room of her own.

Kim arrived with her few possessions and a large bag of washing and proceeded to settle in as if she belonged. She charmed the children with her friendly openness; her willingness to play football or Monopoly; her interest (real or feigned, it was hard to tell) in computer games; her jokes and alternative renditions of their favourite stories. Even though it was the weekend and she wasn't officially on duty she said she was happy to muck in and get to know everyone. She's perfect, thought Roz, perfect. Even Polly, who at first circled her with slight resentment and suspicion, was drawn to her and they were soon talking about hair dye and Camden Market. Geoff was reserved but soon began to thaw, asking Kim about Australia, getting her to show the children on the atlas where she came from. And the children loved her accent. Here was someone who actually talked like the characters in *Neighbours*. And when she told them that she used to hang out in the same pubs and clubs as some of the cast – well, she held the Harper children in the palm of her hand, except perhaps for Sam, who pretended to be uninterested.

Roz settled in to life with Kim even though she knew, and Kim did not, that it was not for long. She initiated Kim into the ways of the various machines in the house and the strengths and weaknesses of the local shops. She told her about the children's favourite foods but said she could experiment if she wanted. She wrote down all the times of playgroup and schools, names of teachers, phone numbers, what to do in an emergency. She was, in effect, handing over the reins. Kim thought Roz was just being extra-helpful and perhaps a bit over-anxious.

Roz introduced Kim to Mrs Baxter. (Geoff thought he'd keep her on for a while, see how things went, but if Kim could handle the ironing and housework too she'd have to go – it would save money.) Mrs B was a bit sniffy at first, threatened by this big girl who either wore those big boots or had bare feet. And she wondered why they needed this extra help. But she warmed to Kim as everyone did. They had coffee breaks together and Mrs B would talk about her husband and her sister who lived in Kent, with whom she was on bad terms. Kim was a good listener.

Kim was sometimes puzzled by her role in the Harper household. She could see that having four children could be a load of trouble but she wasn't sure what Roz actually did. She didn't seem to have a regular job, but after the first few days, when everything was obviously hunky-dory, she began to go out for hours at a time, saying she had business to attend to. Kim didn't ask any questions, it wasn't her place. And why should she worry about whether they really needed her or not? It was up to them. She was happy here: in London, with good wages, nice people, lovely kids. It would certainly be fine for a while, until the big wide world beckoned once more.

Roz began to withdraw further behind her invisible wall. She took advantage of Kim's reassuring presence and saw Alex more and more. They didn't spend all the time in bed. They went to art galleries and museums, wandered around London in the fine weather, went shopping for clothes for Alex, ate expensive lunches in chic restaurants. The weeks slipped by.

Roz and Geoff were still agonising over how to tell the children. Roz had agreed to tell Kim soon. She tried to imagine Kim's reaction – would she be shocked? Angry at being misled? She just hoped Kim wouldn't leave too. She could see no real reason why she should. She'd made friends with Carina, Annie's au pair, and they went out together in the evenings to experience the delights of Camden Palace or Indian restaurants, often returning on the night bus in the small hours. It touched Roz to see them setting off, two girls from opposite ends of the earth, being friends, but she told herself that she was a sentimental fool. She couldn't help it, she spent a lot of time these days feeling emotional. Tears were never far away.

The time was approaching. One day soon she would tell her children that she was leaving and she would go. She moved towards it, feeling the weight of inevitability. Fixed and irrevocable, it would happen, there was no question. Like death.

Roz realised she should put her affairs in order and began sorting through her possessions, deciding what to take. She spent hours going through wardrobes and cupboards, turning up things she hadn't seen or worn for years. She reduced her clothes to about one suitcase-load. That should be enough. Most of her old stuff she couldn't wear with Alex – it smacked of a housewifely life, an old life. She took it all to charity shops. There was one suitcase in the loft which was definitely hers – she'd had it when she went to college. But what in the house could she call entirely her own? Most things had been chosen by both of them, they were joint belongings. Even if Roz had actually gone out and chosen that picture or this bowl and had handed over the money, they were still the family's possessions and Geoff's earnings had paid for them.

She made a short list. There were a few things left to her by her great aunt: a Victorian watercolour of a bluebell wood, some Staffordshire pottery figures. She proposed to take those, plus some of the pottery she'd made; books she'd owned before she met Geoff, mainly old Penguins; some photographs of the children and their drawings; that was about it. There were a few little things she wanted: some shells and stones from various seaside holidays, some pieces of driftwood – no one would probably even notice that they'd gone.

She removed nothing yet. She would show Geoff the list, get his approval – his permission? He would probably be expecting her to want to take more. But as she thought about it, what could possibly be of any real value to her? She was leaving her children behind. If she could leave them, she could certainly leave the rest: the accumulated trivia of everyday life, the collections of consumables, none of them of any significance, not now.

Alex ticked off the days in his diary. The date when Roz was moving in was circled in red. He made what preparations he could, most of them minor and unnecessary but he felt more involved that way. He cleared space in the wardrobes, emptied some drawers, so that she'd have room for her things. He bought new sets of bed linen though what he had was more than acceptable. He cleared out the kitchen cupboards; he scoured the flat for any signs of old girlfriends and lovers, throwing away any postcards or letters he discovered. They were all in the past, pre-Roz, but he didn't want there to be the slightest chance that anything could upset her. She was going to be upset enough as it was.

He could not concentrate on work. He went to his office, was non-communicative to Lynn, answering her questions about his welfare with the mysterious reply, there are big changes happening in my life.

Poor dear, she thought, not really taking him seriously. He was like a cartoon character sometimes, she thought, with his big eyes and long eyelashes and exaggerated gestures and now this moody, broody stance he seemed to be affecting. She took messages and stalled clients and kept his projects ticking over as well as she could, wondering for the hundredth time if the work he did here was really only a hobby. It certainly seemed like it: he told her that towards the end of June he was going to be away from the office a great deal, he'd have other things to attend to. She assumed these things to be personal. Her curiosity was aroused. How intriguing his life was, she thought. She found other people's lives much more interesting than her own.

31

There were only two weeks to go before The Leaving when Geoff had to go to Denmark for a few days, to attend an international conference on sustainable resources. It was part of the company's strategy of keeping an eye on environmental issues without, as yet, doing anything about them.

He went unwillingly, feeling that he should be at home preparing for what was about to happen. Roz came into the bedroom as he was throwing clothes on the bed, trying to pack.

'This is the last thing I need right now, being sent off to Copenhagen.'

'Couldn't someone else go instead? Can't you say no?'

'Hardly. We're all overstretched, and I've already blotted my copybook, remember, by turning down the US job. I've got to be an extra good boy now. Play the keen company man, willing to do almost anything. If there's one whiff that I'm not playing ball, my career takes a downturn and I'll be out. And I can't have that, can I? I've got to keep this whole thing going without you.'

He turned his back on her. He hated her at times, he wanted to shake her. She'd led such a sheltered life. What did she know of anything? She'd never even had to support herself, and now . . . He also envied her. He knew she would feel pain on leaving the children but at least she wouldn't have to deal with their pain, every day. He would have his own pain and theirs to cope with. And she was forcing him to live so many lies – deceiving the children and now Kim. It was like a giant boil he wanted to lance. Her departure would do it.

He made her promise to tell Kim while he was away. That would be a small step in the right direction. God, he hoped it wouldn't make a difference. He could see how much he would be relying on the girl.

Kim was in the kitchen making herself a late night mug of tea as usual. Roz joked with her about her tea consumption, saying it was meant to be the English who drank it so much. Then she took a deep breath and told her what was going to happen.

She said nothing, just stared at Roz in disbelief. Roz waited, not wanting to add any embellishments to what she'd said, it was best to keep it simple. Kim truly did not know what to say. She hadn't known the Harpers long but they seemed to get on OK and the family seemed a happy one. Christ, what a turn-up.

'I'm sorry – I'm just surprised, I don't know what to say.'

'That's all right, Kim. I understand. But this shouldn't affect your position in any way. Things will be the same, except I won't be around.' Like hell they'll be the same, thought Kim. Those poor kids, poor little buggers. How could she?

'The children don't know yet, do they?' Obviously they didn't.

'No. We – I – shall tell them next week, so

naturally I'd be grateful if you kept this to yourself for the time being.'

'Yes, sure.' She was about to say no worries but it didn't seem quite appropriate.

They bade each other good night, more formally than usual. Kim couldn't get to sleep. She just couldn't believe that this woman would leave her children, her home, her husband, for another man. But there you go . . . One thing that Kim had learned in her nineteen years was that anything can happen. How did this affect her? She thought it over. She didn't mind being in the house with Geoff Harper. He was a good guy. Not creepy, like some. Didn't flirt or make remarks or try to take advantage. She could live with him and no wife, just the kids. No worries – except how were the kids going to cope? Could she deal with that? She'd have to wait and see.

Roz had received a postcard from her mother, inside an envelope. She'd almost forgotten that she'd written to tell her that she was leaving. It pictured an ancient stone circle in Cornwall, near where her mother lived. Merry Maidens, it said.

My dear Roz,

Your news surprised me but what can I say? You must do what you think right – or what is right for you. I can see there will be a lot of upset and anguish but I don't suppose there is anything I can do. Let me know what happens – why not come and see me after the event when the dust has settled? The Cornish air might do you good.

Love Mother.

Roz wasn't sure what to make of it. It carefully neither approved nor disapproved. Again, she had the feeling she hardly knew this woman. And 'Mother' was so formal – didn't she usually call her Mum? Perhaps that was another of Maggie's suggestions. Roz shrugged. She didn't rule out the possibility of going to see her mother. She could take Alex – now that could be interesting.

Around midnight she rang him and they had one of their erotically charged conversations, in whispers and gasps, telling each other what they'd like to be doing. It was exciting but ultimately frustrating. She was tempted to go to him for the night but knew she shouldn't. Not long now and she'd be there all the time. They kept reminding each other of that. 'Hang on, Alex.' And he'd said, 'That's what I have to do when you talk to me like that – hang on to myself.' Roz wondered if he did masturbate after talking to her – and that seemed even more exciting and frustrating.

Geoff searched for adventure in Copenhagen. It was, he reflected, probably good for him to have a break from the nightmare of home. All the seminars, discussions and lectures took place in the hotel so he'd hardly been outside into the city, the normal routine for these sorts of events. What was unusual was the range of women present. Women of all ages, sizes, types, from all over the world. He'd seen quite a few he wouldn't mind spending the night with. It was just a question of making contact.

The night before Geoff came back, Roz invited Annie over for a drink. She came about nine and they proceeded to down two bottles of red wine pretty fast.

Kim had gone over to see Carina – they were going to watch a video.

'I wish we'd done this before,' said Roz. She was sitting on the floor, while Annie sprawled on the sofa.

'Other things have got in the way. And we wouldn't be doing this now if Geoff was here, would we?'

'I suppose you're right. What did Martin say about you coming over?'

'When I said I was, the sod announced that he was going out too – can you believe it? I'm sure he said it just to show I shouldn't take him for granted. Not that it mattered, because Carina was staying in anyway. Thank God for her – I don't know what I'd do without her. She's so reliable. I wasn't at that age!'

'Where did Martin go?'

'He *said* he was going to the pub to meet Tim from work, they had some things to discuss. I don't know which pub is the pub and who knows if he's really seeing Tim. I think Tim exists. You see, Martin seems to think everything's acceptable if you dress it up as work. Anyway, I don't give a toss.'

'Here's to not giving a toss!' They touched glasses and drank a toast.

'And he's being really difficult lately. He seems to resent the business, my success – if that's what it is – '

'Annie, don't be so modest. You *are* successful.'

She was indeed going from strength to strength. Now that she had help at home and with basic cake-making – an acquaintance called Liz, a fellow parent at the children's school, was more than happy to do some baking at home and get paid cash for it – she was forging ahead. She concentrated on more clients, better organisation, extending her ideas. She'd got an accountant, Clive, another local parent. He was surprisingly simpatico and obviously liked Annie, even flirted a little, but gave sound advice at a reasonable price. Annie herself was developing a good business sense, a nose for it even. She'd gone to see her bank manager, wearing a suit (but with a short skirt), her hair and smile gleaming, bearing a well-presented business plan (compiled with Clive's help). She got a warm reception and offers of a loan, with further suggestions on how to apply for more money: enterprise loans or small business loans or whatever. So the next step was premises, expansion, more staff.

Roz looked fondly at Annie. She had changed a lot – perhaps Martin was intimidated by that. She looked well and confident. Her hair was now a short sleek shiny bob, like an early Vidal Sassoon cut. It was a gorgeous deep mahogany. Roz wondered what her true colour was.

'I saw that piece on you in the local paper, by the way. It was great – and good publicity, I should imagine.'

'Yeah, I was pleased with it. Though why it was on the women's page beats me. Don't you just get sick of being a minority interest?'

Roz laughed and poured more wine.

'I've been thinking of going in for one of those business awards in *Good Housekeeping* – or is it *Woman's Journal*? God, those titles, see what I mean?'

'Yes, why don't you?'

'I'll see – it may be too early, perhaps next year. Meanwhile, Martin is my main problem. Oh, who will rid me of this man?'

'Annie! Is it that bad?'

'He is. He's still so bloody demanding. *He* has to come first, his needs above all else. His meals, his ironing, his pleasure. I used to hate it before, but I'd knuckle under or do I mean buckle under, and I'd try to please him all the bloody time. But now I'm working, creating a business for Christ's sake, and he still thinks he should be the number one priority! Do you know, I don't think he's ever cooked me a meal in his life?'

'Can't you talk to him, surely – '

'Not really. He sulks, won't talk – or listen. He wallows in martyrdom. And he seems to spend more and more time at work, or out. But then I'm glad – it's a relief!'

She laughed, an angry laugh. She was going to say that she suspected him of having an affair but decided not to mention it – it seemed indelicate, considering Roz's position.

'But Roz – you must tell me what's happening with you. How's it going?'

Roz told her the exact date she'd be leaving. It was only a week and a half away. They both suddenly felt sober. Annie watched Roz's face. As she talked, about the problems of telling the children and when exactly to go, Annie saw an expression cross the surface of her face like a current blown by the wind across water. The enormity of it held them both in its grasp, until Annie sat next to her friend on the floor and held her. She could feel Roz's breasts squashed against her. Roz cried a little, then made a huge effort, swallowed and tried to smile.

'I feel under sentence. It sounds awful, I know, but I feel like someone on Death Row, waiting for the day to come. But, of course, I'll go on living afterwards, won't I, with Alex?'

'Can I come and see you then?'

'Absolutely! I'd like you two to meet each other. And you and I can have lunch, we can be ladies who lunch, your business permitting, of course!'

'Oh, Roz.' Another hug. 'I'll do what I can here, you know, be around if the children – you know what I mean, they know me quite well and if Geoff needs help – '

'Thank you, that's kind. But of course it won't be anything to do with me any more, will it?'

'Hey, come on. You're still their mother, remember. And plenty of fathers leave but still manage to be involved parents.'

'I know, I know.' Roz had told herself these things so many times, she could almost begin to believe them.

Annie went back to her house where Kim and Carina were sharing cider and a joke in the darkened living room. Still no Martin. Fuck him, she thought, who needs him? I need him less and less. And as soon as my income increases, I won't need him at all.

Geoff felt buoyant on the flight home. It had been a fairly good few days. He'd spent one night with a cute Danish researcher in her twenties, who spoke perfect English with an American accent. She did not believe in penetrative sex, viewing it as an aggressive male act, but as she was heterosexual and she liked him she came up with alternatives. It was fun. The next night he'd got totally drunk in the bar with a crowd of men but had somehow ended up in the room of a German professor about his age who wore lacy black underwear. She'd been drunk too but they'd managed to have a satisfactory straightforward fuck. Afterwards he'd wandered down the hotel corridors, his clothing trailing and misbuttoned, feeling like a character in a French film.

His mood changed as he got closer to home.

This was Roz's last week.

They kept going over and over how to tell the children. Geoff realised that the reason why they couldn't agree on the right way to do it was because there was no right way. It should not have to be done, it should not be happening. But it was.

Eventually, at two o'clock one morning, both desperate for sleep, desperate for a way out, they reached some sort of resolution. Roz would speak to the children first. She'd tell Polly and Sam, preferably together, then Matthew and Katy. She'd do it on Saturday morning, provided that the older two were out of bed. Then the whole family would sit down together with Geoff and discuss it. He said they must present a united front – he smiled sardonically – somehow the children must get the impression that, although Mummy was leaving, everything was all right.

They agreed that sometime later on Saturday Roz would go. That was it.

She spent the next few days doing things she thought had to be done. She tidied the children's rooms while they were at school. She sorted through their clothes, discarding anything that was too small or too worn to be passed on. It was a form of torture, sitting amongst the piles of odd socks, faded underwear and T-shirts and bright woolly jumpers. They spoke to her of times past and made her weep. Kim, passing the open door of a bedroom, saw and heard and passed on silently. Polly's room, Polly's clothes, Roz left alone.

Polly would not want anything touched. She stood outside her daughter's closed door as if in prayer.

What else was there to do? When the children came home she suggested a trip to Brent Cross to buy some new summer clothes. Sam wouldn't come, regarding such outings en masse as beneath him (this was a recent decision). Polly had to stay in to revise for her last exam but they both suggested things that could be bought for them, and listed precise details of jeans, Gap T-shirts, a Levi shirt, for Roz to hunt down.

She drove off with Matthew and Katy. The mood in the car was merry: he was telling her absurd stories about his teacher which made her giggle. He is sweet to his little sister, Roz thought. They'll all look after each other, help each other through this, won't they?

They bought sneakers, and T-shirts and shorts, and a hat for Katy, marching from Hennes to Marks and Spencer to Fenwick's to John Lewis. They even managed to get the things that Sam and Polly wanted, hoping they were the right things. Roz used one credit card and account card after another and didn't begin to care who would be paying them off. Anyway these were all necessities.

They ended up in the café in John Lewis. The children had tall, extravagant ice-cream sundaes. Roz looked at them, surrounded by carrier bags. Children with plenty; healthy, happy children. She felt as if she were kitting them out for a journey. Without her.

The next day, when everyone was out, Alex came over. Roz had packed her suitcase and had some carrier bags of bits and pieces. She didn't want to leave on Saturday with a trail of belongings in front of the children. Alex drove her to his flat. He was quiet, kind and sensitive, as if he were admitting her to hospital. He showed her the space in his wardrobes and where she could put her other things, but she didn't want to unpack, not yet. What did it matter if things were creased and crumpled?

They went to Waterlow Park, and walked slowly in the sunshine. Roz had no energy. She felt like someone who was either ill or old, who had to take things easy. They sat on their bench, her head on his shoulder, his arm around her, and he spoke soothing words which she hardly heard, but she needed them, she needed him.

Back home, she prepared several pieces of paper, writing down Alex's address and phone number – *her* new address and phone number. One she'd give to Kim, one to Geoff, and the other (this was written very clearly) she'd pin on the kitchen notice board on Saturday, for the children to know where she was.

She started to make a cake to celebrate the end of Polly's exams, but had to let Kim finish it. Kim was good at cooking, the children said so. She often made them exotic desserts with fruit and cream and grated chocolate. They were very popular. Roz felt she ought to have a word with Kim about healthy eating and the children's teeth, but she didn't want to offend her and who was she to talk about damage?

She went upstairs and lay down on the bed. She wanted to sleep, she wanted to go to sleep and wake up when this was all over. Would it ever be over?

Saturday would be an end but also a beginning. The start of a different life for all of them, for better or worse.

After she left they would all be living other lives.

32

It was done.

On Saturday night Alex tucked Roz up in his bed, stroked her forehead, bathed her eyes and cheeks, swollen with weeping. The celebratory champagne stayed unopened in the fridge. She'd been unable to eat. She'd barely been able to talk, except to moan over and over again, 'I've left, I've left, oh God, I've left them.'

She'd arrived on his doorstep in the afternoon, clutching a large basket and a bag over her shoulder. He'd been waiting, waiting, hoping she'd ring him so that he could collect her but she came by mini cab. He'd filled the flat with flowers – he wanted to welcome her and to mark the occasion but she was in no state to notice anything. She was more than distraught.

She fell into his arms and it was as if she'd fallen to pieces. He carried her to the sofa and held her while she sobbed. Later he'd managed to let go long enough to get her a glass of water. She held him like a drowning woman saying, 'Hold me, please, hold me. I'm sorry, I'm so sorry.' He knew that she was saying sorry to her children, to Geoff, to herself, rather than to him. When she began to fall asleep he reminded her about her contact lenses and helped her to the bathroom.

He led her to the bedroom, undressed her like a child and tucked her up in his bed – their bed now. He watched over her for a while, gently pushing her hair back from her face. This isn't going to be easy, he thought, it's going to take time. He hoped he was up to it. He wasn't sure what he should or could do but he knew he loved her. That should be enough.

He had a couple of brandies before joining her in bed. The phone rang several times but when he picked it up there was silence. No breathing, no sound, just silence after he'd said the number.

At first he couldn't sleep. It was strange having her here. They'd only spent the night together before in Greece. He'd wished for this so much, awaited it so eagerly, yet now Roz slept beside him submerged in sorrow, while to his surprise he was thinking about her children and how things were right now in the Harper house.

He turned to her in the night. He was hot, he was hard, he pressed up against her and held her but she stayed asleep, murmuring words he could not decipher. He rolled over, telling himself to be patient. They had lots of time . . .

In the morning he brought her breakfast in bed with a pile of Sunday papers. She was reluctant to wake, but she wanted to acknowledge his care and kindness.

'Alex thank you. You are good to me.' She held out her hand. He kissed it and sat beside her on the bed. 'That's what I'm here for, Roz.' They gazed at each other for a few minutes and she felt her spirits lighten a little. If she concentrated on him, thought only of him, she might feel better. Later she'd have to share some of the darkness of yesterday, she'd want to talk about it – but not yet.

He treated her so delicately, aware of her fragility. He ran a bath, helped her into it, keeping his touch gentle and his desire at bay (but oh how he wanted her). They would make love when it seemed right. She unpacked while he made some lunch. She ate very little. She said she thought she could manage a stroll and they walked up Primrose Hill, but the sight of children flying kites with their fathers made her cry so they went home. Alex's flat – home? Then while she curled against him on the sofa, she began to talk. It was disjointed, punctuated by cries and gestures, but the horror of it was brought home to him. Words streamed out in a great rush of emotion like stones carried by a rapid river. Part of Roz was reluctant to let the words go – she was ashamed, she could not bear to remember what had happened, she wanted to shut it away. The other part of her needed to release it and Alex encouraged her because he knew she had to go forward. He held her close and listened.

'I told Polly first. Wasn't the best time, she'd just come in from celebrating with her friends the end of her exams. But I had to. She looked as if I'd hit her. Wouldn't believe it. *Couldn't*. Said I couldn't do this, it wasn't possible. I explained about you again. Then she screamed: "How could you? Why, why? What about us? What about Dad?" She's close to him, you see. She told me to fuck off and stamped upstairs. Stereo blasting, slamming around. Geoff went to her but she wouldn't let him in. I stayed up all night, had to, suppose she tried to run away, do something,

something silly. So I sat in the kitchen. I heard her crying.'

Roz paused for breath, gulping, trying to hold back the next wave of tears.

'In the morning she stayed in her room. Wouldn't respond. I tried to explain to Katy that I was going to live somewhere else, but Daddy would look after them. Katy said, "Me come too." Then I spoke to Sam and Matthew, probably shouldn't have done it together . . . Matthew asked lots of questions, couldn't quite grasp it, tried not to cry. Sam shouted at me, said I was a fucking tart – Alex, he's only thirteen – said he hated me, that I should piss off. Then Geoff tried to get everyone together round the kitchen table. Even got Polly downstairs, she looked awful. Sam just stood in the doorway, wouldn't look at me. And Geoff, he behaved so well, he was trying so hard to be calm for them – he explained it all again, slowly and quietly, said that I wasn't going to be far away and they'd still see me, it was just that Mummy and Daddy weren't going to live together any more, it happens, they knew lots of people who only had one parent at home didn't they? Sam muttered something about mothers not usually leaving, mothers usually stayed with their kids and Polly asked Geoff how could he be so bloody reasonable? And they just kept looking at me, looking. They felt betrayed.'

She wept again. Between sobs she told him she'd agreed with Geoff not to make contact for a week, then she described what it was like when she actually left, hearing Matthew sobbing in the hall, Sam shouting; turning back and seeing Polly holding Katy at the window. How dirty she'd felt, horrible and wicked.

Alex rocked her in his arms, saying, 'Hush, hush.' He did that for as long as it took for her to find some peace.

He didn't leave her side for days, it was as if he were nursing a convalescent back to health. He let her talk but when she paused he kept repeating, like a mantra, 'You're here now, with me.' He wanted to remind her, gently, of why she had left. And she turned to him, as if turning her face to the sun to feel its warmth and life.

One bright day Alex got Roz up early and said, 'I'm taking you out for the day, my lady.' He chose her clothes, remarking that he must buy her some more. She asked him where they were going as he buttoned her shirt; he said it was a surprise but she'd see soon enough. She handed herself over to him. What use am I to myself? she thought.

The Range Rover sped out of London. She leaned back and allowed herself to enjoy small things: the sun through the window, the shapes of trees, Alex's warm hand on her leg. They were heading south – she made a guess. 'We're going to Brighton?'

'Yes my love, we are. Isn't it a traditional place for the English day out, especially for lovers?' She laughed. It was good for him to hear her laugh. He was glad he'd had the idea.

They climbed car-park stairs which stank of urine and emerged into the light. Wandering through the Lanes they peered into windows at Victorian jewellery, sepia prints, knick-knacks of dubious parentage – nearly buying lots of things, but not quite.

They disregarded the seediness and signs of poverty and turned towards the sea, strolling along the front, gazing at the ruins of the old pier, walking down the pebbles to the edge of the rolling water. Alex showed off his prowess at skimming stones and she attempted to match him – she used to be good at it. Alex was relieved to see that there were more dogs than children. He didn't want the slightest thing to disturb the tranquillity he was working so hard to achieve.

They lay down on the pebbles as lovers do who have no place to go. It was uncomfortable, the feel of stones in their backs made them groan, but they kissed anyway and he could feel more warmth returning to her. They left the other lovers on the beach, the young, the illicit, the dispossessed, hands exploring under clothing, other clothing discarded in the name of sunbathing. They left them to the pebbles. Roz put one in her pocket – small, grey, striped, so smooth; thinking, how many years did it take to make a pebble out of a stone? She caressed it and thought, this is not what it once was. Like her.

Alex took her for lunch to a fish restaurant off the Lanes. It was wonderfully old-fashioned with white linen tablecloths and elderly waiters who knew all about fish. She was surprised to find she had an appetite and she felt herself coming to life as they drank champagne and ate whitebait. She looked around at their fellow diners, who were they? Antique dealers, businessmen, horse traders, artists' models, photographers? She felt a fondness for them all, a fondness for humanity. It was probably the champagne but it could be the effect of Alex. She looked at him over the table. God, he was good-looking, but he was so much more than that. He was gazing at her with love and anxiety. She felt his hands on hers and decided that some healing had begun. A little. The wound she'd inflicted on herself by leaving her children – God knows what she'd done to them, which in turn made her hurt even more – that would always be there but she could stitch it up, cover it, disguise it. She had to build this new life with him. She could not go back.

They headed home. Home? She would have to think of Alex as home – wherever he was, that was home. Stuck in traffic approaching London, she thanked him for the day. She felt more at ease and less unhappy than at any time since – since Saturday.

'We can do this again you know, we can go anywhere you like. You can open a map, point your finger and off we go.'

She sighed, thinking that this is what you could do when you didn't have children to consider.

'But what about your work? You must have commitments – '

'Roz – you're more important than anything else. I've put things on the back burner for a while. I think we need to be together, don't you?' She nodded, her eyes filled with tears. She rested her head on his shoulder and he managed to drive the rest of the way like that.

In bed that night they lay naked side by side, looking into each other's eyes, appreciating that there was no hurry. Not any more.

It was a wild night. Their sense of each other was heightened. If they could have kissed deeper or longer, they would have. If he could have pushed further inside her, he would have. If she could have held him tighter, she would have. Alex thought he could detect a new dimension to Roz – she seemed to want him to hurt her. 'Bite me,' she said as he kissed her shoulder. 'More, more,' she groaned as he bit her.

'Squeeze me, squeeze me,' she hissed as he caressed her breasts. 'Harder, harder,' she shouted as he thrust inside her. He did as he was told and more. If he'd thought about it, he might have wondered if she wanted to be punished for what she'd done, for leaving her children. Or was she just desperate to obliterate her emotional pain?

They made love for most of the night, losing count of how many times – did it matter? – until their intensity subsided into something gentler. They were unwilling to separate into sleep so they lay and talked. She felt safe and comforted as she nestled in his arms and heard him murmur about places they would go, things they would do. He offered a vision of a life together. Another life. He was building foundations, giving her something to hold on to.

At last they gave in and slept for a few hours. When they surfaced, mid-morning, Alex showered then brought her fresh orange juice. He sat on the bed and informed her that today was to be a get-things-done kind of day.

'Anything you say, partner!' she grinned and went to have a much-needed bath. He sighed with relief. She was getting better. He so wanted to see her happy, he wanted to heal her soul. Then he could be happy too. He didn't know if there was a limit to how long he could go on being strong and supportive – it was something he'd never done before.

He rang his office, checked with Lynn that there was nothing urgent for him to attend to. She sounded amused, he wasn't sure why. He said he'd try to drop in for his mail. Then he turned to the important task of making coffee.

Roz lay back in the bath, enjoying the simple

pleasures of deep vanilla-fragranced water and all the time to soak that she wanted. She contemplated her body, ran her hands over her stomach. She was losing weight. No surprise really – she hadn't eaten much for weeks. She'd never managed to lose weight before without trying (and oh how she'd tried).

She could see the marks from Alex on her body and they pleased her. *He* pleased her. She decided to think of nothing else, she would give herself over to pleasure.

She walked naked into the kitchen. He turned round. 'Roz. Oh Roz.' She stood before him, wanting him to take her up against the wall or on the floor but instead he enfolded her into his towelling robe, moved by her exposure and defencelessness. He held her until he felt her relax. She spoke in a whisper.

'I'm so sorry – '

'What for?'

'If I seem so – so desperate and if I want you too much.'

'I love it that you want me. You're magnificent, you're beautiful – don't cry, my love.'

He walked her into the bedroom, helped her into her robe, tied the belt, found a box of tissues, wiped her eyes, took her back to the kitchen, where he sat her down and insisted she had some coffee and Greek yogurt.

'Listen, my darling. These are extraordinary times for you and whatever you do is fine by me. Remember we're soul mates, there are no barriers between us – all right?'

She nodded, her face shining with tears, love, gratitude.

After breakfast he insisted that they got dressed and said he wanted to talk seriously, about practical things. He asked her if she had her own bank account. She said she did. (She also had a joint one with Geoff – but no more of that.)

'Good. Now this probably isn't the time to have a proper discussion about money – darling, there's no need to look so alarmed! We'll do that another day. This is just for starters – I want to make sure you have some money to use how you like. We could go to the bank and make the arrangements or if you give me your account details I can pay some money in directly every month, beginning today. What do you say?'

She didn't know what to say. She marvelled at his generosity yet why should she be surprised? All she had was what she earned from the work for the council, and that was more or less finished for now. They both knew that he was going to support her – he was just being up front about it. She gave him her account number and he said he'd arrange for two thousand pounds a month to be paid in.

'What? But that's such a lot!'

'Is it? I don't think so. But you needn't spend it if you don't want to! It's for me too in a way – when you buy food or stuff for the home. But it's up to you what you do with it. First you must buy yourself lots of clothes and shoes, things you need.'

She thanked him. What else could she do?

That evening while Alex fixed supper – he said it was going to be a Greek evening, he was making moussaka, she went into the living room and sat by the phone, trying to summon the courage to ring Geoff. Her hand shook. The line was engaged. It was probably Polly talking to a friend as usual. She kept trying every five minutes until she got through. Please let Geoff answer, please. But it was Polly.

'Polly? It's me. Mum.'

'Oh, hi.' She could hear her daughter trying to be cool.

'How are you?'

'How do you expect?'

'Oh Poll. Please. I'm sorry, I'm sorry – '

'Bit late for that, isn't it? Look, I'm – I'm – Oh shit. I'll get Dad.'

Geoff didn't say very much. Things were as she'd expect. The children were all coping, he supposed, each taking it in different ways, at times seeming fine then suddenly asking difficult questions or getting upset over little things. There was a long pause. Neither spoke.

Roz tried to control her trembling and ventured, 'When do you think I can see them? Tomorrow?'

'I think that's too soon. Let things settle down a bit.'

'But I don't want them to think that I've – '

'Abandoned them? But you have!' And me, he wanted to say, you've abandoned me, to this.

'I haven't abandoned them completely. I'm still around, I haven't disappeared – much as you might want me to!'

'OK, OK. Let's think about next weekend. Ah, but Polly will be at Glastonbury. The others then – what will you do, take them out?'

'I suppose so, I'm not sure yet. Shall we talk before then?'

'Yes – ring me on Thursday, we'll make arrangements.'

'Right, I will. Can I talk to any of them now?'

'I don't know, is it wise? Oh hold on. I'll see.'

He supposed he'd better ask them. Neither Sam nor Polly would come to the phone. Matthew did. She asked him about school and his hamster, trying to sound cheery and normal, as if she were just away for a few days. It was stilted and false and he barely responded but at least she spoke to one of them.

'Geoff? Is Katy still up?'

'Kim's just reading her a story, she's ready for bed, so it's probably best to leave her.'

Unfortunate choice of words, they both thought.

'Oh all right then. Regards to Kim. Take care.'

Lame, inadequate words that fell between them. He said goodbye and that was it.

She took several deep breaths and went to Alex in the kitchen. He was singing along to an opera on the radio, crushing garlic, drinking red wine. On seeing the look on her face he insisted she had some wine and then tell him about the phone call.

'Right, so you know you'll see them next weekend. We'll think about what to do and make plans. For now let me introduce you to the secret of making a real moussaka.'

She let him show her what to do even though she'd made moussaka before. Doing things together, as a couple, just ordinary things, was a new delight.

33

Annie knew that Roz had gone. There had been no farewell but Roz had pushed a piece of paper through the door with her new address and phone number – Alex's flat, Annie assumed. She wanted to know how things were across the road – how were the children coping? And Geoff? She saw Kim once or twice in the street but it hadn't seemed appropriate to ask her questions.

Anyway, Annie was a busy woman these days, with a full diary and a growing bank balance. She was about to hire a second helper, working part-time from home like Liz, her basic cake maker, but she could see that soon she'd have to take the plunge and find some premises. She'd registered with commercial estate agents as a start.

She was now the proud possessor of her first van, a zippy little Japanese number, white, with her company name printed on the side. She liked to stand in the kitchen and sneak glances at it parked outside. THE PARTY SPIRIT it proclaimed and underneath: *parties by annie hughes*, with her phone and fax number. Yes, she had her own line with a wonderful machine that was a phone and a fax and an answering machine all in one. The graphics on the van matched her letterhead and business cards – Martin had got them done and it all looked very professional. And I am very professional, she thought. This is me.

Martin had been supportive for a while but he'd obviously found it difficult to maintain. He could be such a pig. Was it just that he was jealous of her because she was breaking out of the mould? She guessed that he might have problems at work. She knew his world, it was rife with competition and rivalry and you had to go on being creative day after day. But he wouldn't tell her anything, said everything was fine, why shouldn't it be? He came home later and later, often after she was in bed. They hadn't had sex for ages and although she sometimes felt randy she didn't want Martin. And he didn't seem to want her. A couple of times a woman (girl?) called Amanda had rung him but he'd dismissed it as work. Annie wondered . . . She had suspicions and soon she'd challenge him – when the time was right for her.

She bumped into Geoff in Sainsbury's during late-night shopping, almost a week after Roz had left.

Matthew was with him, eating crisps, and Sam hovered nearby, looking embarrassed and pretending to be on his own.

'Geoff, hi! How are you?'

'Oh, Annie. Hello. I'm all right. You?'

'Fine. Er – I know that Roz has – '

'Ah, right. You know.' His eyes flicked sideways at Matthew then back to her as if warning her that this wasn't the time to discuss it.

'Well – you know that if there's anything I can do, anything . . .'

He tried to smile. He looked so drawn and pale, she thought, and, felt deeply sorry for him.

'Thanks, Annie. I may take you up on it. Meanwhile there's shopping to do, isn't there, Matthew? I keep forgetting things – Kim has to write me long lists. I can't believe how much food we get through!'

'Food! Don't tell me – '

'Oh yes – I meant to say, I like your van. I saw it outside the house. So everything's going well?'

'Yes it is. Really well.'

Geoff drifted off down the cereals aisle. Annie tried to concentrate on what she needed – this was home shopping, not business shopping, she had to keep the two separate. She approached the task with a lack of enthusiasm as she didn't even know if Martin would be in for supper tonight.

She felt brought down by seeing Geoff. Not by him directly, but by the cloud of confusion and misery that hovered over him.

At times Geoff felt he was coping just fine. He told himself that things weren't so bad, no one had died, the children still had him and he'd do everything he could for them. They still had a mother too, she was just elsewhere. They would all adjust and soon, hopefully soon, they would find a new equilibrium. Their lives had shifted into a different key; changed but not destroyed.

At other times he felt desperate. Things had fallen down around him and it was only by supreme effort that he did not fall apart himself. He had to deal with his children crying and asking why, why, why? Their anger, confusion and unhappiness swamped him. The night after Roz left, Matthew wet the bed – something he had not done since babyhood – and it had happened twice since. Sam became more and more silent and withdrawn, wanting only to be in his room or out with friends. He often smelled of smoke. Polly needed to talk and talk, questioning her father, demanding answers, trying to understand. Katy just kept asking where Mummy was, when was she coming back?

Geoff had to find reserves of strength and energy he didn't really have. He had to keep calm and cool, be patient and affectionate. He had to give, give, give. He would have found it easier if he didn't have to go to work as well. Really he should have taken some time off, but there was too much going on and he had to keep proving that he was worthy. He did try to leave early or at least on time, pushing through the scrum of rush hour crowds and battling with the shortcomings of public transport to come home to – what? Coping. God, he hoped it would get better than this. Just coping wasn't going to be enough. Where was the joy in his life? And laughter? That would come, he told himself. His children used to provide it and they would again.

Kim was a great support but he had to remind himself that she wasn't family, she was hired help. He mustn't rely on her too much. Still, it was some comfort when he came in to hear her call out from the kitchen, 'D'ya wanna cuppa tea, Geoff?' in her broad strine accent. She'd fill the kitchen with delicious smells as she cooked supper for everyone – one great steaming dish of pasta or rice, usually with an unexpected twist to it. There were no deviations, no favourite individual dishes prepared – if you didn't like it, you didn't eat. The children were learning to be more adventurous and less fussy.

Geoff would eventually sit down late in the evening with a drink (he didn't mind drinking alone) and tell himself that another day was over, he'd done his best. They'd got through it, things would get better. Clichés, he knew, but he had to tell himself something.

He tried to keep control of his own emotions. Anger churned inside him, sometimes erupting unexpectedly, such as when he found a pair of Roz's knickers in the washing machine, overlooked when she had last emptied it. They disgusted him, he had an urge to rip them to pieces but ended up putting them in the dustbin. Most of the time he felt drained, empty. He told himself that he didn't really miss Roz – he only missed what she did and what she was to the children. He didn't miss her as a wife.

He made a list of things that would need to be done sometime in the future. Divorce was at the top. Writing the word helped dissipate some of his anger. Then there was custody of the children. Money. The house – it was in their joint names. But it was still early days, it could all wait.

34

Roz fixed the next weekend firmly in her mind, like the finishing line of a race. She would see the children – Geoff had agreed. Now she could allow herself to begin enjoy living with Alex. For she *was* living with Alex, she was actually doing what she'd wanted. Sometimes that revelation broke through, like rays of sun through clouds.

Alex was doing all he could to establish her in this new life. He'd made the arrangements at the bank as he'd said he would. Money had been paid into her account and would go in automatically on the same day every month. Like a salary, she thought. He'd requested an additional gold card for her from American Express on his account. When she told him she had her own credit cards too he suggested he cleared the outstanding amounts so that she could start with a fresh slate. She let him.

He did these things in a straightforward way as if they were no big deal. Roz knew that he had the best of motives – he just wanted to look after her and make things easy. But she was ambivalent – while she was grateful and unable to see any real alternatives right now, she also had the uncomfortable feeling that this was what rich men did for their mistresses.

He presented her with a key to the flat. She

wondered if anyone else had ever used it, then put it on her Parthenon key ring, remembering that night.

One morning there was a flurry of phone calls.

'Roz, it looks as if I've got to go to my office for a few hours. There are some things I have to attend to unfortunately. Look – why don't you go out and buy yourself some clothes and things?'

Was she up to it? they both wondered. She told herself that of course she was, she mustn't be so pathetic.

'OK, that's probably a good idea. I can manage without you for a few hours – but only a few, mind you!'

'Don't worry, I can't bear to be away from you either.'

This is a bit of an adventure, she thought, as she read the bus routes at the stop. It was all new. She went to Oxford Street and headed for Gap. There were so many things she needed as she'd left home with so little. She tried on armfuls of stuff and found she could wear a size smaller than she used to. She bought jeans, shirts, T-shirts, socks, long shorts – basics in complementary colours. At the counter she threw in a brown leather plaited belt – now she was a bit thinner she might start wearing things tucked in. A waist at last. She bought underwear in Fenwick's, some loafers in Bally, then stopped for a cup of coffee in South Molton Street. It was still only eleven-twenty. This is what it was like to have money to spend and no children in tow and no commitments to rush back for, she thought. It was like being on holiday. And this is now your life, she told herself.

She walked down Bond Street, thinking what to do next. More clothes perhaps plus some cookery books so that she could cook new things for Alex, surprise him. Silly of her really, she thought, as everything she cooked was new to him.

On impulse she caught a bus to Harrods – she could look at more clothes and there was a book department. This was indulgence but what else was she meant to do? What was her role? She decided she had enough guilt already, over the children, so she wasn't going to feel bad about a mere shopping trip.

She took the fast lift up to Way In, vaguely remembering when it opened all those years ago. It had gone through several metamorphoses since but some of the clothes looked very similar. She bought a French Connection jacket and some ear-rings and sunglasses then set off to find the books. An Italian cookery book which made her want to go to Italy was added to the collection of carrier bags. She didn't really need anything else but she had to go to the loo and on the way she was attracted by names she'd heard of – Nicole Farhi, Donna Karan – but never thought she'd buy. Then it was too tempting not to try things on. In the cool roomy changing room she turned around and surprised herself in the mirror. She was beginning to look a different person. She acquired trousers and a sleeveless shirt and a cotton sweater by Artwork, long and blue. That was it. She told herself the orgy of spending was over but she had to take something back for Alex. She found most of the menswear pretty boring but found a Ralph Lauren polo shirt in a faded indigo that would suit him.

Last stop was the stationery department for some change of address cards before she staggered out of the store, barely able to carry all the bags she'd accumulated. She put on her new sunglasses and hailed a taxi – she couldn't face the tube, and anyway, it would be embarrassing staggering out into the flotsam and jetsam of Camden Town with all this booty. She reasoned that she'd spent so much that day already that the taxi fare would be a drop in the ocean.

As they drove along Marylebone Road, past the ever-present queues outside Madame Tussaud's, she did some mental calculations. She was shocked to find that she'd spent over eight hundred pounds. That was more than she usually spent on herself in a year.

She used the key – a special moment. Alex was already home and he called out. They hugged and kissed, delighted to see each other, even though they'd only been apart for a few hours. He was impressed with her purchases and didn't seem to find it extraordinary that she'd spent so much. (In fact he was touched by her innocence in these matters. His ex-wife had been capable of spending more than that in two minutes on one designer outfit.)

He loved his polo shirt, insisting on trying it on immediately. She reached out to touch his bare chest, running her hands over him, feeling his muscles, the bulk of him. They went to bed. The glorious luxury of an afternoon devoted to pleasing each other. They took their time, playing and exploring, making sure nowhere was neglected. How they loved it and how they loved each other.

Later he took her out to dinner, insisting she wear some of her new clothes, saying he wanted to show her off. They ate in a French restaurant off Covent Garden and she felt that she was becoming the different person she'd seen in the mirror. It was as if she were living someone else's life.

*

Everyday she took a step forward. She sent the change of address cards to Maggie, to her mother, to Hilary at the council. Her dentist. A few friends. The rest of her long-distance acquaintances could wait for the annual ritual of Christmas cards – they'd get a surprise. Before she'd left she'd copied out crucial details from the family address book. She found that there weren't that many people she wanted to keep in touch with.

A few days later Hilary rang. Roz still found it strange to pick up Alex's phone and say his number as hers.

'You've moved, Roz. I didn't know . . .'

'Well, it was a sudden decision . . .'

Roz decided to keep the facts to herself. This was her professional life. Hilary reported that the guide had gone through the committee with very few suggestions for changes and everyone had been well pleased with it. They were just sorting out how much money there was left for the illustrations and printing. Hilary congratulated Roz and invited her to lunch the following week to discuss the final stage – and something else that was coming up.

She wrote the date in her diary and resolved to tell Alex about it when he came in. He'd gone shopping for food but had insisted she stayed in bed and had a lie-in – she hadn't been sleeping very well. It wasn't just sex – oh the sex – she was plagued by intense complicated dreams which woke her and left her staring into the night, her mind a jumble of half-remembered images and feelings of panic.

She was glad Hilary had called. She was eager to do some more work, to step outside her current preoccupations.

*

When Alex returned they started to unpack all the goodies. He'd been to Selfridge's and Soho and bought all sorts of tempting things. (He was trying to restore Roz's appetite.) She told him about Hilary and the work. He looked a little blank. Surely she'd told him about it before? She prompted him and something registered on his face.

'But you don't have to do that any more, Roz.'

'Alex! What do you mean?'

'I mean you don't have to work – '

'I didn't *have* to work before. I did it because I wanted to, for me.'

He looked at her, hearing the edge in her voice.

'Roz – you can still do whatever you want. Hey, come here.'

He covered her mouth with his, slipped a hand inside her shirt, inside her bra, and got to work. They sank to the kitchen floor amongst the bags of food and fucked furiously.

Her sister Maggie rang the next day. She was going to be in London, working at the British Library, so she suggested that they meet for lunch. And why not, thought Roz. She checked with Alex that he hadn't made any plans for them then agreed to meet Maggie at the British Museum café at one. She'd go alone.

It didn't start off well. It was a very hot day and the café was full, with a long queue, mainly tourists. Roz suggested a pub nearby but Maggie declined, not liking pubs, so they ended up at the nearby Pizza Express. There was a queue there too but they were lucky and were soon sitting at a table for two in the window, drinking chianti while they watched the pizza maker knead the dough.

Maggie looked around. 'I used to come here a lot in

the seventies. I loved it – it seemed the height of sophistication then.'

'I remember! Who was that bloke you were going out with then?'

'Oh God, what an old-fashioned word – bloke. That was Roger, the love of my life!'

'What happened to him?'

'We used to argue so much, over politics, feminism – what *became* feminism. Do you remember when it didn't yet have a name? In the end the fights took over and there wasn't much left. He went off to the States, he was determined to be a professor as young as he could.'

They picked at a salad. Maggie leaned forward. 'But, Roz, tell me how things are.'

There was lots to tell. Roz talked – it was good to have someone who wasn't directly involved and had no stake in the whole thing. And Maggie was her sister, she should be able to talk to her.

She told her about Kim, about telling the children, about leaving. Their pizzas arrived. They were still the best, thought Maggie. She said very little, just listened. She had such curiosity about Roz's life though she disliked herself for it. But other people's lives were fascinating and here was her sister, who had wrenched her life – and the lives of those around her – up by the roots; who was not doing what she should be doing, who had deviated from the path marked out for her. Not that Maggie condoned Roz's behaviour, she didn't.

Now Roz was talking about Alex, so loving, praising his patience, his love, his sweetness . . .

'You make him sound like a saint,' said Maggie sharply, attacking the crust of her Veneziana.

'Well, so far he's behaved like one!'

'So it's not just sex then, he has all these other qualities too?'

Why am I being so waspish? thought Maggie. But I can't help it, she's irritating the shit out of me with all these tales of lovers' bliss.

She must be jealous, thought Roz, why else would she be bothering to be like this?

'No, Maggie, it's not just sex. But the sex is marvellous. If I say he's a superb lover, that doesn't begin to describe him. And what we have together – do together – is the best sex I've ever had, it takes me over, blows my mind. And the thing is, when sex is like that, nothing can really beat it, can it?'

She asked for it, thought Roz.

The waiter kept his expression deadpan but he wanted to say he agreed with her. Maggie was silent. She'd begun to form a barbed reply but some of what Roz said got to her and she thought of Roger, all those years ago . . . His lean body, long dark hair . . .

They had coffee and Maggie asked what Roz was going to do now.

'Do? What do you mean?'

'I thought you might get a full-time job as you'll have so much time on your hands. Then you needn't be dependent on Alex.'

'I do have my freelance work for the council, the writing and editing – that seems to be continuing – '

'That's good. But freelance work is so precarious, isn't it? Have you thought of short courses or training schemes? Some women returning to work find them useful.'

There was a certain sourness in the air now.

'Well, luckily, I haven't got to. Alex is taking care of things – '

'Taking care of you financially? But you know

what that means, you're just a mistress – is that what you want?'

'Yes, though I wouldn't call it that! And stop being so bloody puritanical!' She was angry at Maggie saying such things and alarmed that they echoed the very thoughts she'd been having herself.

'Actually I was thinking of you. Supposing this doesn't work out? Where will you be then?'

Roz didn't answer. The waiter hovered and they asked for the bill. They paid half each but Roz left the generous tip. They walked back towards the British Museum – Maggie had work to do and Roz wanted to buy Alex a postcard.

'OK, Maggie, you've spent all of lunch pronouncing judgement on my life. Do you feel better now?'

'Hey, Roz, there's no need to be so aggressive!'

Maggie smiled with the satisfaction of someone who's at least said some of the things she wanted to say.

'Aggressive, me? If I were really aggressive I'd have pushed your pizza in your face twenty minutes ago!'

They stood on the steps and glared at each other, until the moment passed, saying goodbye with a peck on the cheek. Roz walked off to the museum shop but Maggie paused and watched her sister. She looked different. Thinner perhaps, and her clothes – they weren't exactly smarter – possibly just new and expensive. And now she's returning to her lover, she thought, they'll probably spend the afternoon in bed. For one mad moment Maggie wanted to go too, to join in, make a *ménage à trois* . . .

She turned away and returned to her research but found it hard to concentrate, what with the wine and pizza making her slothful, and the image of the lovers in her head.

OTHER LIVES

35

Alex watched Roz for signs of improvement. She was weeping less although she still had bad days. Crying days, she called them. The life he had imagined with her was slowly becoming reality – but too slowly for his liking. He so wanted them to make a new life together, shedding their old skins. At least they had all this wonderful time on their own, devoted to pleasure, becoming one, forging body and soul. That's how he saw it.

He knew she was becoming nervous about the weekend. She'd rung Geoff and arranged to pick up the children at eleven on Sunday morning but it was only Matthew and Katy who were coming. Geoff said that Sam had refused and would not discuss it; Polly had stated she would ring her mother herself and see her separately at another time. Roz had to accept it.

Then the agonising began – where to take them, what to do? Should she collect them on her own? Alex wanted to go with her; she wasn't sure. If she went on her own in the Range Rover, she'd have to practise driving it first. The discussions went on and on. Alex made suggestions, but didn't want seem pushy – they were *her* children. Eventually, late on Friday night, she decided she'd collect them. Could she try driving the Range Rover tomorrow, would Alex show her? Right. She'd come back here, collect

Alex, they'd all go to the zoo and have lunch there, then back here for tea. They could both take the children home.

Alex did not disagree. Whatever she wanted, he'd go along with. But he could see that he'd have to buy her a car of her own.

She was early picking them up and had to wait at the door of the house, her heart thudding, feeling like an alien, not daring to go inside and not invited. Geoff ushered them out, noting the Range Rover, saying nothing, he didn't need to, the slight raise of the eyebrow was enough for her to know he thought it flashy. He was glad she was alone, but he misinterpreted Alex's absence, thinking lover-boy was afraid to face him.

The Range Rover gave Matthew a point of focus – he loved it. Katy chattered about the teddy she'd brought with her and Roz felt some real cheerfulness replace the false kind she'd been displaying. She was determined to be bright and jolly at all costs.

The zoo gave them something to do, somewhere to go, as it does for countless other Sunday parents. They saw practically everything, reading labels, discussing threatened species, finding habitats on maps. Alex carried Katy on his shoulders and talked to Matthew easily, naturally. It didn't surprise her that he was good at this – wasn't he good at everything?

They had lunch in the café, great piles of unhealthy food, but what the hell, it was only one day. Roz wondered if the other diners thought they were a family. But the children were so fair and Alex so dark.

They joined the throng in the Children's Zoo, stroking the rabbits, braving the goats' enclosure (they nibbled at everything – bags, clothes, Katy's teddy). Alex took Matthew off to see the lions and Roz thought, this is a good start.

Back at Alex's flat things were more strained. They were tired and Matthew became very quiet, making less of an effort. She should have organised things for them to do, she realised. What was the matter with her? Anyone would think she wasn't a mother . . .

She had made their favourite cakes and cheese straws and milkshakes but they weren't really hungry. They ended up watching television while Roz cleared up the mess in the kitchen and Alex read the Sunday papers.

Alex drove them home. Roz tried to relax. Saying goodbye was going to be difficult but she had to get used to this. Matthew asked if she was coming home with them and when she explained that she lived with Alex now, she had a new home, he looked tearful and asked, 'But you will come home sometime? You must.' Katy repeated his words, 'Must come home Mummy.' Roz felt the familiar tightness of her chest and tried to take deep breaths. Alex wanted to say something but knew he should leave it to her. She carefully explained again, told them she loved them and that she'd see them as much as she could. It wasn't what they wanted to hear.

She walked them up the path. Alex stayed in the car, trying not to look, but he couldn't help it – he wanted to satisfy his curiosity about Geoff.

Roz kissed the children goodbye, wanting to clutch them to her chest and not let go, but she controlled herself. Geoff opened the door and Matthew dashed past him into the house. As he picked Katy up, as if to establish ownership, he looked at the Range Rover and saw Alex. Their eyes connected. Alex looked very much as he'd imagined – dark, macho, the opposite of me, Geoff thought.

Roz sensed him willing her to keep this brief. She said she'd call, squeezed Katy's hand then hurried to the waiting car, determined not to look back.

That evening she had collapsed on to the sofa. Alex sat on the floor beside her, insisting again and again that it would get better. She vowed to get organised, to make lists of things to do with the children, places to go. She'd buy some books, games, videos, keep them here for when they were needed. She wanted to perform this new sort of motherhood as well as she had the old.

He wanted to distract her. He leaned over and began slowly to unbutton her shirt and when she tried to sit up, he told her to lie back, do nothing. He removed her shirt, her bra and she lay there half-naked. He applied himself to her breasts, and she relinquished herself to the feelings she never tired of, the experience she could never have enough of.

The phone rang. They ignored it. (It was Polly, having steeled herself to call her mother.)

Roz met Hilary for lunch at a vegetarian restaurant in Crouch End. She assumed a mask of pleasant capable professionalism, accepting Hilary's praise graciously. Hilary handed back the Parents' Guide copy with a short list of comments and a budget for the rest of the work. There were some loose ends for Roz to tie up then she could hand it over to the media resources unit of the council for printing. Hilary said there may be a modest launch party. She spoke of possible future projects – the education committee wanted a leaflet for parents on children starting school and perhaps one on helping your child to read . . . Roz expressed enthusiasm and kept smiling. Suppose they discovered she was a fake, she thought – a woman who knew nothing, a woman who had left her children?

The second Sunday followed a similar pattern to the first: same two children, same time, same procedure, but this time they went to the Tower of London. Alex's spirits dipped as they approached the walls, surrounded by crowds of tourists and the smell of hamburgers in the air. It wasn't how he would choose to spend a summer Sunday. Roz put on a brave face – this wasn't something she would have done when she was at home – but things were different now. They meandered in and out of the buildings and sat for a while by the Thames, hoping Tower Bridge would rise, letting the children climb on the cannons.

She worried about Sam. He still refused to talk to her or even, according to Geoff, about her. Would he ever come round? And how would this damage him? Premonitions of truancy, drug-taking, juvenile crime, flashed before her eyes. Perhaps Geoff could save him. There was nothing she could do. She'd already done it.

At least Polly had phoned her before she left for Glastonbury. It couldn't have been an easy thing to do. It was a stilted conversation. She told Roz she was looking for a summer job, now that her exams were over. They talked about her birthday, which was in a few weeks' time. Roz tried to say the usual motherly things about being careful at the festival, but it didn't sound very convincing. And then she'd tentatively asked when she could see her daughter. Polly said perhaps she'd come over in a few weeks. She'd looked up the address in the *A-Z* and as it wasn't far from Camden Market, perhaps she'd do both and Kim might come as well. Roz was delighted and enthused at the idea, rather too much. But it was a sign of hope.

She functioned enough to complete the Parents' Guide. She made the final changes and corrections, liaised with the media resources people over the layout and illustrations and agreed to proof read it all. Alex was mystified. He looked at the carrier bags of files and the piles of paper spread across the living room floor and tried to take an interest. But what did he know of post-natal depression and the needs of inner city children, the demand for drop-in centres and play schemes? He hoped she wouldn't do any more of this.

Dark days came when grief and a kind of madness overtook her, like a great sweeping wave that comes at you from behind. She began to behave strangely, making purposeless journeys. She'd buy herself a travel card and get on a bus, then another. Often she couldn't say where she'd been.

It was peaceful. She could empty her mind and let random thoughts float through. These were usually connected to the children: memories, milestones, things they'd said and done. She would sit in a trance by a window, preferably at the front, as she travelled across London to places she'd barely heard of, on bus routes she didn't know existed. She preferred the older buses, where you could hop on and off at whim – the newer ones had hissing double doors that sealed you in tight and harassed drivers doing two jobs at once. Sometimes she sat for hours in traffic crawling at lower speeds than the horse-drawn carriages of a hundred years ago.

It didn't matter, she had time. So much time, and hers to decide what to do with. No longer circumscribed by school hours, domestic chores, other people. Only Alex.

Alex had thought she was getting better but she seemed to go forward and then back. What could he do? He wondered if she should see a doctor, perhaps a shrink. Could these journeys of hers be a search for something? He supposed that was obvious. Look at all she'd lost – no, left behind. She could never regain what she'd had but she did have him now. He would be her healer.

He had an idea – a house, that was it. They needed to move. A new place, a new beginning. Somewhere to bring the children, especially if they came to stay. A house would occupy her – choosing furniture, supervising the decoration. She'd be good at it. Money was no problem. It would please him too – he liked change and this place was a bit small for the two of them. He'd suggest it when her mood was right.

36

The invitation for this party had been stuck on the Harpers' notice board for weeks. As it had arrived in the middle of the preparations for Roz's departure they'd ignored it. And they'd been invited as a couple, which they were no longer.

Kim reminded Geoff about it as the day approached. A fancy dress party could be fun, she said. He'd groaned and said why didn't she go instead?

Yet here he was, getting ready. In the end he'd succumbed to the combined pressure of Kim plus his children. Polly had articulated their shared opinion that he should try to get out more. But he'd drawn the line at dressing-up. Over supper last night they persisted in making suggestions – a hippy, a surfer, a new-age traveller – which had been a source of great amusement. They'd even offered to help concoct a costume. He'd looked at his children around the messy table, lively and giggling, tucking into Kim's latest creation, and he felt the ever-present tension in his neck and shoulders ease a little. He would go to the party.

On Saturday afternoon he'd bumped into Colin Wiseman, the host, in Oddbins buying some last-minute supplies.

'But, Geoff – you did get our invite? – we hadn't heard whether you're coming tonight or not – '

'Sorry, Colin – been a bit preoccupied lately – '

'Ah yes, I heard about Roz. We were shocked. I'm sorry – '

'That's OK. But I'd love to come.'

How these small lies keep the social wheels oiled and turning, he thought. But he had to do something like this sometime. He couldn't hide away from the world.

Annie and Martin arrived late. She was dressed as Charlie Chaplin, in a hired baggy suit and a bowler and moustache, but no cane. He was Count Dracula, with the minimum of effort. He'd been reluctant to come as there was a football match he wanted to watch on television. And his plastic fangs, borrowed from Amy, kept falling out.

Colin greeted them at the door, although at first they weren't sure if it was him. He was a solicitor and they were used to seeing him in a suit or carefully-casual weekend wear. But here was someone dressed as a heavy metal rock star: a long curly wig straggled over his shoulders, his eyes were ringed with kohl, his chest was bare under a studded waistcoat and the leather trousers were very tight.

Annie and Martin froze momentarily.

'Yeah, Annie, hi. Hi, Martin. Come in, come in.'

Even his voice was in an altered state.

They followed him, his boot heels thudding on the mosaic hall floor, his armlets and chains jangling. They exchanged a glance and Annie reflected on what a neat little bum Colin had. It was usually hidden. And as for the bulge in front – perhaps he'd put a sock in his Y-fronts.

Smoke and the faint sweet smell of dope filled the air. Colin waved directions, 'Booze and sounds in the front room, eats and talk in the back – or whatever! Wherever! Help yourselves, enjoy!' And he dived off to writhe to the music, something loud and indistinguishable.

'My oh my. So that's why they had this party, to give Colin an excuse,' said Martin, feeling upstaged.

'Well, now we know what his fantasy is,' Annie laughed.

'Do you think all that gear is his? Does he keep it at the back of the wardrobe or wear it in bed?'

'Who knows? You could ask Helen. Let's get a drink.'

'Blood, blood, I've got to sink my fangs into a few pretty necks.' His eyes began to roam.

'Any excuse, eh Martin? Shame they're only plastic and from the toy shop.'

'Sourpuss.'

They squeezed their way to the drinks, past neighbours and acquaintances and people they didn't know – or perhaps just didn't recognise. Their hostess greeted them at the drinks table.

'Helen!' Martin's eager voice said it all. There was Helen, dear, quiet librarian Helen, dressed as Miss Wembley 1980 – or more accurately, undressed. She wore a white swimsuit with high cut-away sides and low back and almost-as-low front. Her cleavage was impressive, like a geographical feature you learned about at school. Ridge? Col? Escarpment? Shiny tan tights ended in white high heels and the pink satin sash strained across her chest. The effect was totally tacky but Annie could see Martin perking up with interest. She wasn't surprised – here was a woman who embodied all his favourite stereotypes: Big Tits,

Good Legs, Great Body, Perfect Figure. Helen had certainly seized the chance to show off her assets but it was a shame she didn't have the face to match, Annie bitched.

She left Martin standing very close and pretending to be a beauty contest compere asking, 'And what are your interests, Miss Wembley? And dare I ask you your vital statistics?' Helen giggled and her breasts jiggled and Martin leaned towards her. He'll be biting her neck any minute, thought Annie.

She felt disgruntled, like an anonymous extra in a cast of thousands. They'd obviously had this bloody party to fulfil their wildest dreams, let their libidos loose. She grasped her glass tightly and looked around, wondering how she was going to pass the evening without getting totally depressed. The fancy dress was mostly fairly predictable, given that most people's aim seemed to be to look as sexy as possible, or what they thought of as sexy. There were lots of variations on the naughty French maid theme – black stockings, suspender belts, little white aprons; and the saucy schoolgirl look was similar. Not all of them were female. Is it only English men who love to dress up as women? Annie thought.

She averted her eyes from a large Superman in tights and suddenly noticed Geoff, leaning against the mantelpiece in the back room, looking pale and tired, listening to Barry, who worked in medical research but tonight was a Roman emperor. Geoff caught her eye and smiled wanly over Barry's shoulder. She decided to go over and talk to him; at least she could ask about Roz – or could she?

Barry beamed at her, patting her bowler, 'I say Annie, can you do the funny walk as well?'

She smiled. 'I might, if you'll play your fiddle.'

He grinned at the joke, hitched up his toga and went to fetch a drink.

Annie turned to Geoff, 'I see you're in plain clothes tonight.' He was wearing faded Levis and a check shirt. 'Or let me guess – are you the Marlboro Man?'

He managed a small laugh. 'I'm undercover. Or I could be the man in the street.'

'Couldn't you be bothered?'

'No, not really my scene.' He drained his glass. 'Of course I should have come as a cuckold with a pair of horns on my head, don't you think?'

She didn't reply – what could she say to that? She could see he was getting drunk, and he seemed different: sharper, perhaps less bland and less inhibited than usual.

'So how are things, Geoff?'

'As you'd expect. Awful at times but we're coping. Look – I don't really want to talk about it. People keep coming up to me and expressing sympathy and asking questions – '

'I'm sorry – I just thought – '

'I didn't mean you. All the others, ghouls, attracted by disaster. Oh what the fuck. I need another drink.'

'I'll get you one,' said Annie. 'What was it, red wine?' He nodded. 'And why don't you sit down – there's a free sofa.'

He dropped on to it and she went off to get the drinks. Why was she being so caring and submissive – was it because it came naturally or because it gave her something to do or Geoff needed some care and attention? Probably all three, she decided.

When she returned he was still alone on the sofa. His threatening gaze had obviously deterred anyone from joining him. Annie sat down and gave him his drink. What nice hands he has, she thought, with long slim fingers.

'Thanks, Annie. But where is Martin and what is he?'

'He's Count Dracula, and I think he's in the other room dancing with Miss Wembley.'

'God, yes, Helen – what a revelation! Our hostess with the mostest.' He laughed then looked Annie straight in the eye. 'Do you sense all the sex in the air? Everyone hot to trot. Where will it all end? An orgy? Wife swapping – not that I've got a wife to swap. Husband swapping?'

'I doubt it!' Annie pulled a face. 'How would they face each other in Sainsbury's or on the train on Monday morning?'

'True.' He almost threw the rest of his wine down his throat and gazed around him. She wondered if he was thinking who he'd like as a sexual partner if there was an orgy . . . And when did he last have sex, surely Roz hadn't been sleeping with them both?

She looked at his long legs stretched out, defying the crush of people, and thought how attractive he was. She'd always liked tall thin rangy types – or she did, before Martin.

Geoff leaned towards her. 'So Annie, tell me all about The Party Spirit – but first do you mind taking your moustache off? I find it a bit disconcerting!'

She obliged as it was feeling itchy anyway, and began to talk about her work, which she loved to do. She saw with surprise that Geoff was really listening and he was taking her seriously. How unusual for a man, she thought, they normally only want to talk about *their* work. Geoff, at a party like this of all places, was giving her his full attention.

'Make sure you keep control of it, whatever you

do,' he said as she paused for breath. 'It's your business, remember.'

'You're right. That's the trick, isn't it, being able to expand but keep hold of the reins.'

They talked about expansion – he was full of good ideas and she said, half-jokingly, 'Sounds as if you'd make a good partner!'

'I'll bear that in mind if I ever decide to opt out of my particular rat race – or if they decide to get rid of me.'

'What do you mean?'

'Companies like the one I work for are pretty ruthless. If they feel you're not pulling your weight, you're for the chop. We've all heard tales of executives arriving at work to find their desks cleared and names removed from their office doors – services no longer required, leave the building immediately, that sort of stuff. And I'm afraid some of them are true.'

'Really? That's awful. But that won't happen to you, surely?'

'I hope not! But I've been letting the side down recently, you know why. Showing signs of vulnerability. Taking my domestic problems to work – that just isn't done. Leaving early, lacking concentration, all because of Roz and – Oh God.' He stopped suddenly, his face crumpled.

Annie put her hand on his shoulder. 'Geoff – '

He put his hand over hers. 'It's all right. Sorry. I'm not about to fall apart – not here anyway! I need another drink. Come and get one with me.'

He took her hand and led the way through the throng. His hand was warm and dry and pleasant to hold. She felt comfortable with her hand in his. Why not? She couldn't see Martin and didn't really want to think about where he might be and right now she didn't care.

Geoff found an almost full bottle of red wine and grabbed it. Their sofa had been filled so they sat on the stairs together. There was a certain intimacy between them – it wasn't just politeness or neighbourliness.

'This is just like being a student again,' he said.

'Oh yes – sitting on the stairs at parties, I remember.'

'And the kitchen was invariably awash with engineering students and a plastic beer barrel . . . God knows why.'

There was a pause.

Geoff leaned close to her and said, 'You know, Annie, I have to say this – I never used to like you.'

'It's OK, Geoff, I know you didn't. And I wasn't sure about you either!'

They both laughed, a little nervously. Geoff continued, talking fast: he wanted to say this and he wanted to be understood.

'I don't know why I thought I didn't like you. I didn't really know you. I just formed an impression and decided that you weren't my sort of person. Just prejudice, of a minor sort. Anyway, I've changed my mind.'

He smiled at her, rather winningly, she thought. This must be the drink talking, Geoff wasn't the sort to start baring his soul. Did he expect her to be grateful that he now liked her? But she found she couldn't be irritated with him. She was enjoying the attention.

He carried on, 'I don't know why I was like that, there were other people I dismissed without knowing them. Well I do know – so much of it comes down to background and conditioning, doesn't it? And my home, my parents . . . Oh, another time.' He paused to fill Annie's glass than drank straight from the bottle. 'So I was a bit smug, I can see that. I judged people too quickly, too superficially. But this business with Roz has turned everything on its head – my ideas about things, possibly my job, my whole bloody life . . . Oh shit.'

He groaned and covered his face with his hands. Annie thought he might be about to cry. She supposed, rightly, that he didn't normally talk about himself at such length. Who did he have to talk to, to turn to? She knew he had no brothers or sisters, but did he have any close friends? He wouldn't unburden himself to colleagues at work. Men didn't, did they?

'Geoff, I'm so sorry.' She felt that was a limp and inadequate response so she supplemented it with her arm around his shoulders and a hug as she would do to a child or another woman in distress. He accepted her touch.

'No, I'm sorry, Annie, for going on like this. It's my problem, not yours.'

Their faces were close and despite his efforts she could see that his eyes were tearful. They were interesting eyes: a mixture of blue and green and grey, yet no definite colour, like the English sea on a cold day.

Martin's voice boomed out. 'Hey, you two! Being neighbourly, eh? Not snogging on the stairs, surely? And where's your moustache, sweetheart? Conveniently removed?' He sniggered.

Annie let her arm slip gently from Geoff's shoulders, looked at the red face of her husband and thought, here's another one who's been drinking too much, too quickly.

'It was itchy. And we're hardly snogging – dreadful word – just needed a place to sit.'

Geoff stood up. He was much taller than Martin.

'Hi, Martin. Left your fangs in someone's neck? Actually, I was just going to ask your wife to dance.'

'Oh, so was I.' Bet he wasn't, thought Annie. 'But I suppose I can dance with her anytime.'

Annie rose. 'What about me? Perhaps I'd like to dance on my own – '

'Yes yes, Annie, we know – it's a woman's right to choose and all that. Go on, have a bop with Geoff.'

Geoff remained silent, using the time to settle his emotions, calm down. He sensed trouble between Annie and Martin – unfinished business, resentment – undermining their relationship. But then what did he know? He was hardly an expert on successful marriages.

Martin pranced off, leaving Annie and Geoff, as if that gave him carte blanche to misbehave. She sighed, unable to decide whether she loved or loathed him.

Geoff smiled down at her. 'Let's go and sample some Sixties nostalgia!' He pulled her towards the music. Sure enough, it was the Stones: *I Can't Get No Satisfaction.* How appropriate, they both thought.

They shifted and turned and twitched together, a foot apart, concentrating on not appearing foolish. She glanced up at him as she threw her head back – she used to be considered a real mover in her art school days, admired for her pelvic thrust. Geoff's eyes were half-closed and he moved elegantly. He really was very attractive.

The music changed to something slow. She recognised the drone of *A Whiter Shade of Pale.* A slow dance? With Geoff?

He saw her hesitation and pulled her towards him gently, slipping an arm around her waist, inside her jacket, holding her other hand to his shoulder. What the hell, she thought. She didn't resist. Geoff had recovered some of his usual composure, he no longer seemed soft at the edges.

'I'm ashamed to say I used to like this song,' he murmured.

'Didn't we all?'

'Yes, and weren't we all pretentious in those days?'

'Were we? Speak for yourself, Geoff. We don't have a common past, remember?'

He held her at arm's length for a moment, sensing a rebuke but she was teasing. He pulled her closer than before and said, 'You're right. Good, I'm glad we don't. That means we can get to know each other now.'

This was nice. A different body, something new. They fitted well together, even though she was much shorter than him. Bone to bone, no flesh in the way. She imagined them as simple bare lines on a piece of paper, a drawing by Matisse. They leaned into each other, she dared to rest her head on his shoulder.

They were as close as they could be now: they moved and bent and rotated fluidly together. She let him guide her. She was very aware of his body and he was very aware of hers. He liked her lightness, her spareness, he could feel her hip bones, he liked that.

They were both hot and their closeness was making them hotter. Annie felt uncomfortable in her suit jacket but didn't want to break the magic of the moment, the moving as one, to take it off. He had begun to stroke her back through her shirt, his thumb moving down her spine . . .

Something needed to happen, there was a tension

between them, sexual tension, it hung in the air. If they were younger or single they would have kissed. They both wanted to, and yet . . .

Geoff let go of her abruptly, mumbled something, put a hand over his mouth and rushed away towards the stairs. Annie watched him, feeling bereft and foolish, but realised that no one was paying her any attention so she shrugged and went off to get a glass of water. Perhaps he'd been feeling sick.

She thought she ought to see if he was all right.

There were several bathrooms in the house. On the mezzanine the bathroom door was open – it was empty with damp towels on the floor and the bath half-full of water. She tried the next one, ensuite to the Wiseman's bedroom. She knocked on the door and a muffled female voice called out, 'Won't be long.' She thought she heard a grunt, a male noise.

She went up to the top of the house to the au pair/children's bathroom, feeling like Goldilocks. The light was on, the door ajar, and there was a smell of sick. Geoff was leaning over the basin, splashing his face with water.

'Geoff? Are you all right?'

She handed him a towel. He cleared his throat, dried his face.

'Yes, I think I'll be OK now. I've been overdoing it – had a few whiskies before I came, then too much wine and nothing much to eat. I'd better go home and get to bed. Roz is coming to take the children out. Some of them.'

They started to go down the stairs and he put his arm companionably around her shoulders.

'Thanks for coming to check on me. Sometimes I

think I need a mother!' Ouch – stupid remark, he regretted it immediately.

Sure enough she stiffened and said sharply, 'Oh thanks a lot,' and tried to walk ahead but he held her arms and turned her round.

'I'm sorry. Please don't take that personally, it was a silly thing to say. Though I do feel in need of care and attention – '

'Don't we all! What you really mean is, you need a wife.' Now she regretted what she'd said – how insensitive and tactless.

He held her gaze steadily and said, 'Or a lover.'

That surprised her. What could she say? What did he mean? The moment passed.

'You've been very kind and understanding tonight, Annie – thank you.' And he kissed her fondly on the forehead.

As they approached the throng at the bottom of the stairs his arm left her shoulders. Annie felt disappointment fall to her stomach. But what had she expected to happen – a quick fuck in the bathroom? Perhaps Geoff didn't fancy her – but then what about their dance? The look in his eyes? Was she so out of practice at reading signals?

He headed for the front door. 'Goodnight, Annie. Let me know how the business goes – if you need a sounding board, get in touch.'

'Goodnight, Geoff – and if you want any help with the children, just ring or pop over.'

She set off to find Martin. He was lounging on a sofa, legs wide apart, his arm around a plump woman dressed as Nell Gwyn, his fingertips resting on the upper slope of her breast, his other hand on her thigh, whispering in her ear. Annie watched him, thinking how he loved soft, malleable women, how he wanted to be admired and cherished and pampered. Nothing challenging or spiky or awkward, like her, she thought. Tough – he can't be a baby forever.

She interrupted.

'Martin. I'm ready for bed. Are you coming home?'

He heard the edge in her voice and was too pissed and lethargic to argue. He struggled out of the opulence of his companion and the sofa, giving her a quick squeeze as he left.

Carina was already in bed, the house was quiet. Martin attempted to focus on the rituals of locking up while Annie checked the children. He looked surprised when she reappeared downstairs.

She started to unbutton her shirt. Her experience with Geoff – or the lack of it – and seeing Martin fondle other women had made her feel really randy. She approached him and started pulling off his clothes, unzipping his trousers.

'Come on, Martin. It's been so long.'

She pressed against him, her shirt falling open.

'Annie – hold on. I think I'm too pissed. And tired. Do you mind if we skip it tonight?'

He carefully removed her hand from his limp penis. He couldn't tell her the other reason why he didn't feel up to it – he'd screwed Miss Wembley in the bathroom. He hadn't meant to, he thought it would be just a quick grope – he'd been keen to see Helen's breasts, get his hands on them that's all, but she'd amazed him by asking for it. And it hadn't been at all bad.

Annie sat in the living room in the dark, punching the cushions, cursing Martin who had staggered up to bed. Bastard. Useless pig, she thought. Her mind raced, her body wouldn't settle down. She fantasised about crossing the road and presenting herself to Geoff.

37

Roz had lost count of how many houses they'd been to see. Fifteen? Twenty? She was trying to be enthusiastic. Here she was, empowered to find a house, *the* house, in which she and her lover would set up home together. So what was wrong?

The echoes of the other house, the home she'd so recently left, plagued her. Shades of her children, even Geoff, inhabited any house of her dreams.

It was hard to concentrate on what needed to be done now. Build a different life, create another home, a new world. A parallel universe.

She ripped open the fat envelopes which had arrived from the various estate agents that morning, grimacing at the language – at first it had amused her but no longer. It was both flowery and assertive, often unashamedly illiterate, reaching heights of absurdity only previously achieved on greengrocers' labels. She felt as if she should be marking these with a red pen.

She quickly dumped no-hopers straight in the bin. She was experienced at this now and able to decode their descriptions with ease. No mention of the garden size indicated that it was tiny or non-existent. A courtyard meant a basic back yard, usually filled with dustbins and the stink of tom cats. Two or more kitchens in a large house signified that it had been let out and probably neglected by the absentee landlord. Fourth bedrooms deemed suitable for a study were in fact too small to be bedrooms, no bed would fit. No wonder they hadn't found a house yet.

She shuffled the pile and tried to retain some optimism. Here was one she'd missed – it had been stapled to the back of some other details. It sounded faintly promising, worth a look anyway. Roz fixed an appointment for later in the day – Alex had said he'd be back by four.

He came rushing through the door towards her, enveloping her in his arms. She laughed, 'No need to rush, Alex – '

'I know, my darling, but I have a need – for you.'

He said it in a mockingly dramatic voice but began to kiss her anyway. She held him at arm's length. 'Let me show you the details of the house – we're due there at four-thirty.'

He sighed – he'd wanted quickly to make love but he sensed her reluctance. Roz didn't offer any excuses. It was no big deal. They couldn't be making it all the time. And anyway, she was being practical, she didn't want to go out with wet knickers. She sighed too – men never knew what that was like, did they?

He read about the house as he drank a glass of mineral water. 'Yes, could have potential. What's the arrangement, are we meeting him there or what?'

'Yes, at the house. Simon – or is it Nigel? I always get those two mixed up. It's empty, thank God. It makes it so much easier.'

He drove them through the North London traffic, that early rush hour when children are coming home from school. Roz kept her head down. She disliked being out around this time as she might see children who reminded her of her own. The toss of a head, a particular school bag, any detail could plunge her into those dark, dark feelings she experienced when thinking about them. Feelings of despair and guilt and sorrow, all churned up in a glutinous mass which had settled inside her, like a heavy meal that she shouldn't have eaten.

Alex was getting impatient with the Volvo in front which was stuffed with overdressed boys in maroon private-school uniforms making faces through the windows – the School Run making its way homeward. These kids were so unlike her own, she thought. She sighed loudly.

Alex put his hand on her thigh. 'We could give up and go back home to bed.'

'We could, but shouldn't we persevere? This could be the house – '

'You're right. Let's hope it is. Sometimes I think we should just buy a piece of land and build our own house – that's meant to be every architect's dream!'

'A piece of land? In London?' She laughed.

'I know! I suppose we do have to stay in London . . .'

His unasked question hung unanswered as Roz directed him through the side streets. They both imagined a piece of land. Hers was a meadow with wild flowers and views across fields and dry stone walls to the sea, a grey-green English sea. His was a bare brown hillside sloping to an olive grove, beyond that an empty beach of pale sand and the shimmering blue-green Aegean.

Simon-or-was-it-Nigel waited for them, leaning against his black Golf GTI, smoking a cigarette with serious enjoyment. They agreed that this *was* Simon, a young man they were seeing far too often, becoming familiar with his suits and ties and shoes, registering when he had a hangover or wore hair gel.

He handed them the keys, suggesting they looked around it by themselves then drop the keys back at the office. Before they had time to agree, he was accelerating away. Alex shrugged. 'He probably has a girl to see or a deal to do. Anyway it's better on our own.'

Roz stood on the tiled path and looked around. The street was a gently curving crescent lined with plane trees and builders' skips. Difficult to park, you needed a resident's permit – but it was all like that round here. Near to Primrose Hill, near the shops. She ran through a checklist in her mind – it was a short one as she no longer needed to think about playgroups, good schools, sports facilities, other families.

Old shrub roses in the front garden scented the air. The house was number nineteen – that was fine, it had no memories or associations. The front door was wide with stained glass panels and an intriguing knocker: an elegant hand clasped over a ball. She'd seen ones like that before – where was it? The Dordogne, in Bergerac? Alex said there were variations of the design on old houses in Lindos on Rhodes. It was a good sign.

Inside it smelt dusty but not damp and wore an air of quiet melancholy which appealed to Roz immediately. They stood in a large square hall with the original tiled floor, geometric shapes of blue and brown and white. Solid panelled doors led off it and a wide staircase turned upwards.

'Roz – come here, look.' Alex was standing in a

well of natural brightness, the rays falling around him to the floor, his palms outstretched, looking like a depiction of Christ in a Victorian painting. She joined him. Up, up the stairwell, at the very top of the house, was a large skylight with a border of coloured glass. It was grimy but it still illuminated the house.

'Ooh, lovely,' said Roz, like a child at a fireworks party. 'What a surprise.'

'Cleverly placed,' said Alex, 'Nice piece of design.'

Roz felt a small leap of enthusiasm enliven her. This house could wake her up, it was something solid and substantial. You can love a house, care for it, bring it to life, she thought as she stood under the dust floating in the beams of light from above.

She followed Alex through one door, then another. A large living room with a massive marble fireplace and the original folding shutters at the windows. A smaller room, then a tiny one tucked away to one side of the hall. Alex laughed, looking at the house details. 'They call this the sewing room.' She pictured past generations of quiet women, heads bent over intricate needlework, closeted together, conversing in low voices.

The kitchen was at the back with French windows to the garden, probably several smaller rooms knocked into one to create a big family room. It had once had some taste and style but now had a neglected, left-behind air. Roz had a good hard look at it, visualising how it could be. With a start she realised that she was picturing it like her kitchen at home (home?); she was imagining it filled with her children.

She took a deep breath in an attempt to conceal and curb her feelings. Alex was suddenly beside her, holding her. Over his shoulder she could see pencil marks on the grubby white wall plotting the heights of children: *Edward* 3 *years . . . Sally* 5 *years . . . David* 6 *years . . . Edward* 4 *years . . . Sally* 6 *years . . . David* 7 years . . . Up the wall they went, charting their progress increasingly haphazardly (children lose their taste for that kind of thing as they get older), stopping at about Roz's shoulder level. Alex followed her gaze.

He held her tighter. 'Hey, Roz,' he murmured.

'Oh, Alex, will it ever be all right? Will I ever get used to not being with them, not having them?'

It all poured out of her in this empty house belonging to strangers. She sobbed, she banged her head on Alex's shoulder, her fists on his back, saying, 'What have I done? What have I done?' over and over.

He stood like a rock, holding her until the frenzy of emotion began to abate. Gulping air for some control, she rummaged in her bag for some tissues and blew her nose, wiped her eyes. With his thumb he smoothed a smear of mascara from her cheek, like a potter stroking clay. She tried to smile brightly and said, 'Shall we look at the rest – the two-minute tour, as Simon would say?'

They climbed the stairs hand in hand, side by side – the staircase was wide enough. Door after door opened off the central landing – five bedrooms, Roz counted them. The place was a mess. It was as if the occupants had managed to hold on to some semblance of civilised life downstairs – but up here there was a sense of disarray. Two bedrooms had sinks and water heaters – had they been reduced to taking in lodgers to pay the way? They trod carefully.

The bathroom was unappetising. They grimaced at each other. They climbed up the final staircase – it was narrower, everything became smaller and meaner as they went higher up the house.

'Servants' quarters,' remarked Roz as they looked at the two tiny rooms. 'This is where the maids spent their lives.'

Alex was rubbing at the grimy window, 'But look at this view!'

It was a perfect cityscape: grey slate rooftops piled behind each other, red brick chimneys, the occasional burst of green where a tree had managed to grow tall enough to show itself. Beyond the houses were the slopes of Primrose Hill, the glimpses of the aviary at the zoo.

'Do you like it up here, darling?' He held her tightly from behind, his arms crossed around her.

'Yes I do. It's somehow very calming, this view.' She turned, they kissed.

'We could make it into a studio for you, perhaps even knock the two rooms together – '

'A studio? For me? What for?' She drew back from him.

'All sorts of things – a place for you to do some pottery, drawings – whatever you like. We could make one room into a darkroom – you once said you'd like to get involved in photography. And I might use it too . . .'

'Yes I suppose so, why not? And I might need a study for my work.'

She tried to grasp why she felt irritated with him. Was he anxious that she wouldn't be able to fill her time without her children? Or was he trying to mould her into some sort of artistic ideal, to make her more interesting? He regarded her with one eyebrow raised. Oh hell, she thought, here was Alex offering her whatever she wanted and she got tetchy with him – she was stupid and pathetic and ungrateful.

He held her by the shoulders and spoke gently.

'What is it , Rozzi? Are you afraid of getting what you want? Someone once said that was the worst tragedy of all.'

He looked at her with love and sadness.

She looked at him with surprise; his sensitivity continued to astonish her. A smile lightened her face.

'Oh Alex. I'll have to work that one out. Meanwhile, I want you and I have you, and surely there's no tragedy in that?'

She kissed him and they gazed down at the gardens. The one directly below was a riot of long grass and brambles and roses. Next door was carefully ordered, with a strip of lawn and flower beds and an old woman slowly hanging out washing. On the other side was a curved brick patio with stone benches and a multitude of pots and small statues and a pond. Neither set of neighbours appeared to show signs of having children. Good.

'What do you think Roz, will it suit us?'

'Yes, I think it could suit us very well. I like the feel of it – '

'So do I. We'll have a great time doing it up, making it ours. Do you think we'll argue over the decor?'

They laughed at such an unlikely notion and went back through the house, beginning to have ideas on how to transform it into a reflection of themselves. She felt positive, even eager, and he felt relieved.

They headed for the estate agent to make an offer. The house stood still and quiet, waiting for them. Roz felt she should ask Alex about money and a mortgage and even if the house would be jointly theirs or just his, but she decided to be still and quiet as well. The questions could wait too.

38

The house was theirs. It had all happened so fast. The owners had been very eager for a quick sale, and Roz didn't enquire about their circumstances – she suspected that they were bleak and she didn't really want to know. She saw too much misery around her these days, she was sensitised to it.

And the house was *theirs*: Alex had bought it in their joint names. One evening, as she was in the kitchen wondering what to do with the swordfish steaks she'd bought, he'd come in waving some papers at her. They were the documents relating to the house. Once they'd signed, contracts could be exchanged immediately.

He went through it with her over a bottle of champagne.

'Roz, I've put the house in both our names, I assume that's fine with you?'

'Of course it is! But I'd presumed it would be yours, you know I can't really contribute – '

'Darling please! Don't talk like that. The house will be *our* home, so it's right that it's in joint names. I know this could be a delicate subject and that other people might say certain things but I see this as a statement, a demonstration that we're together. I'm not expressing myself very well. Do you know what I mean?'

She leaned over and kissed him, ruffled his hair. 'I do, my love. And I'm touched, I'm grateful.'

'Don't be. There's no need to be grateful. But there's something I ought to tell you – '

'Alex?'

'It's all right, don't be alarmed – I just wanted to say that money isn't a problem for me. There's no mortgage or loan – it wasn't necessary. That obviously helped speed things along.'

'Oh. But it was such a lot of money.' She imagined Alex handing over a sackful of cash.

'I got the price down a bit. As I don't have to sell this flat to raise the money, we can live here while the work is done on the house.'

'Money certainly makes life easier, doesn't it?' She didn't want to pry but where did his money come from?

'It helps! And I want to make your life easier if I can. But about the money – it's not that I'm secretive, it's just that I don't particularly like talking about it. Anyway – I've always had a generous allowance from my father, plus I get income from the family business interests – '

'Like the hotel we stayed in?'

'Yes and there are others. Also, we have a travel company in Greece and an import/export business – olive oil, the usual things. Plus I have investments of my own, and property. And I earn some!'

'It's just as well I didn't know this before, you might have thought I was after your money!' He laughed and she kissed him, dribbling champagne into his mouth.

'Ah, but I know what you were after and still are, don't I?'

'Yes – the riches you have in your trousers! Is it so obvious?'

She kissed him again, her tongue in his mouth, her body moving. They went to bed.

Later, he grilled the swordfish while she steamed the vegetables. They often worked together in the kitchen, side by side, companionably. She looked at him and thought, he is rich. He could definitely be described as rich. What would Maggie say now? She'd be able to categorise her sister as not only a mistress but a rich man's mistress too. Roz didn't care. She knew what she and Alex had and labels didn't matter.

As they ate they talked about the house, the things they could do to it, what they'd buy, how it should look. They looked forward to tackling the garden – well, planning and designing it. They'd hire someone to do the rough work of clearing the brambles. Alex said they must have a barbecue – swordfish was wonderful grilled over charcoal, Greek style.

Tomorrow they'd go to his solicitor in Holborn and sign whatever was necessary then it should be completed in about a week, he said. Roz was amazed. She thought it normally took weeks and weeks, but then perhaps she was out of touch, and Alex said it could be done. Money talks, thought Roz. It meant that the house should be theirs by the end of next week.

Alex already had a team of builders lined up for the work on the house, guys he'd used before who, luckily, were available. Luckily. Lucky. Roz contemplated how lucky she was. She had Alex, he had money. And she still had her children, in a way – a different way. Things could be worse. And for some of the time she was happy. The house was going to help. Number nineteen was going to be home and it was going to be beautiful, and she would take her children there. She couldn't wait to get started.

*

Geoff and Katy walked home from playgroup with Annie and Tom. Geoff had taken a day off work and told Kim he'd fetch his daughter, Annie had to collect Tom as Carina was sitting an English language exam. A happy coincidence, they both thought separately, pleased to see each other.

They walked slowly in the sunshine as the children experimented with walking backwards. Annie felt a little shy with Geoff after the Wisemans' party though she wasn't sure why she should. Nothing had happened, had it? But she had seen his vulnerability, perhaps that was it. And she'd found him attractive too.

She squinted up at him, the sun was in their eyes. He looked very appealing today, she thought. Unshaven, a bit rough at the edges, in a blue T-shirt and jeans.

'So how are you – recovered from Saturday?'

He looked embarrassed. 'Oh yes. I'm OK thanks. I hadn't got that drunk for years.'

What's the matter with me? he thought. I want to talk to her but I can't find the words. Is it just that the situation's new to me?

He glanced quickly at Annie who was determinedly watching the children. She was looking very attractive today. She'd changed a lot over the last few months, looking less outlandish, less scruffy. There was something else different about her – was it her hair?

Annie wanted to remark to Geoff how strange it was to be walking along with him instead of Roz but felt it might be tactless. She looked up at him and saw him staring at her hair. He probably hadn't noticed it on Saturday.

'Do you like my new hair, Geoff?' she said boldly.

'New hair?' He laughed. 'Sounds as if you've had a transplant!'

'Well, I hate the word hairstyle, it's so formal. And it's not a new haircut because I haven't had it cut.'

'Ah such mysteries . . . So how is it new then?'

'I'm growing it and I've toned the colour down a bit too. It's all part of being a businesswoman – you know, appearing serious and reassuring to clients and acceptable to bank managers and people like that!' She laughed.

'Oh I see! Well it looks very nice. In fact you look very well, Annie.'

She thanked him. They had reached their road, nearly home. They both felt a little reluctant to part. Was it just that they had been having a friendly conversation and enjoying it or was there something else there that they wanted to prolong?

They went into their respective houses, waving, feeling a little awkward, taking refuge in the children. They were both out of practice in flirting – if that's what it was, the spark of interest that passed between them.

Geoff made his daughter some lunch – fish fingers and chips and grated carrot – and decided to have some too. Afterwards he read her a story. She snuggled close to him, sucking a strand of her hair, joining in, completely happy and satisfied in the moment. Geoff thought how pleasing it was to be able to do this and how he too had to try to find some happiness every day. Impossible maybe, but he would try.

Later he sat in front of the television with Sam and Polly, watching a documentary on inner city crime and teenage gangs. They giggled and found much of it amusing, he didn't ask why.

He looked around the room and thought how things

had changed. It was untidy: he could see an empty crisps packet next to the sofa, there were mugs and glasses left on the coffee table. A hairbrush and several pairs of discarded trainers lay on the floor, alongside a pile of computer game magazines and a Lego model. Before it would have bothered him, but not now.

He went into the kitchen to get another whisky.

Sam began cruising through the TV channels. Polly hit him with a cushion.

'Sam – cut it out! Why is it always you who has the remote control?'

'Because girls are useless!'

'You're pathetic. You're so immature.'

'OK, big sister.' He sneered and held the control out of her reach. He was already taller than her. 'Just because you've been to Glastonbury. Just because you've got a boyfriend.'

'Nick is not a boyfriend – '

'Oh yeah?'

'He's just – he's a friend.'

'Bet you wish he was more.'

They both slumped down on the sofa. Sam stared at the unfunny sitcom on the screen.

'Sam – let's stop this. It's not fair on Dad if we argue and mess about – '

'Yeah all right.'

'He needs our support right now – '

'I know that!'

'I'm sorry, I know you do.'

They sat silently for a few minutes, watching the phoney family on the TV. Sam sniffed loudly and Polly put her arm around his shoulders. He tried not to cry but it was inevitable.

'Why did she leave, Poll? Why?'

'It's as she said – she met this man and fell in love and

decided she wanted to live with him, not with Dad and us – '

'I've heard all that crap, I've had enough of it – and it still doesn't make sense, not to me – I don't get it, I just don't get it!'

'Nor do I, Sam, not really. Perhaps we'll understand when we're adults, we may see it differently then.'

'I'll never understand. I'll always want to know why she left us.'

Geoff loaded the dishwasher, his mind flicking through existing and potential problems. Money. Work. He wished he could work from home. Wasn't that meant to be the trend? People plugged in at home with all the relevant machines, contributing just as much, but freed of commuting and office politics and not taking up the expensive square footage. Could he do that? Was the company ready for it? He doubted it. In his experience, employers still wanted to buy you completely, body and soul. They were suspicious of people working at home – it lessened their authority, they were no longer in complete control of people's everyday lives.

That's what he wanted, Geoff thought, to be in charge of his own life. But how?

He heard Sam rush upstairs and Polly turn off the TV. She put her head around the kitchen door and said she was going to bed. She looked upset but he didn't comment – sometimes you had to let things be.

He had another whisky.

At times he felt like a piece of wood that was being whittled down from all angles until there was hardly anything left. He was under constant pressure at work and at home. Home – even with Kim, it still needed someone at the centre, loving and giving, pulling it all together, being there . . . Roz had ripped herself from the heart of the family and it had left a gaping hole. Could he fill it? Or did it need a wife and mother?

Geoff had begun to have more and more sympathy with working women, those with families. He could now understand what all the fuss was about. Not that most of them made a fuss – that was another burden they had to shoulder, being butch and hyper-efficient and uncomplaining and pretending it was easy. A few women at work, on hearing about Roz, had quietly expressed their sympathy for Geoff, saying that they knew how difficult it was. Up to then, he hadn't even realised that they had children. It was all part of his education, he thought.

He went to bed, exhausted as usual. That night he dreamed that he and the children were on a carousel at a fairground, riding carved horses with hideously grinning teeth. Up and down they went, faster and faster, round and round until he found it impossible to see where all the children were. He'd spot one, then another, but he couldn't see all four. He struggled to get off his horse and couldn't, nor was he able to stop the carousel or get anyone else to stop it – then he saw Roz standing on the ground some distance away, calmly watching the carousel spin. A nightmare.

39

Annie slammed out of the house. Martin was impossible. All she'd done was ask him to look after the children for a few hours while she went to look at possible premises for The Party Spirit with an estate agent. So it was Saturday morning, so what – they were his children, you'd think he'd welcome some time with them. But no, it was grunting and groaning time – Martin was very practised at that.

'Can't Carina look after them?' he'd asked.

'No. You know she has weekends off unless there's an emergency or if I have a lot of work on.'

He muttered something about this being an emergency and what did they have the bloody girl for? Martin had never really warmed to Carina. He had nothing against her personally, it was just that he didn't seem to gain anything from her being in the house – how exactly did he benefit? Annie knew that Carina also disappointed him: she didn't conform to his preconceived idea of a Swedish au pair girl. And Carina did not try to humour him: she was friendly and polite but kept her distance. He found that hard to accept – he expected all women to treat him as special in one way or another, either to find him sexy or interesting or powerful, and to behave accordingly. To Carina he was almost invisible.

*

Annie drove off fast in her van. It felt like an escape.

The first stop was a bankrupt printers off the Holloway Road. She waited ten minutes for the agent, Mark, to arrive. When he did, he failed to apologise and treated her with polite condescension, not taking her or her business seriously. Now if I were a man, she thought, or had one in tow, he'd behave differently. She had a quick look around – it was too big – then they drove separately to something called a light industrial unit on the far side of Kentish Town.

Annie thought of Roz as she drove along, she wasn't sure why, perhaps it was to do with estate agents . . . Roz had told her that she and Alex were buying a house together. What she meant, thought Annie, was that *he* was buying a house. She and Roz hadn't seen each other since Roz left but they spoke on the phone, every week or so. Neither wanted to lose touch but they were both a little wary – Roz because she associated Annie with her previous life and felt that perhaps Annie knew too much about her; Annie because her feelings towards Roz were ambivalent. She understood Roz's actions but her sympathies were with Geoff and the children – she saw the effects on them, even from a distance.

She marched purposefully around the unit – there wasn't much to see, it was just a prefabricated box with a sink in one corner. She threw some questions at Mark about square footage, just to keep him on his toes. The last place was near Gospel Oak, a disused bakery in interconnecting brick buildings, with some covetable off-street parking. It would need a lot of work. She needed to think. She told Mark she'd be in touch (he didn't believe her) and drove slowly towards home.

She didn't feel like re-entering the bosom of her family (not that it had many bosomy qualities) – she felt like going shopping and spending loads of money on clothes or having a long expensive lunch with someone or an illicit afternoon in bed with a lover. Sometimes she envied Roz.

As she negotiated the traffic round Highgate Village, she told herself to concentrate on her work, her business. That was hers, all hers. People envied *her*. She asked herself some hard questions: what exactly were these premises intended for? A shop? Somewhere to meet clients and/or make the products? Who would work there? Had she costed it properly?

She wished she had a partner she could discuss all this with – how far and how fast should she expand, which was the right direction to go? Or just someone level-headed and sensible. Martin was a non-starter, her accountant would charge her. Then she thought of Geoff – he had offered. Perhaps she would see him, ask his advice.

She couldn't believe the mess that greeted her at home. What had happened? All that had happened, it transpired, was that Martin had let the children do what they liked while he had a shower, made some phone calls and read the newspaper. Martin told her this himself as if nothing was wrong. Tom and Amy had been fingerpainting – not just on paper but on themselves, the table, the chairs, the fridge. Afterwards they'd decided to play with water, filling the sink, adding washing-up liquid, pouring to and from bottles and jugs, squirting each other. This was something Annie usually encouraged as being fun and educational, but only under strict supervision. There was more. Amy had slipped on the wet floor and banged her head; Tom had gone to the loo and put far too much paper down it, so that it wouldn't flush.

Annie seethed. They might as well have been on their own and she told Martin so, after she'd cleared up some of the mess and made the children lunch, then settled them down in front of a Disney video. She couldn't blame them.

She was ready for a row.

'Really, Martin, couldn't you have prevented some of this? You were meant to be the adult here!'

She was still cleaning fingerpaint (such lovely bright colours) off the fridge.

'Don't make such a big deal of it, for fuck's sake. Kids are messy, what can you do?'

'What you can do is be involved, for a start. Keep an eye on them, even talk to them and play with them. It has been known for fathers to do that, you know.'

'Yeah well, I'm tired. I don't need this right now. All I wanted was a bit of time to myself this morning, but no, you landed me with the kids.'

'You, you, you! That's all I hear. You don't give a toss about anyone else, do you? Supposing I'm tired and I might want some time to myself, eh? When does that ever happen?'

'You had some time this morning remember, swanning off to look at premises, as you so quaintly call them.' He sneered.

She threw the cloth covered in paint at him. It landed on his denim shirt, fresh on today.

'That's it, I've had enough. Who's the adult now? Pathetic, Annie, pathetic. I don't have to put up with this you know.'

'Oh really, what are you going to do about it then?'

He stared at her for a moment as if carefully

considering what to say next, whether to say it or not. He said it, in a quiet controlled voice.

'I'm going to leave.'

'What? *What?*'

'I said, I'm going to leave. I've been thinking about it for some time. This is no fun any more. I'm not needed here, except perhaps as a provider of cash, but as you keep telling me, you're earning now as well. So I think I'll go.'

'Just like that? Where will you go?'

'Funny you should ask. I've been meaning to tell you: there's someone I'm involved with. She's young, gorgeous, she seems to adore me, she certainly doesn't nag me and bug me like you do and she's said I can move in with her any time I like. So I think I will.'

He stood there, ignoring the paint on his shirt, rising above it, looking smug, hands on hips, legs apart.

Annie was convulsed with rage. She hated him and she hated the fact that he'd said he'd leave before she had the chance to throw him out. She had to restrain herself from hitting him.

'Good! I'm glad. You can fuck off. Go now. I'll be glad to see you go, it will be wonderful not to have you here, dragging me down, undermining me, demanding attention. And who is this darling of yours? That Amanda who keeps phoning? I hope she rings again, I'd like to give her a complete rundown on you, you selfish bastard, warn her of what she's really getting. Is she good at fetching and carrying? At stroking your male ego? But perhaps I'd better not tell her what you're like to live with – it might put her off and I want her to take you off my hands. Now, as a last wifely duty, I'll go and pack your things, dear.'

She ran out of the room, up the stairs. Martin stood still for a moment, surprised at her reaction. He'd thought she'd be more upset, that she might try and plead with him to stay, even if just for the children's sake. But no, she genuinely seemed to want him out. And Christ, what was she doing upstairs, what did she mean by that sarcastic remark about packing his things?

He ran upstairs too. She was in the bedroom and had already emptied drawers of socks and underwear and sweaters in a great mountain on the floor, a testament to his spending power. Now she was starting on his wardrobe, pulling jackets and trousers and suits from their hangers, flinging them on to another pile. Ouch, there went his Paul Smith suit; whoosh, his precious Armani jacket joined it.

'Stop it! What the hell do you think you're doing?'

He started to pick things up and lay them on the unmade bed.

'I'm trying to help, you shit, I'm removing all your clothes. You said you were going – so here you are. And if you're not ready to go in, let's say an hour, I'm going to deposit this lot in the front garden.'

She was breathless from fury and exertion.

'But you can't – you wouldn't! And it's raining!'

'Try me. And that would just be the beginning, sweetheart.'

She stormed off downstairs to see the children. Had they heard anything? But they were still in front of the video, seemingly innocent of what was going on around them.

Annie went into the kitchen, her territory, and tried to calm down. In the past she would have had a cigarette but not now. She wouldn't let fucking Martin make her start smoking again.

Her heart was racing and so was her mind. Did she really want him to go? Yes she did. The bastard had been having an affair, as she'd suspected. He was so bloody predictable. He'd always been half-hearted about being married. Where was his commitment? He'd continued ogling other women, commenting on their bodies, and claiming when challenged that he just couldn't help it, it was his essential masculine nature. She'd never been sure whether he really believed that crap or not, but he found the posture convenient. He hadn't ever really grown up, that was the trouble. He was reluctant to shoulder responsibilities like fatherhood. Would the children miss him? Hardly, she thought. They didn't see much of him at the best of times and he was hardly a hands-on, get-down-on-your-knees-and-play father. No, they wouldn't miss him, and nor would she, and the sooner he was gone the better. She set the timer on the cooker for an hour – she'd meant what she said.

Martin sat in his car outside Amanda's mews house in Notting Hill. He'd tried to ring but her answer-phone was on. So he waited, surrounded by bulging cases and carrier bags. Not very dignified, having all (or most) of your worldly goods stuffed in your car. It had all been such a rush: he'd only said a brief goodbye to the children and Annie said she'd tell them he'd had to go away for a while because of work. He didn't argue, she was so fierce. He was relieved to be away from her. There had been no love or attention for him in that house, he thought. He'd felt he was being squeezed out, what with Annie's little business and that sober-sides au pair and no spare rooms any more – all taken up with Annie's things and no space for him and what *he* might want to do.

He settled down to read *Private Eye* while he waited. Amanda would get a surprise finding him here – a pleasant surprise he hoped. He'd been stretching the truth when he'd told Annie that Amanda had said he could move in. What she'd actually said, when he complained about home, was why didn't he move out if it was so bad? But he was sure she wouldn't mind – the few times they'd been together she'd seemed pretty keen on him. He just hoped she hadn't gone away for the weekend.

Annie felt drawn to Geoff. She wanted to discuss her business with him. She wanted to tell him about Martin. They were now in the same boat – or at least a similar one. On Sunday morning she crossed the road to his house, leaving the children with Carina, who was reading the newspapers – she did it diligently to improve her vocabulary.

Polly answered the door, said her Dad was upstairs, and took her into the kitchen. She was tidying up – it certainly needed it.

'So how are you, Polly? What are you doing now your term is over?'

'I'm trying to find a summer job. It's not so easy. I don't have to be back at college until the middle of September, so I've got plenty of time.'

Annie looked at Polly. She still managed to look wholesome despite the layers of black clothing, the reddened hair, the extra holes in one ear.

'I have an idea! How would you like to work for me over the summer, for The Party Spirit? It would probably be odd jobs – helping with paperwork, phone calls, perhaps some simple cooking . . . What do you think?'

Polly looked delighted, she dropped the pile of junk mail that had accumulated on the table and moved towards Annie as if to hug her. She didn't but her face said it all.

'Oh wow, do you mean it? That would be great! I'm so pleased, I was getting desperate. I'm willing to do anything, I don't mind. Not that I've got much experience – '

Annie reassured her, 'You're bright and sensible and reliable, that's all I need. Why don't you come over later and we can talk about hours and money? But see what your Dad thinks first – '

Annie could hear Geoff coming down the stairs and for a moment was worried that he might disapprove. He came in, holding Katy's hand.

'Hello, what a nice surprise! Polly, don't do any more tidying, love, you've done enough. Annie, would you like some coffee? I'm having some.'

'Yes I would please, but are you busy? I just dropped over to ask you something.'

'No I'm not busy. Only the usual.' He grinned and looked around him.

'Dad, Annie's offered me a job for the summer, isn't that great? Now I've got to ring Laura – OK? See you later.'

'That is good news! And yes, off you go.'

Annie and Geoff were alone in the kitchen. Katy had wandered into the garden to play in the sand pit, Matthew and Sam were reinforcing the tree house that Geoff had built with them last summer. It was quiet, just the sound of children's voices on the air.

Geoff made coffee in a cafetière, put it on a tray with mugs and sugar and milk.

'Let's be civilised, Annie, let's go in the living room.'

She was glad to follow him, as she was used to sitting in the kitchen with Roz, it was full of associations.

She arranged herself on an opposite sofa, watching him plunge and pour the coffee, noticing again his elegant hands with long fingers, quite unlike Martin's.

'I hope you don't mind me popping over like this, unannounced.'

'Not at all, I'm glad you did. It's good to have some adult company.' He smiled at her, thinking how nice she looked this morning. Her hair was shiny like a new conker. She was wearing a sleeveless white shirt tucked into baggy khaki shorts with a wide brown leather belt. What a small waist she has, he thought, and she didn't seem to be wearing a bra. A nice body, he decided.

'So how are things, Geoff?'

'We stagger on. I'm coping! I tell myself it can only get better. But look, thanks for offering Polly a job, it's just what she needs – '

'No need to thank me. There's plenty to do – she's probably just what I need too!'

'And business continues to boom?'

'Yes it does! That's partly why I came over. Remember you offered to help me out, discuss things with me, well, I was wondering if I could take you up on it? Not now but one evening perhaps?'

'Of course. If you think I can be of any use – '

'I'm sure you will be. I just need someone aware and intelligent to throw ideas at, if you know what I mean. To be a sounding board as you suggested – '

'I'm flattered! But what about Martin? Can't he help?'

An innocent question. He didn't expect the response.

'Martin is no bloody help at all, especially now. He left. Yesterday. Things had been getting worse between us and then he told me he's having an affair, which I'd guessed anyway. So I encouraged him to leave.'

She looked flushed but not upset, Geoff thought.

'Oh no, I'm sorry, I had no idea – '

'It's OK. Please, don't be sorry. I'm not, I'm glad. He's no loss, believe me.'

She looked at him defiantly, as if daring him to be sympathetic towards Martin through some misplaced male loyalty. But he didn't feel that. He felt a mixture of things – it made him think of Roz, with sadness and regret; it made him feel sorry for anyone who embarks on a relationship or marriage with joy and hope but ends up on the rocks; and he felt something towards Annie. He could not quite put a name to it but it was a confusing amalgam of admiration and fear – and yes, he had to admit it, desire.

Annie, emboldened by her revelation, seized the moment.

'Tell you what – if you're happy to help me out, how about coming over for supper one evening? Or let me take you out for a meal – we needn't go far, we could try that new Chinese place near the Odeon?'

He hesitated. He could go out, why not? He ought to, everyone said so. He'd start by going over to Annie's.

'Yes, let's do that – I'd love to come over to you for supper. What about Tuesday?'

He'd have to make sure either Kim or Polly was here but that shouldn't be a problem.

'That sounds fine. Shall we say about eightish?'

He agreed. She got up, her small breasts moving inside her T-shirt. He could see her nipples through the cotton. She noticed his quick look, knew what he could see, and was glad.

Annie almost skipped across the road. She felt full of bounce and confidence. Having no Martin around was like being relieved of a great weight she'd been carrying for too long. Now she could go forward in any way she wanted.

Geoff went into the garden and found the boys and Katy up the pear tree in the haphazardly extended tree house. He took a deep breath. It was just as well he hadn't known what they were doing. The sight of his small daughter high up a tree, dangling her legs in the air, shouting with her brothers, made his chest hurt.

'Katy darling, I think that's a bit high for you! Are you sure it's safe up there, boys?'

Sam insisted that everything was fine, he could handle it and they could come down by the rope ladder, no worries. Geoff smiled, hearing Kim's influence. But he decided to stay in the garden, just in case, finding the lawn suddenly needed attention. As he pulled up a few dandelions he listened to his children talk. This is how he'd always wanted it: brothers and sisters playing together, looking after one another, being there for each other.

He sat on the garden bench pretending not to watch over his children and contemplated his existence. If he could sort out work, money, children, the whole damn thing, was there more to life? He wasn't desperate yet, but he wondered if he'd ever have a personal life, dammit – a sex life ever again. There had been Roz and there had been his adventures. Sex with strangers was what really used to turn him on – but was it only as a contrast to sex with Roz? Perhaps his appetites were changing along with everything else. No Roz, no strangers?

He found himself thinking of Annie, the feel of her body when they danced at the party . . .

'Dad! What's for lunch? I'm starving.' Matthew called from the tree. Oh God, lunch. Kim was out with her recently acquired boyfriend so it was up to him. He still couldn't get used to the fact that food didn't just appear on the table as if by magic.

He helped Katy down and summoned the children, asking them what they wanted to eat. The majority vote was for pizzas so he ordered a stack of them over the phone, plus garlic bread and a giant bottle of Pepsi, to be delivered. Once he would have disapproved of such an idea, but now?

Everything seemed to be changing, including him. He decided he might as well just go with the flow.

40

Number nineteen was taking shape. Roz couldn't help being excited – something new was evolving from something old. The builders were knocking down walls, changing the arrangements of space – adding a shower room and another bathroom, and a cloakroom; making a usable roof terrace from one of the flat roofs halfway up the back of the house; digging out the basement so that it could be used for some as yet unspecified purpose. And yet the essence of the house and its original features remained – she'd insisted on that.

Alex had drawn up plans (how that had evoked their beginnings), and they'd discussed them, amended them, until it seemed that the house would be perfect. They'd agreed on all the basics, from the colour of the bathroom suite (white) to the kind of taps, to the additional windows (matching the originals – what else?) to the colour of the front door (blue, to ward off the evil eye). They'd touched on accommodation for her children, or rather Alex had touched on it, lightly, treading carefully. He suggested, and she agreed, that they should set aside three rooms on the middle floor as spare bedrooms and furnish them simply, with futons or pine beds (the kind that could be stored one under another), with built-in cupboards and shelves and the same carpet throughout. It would all be bright but low-key and anyone could stay there – friends, family, whoever.

Roz liked the idea. She didn't want to customise the rooms and make them perfect, more home than home, then have them standing empty and unused, constant reminders of her loss. This way, they were just spare rooms which could be used by her children if and when they came to stay.

Every day Alex, and sometimes Roz, would check on the builders' progress. She never went on her own – she felt uncomfortable with them. They were a cheery band of North London lads, some of them Greek Cypriots. She was amazed at how fast they were working and asked Alex what his secret was. He'd laughed and said it was no secret, just money as usual, they were all on bonuses. The faster they finished the house, the more money they got, providing the work was sound – and he made sure of that.

Afterwards, if Alex had no meetings or work to attend to, they would go shopping. For blinds (no curtains), sofas, chairs, tables, cupboards, rugs, chests, everything. Roz had never done anything like this before – starting from scratch, buying what you like, no saving or waiting, all at once. They started with the big things and worked downwards, to cutlery, bowls, vases, candlesticks, paintings, prints, and those indefinables – objects from another time, another context, which once may have had a real purpose but now served merely to decorate or amuse. Props, Alex called these things: old farm implements, a cowbell, religious statues verging on the kitsch.

They agreed on the look they wanted: a little faded, not brash; a mix of old and new, country and town, a hybrid of Santa Fé with a touch of the American midwest, crossed with rural Greece and Gustavian Swedish plus a dollop of sturdy old British rustic. They made fun of themselves, laughing at the seemingly absurd formula they'd concocted for the furnishing of their house. Nevertheless, they were determined to make it work. They went hunting, in Heal's and the Conran Shop and Liberty's; antique shops at the far end of the King's Road; lifestyle shops near the Portobello; the occasional auction. The accumulated purchases piled up, waiting in the rooms that were ready at number nineteen. Things were delivered, the builders accepted them without comment, getting on with stripping doors, sanding floors, building a one-off wooden kitchen.

The first stage was nearly over. Soon they'd move in, with a few things from Alex's flat, one or two things belonging to Roz. Then they could have fun arranging, displaying, creating, buying the things they'd overlooked. Their home. It wouldn't be long. As they sat in a café off Tottenham Court Road (they'd been ordering things for the spare rooms from Habitat) they joked about giving the house a name.

'Love nest,' suggested Roz. 'Then we could have a carved sign, a wooden plaque with cooing doves.'

'Or Cupid with his bow and arrow.'

They looked at each other, each wondering if they should really do it, would it be too over the top? They giggled and decided it would be.

Alex was delighted that the house was keeping Roz busy. She seemed to have levelled out lately – no more strange bus journeys, less desperate sobbing. Polly had been to see her with an Australian girl in tow. A pleasant enough teenage girl, he thought, although he'd expected her to look more like Roz. The others, still minus Sam, continued to visit on Sundays and he and Roz had taken them to Hampton Court one day, a trip on the river to Greenwich another, the zoo again . . . His knowledge of English history and acquaintance with the sights of London was improving. When the house was ready they'd be able to relax with the children, let things take their natural course.

He could see that Roz was going to need more to occupy her. He was surprised at how quickly she did things – when they went shopping she made rapid decisions, chose things fast. (He didn't realise that this was the result of years of shopping with children, when speed was a necessity.) She still kept talking about this freelance work of hers, the guides she might produce for the council. He couldn't see why she wanted to continue with it – he'd find it depressing delving into that world of the worthy and the needy.

An idea began to form in his mind. She had a good eye for colour and design and a natural flair which impressed him. Some of his architectural projects required an interior design input – so why not Roz? They could offer a complete service, she'd be working with him. You didn't need any training or qualifications to be an interior designer, Roz could certainly do it. He'd persuade her.

Martin was walking along Tottenham Court Road when he saw Roz Harper come out of Heal's, with a man. Her lover, he presumed. A dark good-looking guy. They had several large carrier bags – furnishing their love nest, he guessed. They stood on the pavement, waiting for a taxi, totally absorbed by each other. Martin observed them from behind his shades and thought dear old Roz was looking rather well, almost fanciable, in fact. She looked thinner, different. She'd changed. But then haven't we all, he thought.

He carried on, he had to get some things before the art supplies shop closed. He ran through the list in his mind: sketch pad, pencils, paper, gouache, brushes. Oils and canvases could wait for a while. For Martin was painting again or, as he preferred to say, working. God, it was good to get back to it – it had been so long. How long? Since art school, he reckoned. Since before he lived with Annie, married her, became a family man. Unreal. All that was so unreal. He'd sometimes felt as if he'd been abducted by aliens and forced into that existence. How else could he explain his feelings of being an outsider, of being unrelated to his children and separate from his wife? Even those words stuck in his throat. How *could* he have gone down that road?

He was putting loads of energy into his painting – *work* – because he was steering clear of women, for a while anyway. That fucking Amanda had given him a hard time. Stuck-up bitch. She hadn't been at all delighted when she found him on her doorstep after he'd left Annie. A bit put out, in fact. She'd arrived home at two in the morning and there he was, sleeping in his car, cramped, dying for a pee, expecting a warm welcome, but no. Oh, she let him in, she let him stay for a while, but made it quite clear he couldn't be a permanent fixture.

He'd had one stroke of luck, though. Gerry, a fellow art director, was leaving to work in Hong Kong and wanted to let his flat for six months or more. As Martin was looking for somewhere to live (eventually he'd get his share of the house – Annie would have to buy him out), bingo! It was great, he loved it. Tucked away at the top of an Edwardian mansion block behind Tottenham Court Road, actually in Fitzrovia. That's where he told people he now lived. Never mind that they usually hadn't heard of it. It was enough for Martin to know that it had been the stamping ground of all those old bohemians – Augustus John and pals. And there were loads of pubs and restaurants and still some small corner shops that stayed open late, and he could walk to Soho in ten minutes. OK, so he didn't like cooking or cleaning but he didn't do much of it – he was a bohemian too, wasn't he?

He still had his job but he wasn't so bothered about keeping it. So far, Annie didn't seem to expect any money from him to help support the children or hadn't asked for any. Why should she? She wanted the children and she was doing just fine with that business of hers (he'd even heard her being interviewed on local radio – amazing – though it was only about women in business). Anyway, there were rumours that his agency was going to be snapped up by another, larger outfit, so perhaps he'd get a pay-off or redundancy. Then he could paint all the time.

He remembered how one of his tutors at Goldsmiths', a bearded shaggy guy who drank a lot, had reacted when he heard that Martin was leaving to study graphics after his foundation year. A waste, he'd said, a bloody waste. What was the matter, he'd asked, was Martin frightened of his own talent?

Martin held on to those words of nearly twenty years ago. Talent – did he have any? He was trying to find out. Meanwhile he was happier than he'd been for years. The smell of freshly sharpened pencils, the feel of paint on his fingers, the satisfaction of seeing the work leaning against the walls. Living alone, not having to bother with women (the occasional wank served his needs), doing what he wished, pleasing himself. Wasn't that what he'd always wanted?

41

Geoff and Annie were engaged in something very like a courtship dance. They circled and edged towards each other and displayed different sides of their characters, saying look at me in a subtle kind of way, nothing too obvious. As mating rituals go, it was slow and gentle, but it was beginning to gather momentum.

It started when Geoff went over to Annie's for supper. They talked of her business, she told him about the premises she'd seen, he listened and made some sensible suggestions which coincided with what she was thinking anyway. He enjoyed the attention she paid him, the care she'd taken with the meal – it was a long time since anyone had done this for him. She relished the appreciation in his smile and the looks he gave her when he thought she wouldn't notice. She'd removed her bra before he came over and the top few buttons of her shirt were undone – she knew that he'd catch a glimpse of breast when she leaned over the table with the food. And she wore the Levi's which fitted her bum perfectly so that he'd be aware of that too. They flirted a little and when he left she kissed him quickly on the cheek – for they had become friends, hadn't they?

A week later Geoff asked Annie out for dinner. He

wanted to be with her and he also wanted the children to see that life went on, although differently. This time Katy made a fuss about him leaving and Matthew sulked a little but their behaviour only confirmed his feelings that he ought to go – it was unhealthy not to.

He drove Annie to Covent Garden where he'd booked a table at a French restaurant he occasionally visited at lunchtime. He enjoyed having someone different in the car, he liked the smell of her – Annie mixed with the perfume she wore. He didn't recognise it.

Everything was a new experience: walking along the street with her, discussing the menu, finding out what she liked to eat, her taste in wine, watching her unfamiliar back view as she went in search of the cloakroom.

She spoke of Martin, who kept ringing her late at night, probably drunk or stoned, telling her how he was painting again and how wonderful it was. She was amused at the thought of him living alone and looking after himself. Then she put her hand on Geoff's arm and apologised for talking about Martin, and Geoff assured her it was fine, no worries, and they both laughed. Annie said that he knew that he could talk to her about Roz if he wanted, didn't he, and Geoff replied that yes, he knew and he might but not right now, he didn't want to spoil things.

After the meal they'd strolled around the Piazza, looking in shop windows, although not really interested – they were becoming more and more interested in each other. He put his arm loosely around her shoulders, she slipped her arm around his waist and they settled into a stride that suited them both.

*

It was like a teenage romance. Every time they saw each other, they inched a little further along the way they both wanted to go. Geoff trod carefully – he'd been wounded by Roz and he wasn't sure that he should be doing this, so soon and with a friend and neighbour. Annie went along with this softly softly approach (although at times she was so frustrated she was tempted to buy a vibrator) mainly out of respect for Geoff. She could see he needed tender loving care, she understood he didn't want to be rejected (who did?) and anyway in some ways she enjoyed the waiting. It was excruciating but exquisite.

They went to the cinema several times, the local Odeon, which had been split into three and usually had something they could see. Geoff would ease his arm around her, she would sometimes put her hand on his knee, but not leave it there as she didn't want to frighten him off. By their fourth visit they were more aware of each other than the film (and much later, reminiscing, could only agree on the fact that it was American). Geoff suddenly turned her face to his and kissed her, his lips closed, then opening, until they were kissing each other frantically and deeply. The woman behind them tutted – up until then she had been looking at the screen between their heads but now had to adjust her position. They drew apart for breath and hurried out.

They walked home briskly, their arms tightly around each other. It only took ten minutes. Neither said a word. At the corner of their road they stopped. Geoff looked down at Annie under a street lamp, his hands on her shoulders. Oh, she liked his height, she liked the way he was made.

'Annie? Do you want what I want?'

'Geoff, if you mean, do I want to go to bed with you – yes, yes, I do.'

'Thank God for that. But where shall we – '

'Come to my house. I'm sure Carina will be in bed and the children don't usually wake.'

'Good. I'll just check that everything's OK at home, then I'll be over. Ten minutes all right?'

They dashed into their respective houses. Annie checked the children (asleep), Carina's room (the light was out), surveyed her bedroom – the bed was made, not too many clothes scattered around. She went to the loo, sprayed on some Opium and waited.

Geoff did similar things in his house: checked the children, had a pee, changed his boxers and socks, saw Kim in the kitchen and told her he was just going over to Annie's for a while. And he went.

Kim kept a straight face but broke into a grin when he'd left. She was delighted. Poor bloke – he needed a bit of female company. She and Carina had seen this coming.

He didn't need to ring the bell, she had the door open as he got there. In the darkened hall they embraced and kissed and ran their hands up and down each other's bodies, liking what they could feel and wanting to feel more . . . They were both breathing fast and Annie whispered, 'Come upstairs.' She took him by the hand and they crept up to her bedroom as quietly as they could. She'd left a bedside lamp on.

They stood by the bed, pressed together, kissing, their tongues delighting in exploring each other's mouth. Geoff put one hand over Annie's breast, and oh, how pleased she was. He rubbed her nipple through her shirt with his thumb and she shuddered with desire. She wanted him *now*, but she held back, sensing he would prefer to take the lead. He guided her backwards on to the bed and they lay kissing, getting hotter, more passionate, their kisses wetter, his hands inside her shirt, he loved it that she wore no bra, he liked her small breasts, he liked the way he could cover them with his hands . . . Annie stroked his back, pulling up his shirt, feeling his skin. She ventured her hand downward, expectantly, and it was there, she felt it, his erection. He groaned loudly, saying her name.

She gently removed her hand, stood up and took off her clothes and he followed. They knelt on the bed, looking at each other. She liked his leanness, she had known that she would; his skin was pale, he had little chest hair, but he was muscular about the shoulders, he wasn't puny. She looked down and his cock stood out, it was long, but not thick like Martin's. She wanted to feel it inside her.

He absorbed her body – those sweet little breasts with big nipples, brown and nutty, he wanted to lick them, her flat stomach and delicate hip bones, her thick bush. How he liked her pertness, her sparseness, it was so different from Roz's opulence. She reminded him of someone, one of his adventures – Céline?

He pulled her to him, how good that felt, kissed her fiercely and said, 'Annie, I want you so badly, can we – now?' She nodded, seeing his need and when he hesitated – to discuss AIDS or pregnancy? – she lay back and opened her legs and her arms to him. She didn't need any foreplay, she was wet enough already, it had been ages since she had had sex, and perhaps even longer for him. He slid into her easily, she wrapped her legs high around him, they began to move together. Suddenly he was urgent, crying out, and it was over. He banged his head on to the pillow. 'Annie, I'm sorry, I'm sorry, that was so quick, I couldn't help it.'

She held his head and soothed him, whispered words to console him, said she understood. She told him that the next time would be great and began to describe the things she enjoyed and what they could – and would – do to each other . . . He had stayed inside her after he came, not slipping out and now as she talked he began to harden again. They smiled at each other and began again, slowly. Slow kisses, slowly sucking her nipples, moving slowly and precisely inside her, side to side and round and round and up and down. They turned, staying connected, and she was on top of him, leaning back, slowly rotating her hips . . . This time it lasted much much longer. And the next time even more so.

Geoff strolled across the deserted road to home at four in the morning. They were both satiated and satisfied and pleased with themselves and very happy to have discovered each other.

They didn't formally tell their children what was happening – they didn't need to. Geoff's children had all known Annie for ages and liked her so they accepted her increasing presence without too much comment. And Annie's children accepted Geoff – he was kind and patient so it was easy and they'd always loved the whole Harper set-up, all those children, all those toys, always someone to play with.

Polly was getting to know Annie really well, working with her every day – that's how Annie made it feel, working with her not for her. Every day she'd bound over to Annie's house and they'd run through what had to be done and who would do it. Polly loved answering the phone and saying, 'The Party Spirit, how can I help you?' She took bookings and organised the diary, and made lists of ingredients they needed and liaised with the two women who baked cakes and went shopping with Annie. It was great, and she was being paid well. (Partly because she was Geoff's daughter, but she didn't know that.) She admired Annie and what she'd achieved.

If they were working at home Annie would make sure they had a proper lunch break, sitting at the kitchen table eating salad or ciabatta sandwiches. They'd chat about designs for cakes or new ways of making finger-food exciting. Polly was surprisingly creative, Annie thought, as well as being hardworking and efficient.

Sometimes they talked of other things. Polly hesitantly raised the subject of Roz one day.

'You and Mum were quite good friends, weren't you, Annie?'

'Yes, I'd say we were. We used to see a lot of each other, mainly because of Tom and Katy being at playgroup together. That was before – '

'Before she left?'

'I was going to say before I started the business.'

'Oh. It's just that with us life's now divided into before Mum left and after Mum left. It dominates everything!'

'I can see that it would.'

She watched Polly for signs of distress, and listened.

'But I think things are getting a bit better. Matt's not wetting the bed any more and Katy – well she's just Katy. Perhaps it helps that she's younger? Sam doesn't seem quite so angry. But do you think we're all damaged?'

'Polly – what can I say? Who knows? You seem to be coping remarkably well – '

'Yeah, perhaps. Dad seems happier at least – '

'You do know about your Dad and me?'

'I'd guessed.' Polly grinned. 'I'm glad for him. And I'm glad it's you!'

After that they often discussed her mother and what she'd done. Annie said that despite what had happened, she was a good person – Roz had been very kind to her when she'd first moved here and had been very supportive over the years. Polly found it comforting to hear that – it echoed what she really felt about her mum, underneath the current pain and anger.

She discovered that she could talk to Annie about anything: what she wanted to do with her life; feminism; clothes; sex. She told Annie that she'd slept with Nick just once – so far – and yes, they'd used a condom, but oh how disappointing it was. Annie said that was quite normal and recalled her first time with a boy called Brian – such an anti-climax after weeks of intense petting. She remembered an underwhelming impression of wetness. That made Polly laugh and feel a lot better.

It became natural for the two families to share occasions like Sunday lunch (at Geoff's place but cooked by Annie). Occasionally they'd be joined by Kim and her boyfriend and Carina too. Afterwards they might go to Hampstead Heath together in a great gang to play football or rounders. Geoff would laugh and say they were like a commune, a hippy convoy, but privately he liked it, this loose and friendly crowd, this new sort of family.

Annie and Geoff kept their separate houses – at least for the time being – but their arrangements were informal, they spilled over at the edges. She'd sworn, after Martin, that she wouldn't live with a man again but if there was a man who could tempt her, it was Geoff. She valued him, she wondered how Roz could have left him but she supposed she should be grateful that Roz had made him available. Geoff flourished under Annie's affection. He had all sorts of plans – he would work at home or he'd become Annie's partner or they'd all move to the country, the whole merged tribe. He could actually look towards the future with hope and the prospect of happiness.

One Saturday afternoon Geoff and Annie lay in his bed. As she said, who says sex is only for night-time? Daylight sex reminded them of when they were young – separately.

The children were staying with Roz for the first time, in her new house. Geoff had insisted that they all should go – even Sam and Polly. There were sulks and protestations but he would not give in. It was the right thing to do – things should be done together, as brothers and sisters, as a family. Kim was at her boyfriend's so he and Annie had the house to themselves. Annie had let her helpers deal with today's party – she needed an afternoon off and what better way to spend it? She was going to stay for the whole of Saturday night. She'd boldly told Carina (who was taking Amy and Tom to the cinema this afternoon and who was babysitting tonight) and she'd smiled approvingly.

Geoff and Annie lay naked side by side, idly stroking each other, up and down. They'd just made love and it had been athletic and uninhibited. The sex was wonderful, they both agreed.

Later they would light the scented candles that Annie had brought with her and uncork the massage oil they'd bought together which they were eager to use. They'd open some wine and have a picnic in bed – tonight was to be a hedonistic delight.

For now they rested and recounted in detail how much they liked each other's bodies. They did this a lot, taking turns to touch the appropriate places as they talked.

As Geoff's fingers tripped lightly over her stomach Annie arched her back and thought for a fleeting moment, I used to envy Roz and want to be like her and here I am in her bed, with her husband, but I'm glad I'm me. This is *my* life.

42

Roz would wander through the house telling herself that this was home. She often did this in the early morning before Alex awoke, enjoying the solitude, walking barefoot over the wooden floors. If it was a fine morning she'd sit in the garden in her robe with a mug of coffee, listening to the squawk of sparrows and the growing rumble of traffic streets away, reviewing her life and its progress so far.

They'd lived here for three months now. The kaleidoscope changed less often, a pattern was becoming familiar. Alex and Roz lived in an almost constant state of bliss – but they'd discovered, as everyone does, that living together is not always as easy as loving each other.

Piece by piece they cemented their new life. They sent out cards informing people of where they both now lived, they started a mutual address book. Building blocks, Alex said. He took her to Paradise Place and showed her his office – he enjoyed introducing her to Lynn – and where he kept his personal files with insurance policies, all that sort of stuff. Just in case you ever need it, he told her.

He began to want to talk about the future. Roz was still adjusting to the present. But Alex wanted to marry her and pressed her to discuss divorce with Geoff, to work out a schedule, so that they could make plans. She would stall and say, soon, soon, but she knew that neither she nor Geoff were ready to talk about such things. They'd achieved some sort of equilibrium between them and she didn't want it upset. They discussed the children and their states of mind, their performance at school, who should buy their new clothes or shoes – both large and small details. That was the currency that she and Geoff used for transactions. Later, when they were ready, they'd discuss divorce and the formalisation of the arrangements over the children but not yet.

The children came to stay most weekends – sometimes all of them, sometimes not. Sam would only come with the others and even then he made sure he wasn't alone with his mother. He barely spoke to Alex. She had to live with that – it might improve, it might not. Alex did what he could – he played chess and football with Matthew and discussed art and animal rights with Polly and read to Katy. He sensed Sam watching from the sidelines and waited.

Each time after the children left Roz and Alex would be drained. They'd drink a bottle of wine too fast then have a bath together – in one bathroom they had a large corner bath perfect for two – or Alex would massage Roz, then she'd massage him. Sex would alleviate the remaining tension and obliterate any urge to talk about how it was going with the children. Roz could talk about that for hours if he let her.

One night as they lay together after sex like two spoons in a drawer – one of their favourite positions, his face nuzzled into the back of her neck, penis against her bottom, knees drawn up behind hers, hands cupping her breasts – Alex said something she did not want to hear.

'Oh, Roz, Rozzi. Let's have a child of our own. A baby.'

She was glad that he stayed behind her, nibbling at her ear, so he could not see her expression.

'Oh, Alex. But I'm forty – '

'That's not old, not too old. And you're still so fertile, so fecund, I know, I can feel it.'

His cock pressed against her, growing hard. His fingers slipped inside her.

'Please, Roz, please. Have your coil out. Give me a child, please.'

She closed her eyes as he turned her under him, to enter her. She would not answer.

Alex had to go to Athens for several short trips on family business, a few days at a time. Each time he said she could come, of course she could, but something in his voice encouraged her to say she'd stay at home. Probably just as well, he said, as he'd be in boring board meetings for hours on end, then he'd have to socialise with the family. He didn't give Roz any details but hinted at family squabbles over money and disagreements over future business plans.

While he was away Roz got on with things, all sorts of things. Coloured her hair, waxed her legs, took Polly to the theatre one evening to see *The Doll's House.*

She spent a lot of time thinking about Alex's desire – demand? – to have a child. She visited her new doctor, one of a group practice in Camden Town. Dr Patterson was young, brisk and female and listened sympathetically when Roz explained that although she was very happy with her coil as a means of contraception, her partner complained that during sex he could feel the string in her vagina and it hurt, like a piece of wire prodding his penis. Hop up on the couch, the doctor said, and let's have a look, just relax. Roz spread her legs and breathed deeply and slowly. Dr Patterson said she thought she could do something and inserted an instrument. Click. She told Roz she'd cut the string as short as she could – any shorter and there would be nothing there to get the coil out with when the time came. Roz thanked her. They looked each other in the eye, avoiding mention of men's squeamishness and frailty or the strength and responsibility of women. She reminded Roz of the need for regular check-ups and when her next cervical smear was due and that was it.

As Roz walked home she felt a small twinge of guilt – poor Alex, being misrepresented like that. But he'd never know. It seemed better this way – if he asked, she'd say that she'd had her coil removed and he would never feel anything to suggest otherwise.

When he returned they fell on each other and stayed in bed for the rest of the day. When they came up for air Alex said he had a present for her. He clambered over her and she watched his penis swing heavily, knocking against his legs, as he rummaged through his suitcase. He handed her a small bag with a box inside. She recognised it – it was from the jeweller in Athens. Slowly she opened it. A ring. It was pale and beautiful, was it silver? Alex said it was platinum. She hugged him and thanked him, squashing her breasts against him, her head against his so that he couldn't see her face.

He took her hand, her right hand, and eased it on to

her third finger. (She no longer wore her wedding ring on her left hand, she'd hidden it at the bottom of her jewellery box.) It fitted. He said the jeweller had guessed her size – he'd remembered her, Alex said proudly.

They lay down together and he spoke softly. 'I want to marry you so much, Roz, I want us to be man and wife.' She said nothing but kissed him fiercely to hide her conflicting emotions. He assumed she was overcome with desire. She buried her face in his stomach, running her tongue around his navel, caressing his balls, holding his cock. He murmured, 'And we will have a child. You're so luscious, we'll make beautiful babies.'

He lifted her on to him and thrust up into her. As she moved around him she understood that he was not going to let this idea go. She would have to deceive him. If she had a child with him it would be a betrayal of *her* children, those she had left. She would not do it.

For once Alex climaxed alone. Roz climbed off him and tucked her thoughts away into a private place in her mind. Alex held her hand, fingering the ring he'd bought her. It would be so much easier when they were married – his family would have to abandon their pathetic attempts to matchmake and he wouldn't have to be polite to any more nubile Greek heiresses. (Only Tina really knew and understood about Roz.) And it would make matters simpler from a legal and financial point of view if she was his wife. He just wanted to make things perfect for her, for them, that was all.

The next time Alex was away Roz invited Annie to supper. When Roz opened the front door they gave each other a good looking-over then laughed when they realised what they were doing. Annie thrust a bottle of wine and a gorgeous bunch of flowers – white and blue, very tasteful – into Roz's hands and they kissed on the cheek.

Roz gave Annie a tour of the house. She raved about it and was full of questions about where they'd bought this or acquired that and how did they get the paint looking so perfectly distressed?

They sat in the garden as the sun went down and drank white wine, talking of the changes in their lives. They had a lot to catch up on, although they each kept abreast of latest developments through Polly. They spoke of her and Roz felt a small shaft of jealousy when she realised how close Annie and her daughter had become. Annie spoke dismissively of Martin and then tentatively brought the conversation around to the subject of her and Geoff. Roz had already thought about this and got over her initial surprise – who would've thought it? Annie and Geoff? On delving into her soul she'd found no jealousy whatsoever and nor should there be any, she'd told herself. She reassured Annie, told her she thought it was great, she was glad for both of them.

By the time they were on the third bottle they began to find little titbits to tell each other – as women do – snippets of information that showed things weren't as perfect as they seemed. They didn't compare the sizes of Geoff's and Alex's and Martin's penises, nor did they contrast their performance in bed but rather they revealed things that showed their own vulnerability and that of others. Roz told Annie about Alex's desire for a child; Annie told Roz about Martin's pathetic late night phone calls and his latest idea to return to his roots in Wales and paint full-time. Roz confided her concern about Alex always having to be boss – he liked to make decisions for her and sometimes without her and while she'd been fragile that was fine, but what would happen now that she was growing stronger?

They talked of Geoff's plan to take the combined Hughes/Harper gang on a camping holiday in France. For some reason they found this hilarious and they laughed until they couldn't stop, until it hurt, and there were tears in their eyes.

Alex was about to go to Athens again. Roz wanted to ask him more about why he needed to go – what exactly was going on? He was reluctant to talk about it. She wondered if he saw his ex-wife and daughter but she sensed that was a taboo subject. Sometimes she felt as if there was a part of him she'd never fully know and it was to do with him being Greek.

As they lay in bed that night before he left she pondered on the secrets that lay between them. She'd already told him a lie. When he'd talked again about having a child and asked her if she'd had her coil removed, she'd said yes. He'd covered her with kisses and said, 'Let's make a baby!'

Roz had decided that she'd visit her mother while Alex was away.

'Where does she live, darling, some far away corner of England?'

She pushed him playfully. 'Cornwall, Alex, it's Cornwall, the very *end* of England. Or is it the start?'

Roz thought of her mother in her small granite cottage in a village near Penzance and tried to remember when she'd last seen her. Still, if the damn woman would insist on moving three hundred miles away, she couldn't expect to see her daughter or grandchildren much, could she?

She regretted that the children hadn't seen their grandmother more, she regretted that her mother hadn't been more involved – and yes, regretted that she hadn't been there to help when Roz needed it. She regretted a great deal but now these were mere details.

Roz wasn't sure why she was taking her mother up on her offer to come to stay. Perhaps she felt there was unfinished business or she just wanted to tell her all about Alex (would she be interested?) or maybe she needed to talk about her children. When she'd rung to arrange the trip, saying when she'd like to come, she sensed her mother's hesitation. It wasn't that convenient, she said. Roz thought she could hear the pages of a diary being turned. She was amazed – she'd imagined her mother would be pleased to have a visit from one of her daughters and would be rushing to air the bed. Roz assured her that she'd be no trouble, that she'd look after herself if necessary. In the end her mother agreed.

She caught the train to Penzance. She could have gone by car – Alex had surprised her a few days before with a present, a shiny new blue Golf waiting for her outside the house. She'd been pleased and grateful but did feel that she should have had some say in it. This was just what she'd been telling Annie about.

She left it by the kerb and caught a taxi to Paddington. She enjoyed the long train journey, the hours alone, ignoring other passengers, reading and gazing out of the window and catching glimpses of all those other lives led by other people.

*

There was a satisfaction in arriving at the end of the line, knowing you could go no further – by train anyway. As she stretched her legs outside the station and looked at the sea, breathing in the sharp, fresh air, listening to the cries of the seagulls, she saw someone waving at her. Could this really be her mother? The woman striding towards her bore little resemblance to the mother Roz remembered. She was lightly tanned – perhaps weatherbeaten was more accurate – and her hair was cut in a short bob, naturally grey (no sign of the tight perm and away-grey colourant of old). She was wearing trousers. Trousers! Her mother had never worn trousers, even when on country walks or gardening. And these weren't even smart trousers, but were brown corduroy and baggy and were topped by a fisherman's sweater with a red cotton scarf tied round her neck. The look was comfortable, confident (here was a woman at home in her skin) and a little bohemian and the effect on Roz was startling. Her mother? It was.

'Roz! Hello! Have a good journey? The car's over here.'

She followed the trim bustling figure, wearing, Roz noted, some sort of hiking boots (amazing for someone who used to live in court shoes). They stopped by an old grey Mini.

'Is this yours, Mum?'

'Yes, I picked it up cheap. Wanted a Land Rover really, but I'm a bit small. You can't have anything too fancy down here, what with the salt from the sea.'

Her mother chattered through the ten-minute drive, about cars, local public transport, the rivalry between bus companies, the new superstore outside

Penzance, local unemployment. Roz was very quiet, which her mother interpreted as tiredness. In fact she was trying to adjust to this vigorous, changed woman who happened to be her mother.

In the cottage they had a cup of tea, out of pottery mugs – her mother used to favour bone china – and Roz admired the garden and the new paintings on the walls.

'I did them. I've started with watercolours but I think I'll try oils soon.'

'Mum, I'm impressed! I really like them – perhaps I could buy one for our new house?'

'We'll see. And don't be impressed. I'm not that good yet, I hope I'll improve. But in a way you can't fail down here, what with the light, and the sea and the atmosphere. Now why don't you try calling me Barbara? I think we're past the Mum stage, don't you?'

'Oh. If you want. I'll try. But why? What do you mean, past the Mum stage?'

'Well I hardly see you or Maggie and it seems strange to suddenly hear oneself called Mum. I don't feel like Mum – no, don't be offended, Roz. It just doesn't seem to fit with my life any more. Don't you think there could be a time in one's life when one can stop being a mother – or primarily a mother? There are so many other things to be, don't you agree?'

The days in Cornwall steadied Roz, bringing her peace. She could let herself be. At a distance from Alex, the children, Geoff, the whole situation, she could stop worrying and gnawing at it. She spent some time alone walking by the sea – there was nothing quite like watching those crashing, relentless Atlantic waves to put things into perspective. She spent some time with her mother. Barbara – she tried to call her that – told Roz clearly at the beginning of her stay when she was busy and when she was available. She had a full calendar on her kitchen wall – Roz looked at it when her mother was out. She seemed to belong to a conservation group and the National Trust, then there was her painting group, and some undecipherable squiggles, and someone called Dorothy featured a lot.

Barbara herself did not reveal much of her new life – for that, undeniably, was what it was. All she would say was that she was happy, that she had made some good friends, that the place itself was mysterious and enchanting. She introduced Roz to it, going on long walks to standing stones, Iron Age settlements, barrows and burial chambers. She said there was so much to learn, that she was reading all she could about the history of the area – a very long history. She was planning to learn Cornish – it was still alive and there were courses.

She bombed along the narrow lanes in the Mini, Roz beside her looking out for ancient Celtic crosses concealed in the hedgerows, taking her to truly magical places, secret places where you dipped your hands in sacred water and tied rags on trees and could make a wish. Barbara waited patiently while Roz closed her eyes and thought about what she wanted. That was difficult.

Later in the cottage, in the cosiness of the evening, the sounds of the sea in the distance, they talked of change. Barbara had made cauliflower cheese and Roz had bought some wine from the village shop.

'I never thought I'd have a life like this, you see, Roz.'

'How do you mean?'

'A life of my own, an independent life. I'd always imagined your father and I, together in retirement, pottering about in a bungalow on the South Coast somewhere. But then of course he died just before he could retire.' They were both silent for a moment.

'It took me a while to work out what I wanted,' Barbara continued. 'I was so used to considering others, especially your father. Partly my generation, I suppose, partly me, I did so want to please him.'

'Because you loved him?' Roz ventured.

'No, because I *didn't* love him, not really. Oh I grew to love him in a way and I was fond of him and grateful, but I felt I ought to please him to make up for not loving him. There had been someone else, you see.'

'What, while you were married?'

'No, no. Before. During the war. That really was love, it was very passionate. He was in the RAF. Harry – he was called Harry. And he was killed and then I met your father a while later and I needed someone, and that was that.'

'I'm – I'm sorry, Mum. Barbara. How awful for you – '

'It was but it was a long time ago. Why I'm telling you this, is to try to help you. You see, none of us has the life we'd planned or wanted or expected. And this whole idea of personal happiness, expecting it and searching for it, is a very new one, you know. We didn't think like that.'

'So are you saying I'm wrong in what I'm doing, what I've done?'

'No I'm not. What I'm trying to say – perhaps I'm not saying it very well – is that you're right to follow your desires. Life isn't simple – it's a bit like a

Cornish lane, it twists and turns, and sometimes you can't see over the hedge!'

They laughed. Roz filled their glasses. Her mother carried on.

'I repressed myself for too long, doing what I thought was right. You and Maggie weren't born out of love and I regret that, but children are hardy creatures, they survive. And all those clichés – you've only got one life, it isn't a rehearsal, life's too short – well, I'm afraid they burn with blinding truth as you get older! So do what you want, do what you can while you can.'

That night in bed, as she listened to the seagulls walking across the roof, Roz had a mad wish that her mother would come and tuck her up. Her mother. What a revelation. Perhaps she's become a witch, thought Roz, a wise old witch of the West.

She watched the parallel railway tracks from the window. They seemed to whiz by but of course it was her train that was moving. No doubt her mother could draw some conclusions from that about life. She smiled at the thought.

She unlocked the front door. Home. She seemed to be home before Alex – they'd tried to time their journeys so that they'd arrive about the same time. She realised the phone was ringing and hurried to answer it before the machine cut in. It might be him, he might be delayed.

'Roz? Oh thank God it's you, I've been trying to reach you all day – '

'Who – ?' It was a woman's voice, upset, urgent.

'Roz, it's Tina. In Greece. Oh – '

Her voice rose, there was a lot of noise behind it. Roz froze.

'Tina, what is it?'
'It's Alex. He's had an accident. He's – he's dead – '
'No!' She slid to the floor.
'Roz, I'm so so sorry, but it's true.' Tina sobbed, almost hysterical. 'He was killed last night in a car crash, that awful road – '

Alex was dead.

43

Alex is dead.

She still has to tell herself every morning, make herself believe it.

He will always be dead.

Where is he? Where has he gone?

She remembers saying goodbye, they kissed. The warmth of his skin. She waved from the door as he left for the airport. He turned and smiled and raised his arm. He was wearing pale chinos and a navy linen shirt and brown loafers.

She replays that scene in her mind repeatedly. The last time she saw him. The last time.

Tina said the crash was bad – Roz guessed it was a pile-up. Tina didn't know that expression.

They spoke on the phone again and again and Roz insisted on details. She wanted to *know*. To feel it, understand it.

A lorry carrying fruit. Its load slipped and spilled across the road. Chaos. Alex in the middle of it in the open-topped car. Tina said he died instantly. He died.

Roz wanted something – a scrap of blue linen, a shoe stained with blood, a lock of his hair. Anything to make it real.

He was buried quickly in the family vault outside

Athens, joining his long-dead brother. The family was destroyed, Tina said. Did she mean distraught? Roz wondered. Probably both.

Roz was not there. She did not go to the funeral – his funeral, the last thing that was his. Too soon, too far, and she knew she would be out of place. They would not want her there.

One day she will go and kiss the stone.

A week after the funeral Tina came to London to see her. They stood in the hall of Roz and Alex's house and held each other and wept. Eventually Roz led Tina into the kitchen, sat her down at the table and made coffee.

'Tina – thank you for coming to see me.'

'I had to, of course. Oh this is going to be frustrating, I cannot express how I feel in English. I'm sorry – '

Roz laid her hand on Tina's arm. She had dark shadows like bruises under her eyes, deep brown eyes which reminded Roz of Alex.

'Please, it's all right. I understand. There's so much to say, but how do you say it in any language?'

They managed to smile at each other, their hands connecting across the table. Echoes of other times flashed through Roz's mind, like splinters of light.

'Roz – Alex loved you so much, he was so happy with you – '

'I know. We loved each other. But this is so cruel, we had so little time – '

'Yes. It is so cruel. And I know some of what you've been through so that you two could be together. He used to call me often, just to talk. He told me a lot about you, about what was happening –'

Roz began to cry.

*

Later Tina took an envelope from her bag and handed Roz Alex's watch, his old Rolex. The face was scratched, but amazingly, it was still going.

'Unbelievable, isn't it?' Tina said. 'It's still working, but he's – '

'Dead. Yes, it's like a sick joke.'

Tina took some Greek newspaper cuttings from the envelope to show Roz. She translated the reports of his death: member of the prominent Kostakis family, international career, tragic waste, dangerous stretch of road, lorry driver questioned.

She'd brought some photographs too. 'I wasn't sure if you'd want these, but you don't have to keep them.'

She spread them out on the table. Alex as a boy, in a tree, on a beach. Smiling, laughing. Alex as a student, long curls to his shoulders, a drooping moustache. In all the photographs he was alone. Roz sensed that they had been carefully selected.

'I always told him that moustache was a mistake,' Tina said. And she began to talk about her brother, their childhood, how he always teased her, how she adored him.

After Tina goes home, promising to call, to visit, for they still have much to talk about, Roz loses track of time. She wanders through days, nights, weeks, often not knowing where she is.

She takes lots of baths, stretching out in their corner bath like a starfish. Slips under the water, thinks of her children. Writes *Alex is dead* on the steamed-up mirror. The words frequently reappear to haunt her.

He does not haunt her.

She waits to hear his laugh, feel his touch but he does not come in any form.

She dreams of him. He looks well, intact. He has grown. He wears a golden helmet and says, 'Beware of Greeks bearing gifts.'

In another dream he and Geoff wrestle naked in front of a fire. The thud of their feet, the gleam of their bodies. When she wakes she remembers the scene from *Women in Love.*

She talks to herself. It helps.

She wanders through the house, shedding clothes, preferring the rooms that are emptier, the ones they did not quite finish. For a while she sleeps on a quilt in one of the rooms at the top, stretching out on the pale wooden floor. She wears his watch.

She knows she makes noises, she howls. She doesn't know the neighbours. She doesn't care.

Sometimes she dances – did she and Alex ever dance? She plays Van Morrison and Leonard Cohen and dances alone. It is like the waltz her father taught her as a child. One two three, one two three.

Alex's solicitor writes to her. She takes a taxi to his office. The London streets seem foreign to her. Alex left a will. He's made her rich, leaving her his half of the house, his flat, Paradise Place, all his assets in England, everything in his bank accounts, his investments. All to be hers when the estate is settled. Alex left clear instructions.

Alex left this, Alex left that. Alex left her.

The kaleidoscope has moved too fast. Colours, shapes, patterns, changes, changing. The glass breaks.

*

Everyone is worried about Roz. Annie, Geoff. The children, in their own way, even Sam. Her mother and Maggie. They discuss Alex's death, the shock of it. Somehow it lessens the shock of what happened before. They talk about Roz, and wonder how they can help her and if they can.

Polly arrived. She'd phoned and briskly told her mother that she was on her way.

Roz opened the door and her daughter stood on the step smiling, with her rucksack and bags of shopping. She said nothing about how thin Roz looked, how pale and tired.

She bustled in, unpacking the food on to the kitchen table, full of youth and noise and vitality.

'Now, Mum, how are you?'

'Oh, Polly, you know the phrase – as well as can be expected.'

Her grief was unsettling, piled as it was on top of all the other turmoil they'd already been through. As Polly had remarked to her friends, now I know what trauma really means! But she mustn't let her mother see how nervous she was.

'Mum. Look – I'd thought I'd come and stay for a while, keep you company – ' She wanted to add, look after you too.

'You don't have to, darling. I'm – I'm all right. Really. I will be – '

'But I want to!'

Polly made her mother small tasty meals, surprising her with her cooking skills (picked up mostly from Annie, but she didn't say so). Roz ate very little, but it pleased her to sit at the table with her daughter and watch her eat and listen to her talk and gossip. Polly made her laugh.

Roz began to take steps back into the world.

Winter. November rain, so English, so dreary, yet Roz begins to wake. She watches the weather fom her window, and starts to reassemble herself.

Hilary rang, knowing nothing of Alex or his death, offering Roz more work, wanting a meeting. Roz found her diary, fixed a date and looked forward to it. She would work a lot, as much as she could. Create a career. She might use Alex's office at Paradise Place – an office of her own.

Roz went to see Lynn, still there to sort out the files and papers. Roz liked Lynn and could see she was bright and capable and wondered if she could keep her on in some capacity, as yet unspecified. She'd have to think it through.

She sat at Alex's desk and Lynn brought her coffee, and they talked and talked about him. They cried a little but Lynn made her laugh too, with her everyday tales of office life with Alex. They both knew he wasn't perfect.

Roz needed to go shopping for winter clothes, partly because she'd lost so much weight, partly because – well, she had the money, so what the hell, she thought. She rang Annie and asked her to come. Annie was delighted.

They hit the shops early, meeting at Liberty's, in spending mood.

'A whole day shopping! Such indulgence, Roz, I can

hardly believe it,' Annie said as they collapsed in a taxi, arranging the glossy carrier bags around them.

'We must do it again!'

They dropped into a bistro not far from Roz's house, off Camden High Street, settling into a corner table, leaning their bags up against the wall.

It was an easy-going sort of place: some customers used it just as a café and to read the papers. It buzzed with conversation, people smoked. The waitress was friendly, positively pleased to see two women together without men.

They were hungry and ordered food – was it a late lunch or early supper? Who cared? – and a good bottle of red. It felt just like old times.

'So, Roz, tell me how you are, how everything is.'

'Things are improving, I'm functioning better, I suppose, but – oh, I still have this great hole in my life – I miss him. And we had so little time . . .' Her voice trailed away, but she did not cry.

'I wish I'd met Alex, Roz. Obviously I saw him, at a distance, but I never even spoke to him.'

'Yes, well, there were reasons for that at the time! But I wish you had, then we could talk about him more.' She paused for some wine. 'But sometimes Annie, just sometimes, I almost wish that I'd never met him.'

'Oh, Roz.'

They forked through the large green salad in the middle of the table. Annie knew the names of all the various leaves.

'But none of it can be undone, can it? And I know I've got to look forward, rebuild my life – God, all these clichés!'

'I know, but you're right. What else can you do?'

'Exactly! The funny thing is though, I'm beginning to feel excited, scared but excited – '

'How do you mean?'

'Well, I've never lived on my own before – can you believe it? Here I am at forty, living on my own for the first time. Which is a bit of an adventure – '

'Especially in that beautiful house! Oh, I'm sorry, that sounded superficial – '

'It's OK, Annie – I know what you mean. And that does help, of course it does, and not having to worry about money.' They tucked into their pasta and Roz said she was ashamed to say it, though she knew she could to Annie, but she realised that feminism had passed her by and it had taken all this pain and suffering – *all this* – for her to understand and to wake up.

'Wake up to what?' Annie asked, although she thought she knew.

'To the fact that I'm an independent woman now and it's up to me – I've got to take responsibility for my own life. A life of my own. You know, find my own way, make my own map!' She laughed. 'Oh dear, what do I sound like?'

Annie leaned forward suddenly and put her hand on Roz's arm.

'Do you know, Roz, way back when, I used to think that you had it all worked out, that you had the perfect life, the perfect family. I so wanted to be like you!'

Roz started to laugh – she found this unbearably funny and then unbearably upsetting and tears began to flow down her cheeks, tears of sorrow and regret.

Annie called for the bill.

*

Back home, Roz tried on her new shoes and hung up her new clothes. Alex's things still hung in the wardrobe. She must do something about them, she decided. She'd keep a shirt or sweater for her to wear around the house, but that would be all. The house mustn't become a shrine to Alex, it had to live and breathe as he would have wanted.

She went to bed, their wide wooden bed, and deliberately lay in the middle, enjoying the feel of the expensive cotton sheets, the warmth of the enormous quilt. She thought yet again about what might have happened if she hadn't met Alex – would she have been able to change her life from within her marriage? But she knew that you could wonder forever about the other lives you could have led.

Although it was dark she had an extraordinary sensation of being surrounded by air and light, as if she were lying in the Greek sun.

Alex?

Or was she just dazzled by the possibilities of her life to come?